D0455117

Shifting
Landscape

Henry Roth

Shifting
Landscape

A Composite, 1925–1987
*edited with an introduction
by Mario Materassi*

*The Jewish Publication Society
Philadelphia • New York • Jerusalem 5748 • 1987*

Library of Congress Cataloging in Publication Data

Roth, Henry.
    Shifting landscape.

    I. Materassi, Mario.   II. Title.
PS3535.0787A6 1987   814'.52   87–10019
ISBN 0–8276–0292–8

Designed by Adrianne Onderdonk Dudden

To my wife
Muriel Roth

Philip and Muriel Berman Edition

Acknowledgments

The author and the editor wish to thank the following for permission to reprint:

The New Yorker, for "Broker," "Somebody Always Grabs the Purple," and "Petey and Yotsee and Mario." Reprinted by permission; © 1939, 1940, and 1956 The New Yorker Magazine, Inc. Copyrights duly renewed.

Midstream, for "The Meaning of *Galut* in America Today" (*Midstream* 9:1, March 1963, pp. 32–33) and "Kaddish" (Midstream 23:1, January 1977, pp. 53–55).

Washington and Lee University, for "Prolog im Himmel," from *Shenandoah* 25, Fall 1973, pp. 44–47. Copyright 1973 by Washington and Lee University, reprinted from *Shenandoah: The Washington and Lee University Review* with the permission of the Editor.

The Jewish Federation of Greater Albuquerque, for "Squib" (*Albuquerque Jewish Community LINK*, October 1977, p. 9).

The Jerusalem Post International Magazine, for "Vale atque Ave," October 14, 1977, P.E. This material is published by arrangement with *The Jerusalem Post*.

The New York Post, for Martha MacGregor, "The Week in Books," November 8, 1964, p. 47.

Portland Sunday Telegram, for Frank Sleeper, "Augusta Man's First Novel Scores ... After 30 Years," December 6, 1964, p. 11A.

Life, for Jane Howard, "The Belated Success of Henry Roth," 53, January 8, 1965, pp. 75–76.

WFAU Radio Station, Augusta, Maine, for an interview conducted on January 8, 1965.

Parallel (Montreal), for Don Bell, "A Writer's Dilemma. An Introduction," 1, May–June 1966, pp. 7–11.

Books, for "Faith May Move Henry Roth" [unsigned article], 3, August 1966, p. 3.

Partisan Review, for David Bronsen, "A Conversation with Henry Roth," 36, No. 2, 1969, pp. 265–80.

The New York Times, for "Henry Roth: No Longer at Home," Op-Ed, April 15, 1971.

Literary Review, for William Freedman, "A Conversation with Henry Roth," 18, Winter 1975, pp. 149–57.

Washington and Lee University, for B. Lyons, *Henry Roth: The Man and His Work;* copyright 1973 by Washington and Lee University, reprinted from *Shenandoah: The Washington and Lee University Review* with the permission of the Editor.

Studies in American Jewish Literature, for Bonnie Lyons, "Interview with Henry Roth, March, 1977," 5, Spring 1979, pp. 50–58.

Commentary, for John S. Friedman, "On Being Blocked and Other Literary Matters: An Interview," 64, August 1977, pp. 28–38.

The Jerusalem Post Magazine, for Marsha Pomerantz, "A Long Sleep," 47, September 23, 1977, p. 8.

In Their Own Words. European Journal of the American Ethnic Imagination, for Mario Materassi, "The Return of Henry Roth: An Inside View," 1, Summer 1983, pp. 47–55.

Margie Goldsmith, for an unpublished interview conducted in Albuquerque, N.M., July 2 and 5, 1983.

Europeo, for Antonella Barina, "I miei cinquant' anni di solitudine," 43, February 14, 1987, pp. 106–09.

"Impressions of a Plumber" originally appeared in *The Lavender,* 3, no. 3, May 1925, pp. 5–9.

"Lynn Riggs and the Individual" originally appeared in B.A. Botkin, ed., *Folk-say: A Regional Miscellany.* (Norman, University of Oklahoma Press, 1930).

"If We Had Bacon" originally appeared in *Signatures: Works in Progress,* 1, no. 2, 1936, pp. 139–158.

"Where My Sympathy Lies" originally appeared in *The New Masses,* 22, March 2, 1937, p. 9.

"Many Mansions" originally appeared in *Coronet,* September 1940, pp. 134–138.

"Equipment for Pennies" originally appeared in *The Magazine for Ducks and Geese,* Autumn 1954, pp. 15–16.

"The Prisoners" was originally published in Italian as "I detenuti," in *Lingua letteratura,* no. 8, May 1987. Translation by Mario Materassi.

"At Times in Flight: A Parable" originally appeared in *Commentary,* 28, July 1959, pp. 51–54.

"The Dun Dakotas" originally appeared in *Commentary,* 30, August 1960, pp. 107–109.

The three sections of "Assassins and Soldiers," translated into Italian, were published separately. The first, "Assassini e soldati," appeared in *L'Indice dei libri del mese,* 4, January 1987, pp. 14–16; the second, "La porta a vetri," in *Europeo,* 43, February 14, 1987, pp. 111–112; the third, "Lo stivale," in *Italia Oggi,* 2, January 31–February 1, 1987, p. 28. Translation by Mario Materassi.

"Statement of Purpose" was published in part in Bonnie Lyons, *Henry Roth: The Man and His Work.* (New York, Cooper Square Publishers, 1976).

"The Surveyor" originally appeared in *The New Yorker,* 42, August 6, 1966, pp. 22–30.

"Final Dwarf" originally appeared in *The Atlantic,* 224, July 1969, pp. 57–61.

"June '67" originally appeared in Mario Materassi, ed., *Rothiana: Henry Roth nella critica italiana.* (Florence, Giuntina, 1985).

"Itinerant Ithacan" originally appeared in *New America,* 3, Summer–Fall 1977, pp. 76–85.

"Report from Mishkenot Sha'ananim" originally appeared in *Albuquerque Jewish Community LINK,* 6, October 1977, p. 9.

"Segments" originally appeared in *Studies in American Jewish Literature,* 5, Spring 1979, pp. 58–62.

"The Wrong Place" originally appeared in *New Orleans Review,* 5, no. 4, 1978, pp. 325–328.

"Nature's First Green" was originally published by Targ Editions, New York, 1979.

"Weekends in New York: A Memoir" originally appeared in *Commentary,* 78, September 1984, pp. 47–56.

"Last Respects" was published in Italian as "Commiato" in *Europeo,* 43, February 14, 1987, pp. 113–114. Translation by Mario Materassi.

"The Eternal Plebeian and Other Matters" is an adaptation of remarks made by Henry Roth in Percoto, Italy, on the occasion of the award of the Premio Nonino for the translation of his novel, *Call It Sleep (Chiamalo Sonno),* by Mario Materassi.

The editor also wishes to express his deep gratitude to his wife, Millicent, his son, Marco, and his friend J. Anthony Burton for the sensitive and patient help they have given him in the preparation of this volume. Special thanks are owed to Roslyn Targ, Henry Roth's literary agent, for her extraordinary help and concern.

Contents

Foreword

*I*t was in Albuquerque, in 1985, when he was visiting us in the company of his alert, knowledgeable wife, Millicent, of Korean extraction, that Mario Materassi, professor of American literature in Florence and Italian translator of my only novel, urged me to bring out a collection of my short pieces: people were curious to know what had happened to me, why I hadn't written another novel, why I had ceased to write. Besides giving some indication of how I fared in the interval of fifty years, the pieces were interesting in their own right. Those were Mario's arguments.

I was opposed. I saw no reason why I should publish a bunch of random pieces of various literary value, and some with no pretense to it at all. But Mario had a vision of the whole that I in my slow fashion had not comprehended—and I only began to when he said he would include in the compendium my very first printed piece of prose, "Impressions of a Plumber," printed in the City College of New York *Lavender* during my freshman year of college and written as a required freshman term paper. It was then I realized what his purpose was: nothing less really than to exhibit the continuity within the desolating discontinuity of the frustrated writer's existence—and to show the development that had taken place over all those barren years. He would do this by providing a connective tissue: commentary, interview, reminiscence. He would accomplish something that I had not been able to accomplish, because I had been disabled by that very same discontinuity. In carrying out his purpose, he would be presenting my particular plight, yes, but only as a special case of a quite prevalent one—I called it plight; *blight* would have been a more fitting word, the blight that befell a whole generation of writers who came of age in the thirties, some before, some after, the blight of the one-book or one-trilogy syndrome, followed by creative decline, or even by creative desuetude. I gave my consent.

I think Mario has accomplished what he set out to do. By the setting in which he has placed these short pieces, he has provided an aperture into the workings of a sample imagination, trapped in what appears to have been a widespread collapse of creativity. In my own case, I seem finally to have attained a restoration of some kind, out of which I can again write. But I am eighty years of age. It took a great deal of forgetting and relearning, of perceiving anew. My contemporaries, people often more talented than I was, weren't so fortunate in having such long lives, in having a mate, both gifted and caring, who helped one survive—and in having a devoted surrogate son like Mario to assemble the fragments.

The book is primarily Mario's, not mine. It is a unique document. It provides insight into the state of mind of a whole generation of talented men and women in literature—and very likely in the other arts as well—who suddenly, after a brief spurt of creativity, lost identity, lost certainty, lost faith, lost bearings. Mario Materassi has furnished us with a sketch of an ambivalent and often anguished period, one that we were not able to record ourselves.

Henry Roth
1987

Introduction

Shifting Landscape *collects all of Henry Roth's published writings before and after* Call It Sleep. *They are public statements, memoirs, articles, a poem, a speech, short stories, and a chapter from the unfinished second novel—all told, thirty-one pieces spanning more than six decades, from 1925 to 1987.*

Some of these writings, having appeared in such magazines as Atlantic, Commentary, *and* The New Yorker, *are easily accessible. Others, on the contrary, have been unavailable for years, because they were published either in small magazines with very limited circulation or in periodicals now long defunct. In two instances ("Many Mansions" and "Lynn Riggs and the Individual"), even the author had forgotten about their existence. Yet other writings have appeared in print only outside the United States: one in Israel ("Vale atque Ave," in English) and four in Italy ("June '67" in English, and translations of "Assassins and Soldiers," "Last Respects," and "The Prisoners").*

The virtual unavailability of many of Roth's published writings has meant, unfortunately, that with very few exceptions little attention has been paid to the minor writings per se. Even more regrettable perhaps is the fact that, having based our studies of Call It Sleep *and its author upon an incomplete knowledge of his production, we*

*have risked making inaccurate assumptions and, therefore, arriving
at dubious conclusions.*

*Roth himself has done little to bring attention to his shorter
writings. In most of his known interviews, emphasis is placed on why
he stopped writing after* Call It Sleep—*the interviewers', as well as
Roth's, interest lying less in what the writer had actually accomplished
than in what he had failed to do. Roth has always been more than
willing to examine publicly the reasons for his prolonged silence, but
he has never been eager to remind the public of all those instances
when he had broken his silence. This lack of eagerness is to be
attributed in part to Roth's profound, incurable modesty and, in part,
to the fact that he is his own most severe critic, ever ready to question
the merits of his work.*

*Having reached the highest peak of literary achievement on
his first try, Roth could never be easily contented with lesser heights.
For half a century, his major existential preoccupation has been his
failure to recapture the all-pervading creative drive that had made*
Call It Sleep *possible. This has been his lifelong drama—a drama
punctuated at irregular intervals by the appearance of short pieces
of writing that, apart from their literary worth, interest their author
chiefly as landmarks in what he grimly terms his "desolate discontinuity." Roth's tendency to underrate and minimize his work, arising
from a sense of personal failure, has even led him to refer to himself
as "this dead author."*

But the writer in him was not dead. True, after Call It Sleep *his
career was drastically truncated, and the trauma of the laceration
caused a paralysis that lasted almost two decades. However, since
the end of the fifties, when Roth resumed writing, volume after volume
of typescript has accumulated on his desk. What he has released
for publication, and is here collected, constitutes a small portion of
his overall production, but it is certainly sufficient to prove that he
has not ceased to write.*

The first objective of Shifting Landscape *is, of course, to provide the reader with the totality of Henry Roth's publications. The
second objective, as the title suggests, is to offer as detailed a picture
as possible of the evolution of Roth's views on his dominant interests—namely, writing, literature, family, politics, and Judaism.*

*To this purpose, each piece is accompanied by selections from
his correspondence, from interviews, and from taped conversations.
Besides providing background information, these excerpts reveal
both the constants and the changes in the author's attitude toward
the controlling issues raised in each piece. They also record the role
that writing played in his life at the time the piece was written.*

The result is an informal autobiographical discourse that fo-
cuses primarily on the published writings or, as Roth calls them, the
"points of contact" established with the public, when the decision to
release something for publication meant that he accepted his role
as a writer.

The publications are presented in chronological order according to their approximate date of composition. The supporting com-
mentaries are arranged according to their particular illustrative function and, therefore, in an order that is not necessarily chronological.
They are made to intrude upon the diachronic presentation of Roth's
writings by synchronically introducing the shifts in perspective experienced by the author in the course of several decades. In other
words, the objective logic of straightforward progression is chal-
lenged by the subjective one of retrospection. There is also the
constant shifting of the time frames. Thus, the succession of Roth's
"points of contact" is viewed from a vantage point that is never final
but, on the contrary, always subject to further change.
The logic of change, the logic that accounts for inconsistencies
and turnabouts and contradictions, has long governed Henry Roth's
life, giving it its painfully segmented character. Decade after harrow-
ing decade, Roth looked for something precious that he had lost
when, still a child, he was removed from the East Side: continuity.
He was to find it, eventually, with the state of Israel. Paradoxically,
there is continuity also in the very discontinuity of his experience.
Two remarkable traits have given unity and consistency to Roth's
existence: an insatiable intellectual curiosity that never ceases to
question the self and the world around him and a willingness to pay
the price exacted by total commitment to the answers he has found.
His unbending integrity, both intellectual and moral, took him astray
from the commonsense path of routine and conformity and forced
him to go through life as through a series of disconnected phases,
each apparently denying the previous one. Yet this same integrity is
what gives continuity to the extraordinary existential itinerary of the
East Side boy turned enfant prodige of Modernism, of the acclaimed
writer who buried himself in rural Maine, of the Communist who chose
Israel over the Arabs, of the Jew who found his long-lost Jewishness
through an almost fifty-year-long rejection of Judaism.
The personal cost of this tortuous itinerary is most cogently
epitomized in the burning of his manuscript of the unfinished second
novel. This act constituted the nadir of Roth's hope ever to resume
writing and was intended to put a final seal upon the end of his
literary aspirations. Moreover, insofar as it was also prompted by
practical considerations (he was, after all, under surveillance by the

FBI), the destruction of that attempt at a "proletarian" novel in the middle of the McCarthy era declared also the end of Roth's hope ever to see a socialist society established in the United States. With the "general bonfire of papers in Maine," as he has called it, Roth literally burned his bridges to a past that he felt had led to a dead-end road. Yet, contrary to his intentions, the deep-seated aspirations that had been ritualistically sacrificed were not obliterated in the fire but, phoenix-like, were consumed only to be born anew.

Henry Roth's short writings are invaluable documents of the fascinating existential pilgrimage of their author. Still, beyond and above their documentary relevance, they must be judged in terms of their literary quality. This, of course, does not apply to certain minor pieces that were written for a public not necessarily literary and were meant to serve an ad hoc purpose. "Equipment for Pennies," for example, is a do-it-yourself article; "Where My Sympathy Lies" and "The Meaning of Galut in America Today" are ideological statements; and "Lynn Riggs and the Individual" is a promotional critique. The majority of the pieces, however, were intended to be literary works and should be assessed accordingly.

In judging Roth's work after Call It Sleep, there is the danger of being unduly conditioned by the overwhelming presence of that novel and, consequently, by the haunting image of the career-that-was-not. One thinks of what Roth could have attained, given the promise; one thinks of the monumental figure he seemed destined to become. But by indulging in hypothetical comparisons, one risks underrating his actual achievement and overlooking the excellence of many of these writings. The rare command of language, the tight grasp of the subject matter, the masterly control of structured, balanced inner relations among the component elements—all manifest the solid reality of a superb craftsmanship that deserves attentive, unprejudiced scrutiny.

Mario Materassi
Firenze, 1987

Shifting
Landscape

Editor's Note

When not otherwise specified, the excerpts from Henry Roth's letters are from personal communications to the editor. Likewise, the various taped conversations that are quoted are between the writer and the editor.

Impressions of a Plumber

May 1925

The first published piece of writing by Roth, "Impressions of a Plumber," was written as an assignment for an English course at City College. For many years, before he recalled having written "Lynn Riggs and the Individual," Roth was convinced that, with the exception of another paper for a second English course, "Impressions of a Plumber" was the only writing he had ever done before he began Call It Sleep.

    Roth: I was a freshman—it was the second half of my freshman year. The first half of the freshman year I could not get an English course. City College was already inundated with freshmen ahead of me who had better grades in high school and got their first choice ahead of me. So, by the time I got there, there were no longer any English One courses left open. The second half, I had a choice ahead of the incoming freshmen, so I took English One, which was a requirement—Composition One, or . . . what the hell was it called? I think it was Composition One.

(taped conversation,
Albuquerque, N.M.,
April 24, 1985)

Roth: I was given this assignment in English to write about some experiment or how to construct something. The previous summer, 1924, I had been a plumber's helper, installing pipes in new buildings in the Bronx. So I decided to write on how to install piping. And suddenly it turned into an impressionistic piece. Toward the end of the semester, the instructor announced that one of our themes was so good that he would recommend it for publication in the City College *Lavender.* When he mentioned my name, I almost died— and yet again, I wasn't *too* surprised. It was printed in *The Lavender* and was the first intimation that I had something special. And I got a D in the course.

Interviewer: On what basis did you get a D?

Roth: I didn't do what I was supposed to do: an expositional piece of work. I can't blame the instructor. So I got a D in English my first semester; the next term I got an A.

(Lyons, 1976, pp. 160–61)

Roth: So, the instructor in the course, [Arthur] Dickson, submitted the theme to *The Lavender,* the CCNY literary magazine. They printed it, and he gave me a D for the course. Eda Lou [Walton] read it afterward.

Interviewer: Do you have a copy of it?

Roth: I don't know whether I have a copy or whether my copy is at the Boston University library.

Interviewer: What issue?

Roth: I entered college in 1924, so I would look for it around 1925. I think it had a good beginning—what it's like to be plumber's helper. It goes a little downhill at the end.

Interviewer: The only piece of writing you did before you began the novel?

Roth: That is a fact.

Interviewer: Of course, while at CCNY you did other writing, but it wasn't fiction.

Roth: I did one other thing. There was a course in descriptive writing given by a professor. I received a lot of credit for my descriptions; there was no publication.

(Friedman, 1977, p. 30)

Roth: Believe it or not, a high school friend of mine, for some reason I still don't understand, had kept it. Although he himself was a very solid kind of an individual, and a very good runner and hurdler, he kept everything pertaining to me—my God, I think he kept a newspaper clipping of the time that I was on the rifle team in high school and I made a sensational score shooting one of those .22-caliber rifles. He even kept that; and gave that to me, if I'm not mistaken. I don't understand: why the hell the guy would have kept it? But he did. And he was the one who kept [that issue of *The Lavender*.] And for all I know, it may be the only one extant, unless CCNY kept a file of these publications.

(taped conversation,
Albuquerque, N.M.,
April 24, 1985)

*T*he alarm rings with frightened intensity. It is half past six. I wake reluctantly, shut off the alarm, and yawn. It is chilly even on a summer morning, and my bed is very warm. Ah, if I could lie here just a little longer! But no, experience has taught me that to lie here a little longer would mean my coming late to work. Ah, just a very little bit longer. No! And by a good "no" the flesh is conquered, and I rise.

A hasty toilet, a hasty breakfast, and I am out of the house, lunch under my arm. A short walk and I am in the subway. A wait, the train arrives, and I gain a strap overhead to hang on to. I look around; the car is full of drowsy men like me, dressed in old clothes and heavy shoes like me; in their faces is a look of hopelessness, or in the older ones no look at all, but thank Heaven not like me. Grim Toil has graven on their faces his trademark; he hasn't touched me. With them it's all work and one Sunday; with me it's an experiment. They must earn their bread to live, while I think with selfish satisfaction of my father's apparent good health.

The lights rush past the open window as if frightened by what they see. Soon the train comes out of the tunnel, and the great monarch of this system dazzles me with his splendor, and I avert my eyes. The cool morning air rushes in thru the window and dilutes the fetid breath of the subway. And suddenly I arrive at my station, Bubre Avenue.

A ten-minute walk along the avenue which has by now dwindled away into a road brings me to the scene of my labors. The skeleton houses stand out crudely against the sky. Everything is quiet, it being only twenty minutes to eight. I approach the house where we "knocked off" yesterday and look inside for Hymie, my mechanic. Not in? That's good. Then I slip into my overalls. Raising my eyes, I see Hymie coming. He has evidently been hurrying, for his broad, Slavic face is flushed.

"Hello, kid," he says, "Git the furnace goin'; we got roughin' today."

A day's work has begun, a hard day's work; for our work is "roughing." The "rougher" is the plumber who installs the pipes which lead from bathroom and kitchen to the sewer, not by any means to be considered a very easy or pleasant piece of work. Most of the work is done with six-inch cast iron pipe, and now and then it is necessary to use two-inch steel pipe.

When "roughing," it is necessary to use molten lead to connect pipe; so I cram the little furnace, which we use to melt lead, full of paper and charcoal. Then, as soon as the fire has gained headway, I put the pot of lead on.

The sun has come up now, and as I bend over the hot furnace to get a ladleful of lead, perspiration trickles down my face and neck. Carefully I hand the ladle over to Hymie, who is inside, "corking" six-inch pipe. Two lengths of six-inch pipe are connected by putting one into an enlarged opening of the other and then pouring hot lead into the space between them; this process is known as "corking."

As soon as the pipe is long enough to reach from the cellar to the first floor, I climb up the ladder, squeeze between the beams (for the floors have not yet been laid), and indicate with my hand where the pipe should be; six-inch pipe is always put between the two mold-ings of the wall and so is kept out of sight. A colored day-laborer helps Hymie lift one end of the pipe. Bracing my legs against the floor beams, I reach down and grasp it with both hands; a Herculean heave, and the pipe stands upright, one end resting on the earthen floor of the cellar, the other projecting a few inches above the first floor. The pipe having been braced by nailing straps of tape around it, the "corking" process continues until the second floor has been reached, and since this is a two-story house, it is not necessary to go further. Altho it sounds very easy, it takes about three hours to bring the pipe to the second floor.

I have given the reader the impression that the pipe is merely an enclosed cylinder. If so, how can the sinks and tubs be connected with it? In reality when a floor is reached, instead of continuing straight up with another piece of pipe, a six-by-two "Y" is connected, and then another straight piece of six-inch pipe. Visualize a tree, a poplar, whose trunk extends straight upward but whose branches make an acute angle with the trunk. There you have the six-by-two "Y," the trunk six inches and the branches two inches. To these branches the drain pipes of the wash basins, bathtubs, and flush bowls are connected.

As soon as the proper height has been reached, and the pipe has been properly braced, one of the work-dodging colored laborers digs a two-foot ditch in the cellar, beginning directly under the pipe, and ending at the foundations in front of the house. Where the ditch ends, he chisels an eight-inch circular hole thru the concrete foundations. Then he proceeds with pick and shovel to excavate a hole, next to the front foundation on the outside of the house until he reaches the chiseled hole. Since the floor of the cellar is considerably lower than the ground, he has to dig a rather deep hole. However, he's got all day to do it, so he takes his time.

In the meantime, Hymie "corks" a bend, which is a large elbow, to the bottom of the pipe. The bend permits us to change the direction of the pipe from horizontal to vertical. It is now laid in the ditch so that when the job is done, the earth will again be thrown over it and keep it out of sight; keeping pipe out of sight is the modern philosophy of plumbing.

"We can't wait fer dis guy," says Hymie, pointing in the direction of the noise made by the shovel of the laborer outside, "so you bring in 'bout ten lengt's o' six-inch, an' I'll go up, and git some measurements."

It had rained the night before the truck delivered the pipe, and as a result, the road had become soft and treacherous. The truck driver, fearing that the wheels would sink into the muck, unloaded his burden while still on the asphalt, a distance of about thirty yards from the house in which we are working. That necessitates my carrying eighty pounds of pipe every time we need a length. Now, eighty pounds isn't very heavy, and thirty yards isn't very far, but when the sun has made the pipe as hot as a coal, and you carry on your shoulder piece after piece over a dusty, stony road, eighty pounds begins to feel like eighty thousand and thirty yards is fast approaching the length of a light year. So, it is with hanging head and plodding step that I near the pile for another piece of pipe.

Tooooooot! The whistle screams a joyful announcement. Lunchtime!

My head snaps back, my feet become springy, my heart glad; the world takes on another hue. I run inside the house; take my lunch out of my coat pocket, and climb up to the first floor, where boards thrown on the floor beams constitute the table and seats. Hymie climbs in thru the window with a bag in one hand and a milk bottle full of water in the other. He sits down beside me, pulls a roll out of the greasy bag, and digs his uneven teeth into it. Slowly we munch, Hymie his rolls and salami, I my Swiss cheese sandwiches. Now and then we drink some lukewarm water from the bottle. There is little conversation; both of us are rapt in thought, Hymie probably wondering how long his wife is going to stay away, I speculating as to what time the boss ought to be around. We finish our lunches and lean against the wall of the house. Hymie looks at his big Ingersoll and informs me that we still have ten minutes left. We, as is the case with most house plumbers, have only a half hour for lunch. I prefer that, however, to the full hour lunch, as we go home at five o'clock, one half hour earlier than those having hour lunches. Suddenly Hymie speaks.

"Boy, dat baby diggin' de hole outside sure is slow; he orta go down to de Zoo an' watch de toitles wizz by. Some o' dem boogies ain't got no brains at all. Why, I seen one o' dem drop his coat down a twenty-foot sewer ditch dat was filled wid de doitiest water y'ever seen. Wow! He lets out a squawk y'could hear for a mile.

" 'Hey plumber,' he yelps, 'gimme a wire will ya. I got my coat down dat ditch.'

"I walks over wid him to take a look, an' I sees his coat down on de bottom, all covered wid mud.

" 'Wot de H--l d'ya want de coat fer,' I says; 'it's 'n ole coat anyhow, ain't it?'

" 'Aw,' he says, 'I don't give a d--n fer de coat, I got my lunch in it.' "

I laugh heartily, and I can see Hymie is pleased with himself.

"Well, kid, dere goes de wizel," he says, as the whistle begins to blow. "I wancha to tread a piece of two-inch twenny-tree inches long." And with this he climbs up to the second floor.

Threading two-inch pipe is a bit of work which is even more disagreeable than carrying six-inch pipe out in the sun. In the vernacular of my uncouth mentor, threading two-inch pipe is real "Chinee labor." In order not to confuse the threading of a pipe with that of a needle, an explanation is appropriate.

The first thing done in threading a piece of pipe is to place it in a vise. As soon as the vise is tightened, the stock is put on the pipe. The stock is a long cylindrical steel bar about an inch in diameter. Midway between the two ends, there is a hole which fits snugly around the pipe. In reality, there are teeth projecting from this hole which bite into the pipe as the bar is turned. The best illustration I can give of a stock threading a piece of pipe is to liken it to the letter "T" which has fallen over: the horizontal line is the pipe; the vertical, the stock. Then by pulling alternate ends of the vertical bar, the process of pipe threading is reproduced. It is really too tame to say pulling alternate ends; what I actually mean is yanking your head off.

While I am thus engaged, I hear a step on the ladder. The Boss! Manfully, I tug at the stock, not heeding the warm, salty sweat that stings my eyes. As he climbs up the ladder he glowers at me and, seeing that I am working, climbs to the second floor. Whew! Nearly had me that time. Queer that I didn't hear his Ford. It generally makes enough noise. Mentally, I send up an offering to Heaven as thanksgiving for my having been found working. Voices from above reach my ears. The boss is telling Hymie that he wants the work put out faster. They all do. Hymie's answers are restricted to the monosyllable "yes."

Soon I see the boss's foot reaching down for the next rung. He has never spoken a word of disapproval to me, yet I hope he misses the rung. Why? It's hard to define. He is the boss; I am the laborer. He gets fat contracts, and does nothing but ride around in his Ford, and call down his men, no matter how hard they work. I get twenty-eight dollars a week, which represents the sweat of my body pressed into a solid form. That is how one feels when he sweats for wages. But the boss doesn't miss the rung; he climbs serenely down, without giving me so much as a glance.

Hymie comes down a little later to give me some more measurements of pipes. He scrutinizes my face, but I pretend not to have heard the "bawling out" he received from the boss. He looks relieved and climbs upstairs again. It would have hurt his pride a great deal if he knew a mere helper heard him receive a reprimand.

I hear the laborer outside yell that the hole has been dug. Hymie climbs down the ladder, and we both go down to the cellar, where we run the six-inch pipe thru the chiseled hole to the end of the ditch; but it is slow work and takes us almost four hours. The pipe now runs from the second floor to the ditch outside the house, and our work with six-inch pipe ends. However, the Sewer Department will soon take it up where we leave off. Long trenches will be dug, sewers will be laid, and the house pipe will be connected with them.

It is 4:30 now, and in about fifteen minutes we shall be quitting.

"One more piece o' pipe," shouts Hymie, "an' we'll call it a day. Make this 'un fourteen inches long."

My arms ache, but I work eagerly, and soon the pipe is threaded; I climb up the ladder and hand the pipe to Hymie.

"Put de tools away, kid, and take de lead out o' d'fire," he says.

Gladly I climb down the ladder. Caulking iron, monkey wrench, hack saw, hammers, all are packed into the kit, and the kit put into the locker. The stock, vise, and twenty-pound hammer are thrown in for company. The pot of lead is taken out of the fire and dropped on the sand to cool. I get out of my overalls and go outside to wash. Presently, Hymie comes out, washes also—but with less success, for the dirt has worked its way deeper into his skin. However, it must not be understood that I look like a very dignified person or a picture of cleanliness myself with my coat under my arm to give the air a chance to dry some of the perspiration, which is giving me an uncomfortable and wholly unwelcome bath.

After twenty minutes of plodding we finally arrive at Westchester Avenue, where Hymie, who takes the car, leaves me with the usual, "S'long, kid; anudda day, anudda dollar."

In a letter to the same high school friend who had kept the Lavender *issue, young Roth described his first day on another job he took while in college. The passage concerning the third rail is of special interest in view of the ending of* Call It Sleep.

The Irishman downstairs in the ground floor flat below us, one Reb Mahoney, being informed by his wife who was informed by my mother that poor little R neither spun nor toiled invited me to apply for a job at the Interboro Rapid Transit Company. I accepted with alacrity. And, on the strength of Mr. Mahoney's recommendation that I came from a good family, I was hired, even though the examining doctor said disgustedly, "You don't have a scar on you." Hence for the past week I have been working at the IRT repair barn for nine hours per day—and going to college four hours at night. It might interest you to know that I am a pipe fitter's helper, and like everyone else there always fiddle around "old red mule" (the third rail). I have found out, not by experience to be sure but by hearsay, that a jolt from the third rail doesn't as a rule kill you, provided you've got any sort of physique or constitution. What it does is to play a percussion solo on your teeth, and since I don't relish that kind of music, I am very careful to keep my distance. Another thing, I work in the pit under the trains, and the first day there, I kept wiping my brow with my sleeve, which was filthy with grease. *Frage nicht,* when I came out from under, half the place from the superintendent to the lowliest pit sweeper went into convulsions of laughter. I was peeved at first, but when I looked into the washroom mirror I understood and forgave. I had two black horns of grease sticking to my brow, and the rest of my face had those strange curves of Dr. Caligari beaten all hollow.

(letter to Iven Hurlinger
from New York, N.Y.,
July 17, 1927)

Lynn Riggs and the Individual

1930

This analysis of the work of playwright Lynn Riggs is the only piece of literary criticism written by Roth. Riggs, a personal friend, was a member of the wide circle of writers and intellectuals to which Eda Lou Walton introduced Henry Roth after he started living with her in the Village in 1928.

Although it was written in 1929 and published the following year, this critique is, paradoxically, one of the latest additions to the Roth canon. Roth was reminded of its existence and succeeded in locating a copy of it in the fall of 1986—well over half a century after its publication.

Here's new grist to set the old mill groaning: I went through my correspondence with Harold U. Ribalow and came up with the discovery that he had located a piece of writing of mine on the playwright Lynn Riggs. I was always enthusiastic about Lynn's plays, and friend and admirer of Lynn personally. I thought the piece was to be published by French & Co., Lynn's theatrical agents, as part of their publicity for his plays. Though Lynn paid me twenty-five dollars, I felt at the time that the money was coming out of his own pocket, and the agency hadn't approved the piece, hadn't used it, and neither had anybody else (it was, after all, an undergraduate-level attempt at literary analysis [my one and only]—and yet oddly enough draws an intuitive conclusion that proved valid). . . . Anyway, Ribalow had located it in a now defunct (I guess) magazine called *Folkways*. [The title was actually *Folk-say.*] But he was unable to get an acknowledgment when he directed an inquiry to Oklahoma U. (which I believe Lynn may have attended awhile; it's in his native state, the setting of all the plays I dealt with: the musical comedy hit, *Oklahoma!,* staged in the forties, was based on his *Green Grow the Lilacs,* set in the early days of Oklahoma). I wrote the university library asking whether they could exhume the piece, and *mirabile dictu,* they not only did, but were kind enough to send me a xerox, which I now submit for your delectation.

Don't blame me. How did I know in 1929, when I wrote the "critique," that Mario Materassi would someday single-mindedly scour every obscure niche and cranny of the abode with feather and wooden spoon, in order to retrieve any crumb with the least leavening in it that chanced to escape the fire?

(letter from Albuquerque, N.M.,
October 20, 1986)

I

*L*ynn Riggs is, primarily, not a writer of problem, folk, or realistic drama, but a dramatic poet whose poems are in terms of Oklahoma life. His rich use of folk material is merely a poet's use of his own background. The various scenes, such as the play-party, "shivoree," and courtroom scenes of the several plays, are all developed neither entirely for picturing nor for attacking local or more universal social institutions, but as symbolic of restrictive and leveling forces in life against which the individual bent upon self-development must contend. Indeed Mr. Riggs's plays may all be considered as a cycle concerned with a central and unifying theme, and it is this dominant theme rather than the more obvious folk basis and cultural background of his scene that makes him important as a dramatist. Although Mr. Riggs is indeed an Oklahoma poet, he is just as surely writing of a universal problem as if his plays were set in any other environment. He will be remembered, of course, for his perfect presentation of the milieu of these early plays, but he will be remembered also for his attitude toward life; and it is this attitude which will direct the course of his later plays, for he is already writing about an entirely different milieu.

Before I mention the central theme of the work of Lynn Riggs, it must be made clear that I do so merely for orientation: the life in his plays is too inexplicable, too ramified, too fully alive to be reducible to rigid definition. The issues that appear in Mr. Riggs's plays are not the result of rational thought, but are to him an inevitable arrangement of life itself. This inevitable arrangement, or central theme, expressing it generally, is the conflict between the impulses of the individual and the constricting forces about him, whether they be the demands of other individuals or the organized demands of society. More specifically, it is the struggle life makes to maintain the integrity of life, the right to live by the laws governing its own natural and free impulses and by no other standards. The struggle between this individuality and the external demand of uniformity becomes, when formulated, almost a moral one: the good, which is the genuine expression of natural feeling—the inherent idealism, gentleness, and lyricism of what is fundamentally innocent—resisting what, though it is understandable and pitiful, is nevertheless evil—the expedient, the empty or warped convention, the petrified morality. Tragedy results either when the latter overcomes the former or when the former attempts to adjust itself to the latter.

Once more I wish to emphasize the fact that none of the terms I have been using ever appears in a play. Such an artist as Lynn Riggs does not think in abstractions, but in terms of human life. He expresses his ideas in a struggle between the emotions of human beings.

That his plays form themselves into a natural cycle is brought out by the fact that his first play, *Knives from Syria,* is an escape from the demands of uniformity, and his latest, *Roadside,* a triumph over them, while the six intervening plays are, in one way or another, the defeat of the individual by them. It is as though the author returned to test experience as particularized in Oklahoma again and again before he found his answer.

The problem that faces Rhodie in the play, *Knives from Syria,* is the necessity of adjusting her own natural and romantic impulses to the expedient and the accepted: a marriage with Charley, a typical farmhand, who would then maintain the farm. The solution of this problem is accidental and is effected by the introduction of a foreign element—not as in *Roadside* by the development in the characters of inherent capabilities. The Syrian Peddler in the early play, with his somewhat literary poetic speeches, presents Rhodie with an escape from the monotony of existence.

Knives from Syria is at times rather obvious in its progression. And perhaps because it is only in one act, its characters have only hints of that opacity and fluctuance which give to Riggs's later creations the quality of being self-willed, living entities.

II

Mr. Riggs's next play, *Big Lake,* is a lyric poem, at times almost unearthly in its purity and terror, a play whose characters waver between flesh and symbol. From here on, the author's dramatic poetry is completely in the native Oklahoma speech. The symbols or ideas with which the play is concerned are neither rigid nor bounded, but slip naturally from one identity to another, growing at the same time more rich in suggestion: the idea of innate purity surrounded by corruption is to be found in the innocence of the boy and girl trapped by the evil in men; in the Big Lake surrounded by dark woods; and even in the flower these two children pluck from among the dead leaves.

The tragedy of *Big Lake* is simple and intensely moving. It lies in the destruction of the two children, who represent innocence and purity, by Butch, the criminal, who, in turn, represents bitter necessity. And the fact that Miss Meredith, the strait-laced schoolteacher, has driven the defenseless boy and girl upon the lake, where they are shot at by the thick-witted Sheriff, is an ironic comment upon Morality and the Law. But didactic interpretations are not necessary to an appreciation of this play. Its beauty of wonder and tremulous overtones are sufficient recommendations: the children in the cabin that was "like it growed out of the ground"... "with no sunshine a-comin' in, and no moonlight ever"; the Lake "like ... sump'n you never hoped t' see!" that "holds the sun" like "a cup with gold in it."

Mr. Riggs's next two plays, taken together with *Big Lake,* form a trilogy whose theme is the meeting of youth with existence. In *Big Lake* the corrupt forms of existence destroy the life of youth; in *Sump'n Like Wings* and in *A Lantern to See By,* more realistic in treatment, life remains to each of the protagonists. But tragedy this time is in the struggle rather than in its results. The two plays are almost complements of each other: Willie, in the former, confronted with the force of social attitudes, and Jodie, in the latter, resisting subjection by an individual. Both characters suffer because of their innate differences from the common herd: Jodie's brothers, for instance, are named by their brutal father, Heck, Dick, Nick, Pick, Stick; and Willie is constantly reminded that she is different from her other sisters. Both Willie and Jodie resist the molds into which they are born, and struggle against those leveling forces that would choke the impulses of one and crush the idealism of the other. Their two solutions of life are likewise counterparts of each other, since Willie's is a retreat and the acknowledgment of the inevitable incompleteness of such retreat, while Jodie's is an assertion, the destruction of the embodiment of the subjugating force, his father.

Sump'n Like Wings is diffuse; one by one Willie tries and rejects the separate bonds of her environment: marriage, home, the lifeless moral code of her mother, dependence on others. She attains freedom by organizing herself, and by insisting upon the integrity of her attitudes. *A Lantern to See By*, on the other hand, is concentrated; Jodie's environment grows so intensely oppressive that it has even numbed his thought. Action, desperate action, is his only way to freedom.

III

In *A Lantern to See By*, the farmhouse, the center of Oklahoma country life, was merely background; in Lynn Riggs's next play, *The Lonesome West*, the farmhouse becomes dynamic. Here it is resolved into its elements—living room, partly underground potato house, porch, roof, etc.—each of which becomes a plane for the dominant feelings of a certain character—his aspirations, elemental or unaccountable impulses, transitions, and ecstatic release or vision. The planes are developed with perfect naturalness, so that a realization of them is not absolutely necessary to an understanding of the play. They serve to emphasize and contrast the different worlds, capabilities, and limitations of the various characters. For instance, Ed, an earthy creature and lover of the soil, belongs to the sphere of the partly underground potato house; while Sherman, mad, visionary, and poetic, is the only one to attain the roof of the house.

The characters themselves are among the strangest in American drama; they exhibit that intense self-absorption and psychological isolation in the presence of each other which one finds only in the uncanny reality of Russian creations. To have created such characters as those in *The Lonesome West*, their frustration and tortured ecstasy, is in itself a work of genius.

The play is rich in meanings, but the chief of these is, I think, implied in the fact that each person is isolated from all the others in feelings and desires; therefore, the very attempt at living together of a society whose members can neither coördinate nor sympathize with one another inevitably crushes the finer and the natural impulses under the desires of the strongest. The defeat of the most precious things in the lives of these characters, love, the natural joy of earth, the poetic imagination, becomes in *The Lonesome West* ironic and hopelessly pitiful, since these ideals are defeated through the craving after what is false and relatively trivial. Like most of Riggs's plays, *The Lonesome West* holds many special meanings for the West itself.

IV

The scene in his next play, *The Domino Parlor,* changes from the Oklahoma country to the Oklahoma town. *The Domino Parlor,* to me, is his most anguished and bitter play. So strangely inverted is the world presented there, that what to his characters is the normal and customary seems to us a feverish nightmare; and such deeds as are to them enigmatic or reprehensible are to us the only redeeming acts and feelings in the play. It is better for one in such a world as that in which these characters move to have stifled entirely whatever feelings were genuine and undefiled; but to one such as Toni, the tab show queen, in whom these feelings are not crushed but pent, the realization of their force and truth must suddenly make her life an empty betrayal of them, and her world unbearably alien:

> TONI: If they's ever been anything beautiful in your life, hang on to it, even though it don't stay beautiful. Remember it the way it was at first. . . . Some part of me is gone dead, because I didn't know how to keep it alive. I'm a walkin' nightmare wishin' it'd get daylight.

Yet such a realization gives her the strength to face the impasse with dignity, even though broken and pathetic. Precisely the same situation as that she is caught in confronts Jude, her former lover, so proud of his hardness and disillusionment—walls which reveal themselves as both weak and false.

There are several factors which make this the most heartbreaking of Riggs's plays: the structure itself, which is that of a mystery drama, adds to the intensity; the speeches pierce one with their agony. In this play alone the chief character feels the revulsion of having herself degraded her own true nature, and of having sacrificed something beautiful to the demands of life.

V

From the gray, bitter defeat of *The Domino Parlor,* the dramatist returns again in his next play, *Green Grow the Lilacs,* to the Oklahoma country; but this time to the Oklahoma of the late nineteenth century, when there still prevailed a native romanticism and when the West had not yet lost its joyous freedom nor the consciousness of its own poetry. *Green Grow the Lilacs* is naturally Mr. Riggs's most mellow and golden play; its tragedy lies in the necessary passage of a glorious mood. The formation of attitudes with which to meet life, the acknowledgment of its burdens, and the recognition of change are the valuable acquisitions the characters of this play achieve when forced to live life by common standards; in return they must sacrifice not only a lyric sense of newness and freedom, but the promise in their own natural development as well.

There is a normal temptation to philosophize on this play. One sees in Curly, the cowboy, romanticism, alive to the beauties of the world; in Jeeter, the hired hand, necessity, comprehending only the uses of life and none of its loveliness—and thus symbolically identified with death. Contamination by him is mortality, which one must face with wisdom. Aunt Eller expresses its essence:

> Sickness, bein' pore and hungry even, bein' left alone in yer old age, bein' afraid to die————It all adds up. And you c'n stand it. They's one way. You got to be hearty. You *got* to be.

There is both sadness and ultimate comfort in her wisdom. I cannot refrain from quoting the following to show how completely unaffected and natural is the symbolism:

> AUNT ELLER: Oh well. (*She comes down to him.*) They git to be ole timers soon enough.
> OLD MAN PECK: That's right. Same as us. Tough—like hickory.
> AUNT ELLER: (*Slowly*). No. Not as tough as *that.*
> (*Their wise eyes meet for a moment, understandingly. He smiles*

agreement, nodding his head. Then she holds out the lantern to him to light his way into the dark.)

But if bowing to common standards or to the demands of others touches the individual with mortality, the insistence on the integrity of his own impulses lifts him to an almost immortal plane. In *Roadside,* Riggs's latest play, the inner law of the individual is again confronted by society's demands that he live according to the uniform pattern. But this time the outcome is overwhelmingly comic—and for this reason: that uniform patterns, whether institutions, conventions, or laws, reveal themselves in the light of free human impulse to be a veneration for mechanical procedure, and meaningless taboo; useful guides and restraints to the herd, but useless to the genuine individual, and apt to collapse at the first thrust of human impulse. This collapse of the pattern and the final victory of the inner law is the central theme of *Roadside* and affirmatively fulfills the cycle. Nor do I believe there exists of its kind another comedy so rich, airy, and joyous. Its two chief characters. Hannie and Texas, as a result of the easy largeness and adequacy of their actions, and their perfect freedom, are invested with the timeless and mythical quality which one attributes to a demigod or associates with an epic character such as Paul Bunyan.

VI

Because of lack of space, this inadequate account of the development of Lynn Riggs's themes must suffice; for the same reason, I can barely indicate the qualities of his plays that give them life: their wealth of folk material; their play-parties and songs; their native poetry, its earthy imagery and fine rhythms:

> You'd as soon deny a calf the full udder a-waitin' fer it in the cow-lot.

its fresh, vivid diction:

> Crossin' the crick, ole Daise shied at a cotton-tail. She never done that before. A little ole cotton-tail not bigger'n a minute. I offed plum over her head.

and its pungency and hearty brunt of epithet:

My God, if I ever seen a lantern-jawed cock-eyed idiot that couldn't say "Boo" to a "flyer" you're it! Ever' time I look at you, I git ringworm.

the native "characters," their rich humor and pathos:

> GILLIS: I'm ashamed of my kids, ever' last one of 'em! Plum ashamed! They jist aint no good. You'd think now, a-lookin' at me keerful, 'at I'd have kids an' grandkids that ud git to be the President, wouldn't you?
> HANNIE: Yeow, president of a turnip patch.

Summing up, then, the impression of Lynn Riggs's plays, one is aware that the life of his characters is on earth; none strains toward absolutes; none is driven by ideas; they are spiritual without being religious. Perhaps they lack a full contemporaneous appeal in that they never stand before the abysses of the contemporaneous mind with its search for emotional discipline, standards, and religion. There are two reasons for this: the necessary restrictions that faith to the nature of the author's art imposes, and the fact that his attitudes are directly opposed to the modern search. One does not feel that his chief characters are tragic within themselves; on the contrary, there is an inherent lightness and sanity about them, and their birthright is joy. This, I think, is one of Riggs's strongest beliefs, that joy is the true nature of man, a sign of his true development, and tragedy the defeat of his true nature.

Lynn Riggs is now about thirty years of age and has been writing full-length plays only these last five years. He is already by imagination and sensitivity of equipment the best poet writing for the American stage, and by depth of meaning and definiteness one of the most important dramatists.

In a recent conversation, prior to remembering that he had written something on Lynn Riggs, Roth candidly discussed his peculiar position vis-à-vis the distinguished intellectuals who frequented Walton's home.

> *Roth:* It so happens that once in a while a guy has this good luck, you might say, that one kind of feeling he has fits in with a given period, a given time. But why does the damn thing come in your head? One tries to find some kind of refuge in the fact that some individual seems to resonate with his time. And I think that's probably what makes *the* work of art—the *lasting* work of art: that peculiar resonance. John Synge, the playwright—one of my idols, really—says something similar to that when he writes that talent is not

enough, that the individual has in some way to tap some kind of a stream—I don't know whether he uses the word *universal,* or what—of human consciousness at a given time.

It's sheer luck, really, as far as I'm concerned. So many guys whom I admire, that I knew at the time, in those twenties. . . . Because I was admitted to a much older generation—well, not so much older, but even five years of difference when you are only twenty-two or twenty-three is a hell of a lot of difference. You meet a guy who already has his doctorate and so forth, and he may be teaching, and you are still an undergraduate. And most of Walton's contemporaries were academics and teachers—a number of them with very well established reputations: the Van Dorens, for example; Constance Rourke. Then there were the poets, like Hart Crane, Léonie Adams, Horace Gregory. And critics like William Troy. And playwrights whom I knew, like Lynn Riggs, who wrote the play which later became *Oklahoma!* . . . Actually, I wasn't on their level—I mean, I scarcely had any business *being* there. What I am trying to say is that I saw talents there that were really exceptional. And yet, how was it that this individual, myself—and I speak with due, I think, moderation. . . . I mean, they were brilliant wits. . . . How was it that I should be singled out? It's only because, for some reason or other, I did resonate—and I did, not because it was a matter of my will: you can't do that. But it just so happened that through circumstances, misfortunes, along with everything else, I did feel the vibration of the time, saw the important *sense* of the time, that these much greater intellects, and much greater talents, and much greater social critics, did not.

Now that is something that's almost impossible to explain. I think I told you about the famous remark of Margaret Mead—she was another of those there—who asked almost the same thing: how do you account for the fact that this novel should become, *has* become, a classic of its time? So I said to her, thinking I was smart, "That's a matter of grace"—because to me grace means something you can't explain anyway. And her answer was so . . . in a sense *prosaic.* She didn't realize that I was trying to find a way out and trying to be funny at the same time. She said, "But grace—that isn't a Jewish concept, is it?" I'll never forget that.

(taped conversation,
Albuquerque, N.M.,
February 7, 1986)

If We Had Bacon

1936

"If We Had Bacon" is the only extant portion of what would have been Roth's second novel. It owes its survival to the circumstance of having been published in a small magazine, Signatures: Works in Progress, *now long defunct, where it was introduced by the editors as "the opening section of what is, perhaps, a growing trilogy."*

Roth himself does not recall the exact length of the original manuscript that he submitted to Scribner's. On one occasion he spoke of "about one hundred twenty-five pages"; on another, he spoke of "perhaps seventy five to one hundred pages." The copy sent to Scribner's, which Maxwell Perkins read, was lost after Perkins retired, and the author destroyed his own copy in the late forties.

Roth: About mid-1935, after the trauma of *Call It Sleep* had worn off, I began to get the itch to write again. Now here is where the Party must have had its influence—because I now felt that I wanted to break away from an extension of the immigrant East Side Jewish child and do something from the American Middle West. Now suppose I hadn't known anything about the Party—I probably would have done the adolescent years, perhaps taking it as far as meeting Eda Lou or growing consciousness of artistic abilities. Instead, I broke away and was going to do the proletariat, right out of the American scene. . . . I wrote about one hundred or one hundred twenty-five pages and submitted them to Scribner's. The famous Maxwell Perkins paid an advance to David Mandel, who was a partner in Ballou [the publishers of *Call It Sleep*].

(Lyons, 1976, pp. 172–73)

Roth: So I was sold to Scribner's for a thousand dollars, which Mr. Mandel pocketed and bought a new Dodge with.

(Goldsmith, 1983)

Roth: Even before the publication of *Call It Sleep* I was at work on a new book. I had met a colorful person around whom I was building my second novel. The man was a tough, second-generation German-American who had been raised on the streets of Cincinnati and relied on his fists and his physical stamina to cope with life. Being an illiterate, he had acquired almost everything he knew through his own experience. I was attracted to him because he always took pride in being able to defend himself, no matter what happened. His build and the way he carried himself made me think of a champion middleweight fighter, and as a matter of fact, he had trained with professionals. When he told me that he had never been beaten, I was inclined to believe him. Then suddenly, this man, who had fought and brawled his way through life, lost his right hand in an industrial accident. With that came the terrible shock and realization that he was no longer able to fight the world alone. His personal tragedy and the knowledge that he would have to turn to others for help were terrifying blows that hit him at the depth of the Depression and changed his whole outlook on life.

Like many intellectuals during the Depression, I had become attracted to Marxism and felt the Communist Party to be its true expression. It was as a result of my contact with the Party that I met my German acquaintance and conceived the idea of basing a novel on him. The man and what I learned about him fitted in with what I thought the Party stood for. I carefully gathered the data of his life, as well as my observations concerning him, and wrote about a hundred pages of manuscript.

(Bronsen, 1969, pp. 271–72)

Roth: [The name of the character in the book] was Dan Loem—the guy's actual name was Clay.

Interviewer: So Dan Loem starts off in the book as an adolescent?

Roth: Yes, he starts off in Cincinnati as what you'd call a street tough about to commit a robbery. The first section deals with his waylaying the paymaster of a slaughterhouse. He and his younger brother pretend to be playing baseball, and the guy comes through carrying his little satchel with the payroll in it, and the older of the two brothers bats him over the head and just takes off with the satchel. This guy was already a daring fellow. Later on in his life— probably in his very early twenties—Dan Loem became a sparring partner of a famous middleweight fighter named Stan Ketchel. Ketchel was world champion 1908 to 1910. Dan Loem, alias Bill Clay, was born in 1888.

Interviewer: Did Dan Loem get as far in the book as joining the Party, or hadn't he lost his hand already?

Roth: He hadn't lost his hand yet. He was caught and arrested and sent to a reformatory. That's as far as I got. Loem lost his hand in a factory—in a National Biscuit Company baking machine. He had always suspected it was a deliberate job. The accident occurred at the noon break, when the machinery was turned off, and Loem was wiping the gears at the behest of the foreman.

(Goldsmith, 1983)

What a will [Bill] had. He could bend destiny into a pretzel, especially when he said: "Youze boojwa intellectchels thinks youze knows everything. Youze knows shit."

(letter to Harold Ribalow
from Augusta, Maine,
October 8, 1964)

Roth: [*Call It Sleep*] came out in '34, a time when intellectuals were beginning to gravitate toward the Left almost without exception, and I along with the rest. We believed that the solution to societal ills was a new order of things, a socialist order. So I joined the Communist Party in 1933. Very soon thereafter I thought I had found a wonderful character for a novel: a proletarian I had come to know in the Communist Party, a very colorful guy. He was . . . in his early fifties and sold the *Daily Worker* to eke out a living. It seemed to me that all I had to do was to explore his life's experiences and exploit the picturesque language that he used and I had a novel. I wrote perhaps seventy-five to one hundred pages. Because of Ballou's parlous financial condition, it was submitted to Scribner's, whose editor at the time was Maxwell Perkins. Without any kind of outline, Perkins advanced one thousand dollars for the rights to publish the future novel. That was the end of my literary career. After that came the block.

(Friedman, 1977, p. 34)

*P*lane dawdling out of tempo with the spinning edge, it veered toward him deceptively lolling. He ducked. And his lips twitched wryly because he ducked because it soared above his head above the shadow of the houses and lilted in the sunlight. Hung in the sky, a cored and bronzed and shrunken sun, a pineapple-rind buzz-saw. Hovered, flagged, toppled pell-mell down shirking air currents, whacked on its edge and cracked in half on the wooden sidewalk—the broken brim of a crownless straw hat.

Walter Loem nudged the smooth box of bacon that he carried concealed beneath his striped denim jumper snugly up under his armpit. It had slid down an inch or two, released from the clamp of his bicep, had almost slipped away, in fact, when he threw his arm up to ward off the mincing disk of straw. Loem knew that if the fancy package had fallen to the street in all its unwrapped glossiness, it would have meant only one thing to the faces behind the windows of the dreary, unpainted wooden houses (and he was always aware of faces molded out of the dark under the crust of starched curtains): it would have meant theft. And that's what it did mean.

Not that he gave a hang what the faces knew (drawn faces magnified in narrow windows), or what the disappointed eyes of housewives on the first floor glimpsed, or what the fiercely cheerful eyes of whores on second stories pried into, or the saloon-keeper glancing sluggishly. But when Walter Loem didn't want them to know his affairs, they weren't going to know them, that's all! Now who threw the damned kelly? Just who was trying to get funny?

Under the black slouch hat he wore, Loem's tea-colored brows, thick as caterpillars, still reposed in sunny calm. But in the sandy shade of their shallow sockets, his small, pale-gray eyes glinted with a greenish tinge like the edge of broken glass. He slackened his pace over the wooden planks of the sidewalk and studied the street: The bakery-wagon driver slipping the reins into the ring of the imitation sapling stump hitching post; the old barfly watching a pair of husky teamsters in doormat-colored canvas aprons launch beer kegs down the cellar ways. Nothing out of the ordinary there. But the three dapper, derbied young men, lounging the other side of the faded wooden Indian, were they looking his way? It seemed to him they were. And the one wearing the narrowest cuffs on his pants, Loem recognized: A pimp—the very one he had warned a short time ago not to address remarks to his daughter on her way from school.

Loem snorted ever so softly. Did these skinny birds in spats really mean to tangle up with a real man? That's what he called funny! A tremor rippled through the calves of his legs. He took a deep slow breath that sent his brain into a bright quiver like a bough in blossom. And the memory of former fights floated through his mind, fights while in the army, fights in railroad camps, in mining towns. Shining fists flying like a swirl of petals. (Drop the package first thing off the bat! Never get cornered, stay out in the open! Look out for brass knuckles or a dirk!) Negligently, his right hand slid into the pocket of his jumper, found what it sought, the smooth wagon bolt, an inch thick, three inches long, that fitted neatly into the cylinder of the clenched fist. He could brain a steer with that in his hand. He calculated that two of them ought to be kicking on the ground before the third could even swing. And if the punk did try to pull a knife, then his face would carry the dent of a two-hundred-pound pivoting heel until he died. And tomorrow, Walter Loem would walk through that street with a forty-five under the belt of his jeans.

He watched them closely as he approached, watched their hands. On his face a tawny vacancy was stretched, pinned there like an old slack hide by two glinting eyes and the thin red staple of his mouth. Which one of them would make the first move? To his surprise, not one of them did. No, the dudes were at ease, laughing, toying, as always, with their cuff links and their stand-up collars and the pomaded quills of their mustaches, or studying their well-kept hands, so milky under the fingernails, so free, in the midst of poverty, of the green grime of poverty.

Loem was one acquainted with treachery, but this nonchalance was too natural to be dissembled. He was wrong. Someone must have thrown the old hat from a roof or a window. He relaxed and let the wagon bolt slide from his hand. But as he was about to pass the alley this side of the cigar store, a towhead peeped out, a pair of blue eyes met his, and Loem had just time enough to see the impish light in them change to consternation before the head disappeared. Kids! He smiled to himself. Why didn't he think of that before instead of getting all worked up over a false alarm? The joke was on him. Out of the corner of his eye, he could see a number of kids crouched alertly in the shadow of a stable and flattened against the fences like frogs at the bottom of a spring. He made no sign, and with only a casual glance at the elegant loungers, stepped into the cigar store.

In the back, under the squirming light of a dusty window, the old German looked up from his small, cluttered lathe. He had been boring a pipe, and the aroma of fine old briar in the air, mingling with the odors of snuff, molasses, and cigars, reminded Loem of St. John's bread. The old man grunted in recognition and shuffled to the front of the store. His pink shirt sleeves were rolled up over his meager, knotty arms, his unshaven face, teed high on his celluloid collar, looked hollower and grayer than usual.

"Feelin' kind o' low, Mr. Angstrom?" Loem drawled.

"Vell, I am not feeling zo extra goot," Angstrom answered energetically. "Dot bum heart I haff is actin' ub a liddle."

"It'll git you one o' these days," said Loem gravely. "Then your troubles 'll be over."

"Und den my troubles vill first begin, den ven I meet old Salt-peter." The old man smiled sourly.

"You ain't got nothin' t' worry about. It's a banjo an' a pick for you."

"Ya! Ya!" Angstrom misunderstood him. "If you knew how many polkas I danced ven Bismarck vus chancellor." He forgot his false teeth and tried to suck in his lips. "But vun satisfaction I vill haff—ub dere or down dere! It vill giff no more vurry in all dem new trust cigar stores, no more brofit charing kayoopons, no more two-for-a-penny, t'ree-for-a-penny cigarettes, no more silk flags und gooze-fedder cigarette holders. Only smoke or no smoke!"

"Thet's correck," Loem agreed. "Accordin' of what place He sends you to."

Angstrom rested his sharp elbows on the dusty walnut counter. "But dey're smart fellers, dis American Tobacco Gumbany. Fifty tausend dollars dat Vitney has—und it aint even his—und den he commences to make a hundred million dollar trust. You buy from me now tobacco, he says."

"You call thet smart?" Loem asked.

"Vot else? To make a hundred million dollars, dot's smart. Und to make it on gooze-fedders yet und humbug!"

"You shore like t' be played for a jug-belly," said Loem. "Any kid could see them millions come right out o' your hide."

"My hide?" Angstrom demanded. "Und you?"

Loem grinned. "Not this time. I'm gittin' my terbacker on tick."

"You don't pay cash und you haff de nerf not even to giff cumflimends." Angstrom pulled open a drawer and drew out a long bar of rich, pressed tobacco that was labeled at regular intervals with a small blue lighthouse casting golden beams. He placed the bar on the cutting board, at one end of which a long knife swung on a swivel. "Five cents?"

"Your heart'll beat more reggerle after givin' me a dime's wuth."

"Hmph! It's *my* heart, zo let me vurry about it. Please!" He allowed the knife to rest on the bar of tobacco and pointed up at the shelves. "Vot is the use to go to the expenze und buy good pictchers for a man like you?"

Loem glanced at it. It was the usual diptych, representing Cash and Credit: Miserable Credit crawled on his emaciated, tattered knees and clawed among the moth-bitten papers of a cobwebby, vermin-ridden safe. But Cash, sitting snugly beside the neat strongbox full of stacks and sacks of gold, looked sleek and bloated in his white waistcoat and smoked a big cigar. "Trouble is, you got it hung too high," said Loem.

"But you know vot it means just the same, ya?" was the dogged query.

"Mr. Angstrom," said Loem soberly. "I wouldn't have you look like thet fat son-of-a-bitch fer all the terbacker in the place."

"Ach, you faker!" Nevertheless, he advanced the tobacco another label under the knife and clipped off the bigger piece. Loem would have liked to cut himself a chew right then and there but decided it would be a little awkward with the package under his arm. He slipped the plug into his pocket. The old man opened his big gray ledger and prepared to make an entry.

"Dot's ten. Und fifty-five. Dot's sixty-five cends on de chimney."

"Next time it's cash on the barrel-head," Loem promised. "Er you don't see me no more."

"Now you do me the favor?" said Angstrom disgustedly. "Vy didn't you be zo goot fifty cends ago?"

Loem made no reply. At his back, he was becoming aware of stealthy boyish voices. The kids were coming out of hiding. He nodded to Angstrom, and without haste, sidled up to the door. The towheaded kid standing with his back to him was looking up the street.

"C'mon out fellers," the boy said boldly. "He ain't aroun'."

"If'n he'da ketched you th'owin' it," several kids joined him, "you'da said yer prayers."

"Nearly ketched me, but I ducked—"

"Nearly?" said Loem.

The towheaded kid jumped, but too late. The lobe of his ear was jammed between Loem's thick thumb and forefinger like the cap of a cap-pistol between hammer and breech block. Then the wrist turned casually as though turning a key, and the whorled and rosy ear switched hue and pitch to a twist of lemon peel.

"Ow!" Wound up by the key, the kid's feet tapped mechanically, a shoulder blade hunched up, and he winked long. "LeggO-O."

The others had darted off like minnows at a shred of panic; they returned like minnows, round eyed and blank, and fed with quivering lips upon the scene.

"So it was you throwed it?" Loem looked at his catch serenely.

"Not me, no! Matty done it!"

"Not me, Mr. Loem. He's lyin'."

"Squealin' too, eh?"

"Ow!"

"You'll never grow up to be a real man thet away." Loem shook his and the boy's head mildly. And caught a glimpse of the contempt and amusement on the faces of the three dandies who were still standing in front of the cigar store. "Nope, you'll never grow up with any spunk. Will he, Matty?"

"No, Mr. Loem." Matty grinned with pride.

"No," repeated Loem, "you'll never grow up to be an hawnest workin' man neither." He hitched his belt up with his elbows, sailorwise, to get a better hold on the parcel. "Alluz try to git out er a scrape best y' c'n. Lie, beg, fight, er run. But when ye cain't, when yer ketched, then never squeal on a pardner. Take what's comin' to ye game. Or else," he threw a sidelong glance at the three loungers, "ye'll grow up to be nothin' but a tin horn gambler livin' offa women. Or else, ye'll have to be wearin' sky-boards on yer neck an' shiny shoes on yer feet an' massicurin' yer hands as soft as a baby's ass. And ye'll sink lower'n whale shit."

Two of the men lifted white teeth in laughter. One scowled. They nudged the latter, and he too smiled—venomously. Loem ignored them.

"D'ye know ye might 've easy put somebody's eye out chuckin' thet aroun'?" His hand on the boy's ear relaxed, fingers curling as though holding a mint.

"I wasn't throwin' 'er at you, Mr. Loem." The boy's tight, seamless brow lifted to his. Light lay on the grained hair of the long head with its three curled shavings at the back like light on a pine board; and the penitent blush that flooded the fair skin was itself now like the glow in a pine knot when the sun is behind it. Loem regarded him in oblique meditation and marveled. Marveled at the mobile, fragile enamel of the cheek bones, flesh of split almond. Marveled at the violet eyes in their jet lids, the fathomless, flowerlike, tough purity of them. He was crazy about kids.

"That's all what's gonna be left ye," he thought as he revolved the line of his gaze from askance to askance. "Is yer eyes. They'll be talkin' in yer head mebbe till after yer jaws is lookin' like a fiddle, talkin' like a fiddle." He let himself dream a moment, dipping into the depth of a steady violet hush such as folds about those flowers that distill in perfume. One always sank motionlessly into a boy's eyes, sank endlessly, the way a tree sinks against clouds moving across the sky. "Goddamn! Whur does it all go to?" He could tell already where the wrinkles would lie, there in the hollow between temple and eyelid, "Thicker'n a homemade broom."

"I sez I wuzn't throwin' 'er at you, Mr. Loem." The boy's eyes wavered; the steel gleam above him bored into them too insistently.

"You wuzn't, eh? You come pretty close to nobody else. Know that, pork nose?"

"We didn't see if it wuz you. We wuz jest lettin' her sail."

"Don't make no diff'ence. An' whur did the straw kelly come from? Yer old man never owned one."

"No," another kid offered, "we grabbed it off 'n a swell's head on State Street an' beat it."

"You did? An' who gave you the right to do thet?"

"It's after straw hat time, Mr. Loem. They ain't no more straw hats in the hat stores."

That was a new one on Loem; he squinted for an answer. Somewhere he sensed a hidden connection—something as obvious when discovered as a setting wood cock, but you'd trip over it before you spied it. He let go of the boy's ear and felt as though he were surrendering the idea also and admitting himself baffled. His thumb hooked under the shoulder strap of the boy's homemade overalls, his blunt discolored fingers stretching across the narrow back like tiers of brick.

"Nice pants yer wearin'."

The kid averted his head self-consciously.

"His old lady made 'em out of a ol' awnin'," someone else piped up. "Keeps the sun offa his ass." The others giggled derisively.

"My pants had fancier stripes 'n his first time I bought 'em." Loem looked serious.

"Yea!" incredulously.

"Then I went an' fell into a barrel o' vinegar. That puckered 'em some."

They looked gulled but delighted. "Tell us some more, Mr. Loem."

"I'll tell you some more," Loem said warningly. "When I wuz a kid like you, I once found a piece o' sheet iron—somethin' like that straw hat you throwed—layin' in the road. An' I said to the other kids, bet I c'n take thet rooster's head off standin' there. An' nobuddy believed me. Nobuddy at all 'cept the rooster. An' only part o' him did. D'you know what part? The part runnin' all over the barnyard with his head off. The head wuz layin' in the dirt an' the bill was still sayin' it caint be done! An' funny thing is I never meant it. So the next time one o' you pitches them things my way, don't tell me you didn't mean it, 'cause I'll twist yer ears till I wear out the spring. They'll be flappin' worse'n a blood houn's." He gave the ear a last fillip and turned away.

Almost reverently the little group watched him slouch off. His swaying shoulders seemed wider than the great black seesaw beam above a steamboat.

"He c'n shoot the top off'n a ketchup bottle," breathed one.

"He c'n throw the top of a ketchup bottle in the air an' shoot it right thoo the middle with a big fahrty-five."

" 'Member when that big warehouse over t' Union Avenue burned down?" Another broke in eagerly. "Near the railroad tracks? Mr. Loem borreed George's uncle's horse an' wagon. He told 'em he'd move all their canned goods for two dollars a load, but he fooled 'em—he druv it all home. An' George tol' me his whole family et so much C'lumbia River Salmon, they wuz plumb sick of it. An' all the neighbors too."

"He wuz an Injun-fighter."

"I bet he could whip Jim Jeffries."

"An' that Cudahy meat truck!" another giggled. "That wuz standin' in the alley wide open. My maw got two leg o' lamb out'v it. Everybody knowed Mr. Loem druv it away from the slatterhouse, an'—." The boy dropped his voice to a whisper. The others huddled together to listen.

The three elegant youngbloods standing before the cigar store bent their ears down to catch every word.

II

"Kids," mused Loem as he left the street for the shortcut that wound among the brush and brash of empty lots. "Kids. Feed 'em er don't feed 'em, dress 'em or don't dress 'em, they're alluz up t' somethin'. I seed starvin' kittens already drownin' their troubles in a hank o' yarn." He smacked his lips reminiscently at the wide sky and let the package of bacon slide down to the thumb he linked in his suspender fork. "When I looked at thet little brat, I looked at my own little brother rubbin' the dogs' asses with corncobs an' turpentine outside the Catholic chuch in St. Louis, Missouri. Grownups has their nerve leckcherin' kids." He chuckled to himself. "The way them dogs kiyied an' drug their ass in the ground plumb ruint the services!"

He made his way toward the spur of the Wabash Railroad whose distant semaphores saluted the haze, and crossed the tracks. The brook that purled parallel to the rails was straddled by a two-board bridge, precarious and joggling, that sagged further on one board than the other, as though a man were heavier on the right foot than the left. Rain had deepened the water, into which drooled the soil pipes of nearby dwellings and the waste of a small candy factory on the slope; and deepened, freshened, the continual, equivocal stench that arose from the brook of turds in vanilla and urine in wintergreen was somewhat tempered. The oily sheen on the surface remained though, opaline and glamorous as a hen's viscera. Loem spat into it as he crossed; the brook always put him in mind of a whore.

He turned into the cindery street among the random houses, climbed the green porch stairs of his own and tried the door. It was locked. There had been no rain today, but Juno wasn't going to run any chance of having someone track mud over her clean carpets.

"Keeps the shades down," muttered Loem grouchily as he went down the stairs, "keeps the curtains drawd, keeps the place spicker'n a pebble and darker'n measles, and keeps everybody out. Jest like all the rest o' the damn dutch squareheads." He turned into the alley to make his way to the back door.

Standing beside the kitchen stair, his two sons were speaking in guarded tones. Some magnetic topic had drawn their faces so close together that to Loem their hunched shoulders looked oddly like the prongs of a wishbone. Frank, though younger by a year than his fourteen-year-old brother, was taller if more willowy. His brown eyes were steady, innocent, and responsive, his moist lips fresh and unwarped. A delicate cluster of color stippled his cheeks like a mosaic left by the pressure of fingertips. Under his pointed chin, the bone looked fragile. Dan was stocky, compact. His jaw, already bulging at the base like his father's, hung close to his chest, giving his whole posture a concave, apelike stoop. The gray eyes, well spaced and deep in their sockets, were bold yet wary. A blow had given the bridge of his nose the appearance of being hollow ground. He was thin lipped. His arms and thick hands were oversized like the claws of a lobster.

As the two boys stood facing each other, Loem noted for the hundredth time how, though their knee pants were equally patched and the thick nap of hair under their caps equally in want of trimming, his younger son was the neater and sprucer looking. It may have been his slenderness or his luminous skin that gave him that orderliness and freshly washed gleam. Then too his cap and the knot of his tie and line of his collar were set more precisely, more distinctly, than his brother's. His two suspenders' buckles were always exactly level, his shirt was always flat; there was something less scuffed about his shoes. Dan was as clean in his habits as the other, but he strained and blurred everything he wore, which struck Loem as being a little strange because when it came to making a wagon out of baby-carriage wheels or mending the old bike, Dan was far more methodical, scrupulous, and patient.

At the scrape of their father's footsteps, they snapped sharply around—and then promptly slouched. If his older son had thrust one hand into his pocket and leaned casually against the wall on the bracket of his elbow, Loem would have thought nothing of it. But when his younger son did so, Loem cocked his head a shade. Something was up.

"Hullo boys, what's happened?" he asked casually. "Anything new?"

"No, Dad." Frank was careful.

Dan was candid. "We been wonderin' whur to git some tape fer this baseball. The hide's come off 'n it."

"Kinda late in the year to be wonderin' about a baseball," said Loem. "The other kids is pitchin' other people's straw hats aroun'."

"Aw listen, dad, jest because the season's endin' don't stop us from playin' baseball."

"An' neither does a blizzard I reckon. You wuz figgerin' out a game on snowshoes." If he could prod them into anger they might blurt out what they held concealed.

Frank crouched to the feint. "We wuzn't figgerin' out anything," he said sullenly.

But Dan swayed out of reach with a skillfully offended air. "We wuz jest sayin' mebbe we ought to go over to the five-and-dime an' lift a roll o' tape. Thet's all. What d'you think we wuz talkin' about?"

"Yah!" Loem pigeon-holed the matter. He didn't believe Dan at all, but he had to admire the neat way he had lured his father off balance. The kid was certainly shifty. Well, let it go. Loem knew the incident listed more than a jettisoned roll of tape could right, but he might as well jettison his curiosity along with it. What was the use? What good would it do him anyway if he did tease the head out of the turtle? He knew what it looked like, and it looked ugly as hell. He'd just go off and pawn something and get drunk and break dishes. That would be too bad with money scarce the way it was. But God damn it! He thought when she had given up canvassing Procter and Gamble soap from house to house, she had given up fooling with other men. He never could blame her a hell of a lot—not when he was sober. After all, if he did leave his army coat open fighting off Indians in the Dakotas so the Northern Pacific could survey its lines, and if he did get his privates frozen, it was just his hard luck. Juno was a stout healthy woman, and when he couldn't give her enough she just followed her instincts. Just followed her instincts and made money at it. And there wasn't a bit of use in trying to stop women either. They would always root out a way.

Creeping nuances of the thought tripped him. Where he stumbled he started into flight mothwings of mockery he would never otherwise have noticed. Root out was right. And the bigger the root the better they liked it.

He shared a sour grin with his sons. "Well, boys, are we goin' in?"

"Yeah!" Their alacrity was at variance, dragged slightly before meshing, but Loem ignored even the acuteness of his perception. What was the use? The clinched nail was hard as the devil to pull, but after you did, you generally shook it off the claw. He put his free arm around Dan: the shoulder with the bacon under it nudged Frank affectionately. "Let's see what the old woman's got in the pot?"

"She's turrible cranky," said Frank. "She cain't git tick no more."

"No? Pretty soon somethin'll have to be done about it, I guess. Looks like we're beginnin' to carry more debts and more troubles than we c'n shake our tails with. This'll call for a real pow-pow after supper, full o' thunderin' stragedy."

"I bet she calls it on ye afore supper," said Dan.

Loem laughed and gripped his son to him. They entered the kitchen. A heavy succulent odor billowed about them. Spume of cabbage seethed racily at the crest of a clinging comber of pig. The windows were hoary with steam.

"Hmm!" Loem snuffed up the humid air appreciatively. "Don't

tell, lemme guess." He lifted his head back in feigned surmise, but his sharp scrutiny pried for purchase into his wife's face. "It's the trotters."

Beside the window, whose lower panes had been wiped clean of moisture, Juno was sitting knee to knee with his daughter Agnes. The face she turned toward him was suffused, deeply so, and so richly luminous that for an instant the queer fancy stirred him that the light that rested on her had somewhere been filtered through ruby glass. But the light in the window was as clear as a spring, and yet she glowed as from some secret source like an autumn maple in late afternoon.

"Now what the firation do you call thet?" wondered Loem. "Is they steam in my eye er is thet her Cherokee blood?" But aloud he said, "Wuz I right er is it the spare ribs?"

She smacked her lips as though breaking a spell and drew the corners of her mouth down into a chevron of severity. "Look fer yourself, will you. There's the pot." At the same time her eyelids drooped, unfurling a warning to Agnes, who then sat back in her chair and shut the book she had been reading from.

Loem bent a critical brow over the pot. "Pig's tails!" His head sank crestfallen. "Ef thet wasn't jest what I was agoin' t' say right smack off the bat. Pi-i-g's tails!" His manner became brisk. "Well, my constich-erents, our task is done. We et all aroun' the hawg an' we live t' smell the tail!" He paused. "Cain't I git a wiggle out o' you?"

"Not by bein' sech a ham!" said Juno coldly. "Do you realize what's in thet pot is the end o' the tick?"

"So I heard." Loem had to admire the animation in his wife's square, pink face. He always imagined that anger brought out the Indian in the solid German. "An' I would add, like all the ward-heels an' if-electeds is addin' up now before election, an' I would add that it wuz fittin' an' proper thet we sh'd be eatin' pig's tails t' commemorate the end o' the tick. T'morrer begins a new chapter in the hist'ry o' this fair family—a yunsullied chapter, unsullied by hope, unsullied by pros-pecks, unsullied by —!"

"Shet up!" She cut short his ridiculous posturing. "You always pick the worst time you c'n to be a damn fool!"

"Aw, listen, Juno, be reasonable. We ben in worser fixes'n this before."

"An' it ain't nothin' t' cheer about. I got enough on my han's what with runnin' t' neighbors borreein' a cup o' this an' a cup o' thet, without you actin' like a medicine man sellin' snake oil."

"I allus give you the promise," said Loem earnestly, "ef we cain't borree no more, an' the time comes when I ain't able t' figger out a way o' rustlin' up grub er rent money—which I still c'n—I'll git me a job again. But thet time ain't come yet."

"No," she said bitterly. "It don' never come. I know you don' keer about the kids ner about me. But I'm tellin' you I'm about fed up on this kind o' life—livin' on the town er driftin' from one range to another b'tween here an' the Rockies. Thet's why Dan's never learned t' read an' thet's why Frank's down with the little kids. I want Agnes t' be diff'ent. I want her t' git all the schoolin' she c'n—more'n jest readin' an' writin'. Bookkeepin'. A bookkeepin' gal's got the best chances these days. Settin' in offices an' lookin' neat. But how're we goin' t' do it if you're alluz droppin' so far behind we git switched off—?"

"I explained thet." Loem tried to break in. "I—"

"You're alluz explainin'," she continued remorselessly. "Talk! Talk! Thet's all I git from you. Talk about the idle rich. Talk about the Gold Bugs! Talk about Teddy Roosevelt! Talk about this an' talk about thet. Ef talk wuz all I ladled onto your dish some night, you wouldn't ask fer an extree helpin'."

"No, but they's many's the time I've had t' put it in my pipe an' smoke it."

"Yes, an' you'd dress your kids in it ef you c'd chew enough rag." Morosely, she smoothed her black hair and cupped her hand over the bun above the nape of her strong arched neck. "What I wisht is I'd never give up sellin' freckle-removin' soap. Then we'd alluz be shore they wuz another meal comin'."

The two boys looked uneasily at each other and at their sister. They had seen this little pebble scoop up an avalanche before.

Loem's big sandy face sobered. The heavy muscles at the base of his jaw bulged into white fins. "When I quarried fer granite, we never drilled again into the same holes what had jest been blasted out of." That was all he said, and then the beaked dimples pecked slyly at his sullen chin. "How much flour you got?"

"Darn little." She propped her cheek disconsolately on the console of hands and elbows.

"An' mebbe jest a little sack o' beans?"

"Now what're you after?"

"Ef we got a sack o' beans, we got t'morrer's grub," he announced.

A fresh current of indignation lifted her head. "Do you mean to stan' there an' tell me thet a small sack o' beans an' a little flour is goin' to do fer all day t'morrer? In thet case you c'n stay home an' run this house yourself. Let's see what a taffee-pullin' wonder t' Gawd you are!"

Loem hugged the package of bacon under his arm as though it were a bagpipe. "Juno," he said sadly. "You must be losin' your charms." He had been waiting for this chance to retaliate for her stab about selling soap.

"Oh, is thet so?" She rose to her feet. Her starched white apron cascaded stormily over her bare arms. "I wouldn't be so sure o' that ef I was you. An' what's more you wouldn't like it too much ef I showed you I ain't lost my charms altogether."

Loem smiled cryptically—not so much because he knew he held a surprise in store for her, but rather to conceal the flicker of desire that ran through his face, because she stood before him with lifted crumpled apron. It occurred to Loem that men doffed their coats when they were getting ready to fight, or rolled their sleeves up. Women seemed to want to get out of their skirts. "Yes," he repeated, "you're losin' your charms. Because why c'n I still git tick an' you cain't?" He pulled the plug of tobacco out of his pocket and displayed it.

"Meanin' what?" She demanded dangerously.

"Meanin' nothin'." He pulled the package of bacon from under his arm. "What's left over from the picket fence aroun' my cakes tomorrer ought t' give them beans plenty o' news t' gossip about."

"Whur's the white rabbit, Dad?" said Frank.

"Comin' up," said Loem.

Agnes giggled and promptly pried open the book in her lap and scanned something. But her mother shrugged in disgust. "Ef you think one slab o' bacon is goin' t' keep us t'morrer, you got another think comin'."

"We got breakfas' now, ain't we?" was Loem's reply. "We'll cross the other bridges when we git to 'em." He threw his hat on the wheel of the sewing machine and slumped into the padded rocking chair. Juno whisked away the scalloped white and yellow doilie that swam on faded pillow before his head came to rest on it.

"That's fer looks," she said. "I've tol' you time an' again."

"Well git me a piece o' burlap an' see you don't wash it." He let his head thump back on the pillow. "There'd be some sense to a piece o' burlap, stiddy all day embroiderin' things what needs pertectin' by somethin' else what's embroidered." He rested the package of bacon in his lap and clasped his hands above it in imitation of the way his daughter was sitting.

Agnes wasn't a pretty girl, and Loem knew it, but he was convinced that she would be a handsome woman someday. She was his oldest child—fifteen and fidgety. Her weak and bony fingers were always twisting or gathering something, her handkerchief, the buttons of her white middy, or the worn blue skirt. Her rough nails were always barking something, the binding of a book, the dry skin of her lips. Circling about on heel and toe, spiraling and unspiraling about the leg of the chair, her large feet continually scraped the floor or skated over each other on the edge of her soles. Angular shins in the withered brown stockings teetered tirelessly, jogging the knobby knees. The movement of her arms was random—a spreading fling of elbows, knuckles, wrists. She was long limbed, small headed, pale and freckle strewn. It was only of late that her breasts had really begun to seem deeper than her shoulder blades. When Loem was near her, when he regarded the speckled, irresolute face in the sling of furry brown braids, he was seized by pity. He was always on the verge of lending this tremulous and taut, subdued and capricious creature a helping hand, but by the time he had made up his mind to do so, she no longer seemed to need it.

"Don't, Dad!" Under her father's gaze her freckles had deepened. "Don't!" She wheeled her body away from his till it somehow came to rest in a quirk of book and hands, all on one hip.

Loem smiled into the sulky startled eyes peeping over her shoulder. "What wuz ticklin' you so much in thet book you're readin', sis? Looks like my Inge'soll leckchers." He reached for the volume.

"No!" She squirmed farther away.

"Love in bloom, I guess." He slouched back noncommittally. "Everybody's nursin' secrets today. There's Dan an' Frank what's alluz jawin' so much about this an' that, standin' there like a jar o' somethin'. I'll be damned ef I know what's eatin' this bunch."

"Well, you started it with thet bacon o' yourn," said Juno, "so you needn't complain about the others. An' while we're at it, you might as well tell us whur the supper's comin' from—I mean t'morrer. Fer all we know mebbe you're carryin' a ham under that other arm o' yourn." And then in a very matter-of-fact voice she turned to Agnes. "Put thet book away, hon."

Agnes leaned the book against the rear leg of her chair. It was evident to Loem that both his wife and daughter didn't want him to know what was in it. Discreetly, he measured the distance between himself and the book.

"Cain't git no more hams with Dan and Frank all growed up," said Loem. "Less they want t' put on long baby dresses again an' let me carry 'em into the butcher shop on my arms like I used t' do years ago. Only I expeck you boys'll know better now than t'bawl your heads off an' try t' climb out o' my arms when thet cold ham hits you under your skirts."

Frank looked sheepish: Dan remained solemn.

Loem laughed. "I'll never fergit the day I had t' tell the butcher I guess I better put this kid into his buggy—he's got cranky all of a sudden. You boys'll never be able t' say I didn't learn you t' know good hams early. Your contack with 'em wuz close." He lifted the package of bacon under Frank's nose. "Take a smell o' thet oncet. Premium A number one, and got more stars on it than Irish whiskey."

"Cain't smell nothin' but terbacker an' you," said Frank.

"Aw, what's a slab o' bacon," said Dan, making no move to come over.

"What's bacon?" Loem echoed. "My boy, it's all the diff'ence between a loving pair an' a dog fight." He sniffed the package. "Guess I ben holdin' it too close t' me. An' now about thet supper you wuz askin' about. You know thet gully full o' ashes near the round-house o' the Missouri-Pacific? When I walked by this mornin' I seen some o' them bearin' boxes stickin' up out o' the ashes. They must've fell out into the roun'-house pit, I figger, an' the hostlers jest left 'em there, so ashes an' all is dumped outside. Do you git it? Them bearin' boxes is lined with brass—best quality yaller brass. I know because my uncle Will what used to steal the brass brake wheel right off what they call the observation cars, never waited fer 'em t' throw the bearin' boxes outside. He jest pried 'em out hisself, Uncle Will did. Now ef we root aroun' in them there ashes, it's dollars t' doughnuts there's aroun' a hundred pounds o' brass layin' there. So t'morrer mornin' we take the wagon you boys fetches coal in an' load her up. You an' me, Dan."

"What about me?" demanded Frank indignantly. "Ain't I goin'?"

"You're goin' t' school," said Loem. "Didn' you hear what your maw said? Anyways one feller on the ash heap is enough. After we drag them boxes home we'll knock the brass out an' sell it t' the junkie the same day. They're payin' twelve cents a pound fer good brass. Thet's twelve dollars nearly. Er is it?"

"Talk about countin' your chickens," said Juno. "You got 'em fricasseed."

"Well, we'll have 'em fer supper. An' thet settles t'morrer." He drew out his pipe, stretched, fomenting a luxurious crackle among bunched shoulders, chest, and suspenders. Pipe and parcel hung from his fingertips as from the tips of a Christmas tree—while he shed his yawn. "They's nothin' a pore man likes better'n takin' it from the rich."

He contracted the cactus angle of his arms and tossed the package of bacon on the table.

What happened was odd, trivial but odd. The package didn't land at all with the flabby, fatly cushioned thump expected of it. It clacked glibly, bounced spryly. It didn't sound like bacon.

III

All their eyelids drooped and puckered. Loem rose, picked the parcel up again with long disciplining arm, plowed through waxpaper and flap, and tilted it. A piece of white pine board slid out. It seemed to gleam at them all ingratiatingly; but it faded forlornly when Loem pushed it back into its starry case.

"I jest took it along fer the looks of it," he said persuasively.

"You most certainly did!" said his wife sweetly. "You wanted to build us a little shelf in the outhouse."

"Dad's goin' to whittle us some bacon." Agnes nibbled at her handkerchief. Then she opened the book again and studied it hastily.

"What d' you git fer hookin' a piece o' wood, Paw?" Frank tagged him brightly.

"Git?" said Loem solemnly. "You git started on a lumberyard."

"Aw, you know what I mean. What d' you git ef they ketched you?"

"In thet case, there'd be nothin t' do but have the butcher locked up fer fraud an' malnertrition."

"An' lock yourself up in a bughouse!" his wife added. "An' invite the rest o' the nuts to a plank-steak dinner. Somethin' for the beans t' gossip about! Humph! They'd be the mummest beans you ever heard tell of. Didn' I tell you, you wuz countin' your chickens afore they wuz hatched? I knowed it all the time."

Loem turned to Dan who was spinning his cap over his baseball. Dan had made no comment so far, and his hard young face showed neither ridicule nor mirth, merely tolerance.

"Pretty foxy of 'em, ain't it, son?" Loem felt a little apologetic.

"What're you goin' t' do now, Dad?" Dan was almost like a grown man that way. He rarely argued, rarely urged: he merely asked you, and then he sized you up.

"I got t' git us some real bacon now," was Loem's answer. "Er us won't have no breakfas'. An' I'll git real bacon ef I have t' drag it home squealin'." He meditated a moment. "Mebbe you boys'd like t' come along? Their winders is all chalked so full o' meat prices and tags, them butchers cain't see through 'em no more 'n we c'n see through these winders here. An' out on the rack in front o' the store they got three or four whole lambs hangin' up. What about us takin' the baby buggy along an' droppin' a sheep into it fer the insult they give your ol' man?"

His wife swung into action. "You c'n jest stay insulted, Walter Loem!" she said vehemently. "But you ain't goin' t' take them boys with you. Not today, leastways. An' ef you had the brains Gawd give you, you wouldn't go yourself neither."

"Why not? Are you skeert they'd be lookin' all over the place fer thet parcel o' nothin' I took? Er you think they'd know me from bein' in there before?"

"Thet ain't what I mean at all," she said darkly. "Ef you want t' know, I wuz pretty certain you didn' have bacon all the time."

One side of Loem's face corduroyed with annoyance. "You already done said somethin' like thet before. Now jest what're you drivin' at? You mean I took thet block o' wood o' purpose?"

"Never you mind what I mean. I told Agnes here all about it afore you come in. Ain't thet so, Agnes?"

Agnes nodded and turned her face away, trailing wide, mysterious eyes.

"Thet wuz a mighty big help t' me," said Loem dryly. "A mighty big help. I'll be hossed ef this day an' this house ain't gittin' so full o' the looniest false alarms, it's wuss'n the time the tigers wuz suppose t' bust out o' their cages in Joplin, Missouri."

"Thet's because they's powers an' infloonces t' work what's bigger'n your own," Juno answered triumphantly. "What you know nothin' about, but I know. Ef you'd asked me afore you took thet bacon, I c'd've told you: Whatever looks easy this day is goin' t' be hard, innercent is dangerous, an' vicer-verser, high is humbled an' vicer-verser. Vencher nothin'!"

"Well, I'll be hossed." Loem's thick fingers scraped along the sandy stubble on his jaw till they converged at the cape of his lips. He gazed soberly at his wife. The same hectic light was swarming in her cheeks that had glowed there when he first came in. His own mother, he recalled, used to flush that way somewhere about the time when he was reaching his manhood. Change of life, they called it. Was it that was making her eyes pop out so far you could hang your hat on them, or was it just plain nuts? Maybe one ought to humor women when they reached that stage. It might make things worse if you crossed them. Anyway he could always sneak out on some pretext or other.

"Boys," he turned to his sons, "what I said is all off. Even I ain't goin' back to thet butcher shop t'day."

"Aw, road apples!" said Dan with a sudden burst of impatience. "What're you listenin' t' her fer? She and Agnes'z ben readin' things out of a book."

"You shet your trap!" said Juno sharply.

"I heard you readin' it," Dan muttered doggedly.

"Is thet the book there by Agnes?" Loem asked.

"Yea."

Loem went over and picked it up. His wife reached out to snatch it from him but thought better of it.

"Nobody never hears compliments at keyholes, Walter Loem," she said in exasperation. "Thet book's none o' your business."

"It ain't a dairy, is it?" was Loem's reply. "It ain't private. It's jest a book. An' books is anybuddy's business. Specially ef he c'n read. An' ef it tells you, like you brag about, when you're liftin' bacon an' when it's a fake, then I ahta have it more'n you. Fer very plain reasons." He let a few leaves ripple under his fingers. "Ancien' Lore of Astrology," he read, and then stared straight at his wife. "Is thet what you call learnin' thet gal t' do bookkeepin'?"

"It's more important than bookkeepin' er anythin' else," said Juno defiantly. "You see what I learned out of it. I learned t' know things in advance. I give you the proof, didn't I?"

"You shore did," he answered. "After all I read you about Tom Paine an' Inge'soll an' Darwin, you go an' mess with that tripe. All you proved is thet women is alluz lookin' fer a spiritchell crutch t' lean on."

"Them words in thet book is jest as true an' jest as scientifical as what anybody ever wrote," she said emphatically. "Trouble with you is you think you know all about it w'thout even readin' it."

"I don' have t' read it."

"You jest pick it up and know it all?" sarcastically.

"Jest about," said Loem. "Do you want me t' tell you what I feel like holdin' this book in my han'? I feel like when I wuz a kid, an' they wuz two other kids what stuck a sawed-off broom han'le down a latrine, an' I knowed nothin' about it. Purty soon along they come, argyin' an' callin' each other names like they wuz itchin' t' scrap. An' one of 'em says t' me hol' on t' this broomstick, will you, kid, so I c'n punch thet fathead in the nose. An' me like a boob takes it—well, he drug that there stick right out o' my han' an' I had the biggest fistfull o' what wuz on it you ever seed. An' thet's just the way I feel now."

She turned her head away disdainfully. "C'n you read a horrer-scope?" she asked coldly.

Loem studied the averted face a moment, the fine full curve of chin and throat like the breast of a swimming gull. Women were like children. "You mean all them bugs what's spattered all over this page?" He showed her the chart of planetary symbols and aspects. "Thet's easy. Any bum what's ben on the road fer a couple of years c'n read signs like these. Now look. This one means a big lump o' grub an' two bits throwed in by a nice ol' maid an' no dog. But this little curlikew goes on to say, look out fer the town-clown, boys, meanin' the marshal. Because the one right nex' to it warns you—you'll git et alive in thet jail house. Look again! There's a race goin' on up the wall b'tween the bedbugs an' the body lice, with here an' yon a head louse takin' the bit in his mouth an' hightailin' it up the home stretch. The rest of them figgers on the side is the time they clocked 'em at."

Agnes turned her toes up and tittered against her nails. Frank's derisive tongue curled out like a shoe horn. Dan looked admiringly at his father. But—

"You're jest showin' up your own ignerince!" Juno stamped her foot furiously. "They's smarter people'n you a damn sight what believes in this book: Lillian Russell, Mrs. Cleveland, King Edward! The lady what give me this book knowed the exack day an' hour the Japs wuz goin' t' start fightin' the Roosians—what you're always blowin' about."

Frank crouched down impishly. "Mebbe she started it, Maw."

"I'll slap you, you git sassy with me!" And to Loem. "You even got the kids sassin' me. They's rafts o' big perfessors in the world what'd give their right arm ef they could do like Mrs. Pierce. An' you needn't stand there grinnin' like an eediot!"

"When did you tangle up with her?" asked Loem.

"None o' your business!"

"All right with me. Only I thought you picked it up off a ol' ashbarrel."

"I did not. I met her this mornin' in Ferney's grocery. She seen me git bluer'n rinsin' water when he turned me down fer a little more tick. An' she come over t' me and says, a cloud of care has throwed its shadders over you, sister, a weight is on your speerit. But cheer up, a prosperous time is acomin'. Your husban' will begin t' provide."

"Hmm."

"How did she know I had a husban'? Then we got to talkin' an' she tol' me all kinds o' things about myself, true things, an' give me this book. An' Blanche Henderson what knows of her tol' me Mrs. Pierce had powers what could make a ball o' blue fire hang plumb in the middle o' the room."

"She could?" Loem leaned on a chair. "What does she use fer gas?"

"No sense talkin t' you. Your brain's sot harder'n a hod full o' ol' plaster. You wouldn't believe nothin'."

"I would believe that blue fire bunk ef I c'd light my pipe off'n it!" He clapped on his black hat with a flourish. "Well, boys, I'm goin' back to Haine's butcher shop. Comin' along? The stars has insulted your ol' man."

"No, they ain't comin' along!" Juno planted herself between them.

Loem shoved his hands into the pockets of his jumper and slouched against himself as though he were slouching against a striped hammock. A crooked line of forbearance appeared on his brow and sheared the stratified wrinkles like a fault in rock. "Ain't we had enough o' this damn cat in the cradle? First one minute you're tellin' me they ain't nothin' t' eat in the house but spiderwebs, an' next minute you want me t' b'lieve that biled starlight makes good noodles. We're growed up people, not kids ner bushmen. We're civilized, and I got t' go git some grub fer t'morrer, er we don't eat."

"*You* c'n go. They ain't nobody stoppin' you."

Loem snorted. "Much obliged. But it ain't up t' you t' tell the kids what t' do in this case." He turned to his sons. "Well, boys, what're you doin', goin' er stayin'?"

Frank was on the point of taking an eager step forward, but his brother clipped him with his elbow.

"We ain't goin', Paw," said Dan bluntly.

Loem's mien was very mild. "Ef you really mean t' set home gogglin' into the future, why don't you git yourself a ball o' glass stiddee thet ol' baseball you're playin' around with. That'd make you a first-class crystal gazer."

Dan grew crimson, but he kept his lips tightly shut. Loem went to the door and put his hand on the knob, then he faced them.

"Lemme tell you somethin'. It ain't the bacon what's worrying me no more. It's the superstition. I wuz tryin' to learn my kids t' use they own beans like my old man teached me. But one drop o' moon soup what wuz cooked up by a hose-smokin' crank about the year one is given you worse horrers than a buzzard's shadder on a gopher." He lifted his arm dramatically. "When Jesse James rode out o' the hills t' hold up a train or a bank, he knowed he might git knocked off, an' he laid his stragedy careful. He reckoned the time an' the git-away an' the odds. But it all come out of his own bean. He didn't look up no aspects like thet book says ner no other kind o' ass—!" The door slammed and he was gone.

"Go ahead," said Juno prophetically. "Find out fer your own self what it means t' go buttin' your head into the stars!"

> *Roth:* When I look at what I've written, the only section that survives, it's much too rich, it's nothing like *Call It Sleep*—it's precious, it's stilted. Still, I felt I could do a non-Jewish adolescence, guided by Bill. But . . . after those first seventy-five pages I just stalled, I just wasted time. My excuse for not going forward—and this was really the nub of the disaster: I decided to write a foreword. And in the foreword—dealing with an incident in the life of Dan Loem's father, an incident that took place in the 1870s—I felt I ought to touch on the Civil War; and there I had to come to terms with my own feelings about the Civil War. I didn't have to, really—that was just another diversion. I discovered that I couldn't come to terms with my own feelings about the war—and this is really where I went to hell.
>
> *Interviewer:* Have you come to terms with it now?
>
> *Roth:* I don't worry about it any more. I mean, it's history, and this is the way it happened. But the more I delved into it, then, the more I realized how completely unsure I was as to why the war should have been fought, even when it came to a matter like slavery. It's repulsive to me morally and so forth, but I didn't see any reason why slavery per se should be. That type of plantation economy existed, even had its charm—I mean, you could get into the most confused state of mind, where you absolutely evaporate everything you believed in, all your values and allegiances. And this is what happened. It went on for months . . . going back and forth, rewriting and rewriting. I never got any further, and all I meant to do was write a little introductory piece about the experience of a young soldier whose detachment encountered a band of Plains Indians, that's all.
>
> (Goldsmith, 1983)

> *Roth:* This is the irony: as soon as they accepted the first section, I didn't want to write any more. Here again there are delicate problems all interwoven. There was no necessity upon me to do any more; I was being supported. If they hadn't accepted it or if I had been a poor guy and they said: "Finish another section and you get

another thousand dollars," I probably would have knuckled down. But with no necessity, I just fooled around. Then, having failed to finish *that* novel, I tried to do the adolescence. But this failure was crucial—my will was gone, broken by this first failure.

Interviewer: You actually destroyed what you had done?

Roth: Yes, when I went to Maine in 1946. I was convinced that my whole literary career was over. After all I was a nonentity—*Call It Sleep* just disappeared. I felt my whole literary past no longer had any bearing on *me*. So why keep the stuff? And also the fifties were approaching, and the terror was beginning to fall on all. [At this point Roth looked nervously around and out the window.] You see my reaction? I still look around.

(Lyons, 1976, p. 173)

Interviewer: What happened to the manuscript itself?

Roth: That disappeared. The opening chapter appeared in *New Writing* or *New Directions*.

Interviewer: Do you have the magazine?

Roth: I've got the magazine, not the manuscript. When we moved to Maine, I might as well explain, I still had the manuscript of the first one hundred pages; and then, I'm sorry to say, I destroyed it. I burned it together with a couple of very, very valuable journals during the McCarthy period.

Interviewer: After Perkins gave you the advance, what did you do?

Roth: I had already gone to the Middle West to get material for the first part.

(Friedman, 1977, p. 34)

Roth: So I went to the West Coast with the central character of my aborted novel. He then became my boss—which is part of the whole story. . . . I mean, he told me what to do after that. I spent six or seven months on the West Coast. . . . The isolation was terrible, and Bill was a tyrant, which is a beautiful example of what happens to you when you're under communism, and I came back, mostly by freight train—and that in itself was an extraordinary experience to look back on. . . .

Interviewer: Have you ever thought about going back to [the book]?

Roth: I think it would be a disaster. It's interesting that the entire opening section vanished. I destroyed my copy, and apparently Perkins's disappeared—Perkins retired, and it disappeared from his files.

(Goldsmith, 1983)

Where My Sympathy Lies

March 2, 1937

When "Where My Sympathy Lies" was published, Roth had been a member of the Communist Party for almost four years. This public statement on the Moscow trials was a candid avowal of his deference to the Communist Party's official position on the subject.

Two years before, Call It Sleep *had been the object of a lengthy controversy in the pages of* The New Masses. *At the end of a brief, rather critical article, an anonymous reviewer lamented: "It is a pity that so many young writers drawn from the proletariat can make no better use of their working class experience than as material for introspective and febrile novels." This prompted a number of letters from readers who, although Marxists themselves, for the most part questioned the reviewer's rigid standpoint and expressed favorable opinions on the novel.*

Probably in common with a good many writers, my political development has not reached as high a level as it might—many of my beliefs seem the product more of intuition than of analysis. Nevertheless, I hold, however arrived at, that any writer who longs for justice and brotherhood among men must hate the exploitation of men, the sordidness that rears itself on such exploitation, and the twin pinnacles that cap it, fascism and war. Whoever hungers for justice must ally himself, if only in sympathy, with all those forces that struggle to liberate humanity from slavery and want. Any organization, any impulse of men that honestly and by its acts strives in the direction of such liberation, should enlist a writer's sympathy in direct proportion as there is a struggle for these aims. The recent trials of the Trotskyites in the U.S.S.R. therefore raise this question: to what extent does Trotskyism deserve the sympathy of a writer?

There are several things about this trial about which I am confused. Nevertheless, enough and more than enough has been revealed to convince me of the guilt of the accused; and by guilt, I mean that all their efforts were calculated to nullify or destroy the very growth of the safeguards that would ensure the freedom and fraternity of millions of men. But if I had any remnant of a doubt of this, it has vanished before the steps taken by the Trotskyites in this country to defend their leader. I refer to the libel suit contemplated by the Committee for the Defense of Trotsky against certain Communist leaders and publications in this country.

The Committee intends also to form an "impartial commission" and justifies this act by stating that:

> The Communist Party cannot legitimately oppose the creation of such a commission, if only because of the fact that they themselves inspired the so-called counter-trial in London set up to deal with the so-called Leipzig trial of Dimitroff and his friends. If they have the so-called overwhelming proof against Trotsky they claim they have, let them confront Trotsky with it. (*The New York Times*, February 1, 1937.)

The more one studies this quotation, the clearer becomes the picture of the Trotskyite mentality. The elementary differences between the trial of Dimitroff in Germany and the trial of the Trotskyites in the Soviet Union are apparently no more important to Trotskyites than are facts. Dimitroff was a Communist in a Nazi court, a spokesman and a champion of the working class. In the very shadow of the ax, he maintained the justice of his cause; he enunciated his principles and announced his adherence to them. He maintained his innocence. Before the trial was over, and in the den of Hitlerism itself, he became the accuser of Naziism, the exposer of fascist barbarity wherever it existed, the symbol of heroic struggle against it. He was acquitted.

In what way were the principals in the recent Soviet trials similar? None maintained his innocence there, none became the accuser; no matter how brilliant, none was backed by a principle, all confessed their guilt. Some wept at the loathsome company and the bleakness and obscurity of the pass their historical steps had led them to, some bragged and some jeered, but they all stood convicted, their sentences sustained by demonstrations of Russian workers. I do not believe together with the Hearst press that these men were under the influence of mesmerism or mysterious narcotics; therefore, I believe them to be, as they themselves acknowledged, guilty.

Not only does Trotsky propose to prove the innocence of himself and his associates by a trial of the Soviet Union in which he becomes the accuser, but also by a libel suit against working-class leaders and against working-class publications in a bourgeois court. It is by what such a step aims to accomplish that one can judge what Trotskyism is. Trotskyism becomes the barren woman in the fable of Solomon, the fable in which the king had to choose between the legitimate mother of a child and the spurious one. Solomon decided that the woman who was willing to let the infant live, despite its being fostered by another, was indeed the mother of it. I am not Solomon. But Trotskyism seems to me more an expression of that monstrous kind of ego that, unwilling or unable to go through the pains of bearing and nurturing the growing spirit of liberation throughout the world, would rather see it severed by the sword than not possess it.

As a writer, more than ever involved in the growth of enlightenment and freedom, I can see only one way of accomplishing this, the united front against fascism—and one way sure to paralyze all our efforts, Trotskyism.

> *Roth:* To those of us who were committed to the Left, the Soviet Union was the cherished homeland; but that homeland had become an establishment which was intent on consolidating itself. In the Moscow trials the establishment was destroying the revolution, although at the time we were still loudly professing our allegiance. Events often do not become comprehensible until long after they have occurred.
>
> I am throwing out these ideas as possibilities. The scholar who some day will be making a formal study of the question will undoubtedly find other things to single out. One interesting facet he will have to investigate is the influence such historical factors exert on the

artist. How do they get into the writer's bloodstream and affect his creative sensibility? How are his potentialities inhibited? The world around him after all remains largely intact, but something inside of him has changed.

(Bronsen, 1969, p. 275)

Roth: That's the very example of, the perfect example of conversion, the definition of the very thing I would condemn utterly, today, after I had once completely committed myself to blind allegiance. It's something you have to live down, and it is something that (needless to repeat) continually haunts you. . . .

That piece out of the Marxist phase—thank God I put it down there, no matter how I feel about it now—is a landmark in the development of the individual. Unfortunately he was what he was, but it is a landmark, and without it you wouldn't have known. He could have made a protest that he was otherwise, or someone else, but he can't do that now.

(taped conversation,
Albuquerque, N.M.,
April 24, 1985)

Broker

November 18, 1939

"Broker" was the first of Roth's short stories to be published. Within less than a year, it was followed by two more, "Somebody Always Grabs the Purple" and "Many Mansions." These three stories were the result of his short-lived attempt at commercial writing. Soon thereafter, the long period of creative stagnation began.

Roth: I went to the West Coast . . . in order to break my tremendous dependence on Walton. . . . I had some kind of illusion that maybe I could get something in Hollywood. But that illusion was quickly dispelled, because I'm just not that type. I came back broke. I came back part of the way on a freight train and part of the way by bus. And then I got on WPA. I worked with a pick and shovel and tried desperately to become a commercial writer, someone who wrote to sell, and I did sell a couple of things to *The New Yorker.*

Interviewer: What year was that?

Roth: I think it was '39—'39 or '40. One short story I sold to *The New Yorker* had to do with a Negro, or black, a rough guy who stood there and watched his truck go to pieces under an elevated trestle—you remember the old elevated trains in New York City. The story was called "Broker."

(Friedman, 1977, p. 35)

Interviewer: Your first published story, "Broker," has a Negro for a main character. Is there any special significance to the unautobiographical focus?

Roth: I wrote the story when my relationship with Eda Lou was over. I was now independent, alas. I had to find a way of making a living, and this was the only thing I knew how to do. I probably could have made it as a short story writer if I had just persisted. But again, this didn't have anything to do with my own development. And this apparently was the only thing that mattered. Anyhow, I happened to see an accident like the one in the story and I could spin it out, embroider.

(Lyons, 1976, p. 175)

On Second Avenue just below Forty-fourth Street, under the Elevated, a battered Chevrolet truck had broken down—broken apart, practically—and was slowing up traffic. The truck was headed south and it was loaded with mason's and plasterer's equipment—a plastery clutter of barrels, wheelbarrows, mortar troughs, and wooden horses. The two parts of the truck, body and motor, were still in contact with each other, but the load was tilted sharply upward as if it were still going uphill and the motor was tilted almost as sharply downward. The only thing, apparently, that kept the load from sliding into the street was the single heavy rope that went around the back.

What had happened was obvious at a glance. The truck had been going downtown and the driver, evidently unaware that the rising ground was bringing his rather lofty load closer and closer to the Elevated roadbed, had continued driving under the Elevated until, here at the very crest of the hill, load and Elevated had met.

On the southwest corner, near the truck, a Negro stood, his overalls and tattered gloves caked with lime and mortar like the materials aboard the truck. At times he gazed apologetically at the passing cars, at other times he peered down Second Avenue as though he were expecting someone. Presently the traffic lights changed.

Another Negro, who was driving a car that had just been halted in the van of traffic, leaned out of his window and called, "I never seen that before. No, sir!"

The Negro to whom the truck belonged stepped off the curb and laughed. "You sees it now, don't you?"

"Is that your rig?" asked the other.

"Yeah, tha's my rig! It ain't nobody else."

"Man, tha's trouble!"

"Man"—the owner threw his head back—"any kind of trouble is trouble enough. But that truck just keeps on bein' trouble. Don't pay no more attention to it!"

"What you mean, don't pay no more attention to it?" the other demanded. "I never seen that before. What you call that?"

"I call it broker."

"Broker?"

"Yeah," said the owner of the truck. "Every time somebody look at that truck, it get broker!"

They both laughed richly. Then the one in the car drove off and the other retreated to the sidewalk, where a crowd gathered round him.

"What did she feel like when she broke down on you?" a man in the crowd asked.

"Felt mighty funny." The Negro spread his tattered gloves. "Felt like I was about to fly away. Felt like I was about to sink right down."

"Felt like you was in an airplane?" someone prompted.

"Felt like you needed a parachute?" someone else said.

"No," said the Negro reflectively. "Felt a little slower than that—jitterbug!" The crowd laughed.

A patrol car with two policemen in it pulled up beside the curb.

"Your heap?" asked the cop at the wheel.

"Yes, sir," said the Negro.

The cop nodded. He was a lean-faced man with a sour expression and eyes set close together. "You ought to be locked up for just showin' up on a highway with that thing."

"No, sir, that truck'll haul anything," the Negro assured him. "I've hauled plenty of loads in that truck—up till today."

"Well, when the hell are you goin' to haul it out of here?"

"I phoned up my cousin with a truck in Brooklyn," the Negro explained. "He'll be comin' right along now."

"O.K. So will I," said the cop. "And if I have to look at that heap any more, there's gonna be trouble."

"Yes, sir," the Negro agreed.

The patrol car cruised off.

"Well, you're in trouble now," said someone in the crowd. "You better think fast."

"Thinkin' ain't goin' to do me no good," the Negro replied. "If thinkin' was goin' to do me any good, that truck'd be burned up by now. Thinkin' ain't goin' to help me. It's my cousin." He went to the curb and looked down Second Avenue. Then he shook his head and returned. "What you think that cop's goin' to charge me with?"

"Obstructin' traffic," a man in the crowd advised him.

"Well, that ain't my fault," said the Negro. "Tha's just an accident."

"You know what the judge is goin' to say?" the man said. "The judge is goin' to say, 'Why in hell doncha measure your load before you start out?' "

"You can't measure that load like you would with a tape," the Negro objected. "That load's uneven. You got to measure that load with the naked eye."

"Yeah, I know," said the man. "Why didn't you get a rough estimate before you started out."

"I did," the Negro answered. " 'Bout thirteen feet, I figured." He squinted at the truck. "Maybe a few inches more. 'Bout thirteen an' a quarter. Tha's better."

"Take a look at the sign then." The other man pointed up at the Elevated, at a sign just beneath the Elevated that read, "HEADROOM 12 FEET 2 INCHES." "That's all the clearance you got—twelve feet two."

"Mister," said the Negro, "which way you facin'?"

"East," said the other.

"Which way my truck facin'?"

The other man was silent.

"My truck facin' downtown," the Negro said. "How'm I goin' to see that sign?"

"Well, you could see the 'L' comin' down on you all the time, couldn't you?"

"No, sir," said the Negro. "I could see the hill gettin' higher. I couldn't see no 'L' comin' down. Climbin' a hill always look like it make more room, not less. I've climbed hills before."

The crowd was entertained. "Seems like your truck was wrecked by looks, too," someone said, and chuckled.

"Tha's just right," said the Negro soberly. "An' it keep bein' wrecked by looks. Every time somebody look at that truck, somethin' else go wrong with it. Man come up an' look at that truck an' say, 'Brother, your axle is shot.' Man look at that truck an' say, 'Brother, your rear end is shot.' Man come up an' look at that truck an' say, 'Brother, your universal is shot.' But nobody"—he lowered his voice to a whisper, so his ensuing laughter seemed immense—"nobody come up an' say, 'Brother, that truck so shot, here's a hundred dollars—buy yourself a new one!'"

"Hey! Hey, you!"

The men turned. It was the police patrol car again.

"What'd I tell you?" demanded the lean-faced cop at the wheel. "Didn't I tell you if I came back an' that heap was still there, there'd be trouble? What d'you think I'm doin', kiddin' you?"

"No, sir. I was just wonderin' what to do next," the Negro explained. "My cousin ain't come."

"Ah, t' hell with your cousin!" said the cop. "I don't believe you got a cousin."

"Yes, sir. I got a cousin."

"Listen, you don't need a cousin and you don't need any other kind of relative. You don't need a truck. You don't even need a pushcart. Start unloadin' her, so's we can get her over to the side, out of traffic."

"I can't unload that truck alone," said the Negro.

"Why not?"

"Them girders up there broke all the lines I had around them tubs an' wooden horses. That load's liable to slide if I unlash that back rope."

"Take it off the top of the load first."

"I can't do that," the Negro objected. "There's no room for me on top of that load under the 'L.'"

"Take it off the side then."

"How'm I goin' to take it off the side without somebody to hand it down to?"

"Oh, that's what it is," said the cop sarcastically. "You want somebody to hand it down to. Well, hand it down to yourself and walk over to the curb with it yourself. If you'd of been doin' that all this time instead of chewin' the fat with those guys, you'd of had that truck empty by now."

"Well, I had to wait for my cousin to get here."

"Will you do me a favor?" said the cop. "Will you forget your cousin?"

"Yes, sir."

"All right. Start pilin' it out of the truck."

"But he be here any minute now."

"Like hell he will!" the cop roared. "Not if he moves like you—he'll never be here! Get goin'!"

With the cop watching him from the patrol car, the Negro trudged over to the truck. He surveyed the load anxiously a moment and then climbed up on the side, near the cab. The lighter pieces—gravel screens, buckets, mortar hoes—came off easily enough. He rested them on the cab top and then climbed down again and carried them to the curb.

"Hurry up!" the cop called to him.

"Yes, sir."

He went over to the truck again and climbed up. The heavy pieces—tubs and troughs and wooden trestles—were wedged in tight and he couldn't move them. He climbed down again.

"I got to loosen that back rope now," he said to the cop.

"Well, loosen it."

"Supposin' she slide?"

"She won't slide if you don't get on the back end. Anybody can see that."

"Them pieces are heavy," said the Negro. "I'll maybe have to drop 'em on the highway. Supposin' a car come along an' slam into one of 'em—who get a ticket then?"

"You ought to," said the cop. "Whatsa matter—you weak?"

"No, I ain't weak, but I ain't no derrick," the Negro answered. "Some of them troughs is all caked with cement. They weigh two hundred pounds."

"Well, lemme know when you come to 'em," said the cop. "I'll take care of that."

"Yes, sir."

The Negro went back to the truck and began loosening the rope that went around the back of the load. A wheelbarrow wobbled near the top. He dropped the rope, caught the wheelbarrow, and let it slide quickly to the ground. Then he looked up at the load. Nothing else had shifted.

"I knew that load'd stay there," said the cop.

At that moment there was a crash as two northbound cabs collided. The cabdriver in front leaned out and yelled at the one behind, "What're you—blind?"

"G'wan! G'wan, will you! You're supposed to be drivin' a hack, not sightseein'," said the one in the rear. He threw his cab into gear and shoved the front cab. The man in the front cab immediately threw his machine into reverse and both bumpers were locked fast. It was only when they flung the doors of the cabs open to step out that they saw the cop striding toward them. They shrank back into the cabs.

"All right!" the cop snapped at the cabdriver in front. "I'm gonna burn you for that!"

"What d'ya want from me?" the cabdriver whined. "I happen to slow down and this guy bangs into me!"

"Slow down?" repeated the cabdriver in the rear. "He didn't slow down, Officer. He takes a gander at the truck and he throws his brakes on full. What the hell was I gonna do?"

"Well, what if I did take a look?" said the front driver. "What right's he got to shove me?"

"Lemme see your licence!" said the cop.

"For what?"

"For nothin'! For lookin'! For lookin' out of turn! What d'you think of that?" The cop glanced over at the truck. "What the hell're you waitin' for?" he roared at the Negro, who had stopped to watch the proceedings.

"You said for me to call you when I come to the heavy pieces," said the Negro.

"You picked a fine time! God damn it, I ought to give you the ticket I'm givin' these guys!"

"Why? I didn't do nothin'," said the Negro.

"That's the whole trouble," snarled the cop. "You ain't done a damn thing! Get some of that other stuff off before you call me!"

"Yes, sir." The Negro trundled a wheelbarrow to the curb.

The cop began writing out the summons. By this time another lane of traffic was blocked—one of the two uptown lanes. A general honking of horns began behind the locked cabs. Traffic trickled through slowly. Cars were packed so close the Negro couldn't get out to the truck. He stood there on the curb, shaking his head. "Man," he said, "I seen trouble before, but I never seen trouble that just kep' on makin' trouble."

A cameraman appeared from nowhere and, tagging after him, a swarm of barelegged kids in football helmets. "He's from the *Mirror!*" they cried. "Hey, Mister, take my picture!"

The cameraman stepped into the street and maneuvered his camera for a clearer view of the truck. The kids were already in front of him. Darting recklessly through the pack of traffic, shouting "Take me! Git me into it, Mister!," half a dozen of them leaped onto the tailboards of the truck. The cameraman snapped his shutter.

"Get off there!" bellowed the cop.

The kids leaped for safety as the pile of troughs, barrels, planks, and wooden horses toppled into Forty-fourth Street with a roar.

Not a car could move—uptown, downtown, or crosstown. Horns continued their clamor. Summons in hand, the cop made for the fleeing kids and got as far as the debris on the ground. Then he stopped and took a step toward the cameraman. Then he stopped again and made for the Negro.

"Why, God damn you!" he said. He was almost strangling with rage.

"I didn't do nothin'," said the Negro. "That ain't my fault."

The other policeman, who had remained behind in the patrol car, came running up. "Whatsa matter, Tim?"

"Him! *It ain't his fault!*"

"What?"

"He didn't do nothin'!" roared the first cop.

"What d'ya mean?"

For a moment it looked as though a cop were about to arrest a cop. From the tangle of plastery iron and wood on the ground a cloud of dust rose up to the Elevated—rose leisurely upward through the checkered shade.

"Man! Man!" the Negro marvelled. "Every time somebody look at that truck, somethin' else go wrong!"

> *Roth:* Before we came to settle in Maine . . . I got a couple of things in *The New Yorker.* That was encouraging, of course, because *The New Yorker* is not an easy magazine to print in. But it seemed such hard work, and without the kind of—I've used the word *possession*—possession, inspiration, whatever you want to call it. . . . It didn't seem worth it as far as making a living was concerned. I could do almost anything else, so why sit and sweat over a story to make it fit *The New Yorker* magazine style? If you're going to work hard at one thing, you can work at another thing. If you don't feel this particular something or other is being profoundly expressed, then it doesn't matter what you're doing.
>
> (Bell, 1966, p. 9)

> *Roth:* I felt that this particular creative force . . . that had been efficient in *Call It Sleep* was no longer operating anywhere near the same extent; that I could do what others did, that is, trying for commercial writing, trying to write short stories that were salable, and make a living that way. And I did. I sold a few of them, but I

found that it was awfully hard work, without that particular feeling of inspiration. And there were easier forms of making a living than that, so I gave it up.

(Radio WFAU interview,
Augusta, Maine,
January 1965)

Roth: The first onset of the collapse came about 1940 or late 1939. . . . If there's such a thing as an equivalent or approximate nervous breakdown, that's what I suffered. I was trying to write a short story; it was called "Broker" oddly enough. . . . It was late at night, and I was forcing myself to write the kind of thing I had not been accustomed to writing. Ordinarily, I wrote from a structure that I envisioned internally, not necessarily to please or satisfy a commercial magazine. I have never tried that. Of course, *that's* proof of being a professional writer, and *that* I was not. Somewhere around one or two in the morning I became aware of a terrible feeling of anxiety; I think it was real fear. Sweat broke out on my brow, and I had a desire to just scream. Those are signs of a nervous breakdown. I knew I had to quit everything I was doing and just walk out on the street and walk, and walk, and walk forever. Finally about three o'clock in the morning I calmed down and came home and went to bed. I think it was about this time that I decided, if I ever finish the thing I'm going to be through with writing. The anxiety, by the way, persisted. I seemed to be sort of disembodied. If anything, it seemed to be in the back of my head. . . . It seemed to return whenever I seriously thought to write commercially or anything but a letter, and even, sometimes, in the middle of a letter. The thing would sort of attack me, and the whole quality of the letter, I would feel, was changing. I was no longer writing with spontaneity. And that's another reason I decided I couldn't buck up against that; that's an impossible situation. It stands in front of you like a specter. And you can't beat it, because sooner or later you're going to remember this thing—and merely remembering it seems to invoke it. I have somewhere in a journal set down the very next day what I felt. One of the few journals that I didn't destroy, fortunately. From that point on, the writing almost lapsed.

(Lyons, 1979, p. 51)

Roth: Jesus, it's a shame. I mean, that all those years. . . . It was in 1940, or something like that, that I published something in *The New Yorker.* Well then, the ordinary guy who has all his wits about him says, "Well, here I broke the ice. And like everybody else, I have a mass of experience, of experiences if you wish—go ahead, then.

And I also have power of observation—dig up other stories, print them, and get the income from it, and so forth. You're a disciplined writer, you have some taste and so forth and so on, you've developed . . . you're acknowledged to have some ability—well, exploit it!" Isn't it something that makes sense?

(taped conversation,
Albuquerque, N.M.,
April 24, 1985)

Somebody Always Grabs the Purple

March 23, 1940

For the second of his published stories, Roth again drew upon personal recollections. Unlike "Broker," this short story is autobiographical, the child protagonist being a thinly disguised projection of young Henry Roth growing up in Harlem.

Roth: In 1938, when I was despairing of ever writing again, my relationship with Eda Lou Walton deteriorated. We separated, and almost immediately afterwards I met Muriel Parker at Yaddo, an artist's colony at Saratoga Springs. The following year we were married, but the only livelihood we had came from the WPA and relief. They had me working with pick and shovel laying pipes as well as repairing and maintaining streets. In 1940 I wrote "Somebody Always Grabs the Purple," a story of a boy's visit to the public library. . . . When I notified the relief agency that I had received three hundred dollars for the publication I was reclassified as being no longer indigent, and promptly removed from the rolls.

(Bronsen, 1969, p. 275)

Roth: I did sell a couple of things to *The New Yorker*. . . . One was a recollection of Harlem life called "Somebody Always Grabs the Purple," meaning the purple fairy book.

(Friedman, 1977, p. 35)

*U*p a flight of stairs, past the vases and the clock outside the adult reading room, past cream walls, oak moldings, oak bookcases, and the Cellini statue of Perseus was the children's room of the 123rd Street Branch Library. Young Sammy Farber drew a battered library card out of his pocket and went in. He was a thickset, alert boy, eleven or twelve years old. He flattened his card on the desk and, while he waited for the librarian, gazed about. There were only a few youngsters in the reading room. Two boys in colored jerseys stood whispering at one of the bookcases. On the wall above their heads was a frieze of Grecian urchins blowing trumpets. The librarian approached.

"Teacher," Sammy began, "I just moved, Teacher. You want to change it—the address?"

The librarian, a spare woman, graying and impassive, with a pince-nez, glanced at his card. "Let me see your hands, Samuel," she said.

He lifted his hands. She nodded approvingly and turned his card over. It was well stamped. "You'd better have a new one," she said.

"Can I get it next time, Teacher? I'm in a hurry like."

"Yes. Where do you live now, Samuel?"

"On 520 East 120th Street." He watched her cross out the Orchard Street address and begin writing in the new one. "Teacher," he said, in a voice so low it was barely audible, "you got here the 'Purple Fairy Book'?"

"The what?"

"The 'Purple Fairy Book.'" He knuckled his nose sheepishly. "Everybody says I'm too big to read fairy books. My mother calls 'em stories with a bear."

"Stories with a bear?"

"Yeah, she don't know English good. You got it?"

"Why, yes. I think it's on the shelves."

"Where, Teacher?" He moved instantly toward the aisle.

"Just a moment, Samuel. Here's your card." He seized it. "Now I'll show you where it is."

Together they crossed the room to a bookcase with a brass plate which said "Fairy Tales." Sammy knelt down so that he could read the titles more easily. There were not a great many books in the case—a few legends for boys about Arthur and Roland on the top shelf, then a short row of fairy tales arranged according to countries, and finally, on the bottom shelf, a few fairy books arranged by colors: Blue, Blue, Green. Her finger on the titles wavered. Red . . . Yellow . . . "I'm sorry." She glanced over the books again rapidly. "It's not here."

"Ah!" he said, relaxing. "They grabbed it again!"

"Have you read the others? Have you read the Blue?"

"Yeah, I read the Blue." He stood up slowly. "I read the Blue and the Green and the Yellow. All the colors. And colors that ain't even here. I read the Lilac. But somebody always grabs the Purple."

"I'm pretty sure the 'Purple Fairy Book' hasn't been borrowed," the librarian said. "Why don't you look on the tables? It may be there."

"I'll look," he said. "but I know. Once they grab it, it's goodbye."

Nevertheless he went from table to table, picking up abandoned books, scanning their titles, and putting them down again. His round face was the image of forlorn hope. As he neared one of the last tables, he stopped. A boy was sitting there with a stack of books at his elbow, reading with enormous concentration. Sammy walked behind the boy and peered over his shoulder. On one page there was print, on the other a colored illustration, a serene princeling, hand on the hilt of his sword, regarding a gnarled and glowering gnome. The book was bound in purple. Sammy sighed and returned to the librarian.

"I found it, Teacher. It's over there," he said, pointing. "He's got it."

"I'm sorry, Samuel. That's the only copy we have."

"His hands ain't as clean as mine," Sammy suggested.

"Oh, I'm sure they are. Why don't you try something else?" she urged. "Adventure books are very popular with boys."

"They ain't popular with him." Sammy gazed gloomily at the boy. "That's what they always told me on the East Side—popular. I don't see what's so popular about them. If a man finds a treasure in an adventure book, so right away it's with dollars and cents. Who cares from dollars and cents? I get enough of that in my house."

"There's fiction," she reminded him. "Perhaps you're the kind of boy who likes reading about grownups."

"Aw, them too!" He tossed his head. "I once read a fiction book, it had in it a hero with eyeglasses? Hih!" His laugh was brief and pitying. "How could heroes be with eyeglasses? That's like my father."

The librarian placed her pince-nez a little more securely on her nose. "He may leave it, of course, if you wait," she said.

"Can I ask him?"

"No. Don't disturb him."

"I just want to ask him is he gonna take it or ain't he. What's the use I should hang around all day?"

"Very well. But that's all."

Sammy walked over to the boy again and said, "Hey, you're gonna take it, aintcha?"

Like one jarred out of sleep, the boy started, his eyes blank and wide.

"What d'you want to read from that stuff?" Sammy asked. "Fairy tales!" His lips, his eyes, his whole face expressed distaste. "There's an adventure book here," he said, picking up the one nearest his hand. "Don't you like adventure books?"

The boy drew himself up in his seat. "What're you botherin' me for?" he said.

"I ain't botherin' you. Did you ever read the 'Blue Fairy Book'? That's the best. That's a hard one to get."

"Hey, I'll tell the teacher on you!" The boy looked around. "I'm readin' this!" he said angrily. "And I don't want no other one! Read 'em yourself!"

Sammy waited a moment and then tried again. "You know you shouldn't read fairy books in the liberry."

The boy clutched the book to himself protectingly and rose. "You want to fight?"

"Don't get excited," Sammy waved him back into the chair and retreated a step. "I was just sayin' fairy tales is better to read in the house, ain't it—like when you're sittin' in the front room and your mother's cookin' in the kitchen? Ain't that nicer?"

"Well, what about it?"

"So in the liberry you can read from other things. From King Arthur or from other mitts."

The boy saw through that ruse also. He waved Sammy away. "I'm gonna read it here and I'm gonna read it home too, wise guy."

"All right, that's all I wanted to ask you," said Sammy. "You're gonna take it, aintcha?"

"Sure I'm gonna take it."

"I thought you was gonna take it."

Sammy retreated to one of the central pillars of the reading room and stood there, watching. The same play of wonder and beguilement that animated the boy's thin features while he read also animated Sammy's pudgy ones, as though the enjoyment were being relayed. After a time the boy got up and went to the desk with the book still in his hand. The librarian took the card out of the book and stamped the boy's own card. Then she handed him the book. Sammy's round face dimmed. He waited, however, until the boy had had time to get out of the reading room and down the stairs before he put his worn library card in his pocket and made for the exit.

> *Roth:* Moving to Harlem [in 1914] was a disaster. Judaism was my framework, and striving for material success was a vital, visible aspect of it on the East Side. But this was exactly what my little Gentile cronies mocked: Money! Money! Their scorn helped make Judaism repugnant. And once that happened, my identity disintegrated too. The same thing didn't happen to the other Jewish kids who were living in Harlem, perhaps because they were born in Harlem, or home influences were stronger. I mean, for them, the drive was intact. With me, my world fractured. My mystique went to pieces.
> *Interviewer:* What was it replaced with?
> *Roth:* Well, you just had a mopey, withdrawn kid who spent most of his time reading fairy tales. . . . I don't know how late I read fairy tales. I read every fairy tale, every myth there was in the library. In other words, it became kind of a dream world, kind of a fantasy world, I'm sure. Whereas the other kids at that time, Jewish and non-Jewish, were reading Horatio Alger's *From Bootblack to Millionaire* or what have you. With me, that no longer had any appeal. That was Jewish. Up until that time, as long as I lived on Ninth Street, in the Lower East Side, I thought I was in a kind of ministate of our own. It never occurred to me that the world could be any different. But moving into this Irish-Italian neighborhood, for my type of kid anyway, was a terrible shock. I came to believe that we were all the things the goyim called us.

> (Goldsmith, 1983)

> *Interviewer:* I would like to ask you how you come to choose the titles of your stories.
> *Roth:* Well, I suppose the answer is, these are the titles that pop into my head, as it were. And once they seem appropriate, I don't give them any further thought. Except you can see that there runs through much of this a thread of frustration. . . . "Somebody Always Grabs the Purple," at least in the subliminal area of my own

being, represents the frustration, the loss, the deprivation of some kind of a deep impulse—and the title itself, I suppose, reflects the blocking of, the *frustration* of, the realization of that impulse. And that's how I got the title.

(taped conversation,
Albuquerque, N.M.,
February 7, 1986)

Roth: Frustration, in a word. The frustration reflected from the interior of the writer who, to use the cliché, is up against a block. But it's much more than a cliché. He is unable to convey, he's unable to express the deep desire to create, to exercise his fancy and narrative ability. So it becomes sublimated into kidding, his desire for the fairy tale that he can't get—the purple fable, you know, that he never gets a chance to. . . .

Interviewer: Is there a particular significance to the color itself?

Roth: There is. . . . It's almost subliminal in its associations, because, after all, purple . . . the Roman idea, aristocracy, and excellence, and so forth. These things happen to a literary guy, you know, without his even thinking about it, because he's so steeped in his literary associations. Purple is the richness, the fineness that he *aimed* at, that he thought was his legacy. Ironically enough, purple is also the hue of mourning. Now, whether or not this has any significance . . .

(taped conversation,
Albuquerque, N.M.,
February 8, 1986)

Many Mansions

September 1940

"Many Mansions," the third of Roth's published stories, was completely forgotten for more than four decades, escaping the attention of the scholars as well as practically evaporating from the author's memory. Roth, who preserved neither a copy of the original typescript nor the issue of the magazine where the story first appeared, even forgot its title, retaining only a vague recollection of having sold a third story to Coronet. He never mentioned the story in any of his published interviews and eventually came to doubt that it was ever published.

Some time ago, while going over one of the first letters he had received from Roth, the editor came across the following passage:

In answer to your first inquiry concerning any other published short story: there is one other (one I'd like to forget, and almost have), a potboiler that might be called the last straw of my writing career. This appeared in a magazine called *Coronet* at about the same time—a little later I believe—as the 1940 *New Yorker* sketch ["Somebody Always Grabs the Purple"], i.e., 1940–41. I'm sorry I no longer recall the title. There is another *New Yorker* sketch, prior to the one you mention, called "Broker." That date or copy I have; it's November 18, 1939. Other than that, I believe that is all.

(letter from Augusta, Maine,
May 18, 1964)

Picking up on the lead at last, having unaccountably failed to do so twenty years before, the editor asked Roth for any additional information that would help locate the story. He replied:

No, sorry, I have nothing further on the piece (?) in *Coronet.* When did the magazine expire? I seem to recall a summer in Cape Cod, when the U.S. had not yet entered the war (1940?)—and my agent, who has also departed this life, congratulating me on having sold a story to *Coronet.* I've just asked Muriel whether she remembers my having sold something to *Coronet.* She answered in the affirmative. But alas where it is? Maybe on further consideration they decided against publication. That's the best I can do. It seems to me fairly safe to assume it never appeared in print.

(letter from Albuquerque, N.M.,
November 8, 1985)

With the help of a friend, Professor Louise K. Barnett, of Rutgers University, the mysterious Coronet *story was finally unearthed, to be properly reinstated in the Roth canon.*

W hen I was ten years old I became a collector of mansions. I would walk up and down Fifth Avenue slowly and admire one by one every mansion on what was then called Millionaires' Row. Millionaires' Row extended approximately from Fifty-seventh Street to Ninety-third Street, from Mr. Vanderbilt to Mr. Ruppert. Sometimes I would ask a deliveryman or a coachman who the owner of a certain residence was. Later on I learned I could get all the information I needed from the society columns. With clipping in hand, I often stood in homage before the premises of last night's ball.

Mansions, however, unlike other things that boys collected, had interiors. And after a while I began to long for a peek behind one of these facades I knew so well. Unfortunately, I didn't know any millionaires. But one day, as I was walking along Fifth Avenue—not exactly making a tour of inspection, but more in the manner of a connoisseur lovingly poring over familiar works—I spied Senator Charles Stover coming out of his residence on Seventy-seventh Street. Senator Stover's dwelling had always been one of the chief shrines on my pilgrimages along Fifth Avenue.

The old Mall in Central Park was only a few blocks away, and on late summer afternoons, when Mr. Volpe conducted the band through the Second Hungarian Rhapsody, or Mr. Kaltenborn enthusiastically picked up his violin in a Strauss waltz, I would sit back on a park bench and dreamily watch the glittering roofs of this my prize abode as they wavered among clouds of music. It was the one mansion of all that I would have wished to enter. And now across the Avenue stood opportunity itself.

The senator was a slight man, bearded and old, a little stooped in his tan alpaca suit with its high lapels and his stiff straw hat. For a moment as he stood in front of that vast pile of granite and marble, he looked like the old fisherman in the Arabian Nights who had opened the vase and let out the Djinn. And then he began walking briskly downtown along Fifth Avenue. I set out in pursuit. "Mr. Stover!" I called.

He whirled about. It may have been the sound of running feet behind him or my sudden call, for he gripped his cane as though he meant to strike out. "What is it?" he demanded.

"I didn't mean to bother you." I suddenly repented the whole venture. "I'll go ahead."

"You'll what?" he said. "Come here, young man." The senator had been a schoolteacher early, very early in his youth—before he had gone to Montana to make his fortune in copper. He adjusted his starched cuffs as ominously as any grammar school principal. "How did you know my name?"

"I seen it in the newspapers," I blurted out. "I seen your picture."

"And do you always run after, do you always shout after people whose names you see in the newspapers?" He had a Viking's heavy curved nose and a drastic blue eye.

"No, sir," I quailed. "I never did it before."

"Well, be a man whatever happens." He indicated with a short upward wave of his hand that he wanted me to straighten up. "What is it you want?"

My cause seemed too hopeless for me even to begin. "I know all the houses on Fifth Avenue." I flung my arms out despairingly. "I know them all."

The senator waited with knit brow.

"I know them all from the outside," I said faintly. "I never been inside one."

"Oh." He regarded me obliquely for a moment and then suddenly glanced up and down Fifth Avenue, as though it might have occurred to him that I had an accomplice. Fortunately for me, Fifth Avenue at that moment was apparently devoid of suspicious characters. "You know all the houses," he said. "Why do you know all the houses?"

"I don't know." I hung my head. "Everybody knows something. Some kids know any automobile. Some kids know any penny date. I know any house. I'm sharks with houses."

"Sharks," the senator repeated. "Whose house is that?" he jerked his head abruptly at the white stone house beside which we were standing.

"Oh, that's Mr. Bridgman's house." I was on my mettle now. "Mr. Horace Harding is next to him—by the empty lot." I was afraid the senator would ask me who owned the empty lot—which was something I wasn't sure of. But he didn't. He let his eye run along the row of houses downtown.

"Where does Harkness live?"

"Which Harkness?" I fairly tingled with information. "The Harknesses is trips."

"The Harknesses are *what?*" said the senator.

"Trips," I explained. "Like in marbles. When there's three marbles together, you yell trips. When there's two marbles together, you yell dubs. There's lots like that on Fifth Avenue."

"Oh, yes, yes, yes," said the senator. He said "yes" so many times, I thought he would never stop, as though he were unfolding the years to the time when he had first heard the expression.

"There's even fourples," I offered eagerly. "The Vanderbilts is fourples. The Goulds is fourples. So is the Brokaws."

"Of course there are fourples." The senator crowded his beard upward with the back of his hand. "Do you know where they all live?" And at my confident nod, "All?" he raised his voice. "All the Harknesses, for example?"

"Yes, sir. There's one Harkness lives on the corner of Seventy-fifth Street. Then there's another Harkness lives on number 933. And there's Charles Harkness. He lives on 685, near Fifty-third Street."

"Good Lord!" said the senator.

"You want the Brokaws?" I offered. "They're harder. You want the Vanderbilts?"

"That will do."

"You want to know who lives on the other side of you? Mr. Dietrich? Mrs. Butler? Mr. Schiff?"

"That will do." He quelled me. "I'm quite convinced you know more about the best people than I do about marbles."

"I don't know them," I explained proudly. "They don't know me. I only know their outsides."

"I understand. And now you'd like to go inside, is that it?"

"Yes, sir."

"Why my house?"

"Yours is the wonderfullest," I said simply.

"Hm." His beard lifted. "What is it you want to see?"

"I don't know." I could feel my eyes grow large at the mere thought of all the wonders there were to see. "You got a hundred and twenty thousand dollar organ with four thousand pipes," I reminded him. "It's got wood in it from Sherwood Forest where Robin Hood used to live. You got big lions by the fireplace with rings in their mouth. You got gold on all the ceilings."

The senator had unbent a great deal. He seemed quite a different man from the one I had first accosted—much milder, much more amiable. "You're not the kind of boy who falls over things, are you? You wouldn't touch anything you weren't supposed to?"

"No, sir," I assured him.

"All right. We'll go in."

"You mean you're going to take me?" I stared at him.

"I haven't much time, but you'll see enough."

"Now?"

"Right now." He patted me on the shoulder. "Come along."

I stood there inertly. The prospect of beholding in reality all that I had read in the newspapers and all that I had conjured up out of daydream and music seemed suddenly too much for me. It was one thing to convince the senator that I was worthy to go in his mansion; it was another actually to go in. "I don't know if I can go now," I sagged apologetically. "I think my mother's waiting for me."

"Oh, I have a schedule myself." He took my arm briskly.

I stumbled along beside him. The main entrance was on the sidestreet, not on the Avenue. The nearer I drew to magnificence, the dark bronze carriage gates, the heavily curtained windows, the massive masonry of the lower walls, the less I wanted to enter. I felt as if there was something I already possessed that I might lose if I entered.

Two wide, curving steps led up to the main entrance, and then there were two glass doors, both closed. Through them I could see the reception room within, the big vases and the gilt chairs, and in every corner, a life-sized bronze pickaninny holding aloft a beaded lamp. All this I had expected to see somehow; I had seen it all in imagination. But the thing I hadn't expected to see, the thing that perhaps I had begun to fear I might see when the senator invited me in, was the atmosphere that surrounded all the objects in the room. Shadowy, seemingly hushed, rigorous, it was like the atmosphere in Grant's Tomb or the Egyptian room in the Museum.

I don't know what I expected things did in the senator's mansion—whether they floated or one floated about them. But here, everything seemed decreed, ordained to stay just where it was and nowhere else. I felt as if, were I to go in, I might be decreed to stay just where I was too, and nowhere else, like one of those bronze pickaninnies with the beaded lamps. The senator took out his latch key.

"Do you know what an immy is?"

"Yes, sir," I quavered. "I'm pretty sure it's an imitation."

"Are there immies on Fifth Avenue too?"

"I don't know," I said.

He laughed. Then he turned his back to unlock the door. In that moment lay my opportunity. While he was still talking, I tiptoed down the two steps—and fled like a felon toward Fifth Avenue. I don't know whether he knew I was gone until I was out of sight around the corner. I heard no one call. The last thing I heard the senator say was: "I haven't said that in seventy years."

I have often wondered since what else the senator said that he might not have said in seventy years.

The following is Roth's comment upon receiving a photocopy of his forgotten story:

So here it is indeed: "Many Mansions." What a bit of fluff. As I wrote Louise Barnett: pity I didn't delve much deeper into the background and life of my friend and dentist, Gus, the person whose account of this boyhood quirk gave me the idea for the sketch. *That* would have been a novel, assuming I did justice to the material. I pick a helluva good moment to pine about it.

(letter from Albuquerque, N.M.,
December 17–18, 1985)

A short time later, Roth again expressed his regret at not having creatively "appropriated" his friend Gus's interesting life and written a novel about it. Characteristically, Roth referred to his former self in the third person.

Roth: This all started in the context of the other story—[Gus's] studying eight years at night to become a mechanical engineer, and then he was told, "Of course we wouldn't mind hiring you, even if you are Jewish, but our customers might object." That was the favorite "out" at that time. So I thought, "Well, right there was the yarn"—to try and envisage how the kid went to work in the morning, and at night to an engineering college, probably Cooper Union or some such place as that, for eight long years—and then all of it went down the drain. In fact, as he told me about it, he still seemed stunned that eight years of his life had gone by. Then he said, "There's nothing to do except in the order of a profession, where you can set up your own conditions, as it were." And that's why he took up dentistry.

Interviewer: But you can't write a novel about every interesting individual you come across!

Roth: No. But look how the story reduced itself—what it reduced itself to. . . . The writer was no longer capable of treating, of dealing with and transmitting the wonderful narrative signals, so to speak, that the serious novelist would have been sensitized to.

(taped conversation,
Albuquerque, N.M.,
February 7, 1986)

Equipment for Pennies

Autumn 1954

*After the publication of "Many Mansions," Roth lapsed into an ab-
solute silence that lasted fourteen years. When he finally broke his
silence in 1954, he did so with what he now jokingly terms his "one
contribution to an erudite journal"—a do-it-yourself article for a trade
periodical called* The Magazine for Ducks and Geese.

*The question of why he stopped writing has haunted Roth for
decades. Understandably, the answers he has found are many.*

Roth: I've done a great deal of thinking about that. I think a lot
about truncation, not just my own but the truncation of other writers
of the thirties as well. Some of them, like myself, wrote one good
novel and nothing else. Some wrote a few and stopped. Others
repeated themselves over and over again, like Farrell. I met Daniel
Fuchs some years ago and talked to him about it. He claims that he
went to Hollywood as an act of deliberate choice, that he did it simply
because he wanted to. I don't believe that. If the creative drive is still
there, it's a need and you can't deny it, and I think Fuchs was only
able to go to Hollywood because that urge, that impulse had left him.
And he's not the only one. It happened to many of us.

Interviewer: How would you explain it?

Roth: I've got a number of theories. It seems I develop a new one just about every week. I've explained it to myself in a number of ways over the years, and the explanations keep changing. At the moment I feel it was probably due more than anything else to the tremendous pressure of what was going on in the streets, to the conflict between personal expression and social obligation. . . . [In the thirties] the pressure, I think, was overwhelming, and those who couldn't move with it—some did of course—were broken by it. You can even feel the invasion at the end of my own book where it begins to open up, to shoot out in all directions.

(Freedman, 1975, pp. 152–53)

Your assumption that my aim in changing my point of view in *CIS* when I did is exactly right: as a transition to the choral part; and probably, in retrospect, subjectively I might add, an indication that the form of the novel was being broken, along with the creative psyche of the novelist. The interesting thing to me, today, at any rate, is its prophetic quality—insofar as it forecasts the disruption of the creativity of a whole group of artistic personalities.

(letter from Augusta, Maine,
December 21, 1961)

Roth: I was through. For a long time I thought I was afflicted by some peculiar curse. But I have come to believe that there was something deeper and less personal in my misfortune, that what had happened to me was common to a whole generation of writers in the thirties. One author after another, whether he was Gentile or Jew, stopped writing, became repetitive, ran out of anything new to say or just plain died artistically. I came to this conclusion because I simply could not believe that anyone with as much discipline, creative drive, inbred feeling for the narrative and intense will to write as I had, could, after such rigorous efforts, still be balked.

Looking about, I saw the same phenomenon manifesting itself in practically every writer I knew. They became barren. Daniel Fuchs decided after his third novel that he would write for Hollywood. . . . James Farrell is another example. He had exhausted himself by the time he had written his third novel, and everything he wrote after that consisted of variations on played-out themes. Steinbeck is not radically different, as far as his real contribution is concerned; nothing else he ever wrote came up to *The Grapes of Wrath.*

And Edward Dahlberg—what did he write after *Bottom Dogs* and *From Flushing to Calvary?* There was Hart Crane and Léonie Adams, both of whom ran into the stone wall of noncreativity. Crane committed suicide, and Nathanael West for his part conveniently died. . . .

How does one explain this peculiarity? It happened often enough that I began to reflect on it, and I have continued to reflect on it ever since. I do not have the training to make a scientific or sociological analysis, but it seems to me that World War II, which was already in the making, was a dividing line between an era which was coming to an end, namely ours, and another, which was coming into being. I think that we sensed a sharp turn in historic development. How do writers sense these things? We sense it in our prolonged malaise, and in our art—in the fact that, having been fruitful writers, we suddenly grow sterile. The causes are personal, but they are also bigger than any of us. When so many people are affected in the same way and each one is groping for his own diagnosis, you have to look for a broader explanation.

(Bronsen, 1969, pp. 274–75)

Roth: I remember ["Equipment for Pennies"]. I still was under the depressed state where I began to write with a considerable amount of gusto and then it came back to me again, this thing that had been dogging me all those many years. It would be very difficult for me to describe. . . . It was like—in fact I am writing about it now—it was something like a dybbuk. . . . You could use other words—a kind of nemesis, or something that haunts you, right? And this thing, whenever I would try to write, was always in the back of my mind, always waiting there—this thing would come back. This is something I probably never told anybody. And it's only in the last—what is it now? eighty-five—perhaps in the last ten years, that the thing finally relented. It no longer bothers me. I can feel it, you know. It's a kind of anxiety, a counterdrive *not* to write. Sometimes it would happen in the middle of a letter. I would start off, I would forget this particular anxiety—and then, it won: it had got to be too much of a struggle. In other words, this particular anxiety that would come over me, so possessed—that's the other way of saying—so obstructed, so interfered with me, that I could feel a draining away of emotional esprit, élan.

Interviewer: And when you wrote "Equipment for Pennies," you won over the dybbuk—is that it?

Roth: What I was going to say is that I started off with great enthusiasm, and somewhere near the end I could feel an interference. I persisted despite that, you see, and I can tell that there is a difference in tone between what I was writing naturally before the anxiety struck, so to speak, and. . . .

Interviewer: And that was the first thing you wrote in a long time, right?

Roth: I think so. It was my first intimation that maybe I was coming out of this terrible, terrible bog. After all, I worked in a hospital and I was friends with a psychiatrist there, who also wrote poetry. . . . He said to me, "You are depressed. What you describe to me, these are all signs of a neurotic depression. And what you ought to do is, try and drink a very, very strong cup of black coffee, and then see what it could do to you." I've often thought of that, as a cure. But apparently what happens is that, given enough time, it simply wears off.

(taped conversation,
Albuquerque, N.M.,
April 24, 1985)

*I*f you know what you're after, the local junkyard is one of the most fertile sources of dressing equipment. And it's equipment that will cost pennies. Furthermore, it will prove to be perfectly serviceable.

Here are three basic pieces of equipment that the writer salvaged from the junkyard. In addition to enabling him to do a good job on his own Muscovy ducks, it made possible a profitable custom dressing business.

Scalding and waxing equipment

Neither the scalder nor the waxer needs to be anything more elaborate than discarded washing machines. Wringer, motor, and all other appendages are removed, and only the tub and stand are left. You will find two large holes at the bottom of each tub. Scrape the enamel off and solder a disk of copper or steel over these holes. The covers on small electrical junction boxes will serve. Next, cut a hole in the top of each stand eight inches by eight inches. This is to allow the heat from your appliance to get up through the stand to the tub. In cutting the hole a hacksaw may be used; or if that seems too arduous you may apply to your local garageman to burn it out with an acetylene torch. Your scalder and waxer are now ready and will do a good job.

Incidentally, don't forget to ask the man for the washing machine covers.

If you want to make an extra-special fancy waxer—the kind guaranteed not to overflow and not to catch fire—simply insert a No. 1 washtub into either one of the completed vats. This size round tub will fit perfectly into any washing machine of the standard kinds: Sears, Wards, Easy, etc., allowing an inch or so of water all around. In other words, you've got a water-jacketed job. Put a spacer between the two bottoms so the water can circulate there too. One caution: when you get that No. 1 washtub, don't get the kind with rigid handles because they won't fit. Get the kind with swinging handles.

Heating appliance

It's simple as pie to make this appliance, though it's a little hard to describe. The appliance depends on gas, bottled or otherwise, for its fuel. Again go to the junkyard and pick up the following: two burners with two gas cocks, and one manifold out of an old gas stove with at least two holes or outlets in it not less than two feet apart. That's so that the two burners will come centrally under the two tubs. Total cost of these items should be about fifty cents.

Now arrange your two burners so that they'll come directly under the tubs. That is, they should burn upwards through the openings you've made in the stands. Once you've decided on the arrangement, build a "stove" or stand for the entire thing. This can be of wood—it's just to keep the arrangement rigid.

It may take a little fussing to get this thing right but essentially it's simple: two burners coming out of two holes in the manifold, controlled by two gas cocks.

Now close up any additional holes with standard plugs. Cover your wooden "stove" with sheet iron. Place a piece of sheet iron under the burners covered with aluminum foil to reflect the heat upward and thus get maximum efficiency. The rest will come with use. In my own case the burners were long enough so that I could run the manifold outside the tubs. In that case I ran it on the side opposite the one I was working on so I wouldn't bark my shins, if you get the idea.

If the two burners are short, it might be best to run the manifold under the tubs. Also you may find that the "spuds" in the gas cocks have to be changed to adapt them to bottled gas or whatever gas you're using.

Killing trough

Again in the junkyard I found some discarded metal shelf or bin with two slanting sides and about four feet long, just the thing to hang under the big killing cones. You can make a board backing for the whole apparatus, line it with used sheet iron, and have a blood trough. Since putting mine in I've been looking hungrily at every four-foot fluorescent light reflector. It seems to me that with a little doctoring and patching they'd make ideal blood troughs, because they've got just the right sloping sides. Hang your bar, the one you suspend your cones from so that you will have room enough to get at the heads of the birds. Tip the trough a little so that the blood will flow into whatever receptacle you have placed there.

So case your local junkyard and don't spend over a dollar for anything.

Comments on the above article with some further suggestions for this type of equipment:

If gas is not available, gasoline or kerosene burners, with outlet for fumes, should do the business. And electricity, which is now the most common heat source. Perhaps electrical strip heaters could be inserted. A larger outlet for draining, such as a molasses gate, would be helpful for draining water and feathers from the bottom with sludge after the wax settles. Generally it is believed that water jacketing is unnecessary if the burner is shielded from possible boil-over of wax. The double boiler arrangement is slow and uses extra heat. Also, when you are using machine stripping of wax it's hard to get enough temperature with the water bath system and to get it quickly enough. However, some processors do prefer it.

The motor, reduction gear layout and even the wringer from the old washing machines can be used to make other mechanical gadgets around the plant. A belt conveyor can be driven from wringer connection almost direct, and an overhead conveyor of simple type can be driven from sprocket on upright shaft—and perhaps made from junkyard materials, chain, etc. Operations such as drawing, wax and water dips, "plumping," and even finishing on conveyors are considered about fifteen percent more efficient in labor used than are nonconveyorized operations.

Roth: That copy [of *The Magazine for Ducks and Geese*] is a curiosity, because it was the first time I ever wrote anything on a subject like that. Anyway, that's all it consists of. I discovered that, instead of having to buy equipment, commercial equipment, I could make some of it myself. For example, they sell this big sort of a sink, over which you hang the bird when you cut its throat, so it'll drain into it. Well, I took a barrel, one of those fifty-gallon steel drums—you know the kind I mean—and I had the man cut it in half with his torch so that half made a very nice sink over which I could hang the killing cones. . . . In those days he did it for a dollar. A drum like that, I don't know, I probably picked it up. I probably didn't pay more than a dollar for it either. So there you are. Some of it I did myself, like connecting on pipes so it would drain out, and so on. And a number of other things I mentioned in the article.

(taped conversation,
Albuquerque, N.M.,
April 24, 1985)

Interviewer: Excuse my ignorance: what is a killing cone?

Roth: Above the blood trough hung a rod—not a rod, but a bar. And on this bar—this was all commercial stuff—there were three killing cones. They were about a foot high and open at both ends— an inverted cone, large end on the top and small end on the bottom. You put the bird in there so that the body was squeezed inside the cone but the head projected downward—outward. And then you grabbed the throat. You could feel the windpipe, so to speak, of the poor thing.

Interviewer: Was it still alive?

Roth: Oh yes, it was still alive; that's the transformation, that's what they were paying you for. And that's why people hated doing it, and I hated it myself. You grab the windpipe and just behind the windpipe there's the jugular vein, and you slit that. And the minute you do it, the blood pressure drops so drastically—a kosher kill, they call it—the animal, the bird, the creature dies almost immediately. How the hell I ever did that, I don't know.

(taped conversation,
Albuquerque, N.M.,
February 8, 1986)

Roth: I wrote the novel in 1934, and then it disappeared from sight. And thirty years later it becomes a best seller. I am still working with ducks and geese, I'm still a waterfowl farmer, and now suddenly I have a best seller. Do you know what a freakish thing that is? When *Life* magazine came out, they wanted to take pictures of me killing some poor beautiful little goose or duck. I said, "Nothing doing, I will not do it, that's all!" They were doing it to make me a freak—and I'm freakish enough without that!

(Barina, 1987)

Why does the spider trapped between window and storm sash still spin his web? From whence come his nutrients? What is his prey?

The Prisoners

May 1987

Although out of chronological order, this story illustrates the process described in "Equipment for Pennies."

Feathers! Feathers! Feathers!

The images of that waterfowl dressing business float through my mind like so many feathers—which, by the way, were an important side-product of waterfowl "dressing," i.e., killing and plucking. If I had had sense enough to include some of these details in the following sketch, at the time it was written, I'm sure it could have earned me as much in print as I earned in my "business" for a year. But I didn't have sense enough—or was too tethered to my colossal block to do much else. And even—in passing—had I been serious in my enterprise, in my entrepreneurship, again, I'm sure I could have made a success of it. Mine was the only plant in all of Maine equipped and licensed to "process" waterfowl—and if you've ever tried to pluck a duck or a goose without the requisite equipment (especially the wax, which I bought in hundred-pound lots and kept molten in a discarded washtub) you'll rue the day. The pin feathers on the bird are legion, and you'll be all day trying to get rid of them. On the other hand, if the bird is dipped in molten wax, and the wax cooled, once it hardens, peeling off the wax removes the pin feathers with it, an operation that takes only a minute or two. I've had people come all the way from New Hampshire, in order to avoid plucking a duck (I'm tempted to say), actually, in order to avoid plucking their own ducks and geese. So all I had to do, if I was interested in making my fortune, was to hire some of the local yokels available and go at it. But once you've been bitten by the damn bug, creativity, nothing else will do. There is no antidote for it, not even the prospect of amassing wealth in the waterfowl business.

There were other interesting and amusing touches I could have added to the sketch, if I weren't so depressed myself: The feathers were stuffed in grain bags or in burlap bags, and sent via parcel post to the wholesaler. And two things connected with that operation still stand out clearly in memory: One, the offended manner in which the sallow, bespectacled parcel post clerk in Augusta, Maine, carried out his duties at the sight of one of my burlap bags stuffed with feathers: "Oh, my God," he would exclaim when I heaved the bag up on the counter: "Here come the sneeze feathers! I'll be sneezing the rest of the day!" And to my apologetic "I'm sorry. What else can I do?" his rejoinder was always the same: "Go into some other line of business." His fit of sneezing after I paid the postage made me feel like slinking out of the place.

The other recollection is that of stuffing the dried feathers into the bag. For reasons of economy, I tried to get as much as possible into a single bag. And in order to do this, with one part of the opening of the bag clamped in the vise in the barn and the other parts of the opening held by my two sons, the older about thirteen, the younger eleven, I would ram feathers in until I had stuffed in almost twenty pounds. And every now and then, in the ardor of my task, I would push down with such force that I tore the hem of the bag out of my younger son's grip—poor kid of eleven! Papa would growl at him in wrath: "What the hell's the matter with you? Can't you hang on?" Some Papa. But the boy is a man over six feet now (both are), and perhaps his having had to bear upward on bags of feathers against his father's downward thrust may have had something to do with his height. At any rate, I hope he's forgiven me.

Feathers, feathers. They float in the mind, they conjure up other aspects of the waterfowl business: The building of the dressing plant out of cement blocks, at which I officiated; the two raccoons I shot in the winter who were stealing the duckfeed and grain out of the barrels in the barn (Hapless critters; it was winter and they were hungry. Would I ever forget their hiss of pain when the .22 drilled them); thawing messy pails of water frozen solid after a sub-zero night—thawing them over the furnace register (M loved what that did to the living room!); the boys taking turns weekends doing chores, lugging pails of water out in the bitter cold.

I hatched out goslings in a small hot-water incubator—in the kitchen. (Imagine how happy M was at this intrusion into her domain!) Afterward, the same goslings were brooded under infra-red lights in the barn loft, because the cussed rats attacked them on the ground floor—and what long, weird shadows the fledglings threw on the straw bedding as they ran around cheeping under the ruby-red lights! Ducklings, much less expensive and much less difficult to hatch, I hatched out in a large incubator in the dressing plant—in the spring, when custom dressing was slack. And when my novel re-appeared in hardcover in the early '60s, and I gave up the water-fowl business, I found no better place for storing my haphazard writings than in the numerous drawers of the incubator (*where late the sweet birds sang,* says Shakespeare). All of which struck a fellow writer who happened to be visiting us as very funny. What a rare fancy that was, he exclaimed, to incubate one's ideas in a genuine incubator. With the approach of the holidays, how often I was im-plored to exchange ducks and geese with people who had raised them, but couldn't bear to eat their own pets. Would I give them one of mine for one of theirs? I was only too glad to. Theirs were hand-fed, far plumper and heavier than mine. Oh, it was a great business: The same ducklings or goslings that I had sold to people in the spring were brought back to me to exchange and dress in the fall. So I got my customers coming and going. It was a great business—if I had been a businessman. But I wasn't.

To have been a businessman, I would have had to hire labor. Instead I kept the *gescheft* within the confines of the family. Hours and hours I spent before the holidays killing those beautiful creatures; and then, aided by the kids after they came home from school, plucking and de-waxing (until their suppertime), and again into the small hours of the night, pulling out the greasy entrails of ducks and geese, getting them "oven ready," as it was termed in the trade—and sometimes in my desperation, impressing dear M, school prin-cipal back from a day's teaching and administration, to help. No wonder she developed a severe ulcer in her ankle, as a result of standing so many hours beside her husband eviscerating waterfowl.

(Letter to Diane Levenberg,
June 16, 1987)

Roth: It was a strange situation. In the prison itself they worked on turkeys for guards and prisoners. They had no way of doing a good job with geese and ducks. Geese and ducks have enormous quantities of pin feathers. That requires wax: a composite of wax that women use for canning—for sealing the cans—and beeswax. They sell that wax by the hundredweight.

When it's melted it becomes a kind of depilatory. So the bird is dipped in the washing machine which I adapted. It's full of wax and put into cold water to harden. The bird is then hung up and the wax is stripped off. Now all the pinfeathers come off and the bird comes out almost bald. That's the reason why Maine State Prison came to me. It was such a curious thing that a guard and trusties would come to help me do the job of killing and cleaning. That's the background of the story. It's very autobiographical.

(Telephone interview
with Diane Levenberg,
June 11, 1987)

*I*t was a halcyon autumn morning in the late fifties. They had come to his place in a big green truck with the State of Maine emblem on the side, and under the emblem, the legend Maine State Prison. The guard had gotten out and introduced himself: his name was Buckley. Then the two prisoners had gotten out. There was no introduction for them. Stigman wasn't sure they were prisoners, until he saw the vertical stripes on the shirts they were wearing.

"What do we do?" Buckley asked after Stigman had led them into the cement block building that was his "dressing" plant.

"This is where I kill," he said. "In those killing cones. This is where I scald them," he pointed to a washing machine tub full of steaming water. "We pluck them over here, over these baskets. And then we hang them along the wall to cool and dry. Then we wax them."

"That's what I wanted to see, that wax," said Buckley. "That's something we don't have over to the prison."

Stigman lifted the cover of the caldron full of molten wax.

·"That's what you dip them in?" Buckley asked.

"Right. I let the wax cool in the water a minute and then peel it off. Fuzz, pinfeathers come with it. You don't even have to singe them afterwards."

"How'd you figure that out?"

"I didn't. It's standard procedure in any waterfowl dressing plant. I read about it."

"You been doing it long?"

"Quite a while."

They lugged in the first crates of uneasily quiet ducks and geese, and we set to work. They were very good workers, both the prisoners and their guard. They worked as if they were in competition with one another. They were always in motion, hauling out squawking waterfowl from the crates, or plucking waterfowl, or stripping off the wax, or packing the dressed fowl in boxes. They were careful and attentive too. As they plucked each bird, they shifted from the colored feather basket to the white feather basket, from the duck feather basket to the goose feather basket. They cast the long wing and tail quills into the steel drum, just as Stigman had shown them. They were all in their late thirties, prisoners as well as guard. The prisoner Thibo was a stocky and exuberant man, with dark eyes and thick eyebrows, who spoke English with typical French-Canadian staccato. The prisoner Whitey was very thin; blue-eyed, hair indeterminate blond, he was evidently a Maine Yankee. His manner, even his person, gave the impression of a studied inconspicuousness, as though he sought to blend with his surroundings. Over both prisoners, and over Stigman too, hulked the guard Buckley, six feet in height or more—he had to stoop to clear the electric lights in the ceiling. And yet his manner did much to offset the effect of his bulk. He was matter-of-fact and mundane in his relation to the other two.

They were all impressed with the quantities of feathers they could pluck off the birds, even before they were waxed.

"If anybody told me these geese plucked so clean so fast," said Buckley, "I'd have told him to take a trip to the State Hospital. I had to see it to believe it."

"It's all in the way they're scalded," Stigman said. "A little detergent helps."

"I never saw anything like it," Thibo said. "They pluck slicker than turkeys, don't they?"

"A lot," said Whitey.

"Look at the way them wing feathers come out," said Thibo. "You can't do that to a turkey. You know what you have to do with a turkey?" He turned to Stigman. "As soon as he's stuck, two men have to grab those wings and start pulling."

Buckley wiped the down from his fingers. "Say, I've always wanted a couple of goose feather pillows. They must make wonderful pillows."

"None better," Stigman said.

"It must be like sleeping on strawberry jam," said Whitey.

"It must be like sleeping on a woman's breast," said Thibo.

"I've got to get enough for a couple of pillows. You save them feathers?" Buckley asked.

"Part of my income."

"What do you do with them?"

"When they're dry, I put them in burlap bags and I send them to a feather company."

"No, no. I mean how do you get them ready for a pillow?"

"Oh, put them in a pillowcase in a washing machine. Let them swish around in a little soapy water for a while. Then dry them in the same pillowcase on a wash line or in a dryer."

"Will you save me enough for a couple of good pillows? The missus wants one too."

"Sure." Stigman hung up a freshly scalded goose.

"Why do you guys give me the tail end of the bird?" Thibo complained.

"We don't. You're always lookin' for it," Buckley replied.

"Not that kind. I'm talkin' about the kind you guys are always pokin' at me."

"We wouldn't, if you wasn't lookin' for it."

Whitey got a duck out of the crate, a white Pekin duck. The creature quacked noisily and flapped its stubby wings upside down as he handed it to Stigman. "About how many pounds of goose feathers does it take to make two pillows?" he asked.

"Two pillows? About three pounds."

Thibo grinned: "I can feel the draft from that bird's wings way over here. Kind of cools your brow."

As soon as they had finished dressing the birds—and they worked so expeditiously, the empty crates and dressed waterfowl were in the truck by noon—Buckley sent Whitey back to the vehicle to fetch their dinner.

"You're not going to eat here? In the dressing plant?" Stigman asked.

"Why not? We got our whole meal with us."

"Well," Stigman looked around at the scene of their labors, "what about coffee?"

"We got that too," said Buckley.

"Wait till you see what we got," said Whitey.

"Why don't you come into the house," Stigman urged. "I'll make some fresh coffee."

"It's up to you," said Buckley.

They trailed after him into the farmhouse kitchen, and for a few seconds the two prisoners surveyed their surroundings with a kind of awkward, furtive pleasure. "It's been a long time since I been in somebody's house," said Thibo.

"That's just what I was going to say," said Whitey.

They unpacked their food from a carton and spread it on the table: hamburgers between slices of johnnycake, wedges of pumpkin pie in heavy aluminum cereal bowls, café au lait in a glass gallon jug, large aluminum mugs of the same heavy gauge as the cereal bowls.

"That looks pretty good," Stigman said.

"You want to try any of it?" the prisoners offered eagerly. "We got more'n we'll eat."

"I might try a hamburger."

"Go ahead."

He did. It was rough, it was dry, but not bad; but then he was anything but a gourmet. "How would you like to swap chocolate cake for a piece of pumpkin pie?" he offered.

"Chocolate cake!" they exclaimed.

He brought out the chocolate cake his wife had baked the day before.

"Chocolate cake with white icing," Thibo said with hushed breath.

"That's real chocolate cake," said Whitey.

"You better taste it first," Stigman advised.

"We'll swap you," they said.

"Help yourself." He set the cake before them and placed a knife beside it.

"Now, don't take too big a piece," Buckley warned.

"No." Thibo cut off a substantial slice, and as he transferred the piece of cake to a plate, he raised his eyes to look at Buckley. The guard was frowning in disapproval. What followed was a simple maneuver, yet one that held endless, complex overtones: Thibo slid the plate with the substantial slice of cake on it toward the guard. Then he cut a somewhat smaller slice for Whitey and himself. Stigman brought a pot of freshly brewed coffee from the gas stove. It was almost like sleight of hand the way Whitey poured everyone's prison coffee down the sink drain.

"I won't get the chance to drink a cup of coffee like this for a long time yet," said Thibo.

"I won't either," said Whitey.

The hour they spent together was pleasant, hour past noon of a day in late October, with just enough bleakness about the unheated kitchen to heighten intimacy. Stigman never knew what crimes the prisoners had committed; he never asked. The two conducted themselves like average human beings, no more, no less, just as Stigman expected they would. They talked about the things most present to them, prison life, prison fare, the advantage of being trusties, even what might be called prison norms, the absurdities inherent in them, the absurdities consequent on their infraction. The food the prison bought or raised was good, they said, and in this both prisoners and guard agreed. It was the preparation and cooking that was monotonous and at fault. "They dry the taste out of everything," they said. "Now if you was to fry eggs for a bunch of men, when would you fry them?" Thibo asked.

"I suppose I'd try to fry them as near to when they were going to be eaten as I could," Stigman said the obvious thing.

And received the expected answer: "Well, they start frying them over to the prison at ten in the morning for dinner."

"The trouble is with the cooks," said Buckley. "A man comes in the block and says he's a cook. And come to find out, where do you think he learned to cook?"

"I'm afraid I can guess."

The prisoners laughed.

"Right," said Buckley. "He learned to cook in jail."

Their dormitory was forty feet by a hundred, large living quarters for only fifty men, they assured Stigman, a far cry from a cramped cell. They had hot and cold running water all day, something the cell blocks didn't have, and they had showers. "Oh, they make it easy for you if you want to work," said Thibo. "I'm out in public lots o' times. I'm around women and kids. Sometimes I get whole fields to plow, and I don't see an officer all day."

"How do they know we won't run away?" asked Whitey.

The dinner hour was over. They were finishing their cigarettes. Thibo arose to his feet. "I feel good," he said. "I feel real good." He opened his eyes wide, as if in astonishment, gazed up at the ceiling, and blinked. "I feel like I was home."

"I kind of like it myself," Buckley stood up too. "It's a change, you know? It's like a day off."

In his inconspicuous way, Whitey had begun packing the dishes and utensils in the carton. Suddenly all the articles in the carton clattered.

"What's the matter?" Buckley asked.

"Somebody walk on your grave?" Thibo jested.

"I was just thinkin'," said Whitey. "And all at once it hit me."

"What hit you?"

"Time. Right then I didn't know whether I wanted it to go or stop."

"Lucky you got nothin' to do with it," Thibo declared facetiously. "I only got eight months left."

"If you fellows done differently," Buckley lectured them, "you wouldn't always be thinkin' about time. Time stoppin'. Time goin'. Time still to do. Time you done. If you'd thought first before you did what you did, you'd have other things to think about besides time."

"I found that out too," said Whitey. "I learned my lesson."

"You say you did."

"Why rub it in?" Thibo came to his fellow inmate's defense. "Both of us know if we'd done different, we wouldn't be here."

"What do you mean here?" Buckley queried.

"No, you know what I mean: the prison."

There was silence. For the first time they really seemed like convicts and a guard.

"OK to take this out?" Whitey indicated the carton.

Buckley nodded.

Whitey left. Stigman could see him through the south window of the kitchen lift the carton above the raised tailgate of the truck, and set his burden down. Then, without a glance at the house, he sauntered toward the barn in the rear.

"We thank you again," said Buckley. "Thanks for helping us out with the dressing. We'd never've got the job done alone. The warden told you where to send the bill, right? And don't forget them goose feathers, will you?" He smiled.

"I won't."

"I don't want to steal them," he preceded Thibo toward the kitchen door. "I mean to pay for them."

"I understand. Wholesale rates. You're entitled to them." Stigman followed the two men outdoors.

On the porch stairs, Buckley glanced toward the truck. "Where's Whitey?" he said.

"Must be in the cab," Thibo quickened his step, drew abreast of the cab, looked in the window. "He ain't here," he snapped his head toward Buckley.

"He ain't? Hey, Whitey," Buckley called. "Hey, Whitey."

A pause. A silence of the visual: the clear open rural scene:

October blue sky, brown leaves still hanging from the tree, the meadow across the road sloping down toward the Kennebec River.

"Whitey!"

"Right here, Officer." Whitey appeared from behind the barn. "I been watchin' the birds swimmin' in the brook."

"OK. We're ready to go," said Buckley.

"You got a nice flock of birds, Mr. Stigman," Whitey said. "Good place for them. They must get half their livin' down there while they're playin' in the water."

"Well, not quite," Stigman said.

Their gaze met, and then the prisoner's eyes lifted to a dry leaf suspended from the porch eave by a single glinting strand of spider web. He batted the leaf loose, and it twirled down to the grass.

Stigman shook hands with them.

"I only got eight more months to go," said Thibo enthusiastically. "I'm comin' back to see you when I get out."

"Do that," Stigman said. "You too, Whitey."

"I—I got a lot longer."

"Whenever it is."

The three got into the truck, Buckley on the driver's side, the two prisoners on the other, Thibo followed by Whitey, who let his arm hang out the open window, as Stigman came up. "You mean that?" Whitey asked.

"What?"

"Whenever it is?"

"Oh, sure."

Buckley started the engine. Stigman felt for a moment as if he were standing on the brink of some enormous gulf, enormous abyss. He seemed to be trying to ponder something incomprehensible, to solve something in an instant that comprised eternity.

He could never do it. Whitey lifted his arm in departure. The truck rolled ahead and, still in low gear, growled its way up the hill. The horn sounded once in farewell.

He'd better go back into the house, he thought, cover the chocolate cake, stack up the dishes in the sink. The least he could do for his wife when she came home from teaching school. He gathered up the plates, replaced the bottle of milk in the refrigerator, covered the chocolate cake, and was about to put it on the sideboard under the dish closet when something in the corner caught his eye. He reached out and brought the object into full view: it was one of the heavy-gauge aluminum mugs the crew had brought with them. It had undoubtedly been deliberately stowed out of sight, and just as undoubtedly by Whitey, who had been storing the prison utensils into the carton. But why? What did it mean? What kind of gesture was it? It was a gift, wasn't it? A gift from Whitey to him, a gift from the convict on whose grave someone had walked.

Unlovely, thick, utilitarian vessel of heavy-gauge aluminum, a prison mug, but still a gift. Whether it was Whitey's intention or not, Stigman chose to regard it as a portent, a sign that the long sentence— whenever it was, whosesoever it was—would end.

Interviewer: There seems to be a contradiction here: "The Prisoners" doesn't strike one as the work of somebody who for years had not been able to write—quite the contrary.

Roth: In 1940 I began suffering from a continuous pain in my elbow, so I gave up writing the journal that is now one of the few valuable possessions from the past. As I told myself many many years ago, the trouble with me was, though, that I was always writing, even if only mentally. I was always writing, whatever else I was doing—and, incidentally, it was *that* which impaired my value to others, in personal relations, in business relations, and in any other kind. Reflecting on the matter, I realized I was doing the same thing, without associating it with the process of writing, from childhood on, perhaps from the time my family left the East Side and threw me to the Irish gamins in Harlem, perhaps even before.

(taped conversation,
Albuquerque, N.M.,
December 5, 1986)

Petey and Yotsee and Mario

July 14, 1956

"Petey and Yotsee and Mario" marks Roth's comeback as a professional writer. To be sure, it was a tentative, almost a groping comeback: three more years were to pass before his reawakened will to write would bear a new, solitary fruit—"At Times in Flight: A Parable." Still, as Roth was to put it ten years later, "The old scow [was] becoming unstuck out of the ooze."

*T*here was a dock that stretched out into the Harlem River at about 130th Street, a few blocks north of the New York Central and New Haven station; the trestle of the railroad crossed the river only a short distance from where we swam. To the west was the Madison Avenue turn bridge, and across the river were the freight yards and a large lumberyard. Below us, the big bucket of a coal-company crane pounded monotonously into the hold of a scow and issued dripping lumps of coal. Tugs wallowed by, solitary sometimes, or towing barges, their bow mats like brown mustaches over foam. We went in when the tide was high; the water looked cleaner then and covered the mud flats. We sat on the torrid, splintery dock and slipped into our trunks—tights, we called them—and dived off.

I had just learned to swim that summer, and was already considered a fair swimmer, though nothing in comparison with Petey and Yotsee and Mario, who were there from my block. They swam with a special Sunday stroke, an overhand that slapped the water with a kind of strict flip of the wrist, and they kept their chests above the surface. I hadn't mastered that yet.

One day, I swam out into the river. It looked inviting. And whether the changing tide pulled me out farther than I realized or I allowed myself to be lured out farther, I don't know, but when I turned back, I found myself at a considerable distance from the dock, and also found that I was tired. And then the inevitable unforeseen happened: a passing tug sent a following wave over me that left me gasping and gagging. I tried to regulate my breathing again and move those leaden arms. But if I was gaining on the dock, it wasn't apparent; it seemed in motion itself, away from me. And now the rebound from the original wave slapped me in the face, and I was really beginning to flounder. Consciousness became an alternation between glimpses of sunlight on weathered dock and somewhat longer glimpses of pale-green water. I heard the cry go up from the dock: "Hey, Fat's drownin'!"

They came splashing toward me, all three of them—Petey and Yotsee and Mario.

"I'm all right," I gasped when they reached me. I could feel hands under me as I labored forward. I could hear their laughter. They towed me in toward the dock, swimming on their backs and screaming with laughter. And then they gave me a final shove toward the slimy piles, and I climbed up the makeshift ladder. I sat panting on the dock while they climbed up, too. "Gee, I must have been drowning," I said.

"You musta been," Petey said.

"You wasn't drownin'. You was just fetchin' way down," Yotsee said.

"He wasn't drownin'," said Mario. "He was just tryin' to dive to the bottom and run like hell for the shore!"

And, overcome with mirth, they bellywhopped off the dock.

When I got home, I told my mother and my sister what had happened.

"Thank God!" said my mother. "Blessed Gentile children to save you! May the Almighty bestow on them that joy they bestow on me!"

"You're a dope to go out so far," said my sister.

"I didn't know I was out that far," I protested.

"Why didn't you look back?"

"I know," said my mother. "I'm going to bake them a cake."

"What?"

"I'm going to bake them a cake. Now. A big one." She was already clearing a space on the covered washtubs for her earthenware mixing bowl.

"Aw, Mom," I said. "That ain't what—" I couldn't express it. "Don't bake them no cake."

"Why not?"

"Aw, you bake Jewish cakes."

"And what kind of cakes are not Jewish cakes?"

"Oh, you know. Like in the store. Ward's. Tip-Top. Golden Queen. Like that."

"Go, go," she said. "I'll bake them a spicecake."

"It's Jewish."

"Don't be a fool," said my mother.

She baked them a spicecake. It was embossed with walnuts, dark with crystallized honey, and full of raisins—our typical holiday spicecake.

"Well," she said, exhibiting it when it had cooled. "Who needs to be ashamed of this? Will you give it to them or not?"

"Aw, Mom, they don't understand cakes like that."

"Are they in the street?"

"Yes."

"Then come with me." She slipped the cake carefully into a paper bag, and I followed her reluctantly down the stairs and into the street. "Where are they?"

"There. There's Petey—with the handball. There's Yotsee. Mario is by the cellar. Those three."

"Come."

I trailed her across the street. The three boys were lolling in front of the candy store, just east of the corner.

"You, Petey. You, Mario," she said, and they lifted their tough lean faces.

"And what is the other's name?" she asked, turning to me.

"Yotsee. Yotsee Hunt."

"And you. Yotsee. You should be blessed for saving my son."

"Oh," Petey said. They understood.

"That's nothin'," Yotsee said.

"Fat's— I mean, he's from the block." Mario sent his finger through a curve of explanation.

"You— If I could talk better," she said, "I would tell you. You all got mamas. They understand. Sometime you ask them, they'll explain you."

"Aw, we won't tell 'em. What's the difference?" said Yotsee.

"Here's from me a cake."

They stared at her. "For us?" Petey asked.

"It's for you. You should remember."

They took it from her—Petey took it. "Thanks," he said.

"You're welcome," my mother said.

I followed her back to the stoop, and there we stood a little while, watching them. Petey was brandishing the cake aloft. "Hey, Weasel! Look!" The rest of the gang converged on them. We could hear their avid cries: "What about us?" "Hey, what about a hunk?" The cake was broken and divided and eaten with gusto. Still munching, Mario pointed us out. My mother nodded in acknowledgment.

"You see?" She turned to me. "What were you afraid of?"

"I don't know."

"You were afraid they wouldn't like Jewish cake. What kind of people would they be if they didn't like Jewish cake? Would they have even saved you?" she said, and went into the house.

Interviewer: In "Petey and Yotsee and Mario" the three boys appear to be the same ones as the Gentile boys in *Call It Sleep* who force David to put the sword into the trolley tracks. Does the fact that the boys are anti-Semitic in the novel and not in the story reflect any change in your attitude?

Roth: Yes, I'm sure it does. Because in the interim, my soul had been scrubbed by Marxism-Leninism and the new look about the proletariat. And I think justifiably, after all. I had lots wrong with me to justify antagonism, if not anti-Semitism—kids like everybody else just look for the first handle they can grab. The attitude that I changed—and this was the most difficult one to transform—was the feeling of being victimized to one where I saw that I was as much to blame, as much an active agent as a passive agent.

(Lyons, 1976, p. 175)

["Petey and Yotsee and Mario"] does show, unwittingly, the predicament of alienation-assimilation.

(letter from Albuquerque, N.M.,
December 18, 1984)

Roth: In ["Petey and Yotsee and Mario"] there was a surge of gratitude, contrary to the prevalent Jewish attitude of being put upon by the Gentiles, you know? . . . Because there is that aspect of the Diaspora, of exile, and so forth, which one tends to neglect but must take into consideration, and must acknowledge that you are in this guy's country, or that man's country, or the other person's, on sufferance. And they let you survive, almost two millennia, you know, even though it was sometimes at great cost—the cost of pogroms, the cost of persecution. Nevertheless, by and large, you did manage to survive somehow, and you could *never* have survived without their sufferance. What the story does, it hints at exactly that kind of sufferance: when the Irish kids saw this Jewboy going under—and perhaps I was, I don't know—at least they thought so—they weren't going to let me.

Interviewer: It's a real story, then.

Roth: It's a real story, yeah. Swimming in the Harlem River! How the hell I ever survived *that* is the question. But it's true enough. So one has to acknowledge it, I mean—not make it all just one-sided. And I think that was the impulse that gave rise to that particular story. It's quite different from the general feeling of frustration.

(taped conversation,
Albuquerque, N.M.,
February 7, 1986)

"Petey and Yotsee and Mario" was translated into Italian and published in Linea d'Ombra, *No. 13, February 1986, pp. 21–22, with the title "Petey e Yotsee e Mario"; trans. Mario Materassi. The issue included the translation of "The Surveyor" and an interview with Henry Roth.*

At Times in Flight: A Parable

July 1959

"At Times in Flight" is a "parable" concerning the death of the artist as a creator. It is intended to shed symbolic light on that phase of Roth's life when he had to confront the tragic fact that his imaginative powers had failed him.

The story is essentially retrospective, and yet one discerns in it an intensely prophetic quality, for it anticipates the kind of writing that Roth was increasingly to turn to in later years. It is the first of his many works, both published and unpublished, that focus on the collapse of his creative energy. It is also the first of many that are organized as a two-level narrative, uniting a distant episode dating back to 1938 and the present time, putting that episode in perspective.

Roth: I think that I was asked if I would write a piece. Now, at that time Harold Ribalow came to Maine to dig me out, to tell me that in a year or so the copyright [on *Call It Sleep*] was going to expire. . . . He was a finder, so to speak, and I think it was he, or *Commentary* by virtue of his suggestion, that asked me if I had anything to contribute. And with that as an incentive, I sat down and wrote. I think this piece was the result, as a kind of a parable, if you wish.

(taped conversation,
Albuquerque, N.M.,
February 8, 1986)

I was courting a young woman, if the kind of brusque, uncertain, equivocal attentions I paid her might be called courting: it was for me at any rate, never having done it before.

I had met her at Z, the artists' colony, a place you've probably heard of, where writers, painters, and musicians were invited for the summer, or part of it, in the hope that, relieved of their usual pressures and preoccupations, and provided with abundant leisure, they would create. Unfortunately it didn't work that way, as you've probably also heard. Most of us, it would seem, needed the pressures and preoccupations, since once there, we loafed or spent a great deal of time in frivolity and idle chatter. It was during the time of the Spanish Civil War, in 1938 to be exact, and of course that formed a part of our conversation, the fact that the Loyalists seemed on the verge of victory and yet incapable of gaining it. There was also at that time a kind of projection of the Marxist mood among young intellectuals: a kind of cynicism had entered, worldliness, a kind of sophistication. I mention these things to recall the mood of the time as it seemed to me.

I was then engaged in writing a second novel, which I had agreed to complete for my publisher. I had already written quite a section, and this opening section had been accepted and extolled. It was only necessary for me to finish it, and that was all. But it went badly from then on; in fact, it had gone badly before I reached Z. I can't blame Z for that: they provided me with the necessary environment to write in. It had gone badly—aims had become lost, purpose, momentum lost. A profound change seemed to be taking place within me in the way I viewed my craft, in my objectivity. It is difficult to say. I am, unfortunately, not analytical enough to be capable of isolating the trouble, though I don't know what good that would have done either.

That was the time, the general mood, the predicament—in sketchiest of forms. The young woman I was courting—we shall call her Martha—was a very personable, tall, fair-haired young woman, a pianist and composer, a young woman with a world of patience, practicability, and self-discipline—bred and raised in the best traditions of New

England and the Middle West, the most wholesome traditions. I was, of course, at that time, sufficiently advanced and superior to be somewhat disdainful of those traditions. I wondered whether there was any reality to my courtship, any future, whether, in short, anything would come of it. I was so committed to being an artist—in spite of anything.

The summer advanced. I wish I were clever enough to relate some of the clever things that were said and done there or to re-create some of the clever people who sojourned there, or give some notion of the setting, the place in which we lived and spent our time, the semicloistral mansion, the individual cabins for composition, the walks, statuary, the rest. I think many people know about the place and have heard about its former hostess and its various diversions. That will have to do. A few things come to mind: playing charades in the evening in the darkly furnished, richly carpeted, discreetly shadowed main room, the ample servings of food, the complaints of constipation, the missives that were wont to be sent by the hostess to her guests calling attention to some minor infraction of the rules or breach of propriety. Like all such places, I suppose, it had a tendency to become ingrown.

The colony was close to Saratoga Springs, and I owned a Model-A Ford, and in the early morning before breakfast I would drive down from Z to the spa. There was a kind of public place there in those days, a place where paper cups could be bought for a cent, and a sort of fountain where the water bubbled through a slender pipe into a basin, and I say bubbled because that was one of its attractions, the fact that it did bubble.

Ever since childhood I have regarded carbonated water as something of a treat, something not easily obtainable, in fact, only by purchase, remembering the seltzer water man on the East Side laboring up the many flights of stairs with his dozen siphons in a box. And here it was free, and not only free but salutary. The water had a slightly musty or sulfurous flavor to go with its effervescence, but its properties were surpassingly benign.

I happened to mention to a small group standing in front of the main building of Z the effectiveness and bracing qualities of the waters of the spring and invited at large anyone who wished to accompany me in the morning. The response was almost universally negative. "Drink that water? That stuff?" was the tenor of their comment. "I'd sooner drink mud water," said one of the poets. But one person did reply in the affirmative. That was Martha. She liked the water; it shortly became apparent that she liked it as much as I did.

So we were soon driving together in the morning, from Z to the spa, traversing the mile or so of highway that led past the racetrack under the morning trees. The racing season was due to begin, and as a kind of added incentive to the ride, we could see the preliminary training of the horses—whether this was on the track itself, or a subsidiary one beside it, I no longer remember. But as we drove past in the early morning, we would see what I suppose was one of the usual sights at race tracks, but to us a novelty: the grooms or trainers bent low over their mounts and urging them on for a longer or shorter gallop. A horse is a beautiful thing. A fleet, running horse, and we would stop sometimes on our way and watch one course along the white railing. Enormously supple and swift, they seemed at times in flight. The dirt beneath their hooves seemed less spurned by their hooves than drawn away beneath them in their magnificent stride.

The racing season opened. We had neither of us ever been to a horse race, and we decided it might be a worthwhile experience to attend one, especially since the track itself was so accessible, and as an additional inducement again, in view of the traditional impecunious-ness of artists—free. In other words, the racetrack adjoined Z at one side, and it was just a matter of a short walk through the woods of the estate before one came to a turn of the track—or so we had been told—and what could be more pleasant to lovers, or quasilovers, than a walk through a forest on a pleasant day. We set out in the afternoon.

The path was one not frequently trodden. We more or less sensed its direction, though I think as we approached we could hear a murmur through the woods, and so oriented ourselves. We arrived at a fairly steep embankment which we climbed and came to a halt before the iron palings of a fence. The track lay before us—at a peculiar angle, one might say, to the normal. We were not in the grandstand or near it viewing the activities. We were far away from it. In fact, the grandstand with its throng was mostly a blur of color, and the horses being paraded in front of it were tiny and remote figures. It is perhaps memory that diminishes the scene. We seemed to be, as we virtually were, in some coign or niche where we could behold the excitement in a remote and almost secret way. I can't recall what we said there; I know we were both enchanted by the spectacle, miniature though it was, as though it were a racetrack in an Easter egg. There was an undercurrent of sound that reached us from the grandstand, the band playing, the mingled voices, a certain far-off animation and stir that even at this distance communicated itself.

The horses cavorted, shied, sidled restively as they were brought to the post. The crowd hushed immediately, and the bugle sounded insistent and clear, and suddenly the race began.

The pack headed in a direction away from us toward the opposite curve of the track, and if anything, they were tinier than before, toy horses, toy riders, far off and almost leisurely with distance. Then they rounded the far curve and came toward us, and now they appeared to gain in impetus and gain in size. They were no longer toy horses and toy riders. They were very real and growing in reality every second. One could see the utter seriousness of the thing, the supreme effort, the rivalry as horse and man strained every muscle to forge to the front. Oh, it was no toy spectacle; they were in fierce and bitter competition, vying horse and man, even the mounted man, vying for the lead, and the glowing eyeballs and the shrunken jockeys, the quiet, the enormous suppleness and the cry. They struck the left-hand turn of the track and rounded it; each horse and the whole band centered as one in their effort to stay close to the inner railing. And then my attention was drawn to something strange—I don't know why. Perhaps what was about to happen was already happening—a jockey close to the lead, or in the forward half of the pack, a jockey in pale green silks, seemed to be toppling.

I couldn't believe my eyes, and in fact my mind seemed to cancel the sight and give it another interpretation. But he *was* toppling—and in another moment, he and his mount disappeared. And then in a furious rush the whole pack pounded by, a haze of hues. I glanced at Martha. She was following with her eyes the leaders as they rounded the turn on our right and entered the straightaway, and I was almost tempted to look that way too, such was the suction of their surge, but instead I looked back. The jockey in green was on the ground, still rolling. The horse had fallen a short way from him and was pawing air and ground trying to regain his footing. The jockey arose, ducked under the inner railing, and limped across the greensward rubbing his dusty white riding breeches; officials were hurrying toward him. And now the horse arose and began running after the pack. But he no longer ran like a racehorse. There was something terribly ungainly and grotesque about his motion—and suddenly I realized why; his further hind leg had been broken. It flopped along beneath him as ludicrous as a stuffed stocking and as incapable of bearing weight. "Look," I said. "Look, Martha." She withdrew rapt eyes from the finish line, questioningly. "He's broken his leg."

Her expression changed to one of horror, and that was the word she uttered: "Horrors!"

"Yes," I said. "Just now."

"Oh, that beautiful animal!"

The horse lurched past us, ran a few more steps and careened against the inner railing. His legs milled beneath him, but he no longer could rise.

"Isn't that simply ghastly!" said Martha.

"Yes."

"How did it ever happen?"

"I'm not sure. Jolted I imagine. I could see something break the rhythm of the race, and then—"

"That poor beautiful animal."

"I guess he's done for."

"Why?"

I pointed. Across the greensward, a small truck had been set in motion, a mortuary truck I supposed. There were booted men clinging to the sides of the cab. Martha still regarded me questioningly. "I suspect they're going to shoot him."

"Oh, no!" she exclaimed. "No!"

"Well what on earth are they going to do with him? He's done for."

She uttered a cry and suddenly began running down the embankment.

"Wait a minute!" I stretched out a restraining hand.

"No! Please!"

"What's the matter?"

"I don't want to be shot!"

"You?"

"Bullets ricochet. I'm afraid."

"Just a minute then. I want to see what happens." I had gone a few steps down the embankment, and now I climbed up again. It was more or less what I had expected. The truck was rolling to a stop beside the animal. Men had already jumped off. Some kneeled, others squatted about the horse, examining him. There was a brief conference. And then the cluster of conference opened up into a kind of expectant semicircle, out of which one man strode forward with a pistol and held it close to the horse's head. The report that followed seemed oddly insignificant for so grave and dread an event. I watched them load the carcass aboard the truck, and for some reason a similar scene on the East Side of long ago returned—an image from long-vanished childhood of a cop shooting a horse fallen in the snow, and the slow winch of the big green van that hauled the animal aboard later. So that was the end? *Ars brevis, vita longa*. I came down from the embankment.

She was smiling now, a little placatingly. "I'm sorry I'm such a sissy."

I shrugged. "What's the difference. I hope I wasn't rude."

"No. You were just yourself."

"Thanks." I laughed. "We come here once in a lifetime, and once in a thousand or a million this happens. And so close."

"Disappointed?"

"No. I didn't bet on him. But the odd thing is when I saw him going down, I felt a sense of loss."

She regarded me sympathetically. "We can see another race if you want to."

"No, not unless you do."

She shook her head.

"Well, lead the way back," I said. "You've got a better sense of direction than I have." I followed her into the narrow and rather somber band of trees that bordered the racetrack. Beyond lay a glade with a measure of sunlight, and behind us was a scene that I should muse on a great deal, of a horse destroyed when the race became real.

> *Interviewer:* When did you become aware of the symbolic potential of the horse race you witnessed? Maybe even at the time it took place?
>
> *Roth:* Maybe it had already crossed my mind, I'm sure. You know how it is: for a guy who is sensitized to this kind of thing, he isn't suddenly going to find out later, although that can happen too. But surely, a short time afterwards, it must have occurred to me that this had a certain intense degree of symbolism applying to one's own art. And the writing of it—a pity I didn't do it on the spot, in some way, because then I could have involved all of Yaddo, all the goings-on, all the minutiae . . . the famous Mrs. [Elizabeth] Ames, who presided over Yaddo . . . all of that, all those small details. It would have been fascinating. But you know? 1959 . . . Yaddo was something like 1938, so you have now a lapse of twenty years. So the details would fade. . . .
>
> To me, it's probably one of my . . . if not *the* favorite short piece, it certainly is one of my favorite short pieces: that particular race, and its significance. . . . But, as I say, what could have been if, instead of navel-gazing, I had actually just simply noted. But you know what might have happened: I might have burned it with the rest of my journals.

The story implies that the art itself no longer had any future: the killing of Pegasus, so to speak, the shooting of Pegasus. . . . One of its legs was no good anymore; there was nothing else to do. Except that it also implies that in the death of the art there is a beginning of the acceptance of the necessity to live in a normal fashion, subject to all the demands and all the exigencies and vicissitudes that life will bring. When I say normal, I mean that now he's willing to accept marriage, he's willing now to accept the getting of a livelihood and all that *that* would imply, and so forth. It's certainly not *stated* there, but at least he has someone he loves, who would help him in this particular new role that he had not taken on before and who would probably be in part responsible for his being able to go on—in part. Because all that implies adulthood. I mean, if you examine your own life, you know very well that there was a transition where you knew that you had to expect some of the various buffets that life would give. And there's no other way except to face them, if you are to go on to make your livelihood, if you are going to become an independent person—in my case, not subject to Walton's maternal solicitude.

(taped conversation,
Albuquerque, N.M.,
February 8, 1986)

The Dun Dakotas

August 1960

"The Dun Dakotas," which Roth bemusedly recalls having "done in pencil and submitted in pencil," was the second of his short pieces to appear in Commentary in a little more than one year. Evidently wishing to stress the importance of the writer's apparent reawakening, the editors placed in the same issue, immediately before the story, Leslie A. Fiedler's article, "Henry Roth's Neglected Masterpiece." This was the first lengthy critical appraisal of Call It Sleep to appear in print.

It was appropriate that Roth be reintroduced to the reading public by Fiedler. In 1956, when the American Scholar asked a number of scholars and literary critics to indicate what they thought was "the most undeservedly neglected book" of the previous twenty-five years, Fiedler was one of two (the other being Alfred Kazin) who mentioned Call It Sleep. (No other book had the distinction of being mentioned twice.) The publicity generated by the survey and the resulting reawakened interest in Call It Sleep bore fruit four years later. Shortly after the timely publication of "The Dun Dakotas" and of Fiedler's article, a small New York publishing house, Pageant Books, reissued Call It Sleep in a hardbound edition.

*T*here was something ruinous about the time, or fatal to creative gusto, or so I feel. I have my inklings about its nature, my brief illumination, but just what it was I leave to others more competent at defining abstractions or rendering something definitive out of the multitude of eddies and appearances. The same sort of thing, we know, has happened before, also in a kind of revolutionary age, or one of rapid transition—the Romantics of the nineteenth century who died either physically, or figuratively, on the stump.

I have spent a great deal of time wondering about it; I don't spend so much now. By now, I console myself with the thought that my creative powers, such as they were, even though fully employed, would be on the decline anyway, and by now I would have met myself perhaps with certain volumes published, and conscious of a certain modicum of acclaim, and in possession of certain emoluments, to be sure. What difference does it make? The years would have been over in any event. Poor solace, I know. The mind shuttles and reminds. We go this way only once; and shuttles again and rejoins: once is enough.

I think it's been a tough time for writers, as it is. But on the other hand, when hasn't it been? And yet I know that there are periods of greater and lesser ferment, and inevitably those artists are luckier who have as a booster, so to speak, a dynamic time. We, at least those of my generation whom I knew, had it for a time, so I think, the fag end of it. But enough, you know, to get a sense of heady pioneering, stir, viable horizons. What's done's done, undone's undone; take it or leave it.

I'll tell you. In the whole range of my thoughts on the subject—and who hasn't his private continuum—right now it's morning. The sun is over the stable, and before me, between the house and stable lies the framed bit of snow-covered countryside in the state of Maine. You can see this could be the origin of a great many things that I could say about my life since *Call It Sleep* was published. I can hear the geese bickering behind the stable, and anything I would mention would represent some phase of my present existence—and of course would have its trail all the way back to New York City, the slum childhood, the awareness of some talent, the creative period and the débâcle, and so forth. One has to put a term to things—fill it in as you like. I was a writer once, just as I was an eager East Side kid before that, and a mopey Harlem youth in the interim, who am now a waterfowl farmer.

I don't know—now—how long I'll continue to be that. For one thing, one boy is already at college, and the other soon to go. Who will help around the place, lug in geese to be processed, help pluck, shovel the long driveway, chuck cord wood down the cellar bulkhead, and do the hundred chores of arms and legs. And at fifty-four, one's back begins to feel at times as if the plates had been welded.

I'd like to tell you a story, a yarn. It's sort of importunate at the back of my mind, though I'm not sure it's appropriate. And yet I find that these importunings are somehow more apt to be better guides of my destination than my reasoning.

It concerns an expedition into the Dakotas and more particularly concerns a prologue that I was engaged in writing for the second novel—this, after I had already written a sizable section. I haven't the prologue with me any more and won't even attempt to reconstruct it as it was. The inevitable mule team, the soldiers trudging alongside, led by a captain and a scout, were crossing from the Bad Lands to the Black Hills. They had been commissioned to do a topographical study of their part of the country, and this was during the seventies of the last century. You can imagine the gnarled terrain, or consult an ency-clopedia, or consult Mr. Eliot—the wrenched and contorted land, the lopped pillars, and the grinning gulleys—the scout reined in his horse: "Captain," he said, "did you ever see red cabbage a'growin'?"

The captain reflected: "I've seen red cabbage. I don't know as I ever saw it a'growin'.'"

"You'll see it now," said the scout. "Look around you."

And the captain looked. And on every ridge surrounding them, there were Redskins mounted on their ponies, their eagle feathers against the sky, a veritable paling of feather-crested men.

"Well," said the captain, "what do we do now?"

"We gamble," said the scout. "That's all we can do." He urged his horse ahead a few steps and raised his arm in signal for parley. And down one of the nearby slopes clattered the bonneted chief and some of his braves. "How." No doubt, they said, "How." And perhaps, how kola.

"White man on my people hunting ground," said the chief.

"Chief," said the scout, "we're just passin' through. White Father in Washington send us to make picture."

"Picture?"

"Picture of the land. So all white settler stay out. Keep peace."

"Ugh!" the chief relaxed.

"Chief gamble?" said the scout, producing a deck of cards. "Chief savvy cards?"

"Savvy poker," said the chief.

"Good." They placed a blanket on the ground, and the two men gambled. They gambled for silver dollars, there between the Black Hills and the Bad Lands, among the stupendous shapes, under the stupendous sky. And the chief's luck was extraordinary, and the scout's bad luck equally so. He lost hand after hand, stake after stake, and his pile of silver dollars dwindled. "Never see such luck," said the scout.

"Ugh," said the chief. "Chief heap lucky. Heap strong."

And when his last silver dollar had changed hands, the scout rose. "Chief," he said, "you won all our money. You let us pass now?"

The chief folded his arms across his chest and dreamed a long dream or a long thought—whether of bison, or the bright tepees of childhood, or the game birds of youth I do not know.

But that was as far as I got for over twenty-five years, waiting for the decision of the chief who had turned into stone or into legend, waiting for a man to decide what history was in the dun Dakotas, waiting for a sanction; and oddly enough it would have to be the victim who would provide it, though none could say who was the victim, who the victor. And only now can I tell you, and perhaps it's a good sign— at least for my generation, who waited with me—though perhaps it's too late.

"Will the chief let us pass?" the scout repeated. "Always remember Great Chief."

And the chief unfolded his arms and motioned them the way of their journey. "Go now," he said.

Incidentally, it might interest you to learn that this condition, this loss of a sense of history, had so far intruded into my own consciousness, even though I seemed at the time remote from literary creativity, that in reply to a request for a biographical note from the magazine *Commentary,* I found myself writing a kind of parable dramatizing just that kind of state. It appeared in the September [sic] 1960 issue of *Commentary,* called "Dun Dakotas"—if you care to look at it. And I will add that to my surprise, and even contrary to the way I thought I felt at the time, the piece of writing ended with an intimation that the long period we had gone through during which we had lost the sense of history was coming to an end. I now know what I didn't know then: Cuba is the hope, is the revival of a sense of history— and with it that most important of ingredients in any art: the sense of inevitability. The restoration, shall I say, for some few of us who survived is brief, necessarily, and even frail, but it is a restoration.

(letter to Maxwell Geismar
from Augusta, Maine,
April 20, 1964)

Roth: In "The Dun Dakotas," it seemed to me at the time that I wrote it that the guy was trapped by history, in the same way that Joyce was trapped by history. You remember that famous remark of Joyce's, "History is a nightmare from which I'm trying to awake." That's his remark. But in actual fact, when it comes down to the reality of the thing, I don't think Joyce was trapped by history: I think Joyce was trapped by himself, just as *I* was by myself. And it was his way of justifying his own flight, his own abandonment, shall I say, of the very sources that gave rise, that gave vitality to his writing. In this proud exile of his that he announced—silence, exile, cunning, and all the rest of it—into cosmopolitan society, he abandoned the give-and-take, the vitality, the dynamics of living among your own people that continually feed you. And in doing so, comes an immobilization.

Interviewer: Well, Joyce wrote *Ulysses* when he was away from Dublin, and you don't feel any immobilization.

Roth: Well, yes. There, there's a certain transition period—and the same is true of *Call It Sleep.* I was already away, but there's a transition period when the action is taking place, so to speak, of *distancing* yourself—when you are in the midst (in the mind, anyway—in the creative act) of the removal.

Interviewer: So, the implication is that after exploiting one's material one should go back.

Roth: Well, didn't you mention that, didn't you say that about Faulkner?

Interviewer: But Faulkner never really left.

Roth: You know very well that, in the mind, Faulkner . . . had actually left that limited, restricted area. Faulkner was no longer part and parcel of that world, although he pretended he was. But he did it in order to exploit that world. Faulkner's mind was the mind of the modern cosmopolitan. He had experienced art, in part, but he was smart enough to know that this new cosmopolitan world could not feed him. Why it doesn't feed you is that you don't have a taproot in it, I suppose. And so he went back. And the interesting thing I wanted to add is that Anzia Yezierska did exactly the same thing. She found that she had succeeded with her early work about the East Side, and now that she was an accepted writer in the larger, cosmopolitan literary world, she had no more to say. She deliberately went back and got a flat, or an apartment, on the East Side, where she then proceded to turn out more novels on the same subject. Now, sometimes that world disappears like Atlantis, you know? You left it, and you came back . . . it's under sea. Which is what happened to the East Side. I mean, if you wanted to go back to the East Side, there's no East Side. And I think Faulkner's world also is no longer the same, although he could see remnants of it.

Interviewer: Anyway, he was there to witness the changes.

Roth: Yes. That would have been important too.

About "The Dun Dakotas" it seems to me, just to repeat, that history was the bind. I had to find why did I justify, why did I feel my sympathies lying with the Northern cause as against the Southern cause? Because, as soon as you begin to say, 'Well, were they braver, were they more decent?' you really can find plenty of examples on the other side counterbalancing the ones that you feel a moral justification for. And the moral justification is antislavery. But was that the reason why the North attacked, why the North didn't let the Union disintegrate? Probably not. It would have to come back down to some kind of Marxist way of measuring, and that is to free the productive forces. Now you can imagine how excited you'd get about *that!* And how do you know that after freeing the productive forces, the standard of living would go up? The population would increase, why not? And then look what happens! So where the hell are you? This was a stumbling block of years and years of duration, of years and years ago. Because in effect what I did in order to avoid going on with the novel I'd given Perkins—and it proved to be a disaster, but it also was in a way inevitable because I was not prepared to go on—was to go back and attempt to write a prologue. And in the prologue is where all of my confusion, you might say, came to the surface. So ["The Dun Dakotas"] is a recollection, in part, of both the prologue and the complete blocking.

There, as I originally intended it, was to be a realistic encounter between a band of Indians and the surveyors for a railroad. It was to be a realistic job, done as realistically as I would know how. . . . But since it became a block, for me, in the course of time it moved out of the realistic realm and became a symbolic block that I had to go through, somehow or other—I had to get by, I had to get past. Because this whole thing seemed, in retrospect, to be what had blocked me way back in 1936, you might say. So it became a symbol—and the symbol, these two characters facing each other, in which I suddenly become the petrified figure, the immobilized figure, waiting for an answer. And all I was trying to say was that I felt, somehow or other, for a moment here, at least I passed *that* stage. I don't know what the hell the answer is. I mean, the chief at last lets me through—that's really what it amounts to. Now, who this chief is, or what he represents, I really don't know. It's a subconscious barrier of some kind which has lasted all those years.

The individual that we are talking about, no matter what he says, could not have gone through the creative experience of *Call It Sleep* and not have become so deeply influenced by it, formed by it, as a writer, to be able to cast all that aside. I mean, he was formed for good, you might almost say, no matter what he said or what he thought—burned manuscripts and all the rest of it, because he thought he was all finished. But he couldn't be finished. The very experience of the creation of the novel itself made him a writer, and he never could renege on that, that's all there is to it—no matter what he thought, said, did, or does say.

(taped conversation,
Albuquerque, N.M.,
February 8, 1986)

I have no assurance that anything I envisage will ever take final form. Perhaps I ought to put a period at the end of the word *assurance*. I have no assurance period. I have been mulling and brewing this literary idea for so long until I feel wedded to it. It has become a career, a direction in life and to life. If nothing ever comes of it, then it gave some purpose to living, even if the object of the purpose was illusory. Why don't I simply live, enjoy each passing day for its own sake? Because my enjoyments, if you wish, are simple, not at all demanding: you'd probably laugh if you saw me pushing a wheelbarrow, as I did this morning, loaded with sand to build an embankment around the walls of the spring near the brook. I felt immensely satisfied. This time of the year, with the foliage alive with fiery colors, the maples in flame and the oaks smoldering copper, there's good reason to be satisfied. As I say, I don't require much. If only this nagging thing called literary expression could be exorcised.

(letter from Augusta, Maine,
October 4, 1966)

"The Dun Dakotas" was translated into Russian and published with the title "Nastoiciovji Dakoti" in America Illustrated, *No. 139, 1967[?].*

The Meaning of *Galut* in America Today

March 1963

Roth's short contribution to the Midstream *symposium on "The Meaning of* Galut *in America Today" epitomizes the attitude toward Judaism that he had held since his early twenties, an attitude that was to be drastically revised four years later during the Six-Day War. Here Roth does not even refer to Israel. Perhaps this indicates that, at the time, he identified Judaism with the Diaspora.*

Like "Where My Sympathy Lies," this brief statement constitutes an important personal landmark that helps chart the sometimes contradictory course of Roth's ideological development.

W hat the individual's goals are determines his course of action, and inevitably his outlook, his orientation. On the other hand, one can attempt to "feel" what direction humanity is taking, what would be the best direction. It is my own feeling that this direction, in both senses (assuming survival), is toward the highest cultural attainments. With that in mind, I seek to make my own life conform to those views—or that objective—and insofar as possible (including personal limitations) have sought to condition my own children to that same view. This means that Judaism is only one element in their culture—things being what they are, an inescapable element unfortunately, instead of a freely accepted one. But still only one, to which they owe no more allegiance than to any other that might be felt to be comparable in quality.

That about sums up my view. It follows therefore that the fairly intensive conditioning of my own childhood with regard to Judaism, with its inculcation not only of special criteria, but also of a state of mind, has been abandoned to the extent possible. I would not dare to generalize on what Jews in general ought to do. I can only say, again, that I feel that to the great boons Jews have already conferred upon humanity, Jews in America might add this last and greatest one: of orienting themselves toward ceasing to be Jews.

> *Roth:* From what I can see, they still hang on to old forms, but that doesn't mean much. They seem to be just going through a routine in which the vitality is gone. They're losing that former ability to bring meaning and illumination into their lives. The sooner the Jewish people themselves realize this, the sooner they may make an adjustment in the various countries they are in. I know this is not a very popular view; neither is it a very unique view.
>
> (Bell, 1966, p. 11)

> *Roth:* Being a Jew in the Diaspora is basically a state of mind, an attitude of not belonging. In that sense there are also Gentiles who are Jewish. Only two courses remain open to the Jew in America: he assimilates and disappears completely, while giving the best elements of himself to his native culture—and God knows that he has a lot to give, or he goes to Israel and does the same thing there. The emergence of Israel has proved to be the greatest threat to the continued survival of the Jew of the Diaspora. I do not think the Jew in America can exist much longer with a distinct identity, although he continues to make an attempt at it. I myself do not want the Diaspora. I am sick of it. Isn't it time we became a people again? Haven't we suffered enough?
>
> (Bronsen, 1969, pp. 279–80)

> *Roth:* I've thought about that statement many times because it shows how definitely one can be in a certain phase or stage. I'm

glad I made it, though I probably wouldn't make that kind of statement again the rest of my life. At that time, I thought that assimilation was the only way out for the Jews; I couldn't conceive of any other solution. The Six-Day War changed my whole way of thinking. I still don't have any great attachment to Diaspora Judaism. And I don't think of myself as a Zionist exactly, but I think of myself as a partisan of a country. It's like a regeneration process when a person like me can think of patriotism and valor.

(Lyons, 1976, p. 172)

Roth: It's like "Where My Sympathy Lies." What vast swing of mood, allegiances, illusions the guy goes through! And that's what I think makes this whole piece so interesting: here is this guy saying *this* at this particular point, and he's going to say the very diametrically opposite some years hence. The very word *galut* was for some time a new word for me—I didn't know I was in "galut"!

(taped conversation,
Albuquerque, N.M.,
February 8, 1986)

Assassins and Soldiers: Sundry Epistles from *The Era of Nam*

Written 1963–1964; published 1987

"Assassins and Soldiers" is here published for the first time in English as well as in its entirety. It originally appeared in Italian, the first and second sections in the monthly L'Indice dei libri del mese *and most of the final section in the daily* Italia Oggi. *The sections are translated by Mario Materassi.*

The three sections are dated November 26, 1963, March 25, 1964, and April 1, 1964, respectively. At the time, Roth was engaged in writing his continuum. He later connected the three units to form a loosely knit narrative that achieves unity through the balanced interweaving of two inverse but correlated structures: the encroaching of the outside world upon the individual mind and the simultaneous reaching out toward the outside world on the part of the writer's sons. The backdrop of national and international political violence looms ominously while the two young men receive their military training, one in the National Guard and the other in the army. An implicit question binds all the elements of the narrative: where does the dividing line between "assassins" and "soldiers" lie—if there is one?

I. Tuesday, November 26, 1963

Coda to proverbs by Blake (overlooked by the old gentleman in the flickering candlelight and discovered by Ira Stigman):

Death and history seem to go hand in hand. It would seem that fate and lunacy do too. Why should Kennedy reject a bubble top? Why should an assailant be lurking for him when he does?

The assassin's aim is steadier than the lips of the bugler who blows taps for the slain victim.

There will be more words written about the event and uttered by shrewd and well-informed people than all those already written and uttered by shrewd and well-informed people.

At first glance the man was being framed. It was much too neat: a Marxist and pro-Castro sympathizer cast in the role of the assassin. Much too pat. Afterwards it was realized that anything that can happen happens, especially in Texas.

It seemed odd too that everyone appeared relieved that the assassin had no accomplice. In the past this would have been a source of regret for eager legislative ferrets, Robert Kennedy included. They would have hued and cried connections. What's a Marxist without a Marxist conspiracy? Now the source and center of connections has been destroyed by another assassin, and the case is closed. The FBI, however, promises to investigate further, even indefatigably, in order to confirm its reputation for omniscience, hence unwittingly confirming its implication.

And what does Mrs Ngo say
who lost her husband the other day
in Vietnam to the CIA
though not that way?

The fumes of religiosity in which indignation and, primarily, reason, inquiry, are first stupefied and then borne heavenward are something to ponder. Never has the mind had to fight so for survival against the sway of all-encompassing incantation. We pray the fates spare us from political assassinations of any but Baptist presidents.

From Satan's lost loose-leaf notebook: All these ceremonies, antique masques, these orisons, and this pomp dissipate the energy of the populace better than a lightning rod. I commend your cruciform lightning rod. The concern of the people, naturally converging into a tide for reform, investigation, redress, is pissed away [Satan is not overly careful about his choice of words—The Editor] by a multitude of priests and pulpiteers of all denominations and finally absorbed beyond access in the void. Fortunately for me. Forces that would uncover the rottenness within the realm, and sweep the realm clean, are cunningly volatilized via a multitude of throats vying with one another in eulogy and peripheral pratings. Fortunately for me. So effective and universal are these ministrations that the generality is overcome and falls helplessly to its knees. [There was more, but one of the goons down there *con coda aguta* assailed your correspondent—The Editor.]

"You'd think that something like this would undermine the Church," said M. Again she stood with freshly washed hair lying kinkily on the towel about her shoulders. She wiped my lampshade with a cloth as she spoke. "Instead, it didn't. Here's a man who went to church every Sunday, never neglected his religion. You'd think people would say, 'Go jump in a lake; I don't want any of that.' Instead they don't."

"It's the emperor's new clothes," I said. "It's amazing what they can stuff into the empty set.* Even the soul."

"Doesn't anybody ask where was this God when the bullet came toward you?"

"Oh, no, not ethical. No, they've got an answer for that."

"It's the will of God, they say. Then why do they grieve?"

"I don't know," I shrugged. "It's a mystery."

"Do you know what I think it is?" She gripped the cloth into a ball. "I think it's a good deal like that Judo that Hugh was always telling us about."

"Yes?"

"How one uses the opponent's strength—oh, to one's advantage."

"Oh, yes."

"They use sorrow just that way. Where would the Church be without death?"

The man is as dead as Darius. The Cardinal sounds as if he were conducting an auction in Latin. "The Church is having a field day," said M. "And to listen to the others, nobody was more beloved than our late president. Didn't anybody hate him? I didn't love him. I'd better go on record."

"True," I agreed. "And Goldwater, that bridge between the Irish and the Jews to the presidential chair, what a joke: he's been completely

* A term used in "set theory." [For example: What is the set of restaurants which those restaurants that are *glatt* kosher have in common with those restaurants that are open for business on Yom Kippur? Answer: The empty set.]

lost in the shuffle these past few days. How many of his pretensions as a potential candidate rested on his hostility to Kennedy's policies. He may very well have lost his raison d'être, his chief stock in trade. No doubt he loved Kennedy. Rocky's the man now, it would seem. By the way, according to the rules of wagers, all bets on Kennedy's election are off. Only those who took the long chance of betting on neither Kennedy nor Goldwater have a chance of making a killing."

Another thing: perhaps the Negro will wake up to the fact that the time has come to jettison a good deal of that holy pap purveyed by his reverential leaders and jettison a few of the reverends themselves while he's at it. It goes deeper. His aims as constituted now, if ever achieved, would elevate him into the ranks of the imperialists. He won't succeed, and I don't wish him well. Only if he were willing to assume the leadership of a Negro Socialist Party committed to the radical reorganization of American society, and be in the forefront of that battle and bear its brunt and make the necessary sacrifices for victory, will he make a place for himself in America because he will have remade America. In that kind of America he becomes a social leader by right of conquest, and in no other way.

The heaviest blow the assassin may have struck in striking Kennedy down was against the one man and the one country above all others that Kennedy himself would have directed the heaviest blow against (and had): Fidel Castro and Cuba. Strange unity of aim in ricochet. Such are the forces balanced within the country for and against a massive attack on Cuban socialism that the difference between a Kennedy and a Johnson may make all the difference between peace, however uneasy, and Armageddon. Still I'm not entirely sure. There is also something tonic, something salutary about the unbelievable ghastly violence of this death. We have been shocked out of the repulsive lethargy of our imagination, the spit-wide scope of our feelings. We have never had death, as a nation, we have never had terror so close to home, not even in two wars, as we have had now. We have had an appalling glimpse of who we are, and are troubled, I think. We may even develop a little empathy concerning other lands and places, other people peculiarly uneasy at being the object of our blessings. In short, knowing terror may deter its ready export in the form of Green Berets and bombers. Or is it too much to expect?

Strange, strange again, how one can't buck the juggernaut of history. Almost as if personified, the forms it takes to work its will:

natural, unnatural, long awaited, startling; it's as if it were all one. Joe McCarthy, Dulles, Kennedy. One bubble top that the Secret Service urged would have made all the difference. But it was not to be. By order of the Commander in Chief. After the fact, a life, or a span of time, seems dramatic, seems to lead up to drama, seems to build to a climax; but only *after* the fact. Before the fact, my *New York Times,* which always arrives here a day late, said: "The San Antonio and Houston appearances were the *main* events of the President's tour of Texas, which will continue tomorrow with a breakfast speech at Fort Worth, a luncheon address in Dallas, and a party fund-raising dinner in Austin" (italics added). Before the fact I've seen the same thing in newsreels of prize fights: the telling blow seemed of no particular significance, appeared to possess no singular force, and yet the man went down. Later we hear it was a terrific right-hand punch, a terrific left hook. It all happens in a continuum, and it's only dramatic according to the way we select it, after the fact. "What will Kennedy do after he's served his term of office, or his two terms?" M asked only a few days ago. "He'll be so young still. Will he go into law? Or just enjoy his retirement?"

And the spectacle, Lord, the spectacle! Catafalque and coffin, caisson and Cardinal—I have no TV, but I can well imagine it. Surely it must have occurred to you that granted the sacrifice of Mikoyan, one modest atom bomb, even smaller than that dropped on Hiroshima, well-placed graveside at Arlington, would have wiped out the entire upper echelon of American governmental and military affairs, even our own Maine Governor Reid, Senator Smith, Curtis LeMay. . . .

But all this, though only a few days old, is as old as Darius. Whisk me with holy water, your Eminence, thrice both sides of my coffin, and let the bugler fluff on a note of taps. But what the hell was the point of the Irish honor guard, I fail to understand. I dread the manual of arms. I lost my musket once doing it at CCNY before the whole platoon under the stern gaze of the colonel. ROTC. Jesus, I retrieved the weapon red-faced and mumbling apologies from where it had clattered to the pavement.

How can you eat fried chicken, even Southern fried chicken, and wait for a presidential victim? The man is cool. He relies on a twelve-dollar mail order Italian surplus army carbine for the accomplishment of the deed. "Shall we take a full page ad on our model LO telescopic sight, Sir? For example: 'Try LO telescopic sights. *See* your target. Oswald did!' " All hail, Jack Ruby, thane of strip-tease and avenger of our national hurt . . . (the accursed swine turns out to be a Jew—oh, my prophetic soul!). The buck! The buck! 'T is said there is only one country in that western hemisphere where poor people in any numbers strive not to amass a personal fortune. What manner of monster be they, tell? And these the late lamented did in sooth chastise for to amend their ways, and failing, grieved. And by the rood vowed and swore a mighty oath that he yet would holpen them restore their former system, yclept ye enterprise ye free, where comely, dusky damsels garnered the Yankee dollar amid fun in the sun *galwhore*. Arriba! Arriba!

In the meanwhile the heavens are becoming overcast. The temperature was below twenty degrees last night, and the brook has a film of ice on its south bank, where the bank tilts toward north. On our back steps are three potted plants—Lazy Lucy, chives, parsley—that M deliberately left there to freeze and die. They weren't doing too well as house plants. She is much more decisive and practical in these and in other matters than I am.

Deciduous trees are bare. I wrote a few lines of verse in a letter I didn't send because it suddenly became irrelevant. They are dedicated to Hugh on his military service. Here they are.

Fair is this November noon
the lawn still green
the sky all swept and bare
and flawed only where a jet now flies
ambiguous and gossamer.

Hugh called us long distance Saturday night from Fort Dix, where he is undergoing basic training. (*Basic:* I have yet to like that word.) "Hello, Daddy," he said.

I'm still Daddy. "Hello. How are things going?" I asked.

"OK, I've been made an acting corporal."

"No!"

"Yes. Well—corporal of the training squad."

"Well, I'll be damned. What's on your mind?"

"Dad, I'd like to have my transistor set. I get a little lonesome for some good music."

"Oh, yes. You want us to send that out to you?"

"Yes. And wrap it up in plenty of rags, Dad."

"Rags? You mean against breakage?"

"Yes. But I need the rags too. You've got no idea of the number of rags we use around here. Polishing equipment uses up an awful lot."

"For Christ sake, doesn't the army supply you with rags?"

"No, not that many. I've had to buy them."

"I'll be damned. OK, I'll send rags."

"And my checkbook, please, Dad."

"You want all your checks?"

He laughed. "I want one checkbook."

"OK, the whole book. I thought the army gave you ten bucks to start with."

"They did. But they took three dollars back right off." He mentioned several deductions. "You pay for an awful lot of things, Dad. You've got to pay to have your uniform cleaned. That's money for the cleaners. You've got to keep it clean—for inspection."

"Yes?"

"And you've got to pay ninety cents every time you get a haircut. I get a haircut every week."

"Every week!"

"You've got to keep your hair clipped short. That stuff about coming into the army penniless and having the army support you is just an illusion."

"So I see. Want to talk to Moms?"

"Yes."

"He's a giniral," I rasped stagily, handing M the phone. "But he needs rags."

So it's over.

The Archbishop Cardinal does quite a job. Say what you will, he does quite a job. It was a low pontifical requiem mass, so the little parochial school girl I tutor (the one in the torso cast) told me (Church Latin I tutor, no less). She explained that it was a low pontifical requiem mass because a high pontifical requiem mass would have taken too long: there was TV to consider and the timing of other events. The choir would have had to sing the entire Kyrie eleison, instead of the aged Cardinal making the pitch. Low. High.

It's over. Kennedy is as dead as Darius, and a Chicago Jew racketeer is his avenger. Shit. I'll tell you.

Nothing exists. Nothing indeed does exist. Now listen. Nothing cannot exist alone. That's the whole *crux* of the matter. Nothing cannot exist alone. If nothing cannot exist alone, then something exists. And if something exists, then all the rest in the course of time will exist. Hence all of reality exists because nothing exists, but cannot exist alone. Hence this torment, hence this bliss. Pray for Oswald.

II. *Wednesday, March 25, 1964*

In the morning, after his breakfast of Wheat Chex and the cream from the top of Ernest Cunningham's milk, fried bacon, toast, home-frozen strawberries, and coffee, breakfasting in his morning ensemble, as his mother calls it, pants and pajama top—while the news comes in over the radio, amid our own comments focusing on Vietnam, Malcolm X, and the KKK, and reminders that the shoulder patches of his National Guard uniform are in Hugh's jacket, and his meal ticket and bus ticket are still in Lieutenant W's office where he had forgotten them. . . .

After the ride along Church Hill Road and North Belfast Avenue and Bangor Street, passing the city garbage truck making its rounds of trash collection Wednesday, where receptacles yawn beside the road, through the dubious morning light, amid the thickening traffic of town, commenting on the day's task before him: the seventy thousand crates of dressed chickens to be moved and stowed, the compulsions of large-scale production, the eggs being laid, the eggs hatching remorselessly, the chicks growing to broilers. . . . "But I, I'm a chimney fancier," I remark. "I observe chimney construction. Do you?"

Jeb alights from the car, now halted opposite the brick poultry-dressing plant, behind whose glass doors the young girls are forgathered in pink sweaters (and I fancy clustered there for him, the lank Harvard youth assigned to hoisting chicken crates seven crates high). And I, noting the tightened stance of the girls in pink sweaters as he approaches, perceive what I hadn't known before I had tall sons: how girls freeze into their attitudes for boys, set their bodies into rigid foils. I had always thought it was the other way round. He strides off with his rubber apron under his arm, his blue pants inside the rubber boots, in khaki combat jacket, bareheaded, with his lunch bag in his other hand, striding across Bangor Street . . . between the glass doors, between the pivoting bosoms in pink, toward the dim beyond where the time clock lurks, to disappear into the legend of memory.

III. *Wednesday, April 1, 1964*

There's a patch of plaster in the wall in the library covering a hole. I made it when I threw Jeb's boot against the wall in a fit of rage because I had generously—or fatuously—volunteered to apply the polish to Jeb's boots, and then proposed that he buff them. "There's quite a bit of acreage here," I said jocularly, holding out a boot. "Suppose you rub it a little."

But he let the boot drop from his hand—somewhat petulantly or vexed. He had been in the library when I called him, lounging in a chair behind one of his everlasting screens of the printed page; only this time he was with his brother Hugh, home on a three-day pass from Fort Belvoir. Jeb let the boot drop, saying curtly, "They don't need to be polished." And he returned to the library.

M was standing before the drainboard of the sink, between the sink and the bulky cast-iron Dual Atlantic stove, preparing the little mallard duck for supper, one I had bought from Walter Harriman last Christmas, whose waterfowl I used to dress. She was preparing it in honor of Hugh's visit, a gala occasion, to be celebrated by a duck stuffed with Polish sausage.

(Does he pride himself on his sloppy attire, his wrinkled dungarees, old khaki shirt, baggy sweatshirt, his brother's quilted liner, his slouchiness? I don't know. I suppose so. But this was Sunday, and tomorrow was drill night at the National Guard armory. Saturday we had had a minor crisis: he fumed at having to dress to go to the Little League supper at M's school. . . . He was free to go or not, as he chose, though it would please his mother greatly this last time, if he did choose to go. He had rebelled at first, but since Hugh went—amiably— Jeb went. He behaved like a snob once he was there, tense, transforming the homely approach of neighborliness into the grotesque, with a sudden lampoon uttered aside and darkly: an aristocrat, God almighty; while I crammed in casseroles and baked beans and devoured five kinds of pie in a furor of gourmandizing.)

The boot lay on the floor.

(How can one be so resentful of the military service he will soon have to undergo that will change him, as it has changed Hugh, reduce perhaps his superciliousness and Harvard Brahmanism, his Olympian manner, and his fleering, his superiority—and other traits and propensities he has derived from no one else but his father?)

"How immature can you be!" I expostulated. "When I go to all the trouble of putting polish on your boots—how insolent can you get?"

"I didn't ask you to put the polish on them, Dad."

"True. But I thought it might help out for tomorrow. You've got a drill."

"You could cooperate a little, Jeb," M counseled from the sink. "Dad's done half the job."

"I don't need to be looked after all the time," came his angry retort from the library.

"You better polish that boot." I flung it into the doorway. "I warn you!"

The boot lay there, defiantly, as I applied polish to the second boot.

(He is stubborn as I am, as obdurate, resists correction as I did, or accepts it with as little grace. He is barbed, contrary, caviling, ready to shift blame, and impatient—and wrong, often wrong. But mostly, or what rankles most—no, what has desolated me most—was the feeling that I had been repudiated. After so many expectations and doting assumptions, assumptions that we shared a common atmosphere of views, something tacit and precious, to find, instead of a common bond:

"Socialism means nothing in Africa, Dad. You're mistaken."

"Yes?"

"It's simply a technique that enables those with some education to get control of the bureaucracy."

"What do you mean?"

"Dad," impatiently. "White-collar jobs, desirable jobs, are few in Africa. You don't seem to realize that. If the outs can't find any other way of getting in, particularly if the ins are pro-western oriented, pro-U.S.A., the outs create an opposition by becoming pro-Soviet, you see."

"It's as simple as that."

"It has international significance, yes, which side they're allied with. It has strategic significance for the big powers. But internally, whichever side they're allied with, the public sector of the economy is the dominant one. They just don't have any large private accumulation of capital—"

"And a place like Zanzibar, where they got rid of a feudal oligarchy, of a Sultan—"

"He was just a figurehead. He didn't *do* anything!"

"Well . . . you were there." [He had taught school in Tanganyika, and hitchhiked across Africa to Dakar.] "I don't know. Wouldn't you say that the fact that the people had gotten control of their own destiny was bound to improve their conditions?"

He shut his eyes, wearily, expressively, and shook his head. Never would I forget the sense of desolation I felt, even pity for my son, my son's disillusionment, alienation. "Then you don't believe in a dicta-torship?"

"No. If you saw the result of Nkhruma's dictatorship—the sheer junk in the newspapers. Absolute distortions. Nkhruma a god—"

"I don't know enough about Africa. You don't believe in dictator-ship under any circumstances?"

"I would say not."

"What about Cuba?"

"Oh, Dad! The stupid policies of the United States have made Castro the lesser of two evils for the Cuban people.")

"I warn you, boy," I repeated. "You'll have to polish it."

But the boot lay there untouched.

"You polish that boot!" I heaved the boot-grooming kit toward the doorway but missed and struck the door jamb. "You're going to polish that goddam boot!" I hurled the other boot toward the doorway, and this time I didn't miss. It flew through the doorway and struck the wall beneath the two Phillips Exeter commemorative platters, beneath and between them. Heel-first it must have struck, for when it fell to the floor, it left a circular hole, a darkness in the beige of the wall. An appalling manifestation; it was as though the wall had entered the scene as a character.

"Good shot!" Jeb jeered.

"Hey, Dad!" Hugh exclaimed, and giggled.

I had now picked up the footstool beside the chair. "You polish that boot!"

But M intervened; she stood in the doorway angrily. "This is my house too," she said. "I have a few rights here. I'm not going to let the place be broken apart! You pick up those boots," she addressed Jeb. "And you polish them!" She stood in the doorway like a stern school principal.

"Oh, hell!" said Jeb. But I could hear him rise from his chair, and I could see him climb the stairs to his bedroom with his boots in his hand.

And so I lost my son, my first born. . . . And I patched the hole in the wall with Sears' water plaster, quite cleverly.

Hugh, as I said, was home on a three-day pass, looking very fit and erect, looking like a very pretty soldier, sanguine, and at times garrulous about his duties as acting corporal. He wore his uniform when he came home in order to get his plane ticket at half price, and he wore his uniform when he departed for the same reason. And when he turned to wave to me from the top of the stairs, just before he boarded the plane, when he turned to wave, in his tinted glasses and with his dappled cheeks, I caught a glistening in the eyes of a woman next to me, trim and modishly dressed, watching him with rapt gaze. He was a very pretty soldier. He gets his orders for overseas duty next week, or at least will know the theater to which he will be assigned. And he gets a two-week furlough before he goes. That will be about mid-April. Then he will leave us, our second and last son, conforming and slowly maturing Hugh.

One of my sons, Hugh, the younger, is in Thailand with the Army Engineers, and not liking it greatly. The other, Jeremy, after finishing a period of military training (which has made him a part-time soldier; i.e., he belongs to the National Guard) is now back at Harvard beginning studies in geology.

(letter from Augusta, Maine,
October 2, 1964)

Roth: One of [my sons] was a very nice, pretty soldier. He had a beautiful uniform—he loved everything. And the other one hated being a soldier. So when I polished his boot, you know what happened: he didn't want me to. So I threw his boot at the wall. Poor Muriol!

There's one other place that I know of in all literature where a wall becomes a character—in *A Midsummer Night's Dream,* at the end. The tradesmen put on a little play for the aristocracy, and one is on one side of the wall and one is on the other side of the wall, and one character is *a wall.* That's the only other place that I know of. The wall suddenly becomes a character in the play, and the wall became a character for *me.* I never expected just a wall to become a factor—who ever thinks of a wall? Except Frost.

(Barina, 1987)

Lovely cold March weather with little wind—rather unusual. It has taken the longest time to fill up the two-gallon can hanging from the maple tree outside our north kitchen window. But isn't it good, when the sap finally does get boiled down; we had French toast and bacon with it the other night. Such fun, slurp, gurgle. I wonder what rich people . . . feast on? I mean what sort of tastes do million-dollar novelists develop in food? I ask because last night we had Leo Epstein's fifty-nine-cent-per-pound cold cuts (not gold guts, cold cuts in sandwiches) with Campbell's tomato zoop and I et it like a fiend, with fiendish relish, and pronounced the repast a banquet. If I ever lose that gusto about plebeian victuals, may my right hand, I mean my copyright hand, never go beyond its twentieth printing.

Ernest Cunningham's fences never looked so zany, nor his fenceposts so antic as this morning. . . . No word from Hugh in faraway Thai, and no word from Jeb either, among the minerals in Cambridge.

In Vietnam our Curtis LeMay protégés are assiduously plying their ordnance to keep the war from spreading, while here among King and clergy there's a deal of psalm singing, kneeling, and blessing of enemies—but damn little of friends, the Vietcong. Sometimes I have a sneaking hunch that all this civil rights flurry is a God-given diversion for Imperialists to distract attention from the iniquities they perpetrate against weaker peoples abroad. Right to vote, I murmur; what the hell has the right to vote, exercised by those who have it, done to restrain the caste of sophisticated gangsters who governs us? But then wily vision consoles: some of the nimble youths warding off the truncheons have already learned that, more will, and more will learn more than that.

(letter to Barbara———
from Augusta, Maine,
March 17, 1965)

I have more to say, but will reserve this: about King and the march from Selma to Birmingham now in progress, and about the bastards who dump napalm and noxious gases on other colored people, without eliciting too much from King and the other deacons of the Southern Christian Leadership Conference, except criticism of the youth who *do* make the criticism for being too radical. Oh, I know it's prudent at this stage of the game to remain quiet on that score, or it could be attributed to prudence, but I don't think so. It creates illusions. But there I go, zealous as ever, and I promised not to. The trouble with me is I never could see how one could raise pious eyes to a guy on a cross and derive loving kindness from the spectacle, especially toward my neighbor who raised his with the same piety to the same figure under which he planted a case of dynamite. Hell, I would say, where did you get a *case* of dynamite, and how come the FBI that knows-all, sees-all, knows not? I would say—but I've said enough. Very little is enough. The trick will be to find a way where very little is not enough, where even a great deal is appropriate.

(letter from Augusta, Maine,
March 24, 1965)

Black Power is the present juncture or stage, as you know, of the Negro struggle here. I might as well admit as a defeatist in my own country's efforts, the establishment's efforts, and totally opposed to the survival of the dominant sector, I frankly hope the new unfolding militancy grows. I not only hope it becomes the great stumbling block, even a paralyzing one, of American society, but its ultimate undoing. I don't believe the American society, taking it by and large, deserves to exist, morally; and if it doesn't morally it doesn't deserve to exist in any other way. (In that connection, incidentally, I was disappointed in ———. I might as well be candid there too—charming and admirable though he was in other ways: it seemed to me very much that his attitude or position was opportunistic, legalistic, and integrationist. Whereas I believe the very psyche of the Negro, the only respite for his anguished soul, demands the establishment of a Negro state, and necessarily a socialist one.) . . .

There's a savage transformation that takes place in the contemplation of an aggregate that doesn't apply to the individual.

(letter from Augusta, Maine,
July 25, 1966)

I'm sure [the U.S. establishment] is preparing its own doom and untold disaster for hundreds of millions. That seems to be the price of revolutionary change. My hope is that those I cherish will survive, and that's doubtful, and that the revolutionary change isn't so violent it ends society too, and that's quite possible. Frankly most of the time I operate on faith alone—and live by inertia. The fact is if I were backed to the wall and compelled to answer as to my real beliefs in the future of humanity, I would say I don't see any way out of the impasse.

(letter from Augusta, Maine,
December 14, 1967)

The political situation or nonsituation: I have had some rude shocks lately, very rude; so have many of the Left. The Soviet Union's invasion of Czechoslovakia is the latest. The trap is always open and ready to be sprung, namely the justification: why should the Soviet Union allow U.S. leverage within its Warsaw allies and so close to its borders? But as soon as that's asked, or urged, then one is caught. It's best to think of massive social contention as a-human, elemental, like meteorological forces, and to give up attempting to interpret them in human terms, especially in moral terms; it's best, but not very pleasant. About Israel I wrote you my feelings some time ago. Since then my identification has grown. I now have a country whose future, alas, is as uncertain as its people's future was before they had a land of their own. I have a country, despite all sorts of agonizing reservations, such as the Arab displacement, the danger of Israeli militarism (read Fascism), the nauseating, if necessary, alliance with U.S. imperialism . . . the imposition of a state religion.

(letter from San Cristobal, N.M.,
September 25, 1968)

Politically, ah, there's the really sorrowful state of affairs and state of mind. Contrary to the opinions of my good friends, most of whom expect catastrophe, or even wars of near extermination, the future seems to me far more "comforting." By the next decade, extrapolating (risky but even so) war potentials, the Soviet Union should be so far ahead (plus its allies: deprived Blacks, Hispanics, satellites, etc.) than the U.S. (and China) that no alternative opens except to submit. Maybe a few "minor" scuffles here and there, but the global locking in battle will never occur. Probably the best thing a parent can do for his or her offspring is to prepare the child for some such future, assuming one has a degree of familiarity with the so-called socialist theory and practice. As I'm fond of remarking, the difference between my youthful and senescent attitudes toward "socialism," or "communism," is that once I cheered, and now I mourn; but the belief in its victory remains. And since *all* capitalism will go down before it, that includes Israel too, which may even cease to exist. In short, the absolute end isn't nigh, just coercion for some and a new rule for most, voluntarily accepted—a new consensus, out of which in time a new direction, aesthetically (I hope) will emerge.

And now, with my crystal ball out of the way, and more mundane matters to discuss . . .

(letter from Albuquerque, N.M.,
May 27, 1980)

More than anything else, as I look back, ["Assassins and Soldiers"] reflects the long, long period of imaginative catatonia, or if not that, a pupa stage, one close to suspended animation. And always within an ambience of depression—through which sometimes a rift might open, as in "The Dun Dakotas," and close again. I move uncertainly in a new reality.

(letter from Albuquerque, N.M.,
November 8, 1985)

Statement of Purpose

Written 1965; published 1976

In October 1964, Avon Press published a paperback edition of Call It Sleep. *The book immediately became a nationwide success. Sales were tremendous, soon running into the hundreds of thousands of copies. The critical acclaim was unanimous.*

The impact that the resulting public attention had on Roth was nothing short of shocking. Seeing his secluded way of life threatened by this new development, Roth at first resented it. Yet, within a few months, he found it impossible to continue being the simple waterfowl farmer in rural Maine that he had forced himself to become. As "divorced" (to use his expression) as he felt he was from his one novel, he began to respond positively to the demand implicit in the public attention bestowed upon him that he resume his role as a writer. The flickering urge to write was rekindled by the pressure from outside, and he humbly accepted his new role.

Possibly the most prestigious recognition that Roth received at the time was a grant from the National Institute of Arts and Letters given to him on March 3, 1965. The statement of purpose requested by the Institute is dated March 20. It was published in 1976, minus the second paragraph, in Bonnie Lyons's Henry Roth: The Man and His Work.

Roth: I was at first depressed when all this hullabaloo started with the Avon publication [of *Call It Sleep*] a few weeks ago. When you get used to living like an average guy, you find it's not too bad. I was comfortable and then I was being dislodged all over again. I resented it at first. My pins were being taken out from under me. That wore off some, however.

You can live on a small amount of money, you find. Then something like this comes along and you find you need a new TV and a new typewriter. Actually, however, there isn't much that I want.

(Sleeper, 1964, p. 11A)

And while I was typing this, another clear, attractive voice called up long distance from the *New York Post,* a columnist, a Miss MacGregor, I think, and we had a chat concerning man and antiman, or I should say writer and antiwriter. I don't want to sound pathetic— no, even to mention it is ridiculous and misleading. It was something unsettling to be thrust so from our pivot here, quite, but we're back— a little shakily at times, never again as secure.

(letter from Augusta, Maine,
November 6, 1964)

In a telephone interview, Roth answered questions patiently, courteously. But you had a feeling he wished the reporter would hang up and go away. You even had a feeling he wished the book would go away. "It came out of such a different kind of life," he said. "It seems as if I had spent all these years since in a kind of repudiation of that life. I don't like to make the thing overdramatic. One's feelings as a living, functioning individual change. At least they've changed for me, and they fly in the face of what might be called the imaginative, the creative faculty. I don't want *to create* again in that way— I refuse. All this publicity has had the tendency to kind of stir up what has been in abeyance for a long, long period of time."

(MacGregor, November 8, 1964, p. 47)

First, in more or less the order in which events bulk in my mind: a grant from the National Institute of Arts and Letters, a grant of twenty-five hundred dollars to be presented this May (May 19) at a special ceremonial in the N.Y. premises of the institution "in recognition of your creative work in literature." This is still a secret, not to be divulged, as I have been requested, until April, when the press will be informed. However, within the family I conceal nothing.

(letter from Augusta, Maine,
March 24, 1965)

*T*he grant does two things: it seals off a way of life I have known and been more or less content with for the past nineteen years, longer, twenty-five, from the last time I seriously tried to write. It seals it off simply because, together with the reappearance of *Call It Sleep,* it annuls the necessity and even the internal consistency of that way of life. At the same time it sets a seal of confidence on my resumption of a new way of life based on a performance anteceding the old. Understandably I welcome that confidence, but equally understandably I don't welcome the change. I failed on the ground for which the grant is given. But whether I welcome the one and not the other is immaterial: I can no longer continue to do what I was doing. And that brings me to some indication of what I plan to do: it is, since I knew it so well, to examine the literary potential of exactly that situation, that frame of mind, the precarious equilibrium between the welcome and the loath, to see what resolution springs therefrom.

Your encouragement, your confidence as signified by this grant, is my greatest reliance. I won't fail because I have not tried to vindicate your confidence. On the other hand, the odds are against me. I ask your forbearance if I fail. But more than that, your sympathy if I succeed.

The Surveyor

August 6, 1966

Roth began working on "The Surveyor" (originally entitled "My Darling Surveyor," then "Los Españoles") in Seville during his 1965–66 trip to Southern Europe. He had entertained for some time the idea of writing something related to the Inquisition. This is what he wrote from Guadalajara, Mexico, in July 1965:

As for me, I have dreams, cuckoo dreams of writing another "great" novel. (I'll keep dreaming that till I die.) And the loci of my present fiction, my present envisagings, are and have been for some time Mexico and Spain. I see a wonderful connection between the Inquisition and the conquistadores. There you have it, in a few words. But you know, Mario, I haven't got what it takes. I simply can't swing the scope of canvas I summon up in reverie. I'm either too lazy, or have a crack in my nervous system, or both. That's the sum of it, voilà, cheerio, and all that. My heart is broken, but consolation, amigo, is this: it is and cannot be again. Cheerio, prosit.

(letter from Guadalajara, Mexico,
July 6, 1965)

A few months later, the Roths were in Seville. On the night of their arrival, Roth wrote what he termed a "form" letter. The quip regarding burnings at the stake was an addition typed onto the carbon copy he sent the editor.

I am presently writing in the bathroom of the Hotel Inglaterra in Seville. . . . I didn't see anybody being burned at the stake—yet.

Why did I come? I suppose I came just to make sure—in the flesh, so to speak—that a Spaniard looks as he does, which is not much different from anybody else, perhaps a trifle swarthier. I came to verify something I already knew: that the streets in the old quarter of town are so narrow in some places that you can actually stretch your arms out and touch both sides. (I did and heard a Spaniard behind me laugh.) I came to verify this and other data, but not solely for that purpose. I had to remind myself of that. I came so that in the literary employment of this material I might feel more confident and more intimately assured. That was why I came. But the big question is will I ever employ it?

As of this moment and in this bathroom I have my doubts, vast doubts. And to say, as some of my well-meaning friends have, that failing in my central purpose I shall have had a nice trip to Spain and seen Spain is scant consolation. As of this moment and in this bathroom, who the hell cares for Spain? I don't.

("form" letter from Seville, Spain,
October 5, 1965)

The idea for which Roth was gathering material kept evolving and changing form:

I ought to transfer residence for a while to Madrid and Barcelona. There are two reasons: one, *Call It Sleep* has been contracted to a Spanish publisher, and my agent has suggested I ought to get in touch with them, the firm, and with the translator, both in Barcelona. Something more pressing still is the fact that I ought to spend some time in the museums in and around Madrid, the military museum, the naval museum, etc. I think there's a full-scale model of a Spanish caravel in Barcelona. . . . Needless to say my scholarship is hit or miss, and mostly the latter. But all this bears on what I've been daydreaming about, on and off: the Inquisition, the Jew, Mexico. I think I've indicated at least that much to you before. Not a novel this time but a play.

(letter from Seville, Spain,
December 14, 1965)

Shortly thereafter, "The Surveyor" began taking shape.

I'm in the midst of a short story I should like to show you or send you if and when completed. (Is it ever?) It's the first deliberately objective one I've done in about twenty years, deliberately concocted. It's fun, yields perspectives I hadn't anticipated, just as *Call It Sleep* did, but is awful hard work.

(letter from Seville, Spain,
January 3, 1966)

Have a short story myself, about twenty pages, as I believe I told you (or perhaps not), something really concocted—totally fiction. I didn't believe I was up to that anymore, and am not, really. If it had not been for Muriel, who did all the hard work, supplied the steadiness and encouragement, did the typing, retyping, recasting, there would be no short story. I'll be happy to show it to you after we arrive [in Florence].

(letter from Seville, Spain,
January 31, 1966)

Yes, yes, I mustn't forget, oh, no. We've just received a letter from *The New Yorker* announcing that the story we concocted in Spain is due in print the sixth [of] August; so if you're curious to see how it looks finally and in accordance with *New Yorker* rules of punctuation and orthography (they were very considerate though, highly solicitous and helpful, all contrary to the usual charges), then get a copy—in the Florence public library of course. I hate to tell you what they paid; it would be so crass; it even makes *me* jealous.

(letter from Augusta, Maine,
July 25, 1966)

*I*t was with an air of suppressed excitement that the slight, middle-aged man with the unruly gray hair put down the box he was carrying, snapped open a tripod, and drew out of the box a small surveyor's transit. He swiftly mounted the transit on the tripod. He seemed to work as though he were doing something he was not thoroughly practiced at but something he had rehearsed, adjusting the legs of the tripod and the leveling screws with a certain nervous haste. A short few minutes ago, he and the woman who accompanied him had got out of a taxi with their equipment. He had paid the driver and had led the way at once to the spot they were now on. This, too, he had done with an assurance that indicated the location had been decided on beforehand. In a little while, he had the transit leveled to his own satisfaction and was steadying the plumb bob beneath. The woman, who was also middle aged, but taller and more slender than the man, with a gentle face and a high forehead, was carrying a telescoped leveling rod, which she now extended part way.

They were on the west walk of the short, very wide Avenida del Cid, in Seville, and the man had set up his transit in the middle of the entrance to the Fabrica de Tabacos, a huge, gray edifice, rising only two stories high but sprawling out immensely in length and width. Cigarettes had once been manufactured there; now the building housed the University of Seville. On both sides of the surveyor and his assistant stretched a low stone wall that fronted a deep, wide, waterless moat, overgrown with grass, which ran parallel to the façade of the Fabrica de Tabacos behind them.

"The exact center of the gate. Right?" asked the man, straightening up and adjusting his spectacles. The woman nodded. She seemed more self-possessed than he, not so much because she was under less strain as by temperament. The man drew out of his jacket pocket a small notebook. "No, I don't need that now," he muttered, and thrust the notebook back into his pocket impatiently. "The tape. No, the rod. You've got the work to do."

"I'm ready," she said.

"OK. You pace off about fifty steps along the wall," he said. "When you've gone that far, just turn around. Keep snug to the wall."

Obediently, the woman walked away from him with steady, measured stride, holding the leveling rod as she went. She stopped, turned, and planted the foot of the rod on the ground.

"OK. Now hold it up so I can sight it." She held the leveling rod erect; he swung the transit around rapidly, sighted through the telescope, and began making adjustments. "Lean the stick toward me. Good. Hold it there. Right there. OK. Now come back."

Swiftly, he drew out his notebook, leaned over the protractor of the instrument, and jotted down some numbers. The woman, holding the leveling rod upright before her like a staff, came back to join him.

About them, a Sunday-morning quiet prevailed. Most of Seville had probably not arisen, and the Avenida del Cid was almost empty of people. Few automobiles or buses were in sight. At one end of the wide avenue was the *glorieta,* or traffic circle, of Don Juan de Austria, where the waters of a large fountain glinted intricately in the morning sunlight as they played from periphery to center and splashed from basin to basin. A short distance beyond the *glorieta* a large radial crane stood like a red, ungainly cross in the midst of new government buildings under construction. At the other end of the Avenida was the *glorieta* of San Diego, an open space encompassed by the Maria Luisa Park and buildings left over from the Spanish-American Exposition of the nineteen-twenties. Trees lined the Avenida, and a number of streets entered the *glorietas* from different directions. Dominating all this was the central figure of the area, the monumental equestrian statue of El Cid Campeador, semilegendary hero out of eleventh-century Spain. Horse and rider were poised on a massive granite pedestal that stood in the middle of an oval traffic island on the Avenida. Around the base of the pedestal, there were flower beds surrounded by grass and filled with plants no longer in bloom. High above, El Cid stood in his stirrups and brandished his bannered spear. There was no mistaking what the bronze statue was meant to portray: Spain's martial valor and audacity, the prowess that had rewon the peninsula from the Moors and later subjugated a new world.

There were one or two people waiting for buses at various *paradas* along the Avenida. All of them by now were watching the activities of the surveyor and his assistant. A man walking by, the lone stroller on their side of the avenue, stopped to stare with unabashed curiosity.

"*Buenos días,*" he said.

"*Buenos días,*" said the surveyor shortly. "Now begins the tough job, Mary. You cross. I'll compute the angle."

A woman with a leveling rod crossing a thoroughfare would have been a strange sight anywhere, and Seville on Sunday morning was hardly an exception. A man left one of the *paradas* and sauntered over. A couple of strollers across the street changed course and directed their steps toward the surveying operations. A cyclist teetered on his wheel a moment without making any forward progress, then dismounted and brought his bicycle up over the curb. The tall, particolored staff seemed to be attracting people from a greater and greater distance.

Ignoring all this, the man at the transit worked intently at his computation, swung the instrument in the direction of the woman, who was now standing on the traffic island below the statue of El Cid, and began adjusting the vernier. "A little to the left, Mary," he called. "About two short steps."

"*Qué es esto, señor?*" inquired a young man in the white shirt and tie of Sunday.

"*Un momento.* Mary, a little more left!" he shouted to the woman across the street. "*Por favor, señor,* do me the favor of standing to one side." The surveyor immediately crouched before his instrument. His spectacles had apparently fogged. He snatched them off. "A little more," he directed. He looked up from the telescope. "Where are you? Good! Mark it right there." The woman crayoned a cross at the base of the leveling rod. "Come on back," he called. "I can't leave the transit."

"*Fotógrafo?*" a woman in black asked him.

"*No, no,*" he replied. "*A grimensor.*"

"*Por qué? Es extranjero,*" she said. The man shrugged his shoulders.

"*Señor.*" One of the bystanders, a man in a Basque beret, came forward. "*Qué está usted haciendo?*"

"Measurements," the surveyor replied in Spanish. His assistant was approaching. "OK. I'll take it," he said to her, and stepped forward to relieve her of the leveling rod. "Now," he said grimly, handing her the tape. "Fifty-six and three-fourths meters."

"Yes, I know the number. Don't get rattled, Aaron." She was already backing away from him, unreeling the tape, one end of which he continued to hold.

He laid the leveling rod down, hurried back with his end of the tape to the transit, and knelt at the plumb bob beneath it. "Are you there, Mary?" he called.

The tape was now across the highway, and the woman had reached the traffic island and was aligning the tape with the mark she had previously made. The bystanders' wonder increased, and so did their numbers. Newcomers began to ply those already there with questions. "*Ingleses? . . . Me parecen americanos. . . . Qué hacen?*"

"A car!" The woman's warning cry came from across the Avenida.

"Lower the tape!" the surveyor yelled from his stooped position. "Lower the tape, Mary. Wave him on!"

The woman, at her end of the tape, smiled pleadingly at the driver of a small Seat that had stopped before the narrow ribbon of metal. "*Por favor! Pase, por favor!*" The driver proceeded reluctantly.

"Where are you?" said the man at the plumb bob.

"Fifty-five and one-half!"

"It has to be fifty-six and three-quarters!"

"That's the flower bed!"

"Oh, hell! Note the number! Mark the edge!" The woman quickly made a cross where the pavement of the traffic oval met the grass border of the flower bed. With one accord, they arose, the woman reeling in the tape, the man walking toward her. "Did you have the tape tight?" he asked her. He was perspiring.

"Yes. I made two marks, one behind the other."

"Wonderful," he said, a little breathlessly. "There! Let's scoot out of here." He had already taken the reel from her and was winding in the ribbon of tape with a rapidity that made it writhe and slither on the ground. He shoved the reel into his pocket. "Telescope the rod. I'll dismantle."

With the small crowd still watching them, as puzzled as ever, the pair packed their equipment, and in a few minutes they carried it to the curb. "Taxi!" the man called and waved.

The driver of a cab going by on the other side of the traffic island waved back, circled about the oval, and came their way. The surveyor swung the transit box into the cab as soon as it came to a stop. The driver, who appeared to be accustomed to the strange ways of tourists, got out and helped him mount tripod and leveling rod on the carrier above the cab. "Hotel Inglaterra, *por favor,*" said the surveyor, and then, settling in his seat, whistled with relief. "I wasn't any too soon, you know."

"Why?" the woman asked.

"Look back. I think you can still see him"

At one of the corners of the Glorieta de San Diego stood a gray-clad member of Spain's Policia Armada.

"What rashness!" Aaron Stigman reflected aloud as he and his wife approached the Avenida del Cid once more, this time on foot. "Why didn't I pace it off and let it go at that? No, I had to find the very spot. As rash as anything I've ever done. Was it my passion for accuracy, do you think? Or am I turning into an absurd old man?"

"No, I just think it's Seville," she replied.

"Why?" He was carrying a raincoat over his arm, and reached under the coat to adjust something beneath it.

"Too many cathedrals, too many *retablos,* stained-glass windows, saints, crucifixes, Virgins—Virgins! Even a Protestant mind like mine rebels at it." She laughed. "It's just too much."

"Yes, too many martyrs of their faith. None for mine—or what used to be mine. Why shouldn't there be some acknowledgment?"

"Well, of course, Aaron. That's why I approved."

It was now about two hours later, and the Avenida del Cid presented a livelier appearance. Amorous couples, the young man's hand often resting in Spanish fashion on his sweetheart's shoulder, strolled along in and out of the shade of the acacias. Short, robust infantrymen in their coarse khaki uniforms mingled with sober Sevillians returning from Mass. On one corner, before the Fabrica de Tabacos, a street vendor had opened his little stand and was arranging his candy and loose cigarettes. Tourists in a yellow-wheeled, horse-drawn cab gazed diffidently about while the coachman leaned sideways to comment on points of interest. Three tall, obviously Scandinavian youths, their bare heads shining like brass in the Sevillian sunlight, turned the dark heads of the Spanish *señoritas* who passed them. All the *paradas* on the Avenida now had their queues of people waiting for the bus. Traffic moved in all directions to and from the *glorietas;* jaunty little Seats droned along, interspersed with buzzing scooters and suddenly out-distanced by snarling motorcycles. From his traffic island in the midst of all this, the monumental El Cid still stood in his stirrups, brandishing his bronze spear.

"I'm sure no one will notice," said Stigman as they waited at the curb.

"I'm sure no one will."

"I could have triangulated it to be absolutely certain, but I guess one measurement was enough. All we had time for." He took his wife's arm. "We can cross now."

"I was only afraid the measurement would end at that catch basin over there."

"Oh, no! What a grisly thought! And yet you know they *have* found bones in the most unlikely places. Anybody watching?" They had reached the traffic island and were standing by the marks his wife had made on the pavement earlier.

"No, I don't see anyone," she said.

"I'll just lay it here. All right?" He had stepped over the grass as far as the flower bed. "OK?"

"OK."

He took a small wreath of fern and boxwood from beneath the raincoat over his arm and placed it on the flower bed. "There! I've done it." He stepped back to the pavement. "A little tribute where it was due. It's scant enough, isn't it?"

"I'm surprised how much I feel about it, Aaron. I didn't think I would."

"Yes?" He stood looking at the flower bed. "What kind of flowers are those?"

"Canna lilies, I think. They've been cut."

"Canna lilies—I don't know them." There was an expression of contemplative sadness on his face. "The gardener or somebody will find a wreath here and wonder why. He'll probably move it to El Cid, but there's nothing I can do about it. There's little one can do against oblivion, anyway." He was silent. "And now?" He finally turned toward his wife. "Where shall we go now?"

"Anywhere. Maria Luisa Park?"

"All right. Let's find a bench there and sit down."

They skirted the base of the monument—and saw, walking toward them, a gray-clad policeman. He still had a few steps to go before he reached them. *"Buenos días, señores,"* he said, and saluted.

"Buenos días," said Stigman.

"Are you by any chance the same English couple who were seen surveying here this morning?"

"We are Americans, not English," said Stigman, speaking in Spanish. "But we were surveying."

"In that case, I have a few questions to ask you."

"Yes?"

"I am sure you can answer them easily. Can you explain why you were surveying?"

"Yes. I was attempting to locate a spot of some sentimental value to myself," said Stigman. "A place no longer shown on the maps of Seville."

"What place is that, Señor?" The policeman was a stalwart figure. Gray hair showed under his scarlet-ribboned military cap. The skin of his large face was pink, as though freshly shaven. His competence and good judgment were manifest.

"It is a—well, I would rather not say. It is a private matter."

"Señor, surveying in public places among public establishments is no private matter. I could point out further that you laid a measuring tape across a highway, impeding traffic—"

"It was only for a minute."

"A minute is enough for an accident. You attracted a crowd."

"I could not very well help that."

"No, but these are not private matters. Do you have a permit from the proper authority to do this kind of work?"

"I did not know I needed one," said Stigman.

"It is customary to have a permit from the proper authority to avoid difficulties such as those I have just mentioned. However, you are a tourist, and sometimes we overlook what tourists do. But what is this surveying about?"

"Well . . ." Stigman took a deep breath. "I said I tried to locate a place of some sentimental value to myself. I had no other reason for doing so. In fact, I have just laid a wreath over there."

"A wreath?" The policeman turned and looked at the flower bed.

"Yes. Do you want me to remove it?"

"Naturally. I would like to see it." All three of them moved toward the flower bed. Stigman picked up the wreath and showed it to the policeman, whose face gave every indication of extreme perplexity. "Señor, you realize that you have not yet explained yourself."

"I have tried to."

"But what you have told me is no explanation. I have asked you what the surveying was about."

"I have already told you what the surveying was about. What explanation do you want me to make?"

"Aaron . . ." his wife cautioned.

"No, I haven't anything more to say to him." Stigman reverted to English. "I told him all I could. What does he want?"

The policeman showed signs of impatience. "Señor, once more, will you explain what you were doing?"

"I have already told you what I was doing."

"You have told me nothing. Nothing I can understand."

"That's not my fault!"

"Señor!" The policeman raised the hand that held his gloves. "Please accompany me."

"What for?" Stigman braced his legs against the ground.

"There are too many private matters involved here. Too many things that need explanation. This way, *por favor.* The Señora, too."

"Well, for God's sake," Stigman said, looking bleakly at his wife.

They crossed the Avenida to the low wall before the Fábrica de Tabacos, and there the policeman turned to lead the way toward Menendez Pelayo, the main thoroughfare. Two monks who were at that moment striding toward them, vigorous, bearded young men with bare feet in sandals and white cord about brown robes, noted the wreath in Stigman's hand and looked at the trio alertly. It was evident they thought the policeman was escorting two tourists bent on a commemorative act. And so others appeared to think—those they met strolling along the Paseo, and those sitting among the colored tables and chairs of the outdoor cafés. Street photographers arranging their miniature horses and black bulls nodded in deference, and a chestnut vendor halted his stirring of the chestnuts to peer at the wreath through the white smoke. Between the traffic and the wall—between the rumbling of vehicles on Menendez Pelayo, reverberating against stucco buildings and store fronts across the street, and the ancient wall of the Alcázar deploying its series of pyramidal caps—the three passed the double pillars of the monument to Columbus and drew near the orange trees of the Jardines de Murillo. In the distance, above the Cathedral, the weathervane Giralda, frail and diaphanous against the blue sky, seemed to accompany them as they walked. Stigman glanced at his wife as if seeking reassurance. With parted lips, she seemed to be drinking in the scene. She seemed to be enjoying it.

There were two men behind the railing in the drab *comisaria,* one man at the desk and one standing. The man at the desk wore a blue sweater and large tinted glasses. His head tapered, and this, together with the large glasses and his heavy torso in its dark sweater, gave him a froglike appearance. There was a touch of the forbidding about him. The man standing wore a business suit and a white shirt. He was uncommonly tall for a Spaniard, and the way he stood, in a stooped, hollow fashion, was even more uncommon. Under thick, iron-gray hair, his features seemed to wince, as if his face were too close to a hot fire. Behind the two men hung a fading portrait of Francisco Franco, in which the Caudillo looked out at the newcomers with benign eyes. Below the portrait, a large map of the district was tacked up. A ring of heavy ancient keys on one wall had scored an arc in the plaster; on the opposite wall, the hands of a new electric clock neared noon. The two men on the other side of the barrier stopped talking.

"*Buenos días,*" said Stigman mechanically. His wife repeated the salutation.

"*Buenos días,*" the two men before them replied.

The policeman saluted the man at the desk. "Señor Inspector," he began. "On two occasions today, I was at the Glorieta de San Diego when I saw this gentleman and his wife doing what seemed to me very strange things. On the first occasion, they left in a taxi before I had an opportunity to question them."

The two men behind the railing regarded Stigman and his wife noncommittally. The policeman went into a detailed description of what he had observed and the information he had gathered: that the couple had used surveying instruments on the Avenida del Cid for purposes they refused to disclose; that they had carried out this activity in a hurried and surreptitious manner; and that later in the day they had allegedly placed a wreath on one of the flower beds near El Cid, a wreath that he had not even seen them bring. "The Señor is carrying the wreath," he concluded.

Stigman held it up.

"May I see it?" the inspector asked. Stigman handed over the wreath; the inspector examined it briefly and then set it down on the desk.

"And the surveying instruments—where are they?"

"They are at our hotel, the Inglaterra."

"You travel with surveying instruments?"

"They are not mine. I rented them. If you wish..." Stigman brought out his wallet, produced a slip of paper, and passed it across the railing. "This is the voucher for my deposit for the use of the instruments."

The inspector examined the voucher and laid it on the desk. "And your passports?" The documents were produced and surrendered. After a glance at each booklet, the inspector placed them on his desk.

"You have been conducting surveying operations on a public thoroughfare in Seville, Señor. What is their purpose?"

"Their purpose was to find the place for that wreath."

"And that place was the flower bed beside El Cid. What lies in the flower bed?"

"Nothing that I am sure of, Señor Inspector."

"What did you think was there?"

"That is something I do not care to discuss."

"Come, Señor."

"No, I do not care to discuss it," Stigman said. "If there is a fine attached to what I have done, I am prepared to pay it. If the case is more serious, I demand my right to speak to the American consul."

"We are not at that pass, Señor. I am merely asking for clarification of certain mysterious activities that you have been conducting in public. The police have a right to inquire into their meaning."

Stigman moved his head abruptly to one side and looked up. "Señor Inspector, what would you think of a person who was a guest in your house and insulted you—a guest who insults his host?"

The inspector made a deprecating gesture. "Obviously, I would feel contempt. What has this to do with you?"

"I am attempting to refrain from insulting the country I am visiting."

"Let us not worry about insults, Señor. All I ask for is a little clarification. Why were you surveying? What lies in the flower bed? What are the facts?"

"I have already told you all the facts that are pertinent," Stigman said. He gripped the railing. "The rest I refuse to tell you. I have done no one any harm."

The inspector sat back. "What is your occupation?" he asked quietly.

"I am a general-science teacher, retired," said Stigman. "My wife gives music lessons in private."

"I note that you speak Spanish very well."

"We have spent many summers in Mexico."

"And what possible reasons can you have, Señor, for refusing to tell me what was the object of your surveying?"

"I did tell you. It was to place a wreath. Nothing more."

The inspector looked up at the man beside him as if at one with greater authority. Wincing and unwincing, the tall man's difficult face seemed to belong at times to two different individuals. He had studied Stigman for a while and then Stigman's wife. Most of the time, his eyes rested on her, and when they did his features became lighter. He now addressed a question to the policeman. "Where, once again, was this wreath laid?"

"There, Señor Abogado, at this end of the oval." The policeman leaned over the railing and pointed at the wall map. "The end toward the Glorieta de Don Juan."

"Ah."

The inspector swiveled about. "There is nothing there of importance," he said, pointing to the wall map. "The Capitania, the Portuguese Consulate—nothing more. The Palace of Justice is only in its foundation."

"Right here?" The tall man put his finger on the small end of the oval and looked at the policeman.

"*Si, señor.*"

The lines in the tall man's face cleared. "You need not detain them any longer," he said to the inspector.

Not the slightest shade of expression came over the seated man's face. He picked up the passports and the voucher and handed them over the railing to Stigman. "I would caution you against continuing to use surveying instruments in public without a permit," he said.

"Then we may go?"

"*Si, señor. Adiós. Adiós, señora.*" They were free to leave.

The tall man had brought the wreath through the gate of the

wooden barrier. He handed it to Stigman. "You know your way back?" he said.

"Oh, yes," said Stigman. "The way we came."

"It would be a privilege if I could accompany you for a while."

"By all means, if you wish," Stigman said.

The three paused for a moment outside, under the red and yellow flag of Spain over the doorway. "I am Miguel Ortega," the tall man said. "I am a state attorney."

"I understood as much," said Stigman.

"We can go to the Inglaterra this way"—he indicated Menendez Pelayo—"or this way, through the Barrio de Santa Cruz. It is more picturesque." His face unkinked as he spoke to Mary Stigman. "Every Sevillano fancies himself a guide."

"We shall need a guide, Señor Ortega, if we go through the Barrio de Santa Cruz," she said.

"And I shall be delighted to conduct you."

"I am sure that no one will mind if I throw this raincoat over my wreath," said Stigman.

The little café to which the lawyer had invited them was, as he said, something more like old Seville than new. The espresso machines were there, as they were in all Seville cafés, and the barrels of wine and sherry as well as the ranks of colorful bottles on the shelves in the rear. The usual paper wrappers of sugar cubes littered the floor. But the atmosphere in the place was more neighborly than in any of the cafés Stigman and his wife had been to. To the right of the bar, in the rear of the establishment, was a small provision shop. Aging hams covered with gray mold hung from a pipe near the ceiling, and next to them was an assortment of smoked sausages equally aged. There were basins of chick-peas visible on the small counter, lentils, rice, a large slab of brown quince jelly, and a crock of olives. A youngster with a fresh roll in his hand stood before the counter while the proprietress cut russet slices of *chorizo* for a filler. Three or four men were leaning on the bar in the café, one of them quietly shaking a dice cup. There were only three tables in the place; at one of them a bespectacled old man was busy filling in some sort of form. He had a large glass of white wine and a bundle of lottery tickets in front of him. On the wall behind the bartender hung a slate with the appetizers for the day chalked on it.

"Yes, I do like it," Stigman's wife replied to the lawyer's question. "It has all the appeal of something long lived in."

The lawyer nodded. "Ever since my youth and long before," he said.

The waiter brought the three cognacs they had ordered. "*Salud,*" Ortega said and lifted his glass. Stigman and his wife lifted theirs, and they drank.

Ortega put his glass down. "You know, Señor Stigman, I quite appreciate your feelings," he said. He tilted his head slightly toward the wreath, which Stigman had put on a chair under the table. "In fact, if you wish, I will escort you back to the Avenida del Cid. Would you like to leave it there?"

"Oh, no," replied Stigman shortly. "I have made my gesture, for whatever it was worth."

"You found this place to your satisfaction? I mean, you are reasonably satisfied with the accuracy of your location?" Ortega's face knit and darkened.

"Oh, yes. Shall I say, within a half meter?"

The lawyer shook his head. "You intrigue me enormously."

"Why?"

"That any man would be so—I hesitate to use the word—so naïve. I do not know what word to use."

"I was determined that I was going to make my gesture. I made it."

"Of course." The man's face, wrinkling and unwrinkling, must have been a formidable thing to confront from a witness stand. "Señor Stigman," he went on, "I have old maps on the wall of my study. They are not maps, no. They are old views of Seville. Have you seen such views?"

"I have seen reproductions."

"I have three. In two of mine there is shown a certain landmark of the city, outside the walls. Where El Cid now stands. Approximately."

Stigman sat back listening.

"It is no longer there."

"No, it is no longer there," Stigman conceded.

"And this is the *quemadero,* where criminals were burned to death."

"That is where I laid the wreath."

"So I concluded."

In the pause that followed, only the dry rattle of the dice in the dice cup could be heard, and the scratching of the pen of the man doing his accounts at the table nearby. The café door opened, and three well-dressed patrons walked in—Spaniards with placid faces.

They ordered *café con leche* and looked about. A hum of conversation began. A hissing sound came from the espresso machine.

"That is where I laid the wreath," Stigman repeated. "Your conclusion is correct. But do you know why I laid the wreath?"

"Yes. Because this was the same *quemadero* where heretics found guilty by the Holy Inquisition were burned—among others, relapsed *conversos,* those Catholics who secretly clung to their old Judaic faith."

"They were men and women who were put to death because they would not renounce their faith," Stigman said. "They were martyrs. I honored them because they deserved to be honored, because of their heroic constancy in the hour of trial. I honored them because no one in Spain honors them."

"I understand," said Ortega. "I am not offended, if that is what you were concerned about. All this is part of the Spanish heritage, along with her age-old greatness."

"I am happy to hear it," said Stigman. "I am happy you were not offended. It was a small enough tribute I paid—but, even so, it seems to have had some consequences."

Ortega's squint might have been a smile. "Among them, I have had the pleasure of meeting you and your charming wife."

"Thank you. It has been a pleasure for us, too."

Again there was a pause, this time an awkward one.

"Señor Ortega," Stigman said finally, "it seems to me a strange thing that a gentleman in your position, even with such views of Seville as you have on your walls, should have fixed so immediately on the *quemadero*—should have focused on that spot at once. No one else realized what it was. Not the crowd around us this morning, not the policeman, not the inspector." He hesitated. "You say this is part of the Spanish heritage. Why is everyone ignorant of it but you?"

"There may have been personal reasons. An idiosyncrasy."

"What, for example? I am eager to know how you could locate a thing like that so quickly. I had a good deal of research to do before I could be sure."

Ortega grimaced. He seemed to be deliberating. He brushed a small flake of cigarette ash from the table. "You have a point," he said.

"But how?"

The Spaniard clouded his eyes briefly with his hand. "Señor Stigman," he said, "what if I informed you that my grandfather told me that his father, when he became very old, would light a candle on Friday nights—would do it as a matter of compulsion? Would light a candle and put it in a pitcher?"

"Ah, so that is why," Stigman said. "That is why you knew where the *quemadero* was."

"In part. I knew where the *quemadero* was because I feel the same way about the people who died there that you do. Because I cannot forget their heroic constancy, as you call it. It was the heroic constancy of Spaniards who were also Jews."

"Spaniards!" Stigman looked at the other man with a startled expression. "It was the heroic constancy of Jews who were also Spaniards!"

Ortega sat motionless. For once, his uncertain face seemed at rest.

"And do you light a candle on Friday nights?" asked Stigman.

The lawyer shook his head, almost as if disdaining the thought. "A candle in consciousness is enough, is it not? And you?"

"Oh, no," Stigman said. "I left the faith of my ancestors many years ago."

Their glasses were empty. Ortega signaled the waiter, who brought three full ones and removed the others.

"I think the word now should be *'l'chaim,'*" said Mary Stigman.

"Do you know it?" asked Stigman, lifting his glass.

Ortega lifted his. "Of course. It is the equivalent of our Spanish *'salud'.*"

From some open window or café door, a male voice hovering in a flamenco quaver reached the Stigmans as they walked through a cramped street of the Barrio. A thin reek of urine emanated from the unsunned cobblestones. Huge doors supporting other doors within them and studded with brass nipples in showy array opened on the flagstones of tranquil patios. Inside, copper salvers gleamed amid the potted plants; there was a courtyard well in one patio, vases and conch shells in another. Above their heads hung the shallow balconies of the houses, glassed in or laden with greenery, and above these the very roofs grew moss and weeds among their curved tiles.

"This is charming," said Mary Stigman. She was walking close to her husband's side along the narrow pavement.

"Are we going all right?"

"Yes, I think so. The next should be Mateos Gago, and then we should see the Cathedral."

"Quite a remarkable man, Señor Ortega, isn't he?" Stigman observed. " 'Spaniards always pay,' he said when I tried to pay the waiter. *'Los españoles siempre pagan'*—as if it were a tradition." He looked at his wife. "I'll think you're remarkable, too, if you can find a way out of this maze," he said, smiling. "I wish you hadn't been so insistent with him about our ability to find our way without his help."

"I've got the city guide to Seville in my purse."

"So you have. I don't know whether there's something wrong with my sense of reality or my sense of direction," Stigman said. He took his wife's arm. "It must be those two cognacs," he added lamely.

They reached the corner and turned into Mateos Gago. The orange trees that lined the street were in the way for a moment, and then they saw it—the Giralda, *la Fe,* the weathervane. Faith stood on her high pinnacle above the Cathedral, pointing at every wind with her palm branch of triumph. A few more steps and the lofty Moorish minaret that supported her came wholly into view, rearing high its small balconies and sinuous arches, its marble pillars from whose capitals delicate brickwork tracery rose like spreading smoke from a brazier.

"Yes, there it is. You found it," said Stigman. "Now I know where the hotel is." They walked confidently ahead. "Wait a minute!" he said, and arrested his stride.

"What is it?" Involuntarily, his wife looked back.

"Oh, no, no one is following us. Do you know what I did?" Stigman held up his raincoat. "I forgot the wreath."

Roth: The Jews were devoted to their faith. The Aztecs were devoted to their faith. It's rather contradictory that I, an atheist, should be interested in a phenomenon called faith, but the idea of faith interests me most. Those two sixteenth-century events are epic in quality.

One happy result, a dividend, of my stay in Spain and Mexico is a short story I'm calling "The Surveyor." It takes place in Seville and is related to the Inquisition. I'm almost amazed that I can still write good publishable stuff.

(anonymous interviewer, August 1966)

We're sort of writing—note the we. Muriel has become indispensable in the process. I just couldn't have the forces to make the effort without her. Sort of writing a play—along the lines I once broached to you. It, the play, has taken many unforeseen hops, skips, and jumps, as though I have gone through the "stages of my youth and childhood," writing in outline and sketchily all the novels and stories and dramas I should have written in the years of desuetude as I call it, sterility to be fancy. It's interesting enough that I have to recapitulate, and finally arrive at little more than adolescence, at the same time as I reach the old age. Well anyway, it's been anguish at times, to synthesize the material, marshal all the elements of suspense, stuff that I was supposed to have learned many years ago, to get everything in I wanted to get in (much is still sketchy) (and all of it is still dubious). So there we stand. We have been in Mexico these more than four months doing it—and I'm sure that not until the last moment, when somebody says we'll print it, and even after, will I feel I have finished it. And then I'm going to quit—absolutely, ultimately, and cheerfully.

> (letter from Mexico City, Mexico,
> March 18, 1967)

My writing? Well . . . very engrossing to both of us, Muriel and me, as I run through and discard a whole gamut of potentials. We've sent something to the agent at long last—thematically the sixteenth-century material I broached—and are now waiting for a reply.

> (letter from Guadalajara, Mexico,
> July 19, 1967)

By the way, "The Surveyor," published in *The New Yorker* last year, has been included in Martha Foley's *Best Short Stories of '67.* Why '67?

> (letter from Augusta, Maine,
> December 14, 1967)

Roth: In 1965 when I was in Seville I felt this strong urge to do something about the Inquisition. What I finally got out of it was "The Surveyor." But essentially what I was interested in, as I look back on it now, was trying to find my way into something related to Judaism. It's like a blind force looking for an outlet.

> (Lyons, 1976, pp. 175–76)

Roth: Again, a guy thinks he's very self-aware, and he isn't. What the hell am I doing there in Spain, looking for vestiges of the Inquisition and vestiges of Marranos escaping Inquisition—what am I doing? Do I know that I'm trying to find a way to reunite with Judaism? I didn't know it. If you wish, the fascinating aspect of it is that this much touted self-awareness is nonsense, in many cases. . . . That I should be doing all this at the same time not realizing that that's exactly what I'm doing—to try and find some reunification, on a new basis.

> (taped conversation,
> Albuquerque, N.M.,
> February 8, 1986)

"The Surveyor" was included in Jewish-American Stories, *ed. Irving Howe, New York and Scarborough, Ontario: New American Library, 1977, pp. 51–66. It was translated into Italian with the title "L'agrimensore" and published in* Linea d'Ombra, *No. 13, February 1986, pp. 22–28; trans. Mario Materassi.*

A nonfictionalized account of Roth's visit to the former site of the quemadero *in Seville is to be found in "The Wrong Place" (see later).*

"...the final dwarf of you
That is woven and woven and waiting to be worn..."

—Wallace Stevens

Final Dwarf

July 1969

The genesis of "Final Dwarf" was particularly laborious. Roth wrote the first version of the story—then entitled "What Kind Journey"—in the late spring of 1964; subsequently, he set it aside for almost two years. In the spring of 1966, after the successful completion of "The Surveyor," Roth was able to go back to "What Kind Journey" and reshape it into its present form.

As his letters at the time intimate, he had some difficulties in establishing a satisfactory distance between himself and the personal elements present in the story. The main difficulty, however, lay in recapturing the "creative moment."

In the meantime my father had arrived for his annual summer visit, and his advent is both a trauma (as *I* said) and a drama (as *Muriel* said.) His stay, a short one, but an unusually stormy one, lasted for one week. And he departed. (I may have something for you to read on that score in a few weeks. But it's too soon to say.)

(letter from Augusta, Maine,
June 12, 1964)

In September of the same year Roth sent the editor a copy of "What Kind Journey," dated June 12.

That sketch I sent you—I've been trying to knead into the dough of my prose a kind of informed, partly responsible sociology. Whether the dough rises is another matter.

(letter from Augusta, Maine, October 2, 1964)

Only an odd proviso: I don't want the story to appear in English anywhere, that is, as a whole.

(letter from Augusta, Maine, October 2, 1964)

Later in the fall, Roth wrote a four-page letter almost entirely concerning "What Kind Journey." As usual, his comments show him to be his own most merciless critic.

My central core, kernel, is—not missing—I don't want to be hyperfigurative—not gone, but as it were twisted out of proper orientation. I don't want to carry the figure any further. I know the story has in it elements which are superb. But the elements themselves are not enough, not enough, as anyone knows.

I know that here in myself is tremendous but now random imagination, imagination I can't control or bring to a focus. That's one thing; the other is that I am hung with the albatross of myself. And by myself, by my own efforts I know in my clearest moments I cannot escape. On the other hand obviously it's too bad to let an imaginative sensibility, something possessed of a sense of grandeur, just go to waste.

(letter from Augusta, Maine, November 6, 1964)

At long last I seem to have begun cooking again. . . . (I sometimes think the frenzied motions I go through in the effort to recapture the creative moment are nothing short of crazy.)

(letter from Augusta, Maine, January 4, 1965)

While visiting in Florence, Italy, in February 1966, Roth worked on the story again, using the copy in the editor's possession. He returned the copy before going back to Spain but soon cabled from Barcelona to borrow it.

Your copy of "What Kind Journey". . . arrived promptly, and Muriel and I have been working mostly out of it. . . . After three or four trials along other lines of narrative, I was finally compelled to admit that the maximum human content was in the version you had; and since then Muriel and I have been working on that, attempting to give more direction and cohesiveness to it, but keeping the general framework and content intact. We're within a few days of a "final" draft; will have to defer that until we settle in the new hotel.

(letter from Casteldelfels, Spain,
April 9, 1966)

Thanks for the loan.

Tried to improve on it, but don't think I have succeeded. Have sent off a draft to my agent.

(letter from Madrid, Spain,
April 24, 1966)

*H*e was so pleased with the reading glasses he had ordered through the catalog and he was so ingenuous in his enthusiasm that the woman behind the counter, the Sears mail-order clerk, asked his permission to try them on. She was middle aged too, or past middle age, like himself, and wore bifocals, as he did. He tendered them to her, and she put them on; but apparently they didn't procure the same results for her that they did for him. She looked down at the invoice in her hand with a rather bewildered expression and handed the glasses back.

"Not strong enough?" Kestrel asked sympathetically.

"I don't know what they are." She took refuge behind her own bifocals as if she had been disturbed by what she had seen. "But they're not for me, that's for sure."

"I was told by an optician some time ago that my eyes were still fairly young according to my age. So I got the weaker ones: forty to forty-five age group instead of my own, fifty-five to sixty."

She no longer seemed to be listening and had begun totting up the price of the glasses, the shipping charge, and the sales tax. "That's four twenty-one, please."

He smiled, placed a five-dollar bill on the counter, and while she made change, he slipped the glasses into their case and pocketed them. At least fifteen bucks to the good, he thought triumphantly: that's how much more the unholy alliance of opticians and the American Optical Society would have soaked him. True, the lenses weren't prescription lenses and did nothing to correct his astigmatism. But that was a minor matter compared with the boon the glasses would be when he hunted up a word in a dictionary or read a carpenter's scale. He received his change, thanked the clerk, and folding the invoice, walked briskly through the center aisle of the store toward the doorway. Sears retail store, compact with merchandise and glistening under its many fluorescents, was always an interesting place to Kestrel, especially the hardware department, with its array of highly polished tools. But he had no time to stop and browse today; his father was waiting for him in the car.

The street he came out on was Water Street, the former commercial center of town. For many years Water Street had tried to keep abreast of the times by fusing new chromium trim onto old brick facades. With the advent of the shopping plaza, the street seemed to have given up and become dormant, as if waiting for a rebirth. His car was on Haymarket Street, the next street west. He crossed with the WALK of the traffic light and made his way up the inclined sidewalk that led sharply around the corner. Haymarket Street served as a kind of ancillary to Water Street. It provided extra room for parking meters, ventilating ducts, and traffic circulation.

"Where to, Pop?" He opened the car door and slipped in behind the wheel. "My errand's all done. What are yours?" It was always necessary to shield Pop from the idea that the trip to town was being made on his behalf. Otherwise he would balk at going and then sulk.

His father continued to bow over his homemade cane. "I would like to go to the First National. First to the First National in the plaza. I need a little meat, a can tuna, a couple oranges. Then I want to go to the A & P and buy coffee." Pop always adopted a whimsical, placating drawl when he wanted a favor.

"Why the A & P?" Kestrel sensed an old ruse. "Why not the First National coffee?"

"I like A & P coffee better. I like better Eight O'Clock coffee. It ain't so strong."

"Oh, yes." Eight O'Clock coffee was a cent cheaper than any other brand in town. The usual guile was at work. "I think you'd better shop in one place, Pop. No sense running to two places just to buy a pound of coffee." Kestrel hoped that the gravel that had entered his voice was lost in the starting of the motor. "You get better trades at the A & P anyway."

"OK. You want A & P? So A & P."

Kestrel fastened his seat belt. The old boy would have him run all over town for a couple of cents. To save *him* a couple of cents, blind to the expense of running the car. As Norma said, Pop certainly had a knack of bringing out the worst in people. Kestrel smirked and steered right to cross the railroad tracks. Just a few days ago, before Pop arrived for the summer, she had proposed a scheme of levying a fifty-cent toll on everyone who accompanied them to town and then suspending the rule for everyone except Pop. And this coming from Norma, the most generous of women . . .

Behind them the bank and the abandoned theater, behind them the bowling alley and the car wash, they climbed Winslow Hill to the traffic light on the terrace and then drove on past the porticos and the fanlights, the prim round windows of the fine homes of another age, to the rear entrance of the A & P parking lot.

"OK, Pop?" Kestrel undid his seat belt and got out of the car on one side as his father got out, more slowly, on the other. "Norma didn't want anything special. Cigarettes. But I've got plenty of time. So shop for everything you need." He preceded the old man to the glass door and held it open. Pop hobbled in on arthritic legs. "You know where the car is. I'll be around somewhere."

"Yeh. Yeh." The old man dismissed him with a curt wave of the hand. "I'll find you." He hobbled over to the telescoped shopping carts in front of the brightly arranged aisles, separated one, and trundled it inside.

Kestrel debated with himself for a moment. It was just barely possible that Grant's in the shopping plaza across the avenue had the kind of lock he was looking for, a freezer lock. He hadn't thought of it while he was in Sears. On the impulse, he hurried to the edge of the A & P blacktop and crossed the highway to the immensity of the plaza parking area opposite. The First National where Pop had wanted to shop lay directly ahead, to the left of Grant's, and Kestrel realized he could as easily have stopped there as not. But it was the principle of the thing, he argued with himself. He resented being gulled, being cajoled into doing his father a service for the wrong reason, for spurious reasons. It came back to what Norma said: Pop brought out the worst in people.

Grant's had no freezer locks. They had bicycle locks with inordinately long hasps, but no freezer locks. Leaving the emporium, he hurried back toward the avenue, meanwhile trying to descry the car from a distance. Was his father already in it and observing his son's breach of faith? No, he had beaten the old boy to it. He waited impatiently at the curb for an opening in the flux of traffic, crossed in haste, and panting slightly with exertion, leaned against his car. "Oh, the cigarettes!" He started toward the A & P and reached the door just as his father emerged with a bag of groceries on his arm.

Kestrel hesitated. "Want a hand, Pop?"

"I don't need it." The old man elbowed the extended hand to one side. "Here." He pressed a batch of trading stamps into the empty palm.

"Why do you give me these?"

"I don't want them. You save them."

"I don't save them."

"Your wife saves them."

"OK." Kestrel followed his father to the car. "Now where?" They both got in.

"Maybe I could get a few day-old cookies down at Arlene's. I like a few cookies in the house."

"I suppose so." They had been on Water Street once, Kestrel was about to remind his father, but checked the impulse under a fleeting yet complex illumination of how the old man continually led away from any objection. Who could object to a few cookies in the house? "OK. Arlene's."

"We don't have to go if you ain't got time. If you're in a hurry to get home—"

"Oh, I'm in no hurry," Kestrel said resolutely. "No hurry at all. What else?"

"Onion sets," Pop took out his shopping list. "Onion sets at Russel's Hardware Store. One pound." He read the words as if the list shielded him from responsibility. "And that's all."

"Onion sets at Russel's." Kestrel started the motor.

"They had hamburg." The sign in the A & P window caught Pop's eye. "I didn't see that."

"That's the come-on for today. Do you want any?"

"That ain't bad. Forty-nine cents a pound. I could have used a little hamburg."

"I can still stop." Kestrel made a token thrust at the brake pedal.

"No. Too late. If I had more time to look around—" Pop sat back in regret.

"Who said you didn't have time?"

"You don't have to say. I can tell."

Kestrel took a firmer grip on the steering wheel.

"Instead I paid thirty-three cents a pound for chicken wings. Thirty-three cents," the old man intoned. "Nineteen cents a pound, twenty-one cents a pound, most twenty-five cents a pound they charge in New York. Here in your state where they raise chickens, thirty-three cents a pound!"

"Pop," Kestrel grated. "Your seat belt."

The old man felt behind him for the buckle and pushed it out of the way.

They drove back to the center of town. Arlene's was at the south end of Water Street. Kestrel spied an empty parking place, but it seemed too tight. He chose to drive on. "Best I can do, Pop," he said apologetically, and parked the car beside a twelve-minute meter in front of the post office.

"I saw back there a nice place near Arlene's."

"Too many cars behind me. I didn't want to hold up traffic."

"For them you got consideration," Pop muttered. "But for me—" He got out of the car and hobbled in the direction of Arlene's. There seemed to be a special emphasis about the way he hobbled, as though he were trying to impress the pain he felt on his son.

Oh, hell, Kestrel thought as he waited. He never could do anything to please his father. Ever since childhood it had been that way. Still, he had to get over it. It was ridiculous to bear a grudge against the old guy. There was nothing left of him. A little old dwarf in a baggy pair of pants. *The final dwarf.* Kestrel smiled.

The car door opened.

"That was snappy, Pop!" said Kestrel.

His father slid into the seat with a self-satisfied look, shut the door, and picked up his cane.

"What about the cookies?" Kestrel asked. His father seemed to be flaunting the fact that he had made no purchase.

"Another time," said Pop airily.

"Why? Didn't they have day-old cookies?"

"They had. They had."

"Were they too high?"

"No, they was the regular half price."

"Then for Pete's sake why didn't you get some?"

"There was only one girl behind the counter and maybe ten customers."

"Oh, please! I come down here for you to buy cookies, and now you come back empty handed." Kestrel was sure the old man was retaliating for the way his son had parked the car.

"*Noo, nischt gefehrlich.* I got yet a few cookies in the house."

"Wait a minute." Kestrel was loath to start the engine. "That isn't the point. You wanted to come down here to buy cookies. I brought you down. Now you tell me you've got a few in the house. Why don't you buy some while you have a chance? You're down here."

"I don't need them. You would have to wait a for-sure fifteen minutes."

"I don't care. I waited this long."

"I don't need them!" his father snapped. "Meantime the money is by me, no?"

"Well, for Christ sake!" Kestrel started the motor. "That's a fine trick. The whole trip down here is for nothing!"

"So you'll be home a few minutes later to your wife. She won't miss you." His voice reeked with contempt.

You son of a bitch! thought Kestrel. There it was again, the same mockery that had rankled so in childhood, in boyhood, in youth, disabling mockery against which there was no remedy and no redress. Furiously Kestrel steered into the near lane of traffic. Penney's clothing store passed on one side like a standard of his wrath and Woolworth's across the street like another. And so did McClellan's and Sears and the pawnshop. He made a right turn at the traffic light, crossed the low bridge over the river, and climbed the opposite hill. He had almost reached their destination before he could force himself to say, "Now you want onion sets."

"Yeh, if he's got," said his father.

Kestrel stopped the car. The hardware store was across the street. He shut off the ignition and waited. His father made no move to go. "Well?" Kestrel asked.

"There's so much traffic," said his father.

"Do you want me to go?" Compassion now made headway against his anger. "I suppose I can get across the street faster than you can."

"Go if you want to go. I'll pay you later."

Kestrel got out of the car. "Onion sets, right?"

"One pound, not more. You hear?"

Kestrel's lip curled. With his back turned to his father, he could safely sneer. As if he would deliberately buy more than a pound.

They were on their way home now. Kestrel had bought the onion sets—and the freezer lock too, even though he had taken a longer time to shop than his father had anticipated. When he came out of the store, Pop was sitting half turned around in his seat with a frown on his face, gazing fixedly in his direction. Fine, Kestrel had thought with a certain nervous malice as he quickened his step toward the car, it's your turn now. And he had made some remark about how few clerks there were in all the stores on a Tuesday.

"Oh, sure," was his father's neutral reply.

Town slipped past at a leisurely twenty-five miles an hour: shade tree and utility pole, service station and abandoned cemetery.

"This time I got my supply of matzos for the summer. I brought five pounds from New York."

"Five pounds! All that way on a bus?" Kestrel felt a little indulgent after his own retaliation. "You must really like them."

"Oh, for a matzo I'm crazy," said his father. "I eat matzos not only on Passover."

"That's evident."

"With a matzo you got a bite or you got a meal," Pop continued sententiously. "It's crisp, good, or you can dunk it in coffee. There's matzo-brei, matzo kugel, matzo pancakes. You can crumble it. Dip in it. It's better than cracker meal. A lot cheaper too, believe me, especially if you go down to the East Side to get the broken ones."

"Marvelous. Can you wipe up gravy with a matzo?"

"Of course you can wipe up gravy. You forgot already. You wet the matzo before you sit down to eat, and it becomes soft like bread."

"The stuff's universal," Kestrel twitted. "Khrushchev should have known better than to ban them."

"Oh, that dog!" said Pop.

The Gulf station was passing, with its used-car lot in front and its desolate auto graveyard in the rear. "You know, Pop—" Kestrel began, and then stopped. He had been on the point of remarking that matzos could be bought in the chain stores in town, but they would be more expensive. "Oh, well—"

"What?" his father asked.

"Nothing."

They drove on in silence. Some of the newly constructed houses slipped by, the cute little boxes, as Norma called them, gray and brown and red, that had begun to line the highway.

Pop fingered the onion sets in the bag, picked out a withered one, and let it fall back significantly. He still hadn't paid for them. "Noo, there was a big fuss here over this Kennedy?" He put the bag to one side.

"This Kennedy?" Kestrel was startled. "Which Kennedy?"

"Bobby Kennedy. About John Kennedy I'm not talking."

"Of course. Everyone was shocked, just as with John Kennedy. Why?"

His father leaned on his cane and smiled. "I'm only sorry the other one wasn't shot too before he became president."

Kestrel's face furrowed as he glanced into the rearview mirror. For a moment it seemed to him that the old man's tone of voice was almost solicitous, as though he wished John Kennedy had been spared the trials of the presidency. He turned to look at his father, still smiling ambiguously. "What do you mean, Pop?"

"I mean both of them should have been shot before they became president. We would all be better off."

"Why? I don't get you. I was no admirer of the Kennedys but—"

"Why?" The new sign advertising the Grand View Motel 6 Mi. vanished on the right among second-growth trees. "The Niggehs!" Pop said vehemently. Where the sheep had once ranged, the juniper-studded field on the left reeled about the corrugated-ironsheep cote in the distance. "The Niggehs, that's why."

"The Niggers?" Kestrel repeated stunned.

"Yeh, the Niggehs! What they made such a good friend from the Niggehs! You're such a good friend from the Niggehs? There!"

"What's that got to do with it?"

"Good for them!"

"But that's got nothing to do with it!" Kestrel's voice sharpened. "That wasn't why they were shot."

"No. But that's why I'm glad they was shot."

Whew, Kestrel whistled silently to himself; you goddamned venomous little worm!

"You know, you can't talk to a Niggeh no more since the Kennedys?" his father demanded. "Not to a man, not to a woman, not to a child. Even a child'll tell you: go to hell, you old white fool."

"I see. I wish you'd put your seat belt on, Pop." Kestrel tapped the buckle of his own.

"I don't like it."

"You'd like going through the windshield less."

"I don't wear that kind. I told you. When you get them so they go around the shoulder, then I'll wear them. They press me here." He rubbed his abdomen.

You damned idiot; Kestrel stared straight ahead.

"The Kennedys," said his father. "There's where the mugging and the robbing started. Only Kennedys. *Noo,* sure, they know a president is their friend. So whatever they do, he'll say: Nebich! It's a pity! So they rape," he slapped his hands together, "so they rob, so they mug, so they loot. That poor Jewish man what they hit him in the face with a bottle last week in the subway—a plain Jewish working man—the Kennedys is the cause of all that!"

The side road where they lived was only a short distance away, and peering deeply into the rearview mirror, Kestrel saw himself forbidding and ominous against the empty highway. Was the old man baiting him this last time in retaliation for having been made to wait, or were his own thoughts about his father of such force that they communicated? He could almost believe it. "Nobody is the cause," said Kestrel. "Nobody in particular. All of us."

"All of us? Go! You and the other *philosophes*. I had something to do with that Niggeh what he mugged me in the elevator and took away my watch and two hundred and eight dollars? And put me in the hospital? And who knows, gave me this arthritis? You should have seen that detective how he beat his fist on the wall when he seen my face. And the others what they get mugged and beat up—and raped. *They* the cause of it? With you *philosophes* you can't talk."

"OK."

"Come live in New York a few months, you'll see. Let's see how you'll be a *philosophe*."

"OK." Kestrel braked the car gently, made his left turn into the side road with a minimum of swerve.

Pop glanced at the crowds of white cockerels behind the screen in the big doorways of the three-story broiler plant on the corner. "You should see them in the waiters' union, how they push us away when there's a good job—in the Waldorf or where. The best is for them. Old waiters like me, white waiters—throw them out and make jobs for *them*. They come first!"

Oh, shit. Kestrel pressed his foot down on the accelerator.

"Everything all at once," Pop continued. "More, more! Colleges and schools and beaches and motels. Regular princes make from them. And yesterday they was eating each other."

The stretch of road they were approaching had been cut through ledge—straightened out—leaving a few run-down buildings stranded in the bend on the left. On the right was the ledge. On top of it, in the gloom of overhanging trees, he had once seen two pretty deer, a buck and a doe, poised for flight, and the memory of the sight always drew his gaze to the spot thereafter. Two inches to the right, he thought, two inches that way with the steering wheel, and it would all be over with the old fool. Just two inches *now;* he'd go through the windshield like a maul, he'd slam that rusty granite. And who would know? Instinctively Kestrel shied away from the rough shoulder of the road. "Don't you think that's enough of politics, Pop?"

"Sure. On another's behind it's good to smack, like they say. Here in the country you don't see a *schwartzer* face for I don't know. A mile. How will it be if they moved next door?"

"Oh, please!"

"Yeh," his father nodded. "You'll be just like me in a few years. Just wait. All I'm saying you'll say."

A truck came over the brow of the hill. Topheavy and loaded with logs, it picked up momentum as it rolled downhill toward them, lurched at the road's shoulder. And once again Kestrel heard himself urge: two inches on this wheel, a glancing blow, and the brakes. He skirted the other vehicle, glimpsed its driver, Reynolds, owner of a nearby lumber mill. "That was Reynolds," he said to Pop.

Pop rejected the overture with a slighting gesture. "You'll be just like me. Wait. I seen already *philosophes* like you. Your cousin Louis Cantor when he lived was a *philosophe,* a socialist. Every time he came to the house he brought the socialist *Call.* So what happened in the end? He laughed from it. 'What a fool I was,' he used to say."

The top of Turner's Hill was open on the left, open and sloping downward over sunlit boulders toward the woodland and the river valley. Almost inviting it seemed, inviting for a hideous spin and a rending of metal. Who would survive? Kestrel held the car grimly to the center of the road.

"And that's what you'll say," said Pop.

"You think so?"

"I know it."

"All right. Then let's drop it. I'm driving a car."

"Ah, if there only was a Verwoerd here like in South Africa," Pop lamented. "A Verwoerd. He should be like a bulldozer for those brutes. Even a Wallace. A Wallace I would vote for."

Kestrel could feel his jaw tremble. Christ, if the old fool didn't stop— They still had two miles to go. "That's enough!"

Pop hitched a scornful shoulder, crossed his legs over his cane. "So what did you get at Sears?"

"At Sears? Oh. Reading glasses."

"Reading glasses? At Sears?"

"Yes, they have them. I've been getting my bifocals chipped working around the place."

"How much did they cost?"

Brusquely Kestrel pulled the case out of his pocket, handed it to his father. "Here. You tell me."

The old man took the spectacles out of their sheath, appraised them, and adjusted them on his nose. "Oy!" He recoiled.

"What's the matter?"

"You're going right into the stone wall." Pop pulled the glasses off.

"I am?"

"Into a stone wall. I mean they look like it. Pheh! Only from Sears you can buy glasses like this." He slipped them into the case, handed the case to his son.

Kestrel sighed. He felt shriveled. He removed a hand from the wheel, replaced the glasses in his pocket.

"Boy, you gave me some scare!" The old man groped beside him for the seat-belt buckles.

[In this story,] there's a continual retaliation too: Kestrel finally gets the lock at [Russel's] deliberately in order to make his father wait; it is almost subconscious that he compulsively takes his revenge. [This] again accounts for his being more amiable on the drive home, because he has taken his petty revenge. Which in turn very likely leads his father to deliberately broach views that he full well knows his son is in bitter opposition to. He knows his son's position. . . . Actually, you know, the thought occurs to me, realizing the intensity inherent in the whole situation, the son has for all intents and purposes killed his father, as in fact he should. The mere physical continuity of the old boy is of no great account. (And it so happens that when he left, as he did within the week, I felt he was . . . crawling off to die. I have a beautiful account of the morning that I took him off to the bus, the strange, apparitional falling of the maple-tree seed, like an autumn in the spring, and for a change, his decent raiment, as if he were his own mourner, and his subdued manner and more than usual lucidity like the proverbial moment of truth before death.)

(letter from Augusta, Maine,
November 6, 1964)

Interviewer: In "Final Dwarf" the relationship between Kestrel and his father seems murderously hostile. Do you think that reflects your adult relationship with your father?

Roth: This was a relationship that could not be resolved—and will not be resolved in my lifetime. And that's all there is to it.

Interviewer: How autobiographical is the story?

Roth: Not very, but I'll tell you a funny thing. It seems to me sort of prophetic. because to me it meant the shrinking of the liberal. The retreat of the liberal from his own position without his knowing it. Oddly enough, what Pop was seeing was what his son later saw.

(Lyons, 1976, p. 175)

Roth: The reaction of my father [to *Call It Sleep*] was: "I shouldn't have beat him so much."

Interviewer: Did he feel betrayed?

Roth: He felt remorseful. Later in Maine, I wrote "Final Dwarf," . . . In this story, he began to understand the essential and irreconcilable animosity that existed between us.

(Friedman, 1977, p. 32)

"Final Dwarf" was included in A First Reader of Contemporary American Short Fiction, *ed. Patrick Gleeson, Columbus: Charles E. Merrill, 1971, pp. 147–57.*

No Longer at Home

April 15, 1971

In the spring of 1971, The New York Times *asked Roth to discuss the reasons for his prolonged silence. The result was "No Longer at Home." This was the first time that Roth publicly expressed in writing his new commitment to Israel.*

*C*ontinuity was destroyed when his family moved from snug, orthodox Ninth Street, from the homogeneous East Side to rowdy, heterogeneous Harlem; normal continuity was destroyed. The tenets, the ways, the faith were discarded too drastically, too rapidly. That may have been what he sensed when he wrote his novel, that may have been a kind of subliminal theme, dominating him without his knowing it. And once continuity was destroyed, there would always be a sense of loss afterward, an insecurity—even though he might ultimately say good riddance to all that was so abruptly terminated. Therein perhaps lay the explanation for the failure, not only his own, but of so many gifted literary people, his contemporaries, who in one way or another, for one "reason" or another ceased to develop creatively. The whole question needed exploration and study. . . .

He unscrewed the brass-plated top of his mini-cuspidor and spat. A new, unexplored realm, this of chewing tobacco—for the modern writer (now cramped and irked by the awareness that everything pertaining to the minutiae of smoking had been exhausted). A new unexplored realm. For example, the liquid in the glass cuspidor gradually accrued in amber. Yea. He had forgotten in the preoccupation of writing the foregoing a thought of greater significance than the one he dwelled on, a thought, an insight, rather, into the meaning of an event long past. It had to do with his writing of thirty-five years ago, with his second novel, the novel he had destroyed unfinished. (He could still visualize himself in his study in Eda Lou's Greenwich Village apartment, seated at his desk, writing.) A peculiar dichotomy had asserted itself, only vaguely apprehended at the time, a dichotomy of purpose, or was it direction? between his striving in the novel and his personal inclinations. It was an interesting revelation—he gazed absently at the diminished waters of the pond—about thirty-five years too late, but would it have helped any if he had realized it then? In the novel, based on the life of a certain Bill Clay, an illiterate and picturesque proletarian, the central character was essentially a wholesome individual, for all his rugged experiences still sound at the core, seeking a better world for himself and his fellows. (His pilferings and shopliftings, the armed robberies he committed in his younger days, and his brawlings either were justified or could be justified by the compulsions of capitalism, committed before the illuminations of communism, of Marx, the man with the busted mattress on his face, as Bill called him, before classconsciousness, in short.)

While on the one hand the author dedicated his creativity to the portrayal of proletarian virtue, on the other he desired what his character eschewed. He yearned for the tainted, the perverse, for the pornographic, as it would be termed today, and detested himself as degenerate for doing so. This was the dichotomy. More and more drawn to things sensual, more and more imaginatively kindled by vileness, at the same time as he strained to project a Party hero. And with apparent success in this latter aim, be it said, for none other than Maxwell Perkins approved the opening sections of the author's novel.

He sat examining the gilt imprint on his pencil. Eagle Mirado 3. Gilt, yes guilt. What guilt that dichotomy could engender! A Party stalwart in letter, a satyr in proclivity. The proclivity condemned as degenerate. Perhaps it was. Perhaps pornography was degenerate, pre-saged another Rome in decline. At all events the outcome was stasis, stasis, immobility, desuetude. It was time to eject his quid, rinse his little cuspidor. Shaped like an hourglass, wasp waisted, why hadn't that ever been used as a simile for the svelte female figure of a corseted bygone age? His landlord's gray guinea fowl paraded before the window snickering raucously. . . .

That which informed him, connective tissue of his people, incul-cated by *heder*, countenanced by the street, sanctioned by God, all that dissolved when his parents moved from the East Side to Mick Harlem. The struts went and the staves. It would have to follow that the per-sonality became amorphous, ambiguous, at once mystical and soiled, at once unbridled, inquisitive, shrinking. No longer at home. I guess that's the word, after this smother of words. *No longer at home.*

I'll tell you though, I have now adopted one, out of need, a symbolic home, one where symbols can lodge, whatever it is in ac-tuality, whatever waverings and residual reservations I may have: *Israel.*

> I denigrated the loss of the ancestral ones, their vast impor-tance, something I had originally stressed. Fact is they were the important ones, however lightly I seemed to part with them. They transmuted themselves into a kind of pervasive mysticism that in-fused the youth, gave him a kind of singular vision all the years of poverty and worse in Harlem's 119th Street. There was never a moment that I strayed from the mighty Hebrew conviction that this suffering meant something, must have a meaning; suffering that I myself invoked, brought on by myself, was meant for me as one chosen to discover the meaning, unfold it.
>
> (letter from Augusta, Maine,
> November 6, 1964)

> *Roth:* In the early thirties, when I became a writer, my attitude was one of complete detachment, at least I thought I was detached from everything—country, or class, or people certainly, even my own. And everything was just objects, in very much the sense, in very much the tradition, of the writers of my time, Joyce in particular. And the solution (Joyce actually went to live in another country) wasn't necessarily for me to become an expatriate: all I had to do was just go a few blocks downtown, in New York's megalopolis, or a few blocks uptown, to leave my milieu, to obtain that kind of detachment in which everything, including your own folk, become elements for art, without a feeling of being profoundly committed—to them, to their exilic struggle. For a while, I thought that I was committed to the

proletariat. That's also the second change. But it was not a profound change. . . . For a while I *thought* it was a profound change, I *acted* as if it were a profound change; and I think it affected me greatly to be identified with a revolutionary movement in the United States, as I was in the thirties, near, or thereabouts, the mid-thirties on. Yes, I mustn't underrate that. I was deeply and emotionally committed.

But it's interesting that, as I look back, I was not committed in a way that you would say was functional, in which I acted *dynamically* within the revolutionary movement. I am not talking about the writer. But I didn't come up with ideas that in any way would have any bearing on the revolutionary movement, on what the proletariat might do or might not do, or what the unit that I belonged to, the cell as it was then called, might or might not do to influence the people in the neighborhood or in the shops or what not. This is very significant. I was passive about it—I mean, I took my orders from above, or from people who *were* dynamic, who *did* come up with ideas, and I helped to carry them out. But as far as *living* the thing, you know, so that the very living of it would produce, would *spin off,* if you wish, suggestions, proposals, ways of going about revolutionizing greater circles, this didn't happen.

Whereas now, it seems as if I'm continually spinning off ideas about what Israel should do—I mean I daydream about Israel. I know that many of the things I think about have no value politically, but they have value for me spiritually, they have value for me even literarily, so to speak. If they are not practical, they are quaint, you know—but they at least show a real involvement that I can only label as a *living* involvement; the way, let's say, a true musician lives in his music or a true mathematician in his field—somebody who is really involved, so that his life connects in myriads of places with the object of his involvement. And this is how I feel about Israel today.

(taped conversation,
New York, N.Y.,
October 24, 1973)

June '67

1985

"June '67" is Roth's contribution to Rothiana: Henry Roth nella critica italiana, *a collection of essays on* Call It Sleep *and its author written by Italian scholars and critics since 1962, when the novel was first introduced to the Italian public.*

This segment from a journal kept during the Six-Day War re-cords the lacerating conflict of loyalties that brought Roth to his present standpoint vis-à-vis Israel, and, ultimately, to his new sense of himself both as a Jew and as a writer.

When the June '67 War broke out in the Middle East, my wife and I were in Mexico, in the city of Guadalajara. We—or I—had chosen Guadalajara as a pleasant ambience in which to live while I embarked on a novel I hoped to write about a Marrano, a crypto-Jew who had managed to slip through the net of the Spanish Inquisition and smuggle himself into Mexico along with the conquistadores. The notion of the crypto-Jew caught, as it were, at the center of a struggle between zealous

Catholicism and equally zealous Aztec paganism fascinated me. Needless to say, the novel never got off the ground. I was incapable of achieving both the ideologic levels necessary for the task, incapable of the necessary historical scholarship as well.

Nor did I realize that in seeking to write that kind of book, I was all unwittingly groping toward a return to Judaism. When the '67 War broke out it acted upon me like a second vector, to borrow a term from mathematics, a second impulse acting in the same direction as the first, and reinforcing it. The Jewish identity came to the fore, asserting itself in consciousness. Not only that, but something else was being catalyzed, a changed personality, at last, an individual with an increasingly firm point of view, an ideology, however spotty, but durable, tenable, a new bond with tradition, a new reunion with folk.

What follows is an excerpt from a journal which I began at the time, as if the '67 War were prodding me into portraying the confused debate going on within me:

The Arabs would overwhelm the Israeli, one of the artists R had met in San Miguel had told him; and R had agreed. How could it be otherwise? Two and a half million Israeli against a hundred million Arabs. And yet the newspaper dispatches [and] the radio broadcasts weren't bearing out the prediction. The Israeli seemed to be holding their own, and even advancing in the face of three Arab armies. Or were these reports, these dispatches from Israel mere fabrications: Israel cheering itself on. And what? (he thought): they had a right to exist. No, he was anything but a Zionist (he answered himself impatiently). But they were entitled to some refuge of their own, some parcel of land they could call their own, to which they could retreat— in the event another maniac like Hitler threatened their existence—a state to which they could appeal for diplomatic action, or forcible measures to avert another Holocaust. He recalled an analogous situation at the time of the expulsion of the Jews and Moors from Catholic Spain. The regime had treated the Moors—or crypto-Moors—far more leniently than they had crypto-Jews. Why? Because of the threat of Islamic reprisal. As for the Jews, Catholic Spain could do with them as she willed. It was intolerable that they should lose that little parcel of desert they were working to reclaim. And with scarcely anywhere to go now, no sanctuary. It made him sad, sick at heart, despairing—but what the hell, they had asked for it, opted for a capitalist state, allied themselves with U.S. imperialism, depended on wealthy U.S. Jews promoting Bonds for Israel. He knew a few of them, very few, of the Lermot Bros. type, poultry-processing magnates, whose youngsters he had tutored in math back home in Maine, poultry magnates exploiting the dumb natives (as Pound might have alleged). "Those Arabs don't need much," said one of them. "A blanket or two extra makes them happy." But did that make Israel like them, did that make Israel the same? Weren't there wage earners, farmers, cooperatives? (he asked himself irritably). Were they to be annihilated too, or driven out into the sea, as the Syrians bragged, forced to wander again, seek a foothold in foreign lands, live again on sufferance? There would scarce be alternative now to assimilation. Well, then assimilate! Get lost. He was married to a Gentile wife, and never could have known anyone gentler, kinder, more considerate, devoted, intelligent, perceptive, and companionable. But Jesus, that was no solution either. Who were more assimilated than German Jews? Even when they fled here they behaved like a superior race. What good did assimilation do them? To what lengths Nazi insanity had gone! A single Jewish grandfather was enough to send you up the chimney—but damn it, they had asked for it, Israel had asked for it—their extinction would be the result of their capitalist commitment, capitalist social structure. That there were workers and farmers, producers among them was irrelevant. Still, he felt troubled.

Here, far away from the carnage, snug in Mexico, he grieved, and hardly knew why.

Roth: Strangely enough, this dead author may be going through a resurrection. I started writing again in the summer of 1967, simultaneously with the outbreak and conclusion of the Israeli-Arab war. I was in Guadalajara, Mexico, at the time, where I followed the daily events of the war in the local newspapers with great avidity. I found myself identifying intensely with the Israelis in their military feats, which repudiated all the anti-Jewish accusations we had been living with in the Diaspora, and I gloried in their establishment of themselves as a state through their own application and resources. An intellectual excitement seized hold of me that forced me to set down what was going through my mind, to record my thoughts about Israel and my new reservations about the Soviet Union. What I wrote seemed to reflect a peculiar adoption. Israel did not adopt me; I adopted my *ex post facto* native land. What seemed important was that I identified with Israel without being a Zionist and without having the least curiosity about Israel as a practical, political entity. Suddenly I had a place in the world and an origin. Having started to write, it seemed natural to go on from there, and I have been writing long hours every day since then. I am not yet sure what it is leading to, but it is necessary and is growing out of a new allegiance, an adhesion that comes from belonging.

I had the need for us to be warriors; I had the need for us to be peasants and farmers, for us to exercise all the callings and trades like any other people. I have become an extreme partisan of Israeli existence—for the first time I have a people. All this has made me conscious of my latent conviction—that the individual *per se* disintegrates unless he associates himself with an institution of some sort, with a larger entity. I could not find that kind of bond in religion, and I do not think the Israelis do either. I found it in the existence of a nation. I have not been able to turn for that to America, which is presently committing the folly of destroying itself, so at least for the present I have adopted a people of my own, because they have made it possible for me to do so. And I am further indebted to Israel because I am able to write again.

If there is anything dramatic about all this, I suppose it can be explained as the way a fictioneer does things. Significant for me is that after his vast detour, the once-Orthodox Jewish boy has returned to his own Jewishness. I have reattached myself to part of what I had rejected in 1914. Even before the Israeli-Arab war I was beginning to feel that there might be some path that would lead me back to myself, although I realized there was no returning to the Jews of the East Side of more than a half century ago. Then suddenly I discovered that I could align myself with a people that is forward-looking and engaged in the vital process of its own formation. And with the resumption of writing I find that I myself am reabsorbed into something that is immediately vital. One of the little—or big—projects I have undertaken is a work dealing with the artist responding to his world.

(Bronsen, 1969, pp. 278–79)

Roth: In '67 the June war broke out in the Middle East. Now, I think this is an important point. Quite contrary to party discipline, party program, party line, I felt myself turning away from party directives and turning toward Israel. Despite what I thought I should be doing or feeling, I nevertheless began to side more and more with Israel in the months and days preceding the war. You remember, in May, the Syrians were going to drive the Jews into the sea. I felt a greater and greater sense of sympathy with Israel. Now, whether the Holocaust had something to do with it or not, I don't know. As a matter of fact, I was not so much affected by the Holocaust, but I began to feel a terrible anxiety on behalf of all those Jews who were going to be driven into the sea, and who apparently were going to be annihilated, and I couldn't stand the thought that at the same time I was supposed to say hoorah.

According to the party line, the Arabs were anti-imperialists and they were only fighting for their own freedom from imperialists. As a good Communist Party member, it was my manifest duty to support them, but on the contrary, it was for Israel that I felt a tremendous sense of concern. It was Israel that I hoped would prevail in the coming war, and that marked the beginning of a great change in myself in every respect. When Israel defeated the Arabs in a matter of a few days, my exaltation knew no bounds. I felt at last that Jews had redeemed themselves by self-sacrifice and sheer valor. From that point on, and there were other reasons, I experienced a resurgence of my long dormant literary vocation. I began to try to set down my thinking on why I felt this way about Israel. By the way, we were in Mexico at the time. The reports I read—the first one was that the Israelis had destroyed the Egyptian air force—were all in Spanish. My Spanish wasn't too good, so I had to dig it all up and go back again and read it over—and exult!

For the first time, I began to write along entirely different lines. No longer was it merely narrative, and no longer merely perceptions or impressions, but rather trying to think what the hell do I feel about Communism, what do I feel about Israel, what do I feel about Judaism, and why. That marked the beginning of the resurgence of my own writing.

I now write. It's no longer recognizably narrative, although it may include narrative elements. I no longer attempt to maintain an inviolate continuity. But I write and that's the important thing.

The gestation period of an individual's rebirth is of indeterminate duration. The only valid proof for a writer is to produce something of literary merit. When that happens, I shall certainly seek publication. Israel is my chief concern now, and any work of literary merit that I can achieve would be in her behalf, to muster sympathy and support for her struggle for survival and security.

(Friedman, 1977, pp. 37–38)

Interviewer: In an earlier interview you said that the Six-Day War changed your whole way of thinking. Did the Yom Kippur War have any particular effect on you?

Roth: Only insofar as it caused me profound grief. But it didn't change my view of anything. It confirmed it all the more by taking some of the complacence away.

Interviewer: Could you say something about your current views of Israel?

Roth: I have become a little more sophisticated than the individual who saw pretty much black and white in 1967. I now see Israel society has some serious problems within, not only the Arabs but also a class problem. It's badly stratified. Still I feel that the Diaspora is headed for assimilation, and all that is left of Judaism in the future will be in the state of Israel. And that is the one thing we should try to preserve.

(Lyons, 1979, p. 56)

The American people have finally caught up with [the Jew], in the sense that they have assumed some of his characteristics. And this, this is the most peculiar and ironic part of it all: they have done so at the same time that he is on the verge of disappearance, of shedding his historic role. (How can he maintain it with a bona fide modern state of his own in existence?) He has now become the trope of the other exiled, the Americans. Hence the vogue of Jewish writers in the U.S.A. and the revival of *Call It Sleep*.

(letter to Bryon Franzen
from Albuquerque, N.M.,
November 4, 1968)

Hat der begrabener schon sic nach oben . . .

Faust, Goethe

Prolog im Himmel

Autumn 1973

"I really put it down as a whim, as an ironic commentary," says Roth about the title, which he borrowed from Goethe's Faust.

"Prolog im Himmel," like "No Longer at Home" and others that were to follow, is a piece of writing that defies definition. It is neither consistently narrative nor strictly autobiographical. It is an apparently haphazard collage of snatches from a journal, impressions from a trip to New York, the author's thought about the Yom Kippur War, his comments on his own writing, etc. What keeps these heterogeneous elements together is the underlying search for coherence in the face of the seeming fortuity of experience, the insistent groping for order through the chaotic onslaught of outside pressure.

Roth has often referred to this form of writing (which he began sometime in the late fifties) as a continuum, *a term meant to describe his day-to-day exercise in what he calls "the rambling account of myself." This particular form of writing was born out of Roth's need to recapture the daily discipline of his craft, at a time when he did not have any specific "fable" to tell. Once, in 1964, he told the editor: "I can't think of a structure, a plan. The moment I have one, I would no longer be able to write. I would feel trapped." In this sense, the term* continuum *aptly suggests an écriture that by its rhythms and modalities mirrors the mind's constant search for its lost identity.*

Creative writing, ah, that *via dolorosa*. No, only that genre of which I showed you a fragment, a kind of continuum, about which much can be said, or very little. A landscape of the self; to epitomize its meaning for myself and others, I offer you the title, Portrait of the Artist as an Old Fiasco. (*Meaning* is perhaps the wrong word; *trend* would be better.)

(letter from San Cristobal, N.M.,
September 25, 1968)

I still write my perpetual continuum; it's like a meat grinder.

(letter from Albuquerque, N.M.,
March 27, 1969)

I write, yes . . . frequently disjointed and I fancy posthumous things, a kind of continuum whose only internal structure is a play the author is engaged in and sometimes actually writes. It goes on and on, the continuum, like a huge cocoon about a larva.

(letter from Albuquerque, N.M.,
November 18, 1971)

He had awakened several times during the night quite disoriented, imagining himself in motels on the way to places he had visited the past month, or at the destinations themselves, anywhere but home. The light he saw shining under the bathroom door (a pink glow because M had neglected to turn off the infrared lamp before retiring) suggested by turns that he was still in Maine staying at the home of former neighbors, or in Rochester to pay a last visit to M's dying sister, or in the farmhouse in Canaan where he and M had forgathered with their son and daughter-in-law, and where he had first learned of the outbreak of the new Middle East war ("Dad, you'd better have your breakfast first," advised his pert daughter-in-law, "before I tell you the bad news from Israel.") Or yet again, the place he had stayed in longest in order to absorb as much of the New York milieu as he could, the apartment of Lucy, widow of one of his CCNY classmates. Only when R got out of bed and went to the bathroom did the drifting domiciles come to rest. He was back in the mobile home he shared with his wife in the Heaven Hill Mobile Park in Albuquerque. Relieved to be home, and now awake in his relief, as though he had escaped from the zodiac, he took half of a .20 gram barbital tablet, went back to bed, and awoke in the morning refreshed. . . .

So the Yom Kippur war, Israel's fourth ordeal in 25 years, was formally declared in abeyance, this phase at any rate tapering off with a cease-fire in place, with the dispatch of U.N. personnel to keep the peace on desert and height, with negotiations between senior officers of Egypt and Israel for the first time in seventeen years, with passage of food and medical supplies to Egypt's beleaguered 3d Army Corps, with the consent of Israel, with S.U. observers matched by U.S. observers, and with Palestinian terrorists reserving all rights of perpetration. This round of killing and destruction was pronounced closed.

The truce was described as offering the most hopeful prospect of peace in that part of the world in many years, proof of the viability of the détente between the two superpowers, and begotten of that détente, although not without duress. A grave crisis had been averted, a great reprieve had been won, the globe had been spared nuclear immolation, Kissinger had spoken, the U.N. had acted, leaders of every nation in the world awoke to their involvement in the conflict and to their responsibility for preserving the peace. And all this, one might say, because of a pack, well, a parcel of Jews, less than three million, determined to defend their national restoration against ten times their number. How could one doubt they were a chosen people, how could one fail to entertain the notion, or at least toy with the idea? Still there were other explanations for the singularity of Jews. The question wasn't important at the moment and only deflected from something that interested R much more.

Such as the feckless way he spent Thursday, October 25, the day of the great Alert, with his new mini–tape recorder in his bosom, the button mike at his throat, traversing New York streets and commenting on what he saw, collecting material he hoped to exploit later in a projected novel: only to discover after hours of peregrination that his tape recorder had consistently malfunctioned. All his observations, all his remarks, all that he had thought safely stowed in the instrument returned to him distorted beyond recognition. Cursed electronic gadget! Not even the huge rally of Jewish youngsters gathered in the vicinity of the U.N. chanting slogans and singing *hatkiva* had registered. Nothing of all that impassioned tumult could he identify. Nor any of his comments on the changes he noted on Second Avenue as he sauntered from the East Side Terminal to the YMCA building, faithfully following the route his character would take. And those vivid impressions he had impounded during his stroll along Forty-second Street past the Public Library. The throngs, the beards, the costumes of blacks. And above all, those potentially comic mini-dialogues with the Jewish vendors of pornographic literature, films, and other lewd objects in the sordid little stores west of the Avenue of the Americas. Nothing. A grinding roar, an impenetrable gargle. What a waste of time. If only he could have salvaged a rude word, an expletive, a few curt phrases, a single insight, anything. Well, no use mourning over addled speech and voices. Memory would have to serve, and his written notes, though entered in other connections.

Friday morning he had taken the plane back to Albuquerque, boarded it at the Newark Airport, something he had never done before (and vowed never to do again if he could help it). Still, thanks to the unwelcome opportunity afforded by the interminable delays encountered in reaching the terminal, he had something to show for it:

Friday, October 27, 1973
The taxi ride north through lower New York from Lucy's apartment on Park Row to the East Side Terminal in morning murk through a welter of trucking was sufficiently unnerving in itself, but easy compared to what followed: First, a fifteen-minute delay in starting because the regular bus driver failed to report for work. Then an excruciating, slow inching across town hemmed in by traffic that appeared to mill rather than to move. And at the Hudson Tunnel utter stasis. Vehicles choked to immobility by two simultaneously stalled cars at the tunnel approach, cars that had to be towed away before anything else could move. Minutes spent twisting fingers, waiting with mounting anxiety, contemplating fretfully coil upon coil of interstate buses on the spiral ramps leading from the Port Authority Building, and the chains of private cars clogging the streets. To this appalling press of vehicles crammed to paralysis came the final irony, the rangy steel frame of a multiple-car conveyor, a piggy back truck loaded with autos on every level and incline, barging in from some assembly line in the Midwest to contribute its mite (truly) to an already infested city. At long last the line of those ahead segmented like the legendary glass snake; our bus too began to move forward, gained momentum and at last sped through the tunnel. And out into daylight smog again. And over the New Jersey marshes. Yet so great was the tide of incoming vehicles that a lane on our side of the highway, the outbound side, was closed off to us, usurped by those whose exhausts sent them hurtling toward their quarries in the city. The disquieting thought seizes one that civilization is battening on its own entrails, its own confines. Or civilization is battering its own dikes, its own limits. As I once long ago, the youthful novelist, sensed in rupturing the envelope of my narrative that spilled over into apocalyptic chaos. As that incomparably greater artist Joyce must have known, consuming the very medium of his prose. Was all that a foreshadowing of this to come? And what will come out of it? What will emerge?

Nobody else would have thought of a traffic jam in this peculiar manner—R shook his head pityingly after he entered the note in his journal—nobody else would have warped the perception around so self-centeredly to bear on his own personality and its preoccupations: that image of congestion and inexorable increment! Only he in his self-engrossment. Anyone else would have drawn practical conclusions or realistic ones: found in the scene an example of the stupendous quantities of petroleum expended, with its corollary of universal dependence on Arab oil, and the woe this spelled for Israel. Or at the very least, called attention to the waste, the rank pollution, the disfigurement of the human ambience; and once again perhaps hinted that Israel might be rendering mankind a service, however unwitting, by accelerating research into more benign fuels and energy sources; hydrogen for instance, or the thermal energy in vulcanism. R sighed shortly... Wryneck as always. Adrift... and transcribed his last jotting:

> Observers are being sent to Egypt to assess the extent of the 3d Army Corps' entrapment by the Israeli. (See *The New York Times,* Thursday, October 25, 1973 on the Mideast.) How this latest crisis changes my attitude toward the U.S., my home country! Despite the fen of Watergate, and a president sunk in it, and distrust hovering above it like a miasma, I am become to a degree reconciled with this land and its people, to a degree have shed scale of alienation. And all this because of Israel.

This piece appeared in the Fall 1973 issue of Shenandoah: The Washington and Lee University Review, *in response to a request by the editors for a piece to accompany Bonnie Lyons's interview with the author.*

> *Roth:* Until about a year and a half ago, I was writing a kind of "continuum" journal—what someone called "awarenesses." These "awarenesses" were reminiscences and observations about my surroundings—and I had written a pile of them, notebooks at least a foot high. Then about a year and a half ago, I began to write something that was a continuity, also in the past, and with this I became more and more curious. First I tried to write it as a play—then I thought it's about time that you acknowledged that one goes on in an art. You don't just break away into a different form—you use the techniques you have developed even if they are a bit rusty. And that's what I'm doing now.

> (Lyons, 1976, p. 176)

Squib

December 1975

*This barbed bagatelle was signed "An anonymous reader." It was
written in reaction to the resolution passed by the United Nations'
General Assembly on November 10, 1975, that defined Zionism as
"a form of racism and racial discrimination." This resolution had been
preceded by two others that were strongly pro-PLO and pro-Pales-
tinian.*

If as forecast
   the great Arab democracies
   cajoling their sulky cohorts in Africa
   and bullying the nonaligned
   by greater bullies incited
   and led by the upholstered and ineffable Amin
   (whom erst his Moslem masters had castrated
   to guard their harems)
   succeed
   in ousting that "imperialist agent" Israel from
   the halls of the U.N.

wouldn't that warrant razing the edifice to ground
and dumping the rubble into the East River?
At least from the esplanade thus founded
kids could dive bare ass
and septuagenarians bask in sunshine
while they angled for shad.

Roth: What ["Squib"] does—it represents a stage in the development of the individual in his allegiance. It's one more stage in the development of the individual *away* from his original Marxist "orientation," to a reunification with his people, to a politicization—in fact, to a level in which he is now willing to accept things in the nature of political economy that the pure writer once would *not* accept. I mean, such things as U.N. debates and other aspects of international politics—all of which, in the Joycean tradition, would have been completely blocked out. That's all I'm saying: one more stage in his development of a commitment to Israel.

(taped conversation,
Albuquerque, N.M.,
February 10, 1986)

For two other examples of Roth's dabbling at versification, see "Assassins and Soldiers," Section I.

Dear Eldridge Cleaver:
Let me offer a response to your excellent statement on racism appearing in the overseas *Jerusalem Post* of January 20, 1976.
During World War II, before the Soviet Union was attacked, the U.S. Communist Party strenuously opposed this country's involvement in the war against Nazi Germany. In retaliation, the U.S. government incarcerated Earl Browder, spearhead of that opposition. On June 22, 1941, when Nazi Germany attacked the Soviet Union, the U.S. Communist Party declared that the character of the war had undergone a qualitative change: instead of an imperialist war, it was now a war for national liberation. Earl Browder, who now supported the war, was soon released from prison. A similar qualitative change seems to have occurred in the case of Eldridge Cleaver. He who once imperiled U.S. democratic institutions now supports them. By the same token the U.S. self-interest requires his release from prison. . . .
Any substantial voice among the Blacks that speaks out in defense of Israel and speaks out against the infamous racist equation promulgated in the U.N., that voice ought not to be pent up in prison, but given full range to transmit its message. . . .

Your statement on racism coming so close to the announcement of Paul Robeson's death brought to mind the vast and hazy notion I once entertained about a better world created by a Black-Jewish-Labor-Intellectual coalition, to all of which Paul Robeson's song gave incomparable resonance. Vanished away of course, frittered away. Nevertheless that particular vision left an indelible imprint that still lingers on as a kind of constituent of present hope. It is doubtful that such a coalition will ever be re-formed. And yet, in spite of realities, hunger for reconciliation remains as imperious and unappeased as ever. It seizes upon your statement as a first harbinger.

(letter to Eldridge Cleaver
from Albuquerque, N.M.,
February 1, 1976)

Kaddish

January 1977

The year 1977 was a most fruitful one for Roth: in ten months he had four pieces published—as many as had been published throughout the sixties.

"Kaddish," the first of these four pieces, appeared in Midstream *and was later reprinted in the* Albuquerque Jewish Community LINK *(May 6, 1977, p. 9). Thirteen years earlier, participating in the* Midstream *symposium on "The Meaning of* Galut *in America Today," Henry Roth had called upon Jews to orient themselves "toward ceasing to be Jews." By 1977, as he candidly avows in "Kaddish," Roth had reversed his position on Judaism and had become a staunch supporter of Israel.*

The final sentence, "A good morning to you, Lord God Almighty," is a quotation from a traditional Hasidic Kaddish.

In a Zionist magazine called *Midstream,* and scarcely accessible to you, you'll find the first stirrings of the Roth rebirth. . . . Others are in progress, now that the direction has been established, but all a bit late—pity I'm so sluggish in the mind.

(letter from Albuquerque, N.M.,
May 24, 1977)

At his wife's suggestion, and while she waited, tall and gray in postman-blue bathrobe behind the screen door of their mobile home, R hauled the child's old red wagon, loaded with recently picked squash, out of the shade of the cottonwood tree into the New Mexico sunshine to cure. Eyes askant for the bloated and horrid horn worm, he picked a dozen or so of cherry tomatoes, flushing swarms of grasshoppers from the garden patch at his every tread. He shifted the trickling hose from the scrawny mint bed to the thriving carrot rows. And setting out the bulky plastic bag for the Tuesday trash collection, noted that new irrigation dikes now trisected the field across the road, and above the lean adobe, how drab against the sky stood the elm, ravaged by beetles.

Three cloudy areas within himself overlapped, merged—and separately or together, continually preoccupied him. If he had to name them, he would have said the first was the growth of literary self-awareness in the latter part of the twenties. The second was the Communist Party experience, the revolutionary transit—and its impact. The third was all that matrix of tutelage and dependence bonding the young writer to the older woman. And the fourth—he now realized there was a fourth—was his determined reorientation toward his own people, outcome of Israel's will to survive—and his own partisanship in that survival.

These were the cloudy lists wherein he contended and strove for conclusion.

In the twenties he had felt snugly ensconced in his milieu, estranged from it, but spying on it, exploiting it, and yet without the least sense of obligation to it. In modern terms he would have said that he and his society were polarized: a steady current of impressions, a negative one, flowed from it to him, which in the transformer of his sensibility he converted into art. Autonomous art: *silence, exile, cunning.* Apparently, that kind of exclusion or foreclosure of milieu, that kind of polarity, favored the creation of art. The twenties were vivid with innovations, with brilliant advances in all fields of art. Had the society remained the same, a great tradition of twentieth-century art might have grown up, a great style might have flourished. But the society did not remain the same. Before the decade was over, the stock market crashed; the economy buckled. By the thirties the great Depression had set in—like a tide of misery. Much touted Normalcy sat naked from the waist up in some deserted railroad freight yard, and scanned his shirt with all the care with which he had once scrutinized the stock market report.

What were the consequences for the artist, for R? Polarity was gone. He could not longer snugly, or smugly, separate himself, the creative, the expressive personality, from the rest of suffering humanity. They clamored to associate with him in their affliction. Far from being the mundane, philistine mass he had regarded them before, commonplace drudges and traffickers, they were a million eloquent voices protesting against callous institutions, the very institutions he himself had inveighed against, although cynically. They, the hungry, the impoverished, the dispossessed, were not cynical. They were in deadly earnest. They began a milling within themselves, as if readying for an attack, for a charge. And now he was aware in a single blur of a vast soberness descending upon him, flooding him, extinguishing irony, snuffing it out in a terrible pervasion of his being. And now he was aware of his own dilemma. This was, or this augured, revolution, and he had joined the Communist Party. But where now would he fit? The kind of writer he was, whose inveteracy a novel had but now reinforced? Retiring, detached, ambivalent, who made no distinction between conditions, to whom the sense data of the world came untagged and wayward, the nostalgic wreaths and fruit printed on the sheet metal under a tenement eave as valuable as the rich verdigris on the copper gable of a Fifth Avenue mansion. Phrase was his criterion, artistic integrity his obligation. Castigated by the Communist press, lauded by the Capitalist, where the hell did he fit? Nowhere. The very narrative he was engaged in writing, with wholesome stalwart proletarian as hero, became sicklied over with eroticism, veered toward pornography. Jesus. He had a vested interest in the sordid, the squalid, the depraved. He became immobilized.

So much for art. He had been living all this time with Eda Lou Walton, professor of English literature at a New York university, and generous to a fault in her support of youthful talent. When his art languished, his dependence festered. The relationship, or the affair, terminated. And now he would have to make retribution, multiple retribution for all the privileged years he had enjoyed, his years on Parnassus, whose emblems were his English tweed jacket, his Dunhill pipe, and his private study looking out on a Greenwich Village backyard. His fellow writers had grubbed for a living during that time, had long since learned the knack of converting their craft into wares; he hadn't. And the thirties was no time for latecomers and slow learners. So it was pick and shovel for him on a project in Queens for the WPA.

And all this time too, he had watched, with the peculiar foreboding of self-relevance, the strange evolution of T.S. Eliot; the modern man, the enlightened American, converting into an Anglo-Catholic, eschewing his democratic heritage in favor of monarchism. A long time R had pondered on the anomaly; what did it mean? What had induced Eliot to take the step? And slowly, over the many years, the answer became clear: he was driven, not induced, out of supreme necessity, out of the need to extricate himself from that very wasteland, which otherwise would have destroyed him as an artist. The step was taken to retrieve that art, to regenerate it—for in no other way could it be done, in no other way *could coherence be saved.* One had to admire the man for his astuteness and resolve. But who could follow him— there was the rub—who could emulate the bastard, preeminent poet though he was? Brahmin, evasive Jew baiter, or at best deprecating anti-Jew, royalist, reactionary. And yet, emulate him one had to; for all, all who had come of artistic age by, and especially in, the thirties, had suffered a parching of their means, all were in that wasteland. . . .

And then came the 1967 War in the Middle East, and the gloom that settled on him, despite his so-called Marxist orientation: the Arab states, the progressives, were going to drive the Jews, the Zionist-imperialist-pawns, into the sea. Jesus Christ, another holocaust of Jews! Sympathy flared up in the face of doctrine. And lo! the forlorn hope: by skill, by daring, by valor, Israel prevailed. A miracle! The pall lifted that had so long encompassed him. What the hell was he waiting for? Here was a people reborn—*his* people—regenerated by their own will. Was he mad not to share in that regeneration? He had been seeking it these thirty, almost forty years, ever since he had first opened *Ash Wednesday.* (And how many times had he thought with pity of his great master, Joyce, who couldn't make it home, and ended in that blind alley corruscating with his genius.) Here was regeneration, tenable, feasible, rational—not in the direction of grandfather's medieval orthodoxy, but in the direction of a renascent Judaism, a new state.

The hummingbird poised in marvelous miniature between the steel thorns of the barbed wire fence separating the mobile home court from the neglected strip of land adjoining, the weeds, the random building material, the nodding, sulphurous wild sunflowers—poised in quintessential pugnacity, and then sped off at R's approach as if loosed from a sling. Two conclusions reared in his mind inescapably: his life was saved by M, whom he had been so incredibly fortunate as to meet at Yaddo in the midst of crisis. Through her, her affection, her constancy and understanding, and above all her native steadiness, he had learned to meet necessity with persistence—and attain thereby an approximate adulthood. And it was Israel, a revitalized Judaism, that revitalized the writer, his partisanship a new exploration into contemporaneity, a new summoning of the word—however inept in the service of a cause. Threescore and ten, he climbed the stairs to the screen door. A good morning to you, Lord God Almighty.

About 1980 or 1979 [sic] I wrote a very short piece called "Kaddish" for *Midstream*. . . . I meant to call it "Mobile Home," but I called it "Kaddish" at the last minute. It's just a very short appraisal of presumably a few minutes being spent in and around the mobile home court where we lived on North Fourth Street, called Paradise Acres. We lived there almost ten years.

Interviewer: Why did you and Muriel decide to live in a mobile home?

Roth: Well, I think it was Muriel's wisdom that decided us to do that, because we had a chance in 1972 to buy a house quite reasonably. But we had had enough of owning real estate in Maine. Here the land is not ours. The dwelling is, but the space isn't. If you don't like where you are, if you don't like your neighbors, you call up the trucking company and ask them to move—the neighbors!

(Goldsmith, 1983)

Except for one little volunteer cluster of marigolds, I lack the flowers, or the horti-(flora?)-cultural impulse your letter speaks of. Harvested yesterday some enormous pods of cultivated sunflowers (a cunning addiction on the East Side of yore, the entirely oral splitting of the shell, extracting seed, expelling the shell: crack, ptooh, which I never mastered). Anyway, long after the cultivated sunflowers nodded their heavy heads in autumn drowse, lo, just outside the fence an upstart wild sunflower popped its saucy flowers pyrotechnically. Must be a jillion on the one stout stem.

(letter to Luther Cressman,
from Albuquerque, N.M.,
September 13, 1978)

Interviewer: In a recent piece in *Midstream,* and in an earlier memoir in *Commentary* (August 1960), you stressed the influence of Eliot and "The Waste Land." I wonder if you could talk about what Eliot meant to you personally and what he meant to your generation.

Roth: I first came to know Walton through a young man Lester Winter, who had a lyric gift of a limited and conventional sort. At the time Walton had already initiated a course in modern poetry which was quite an advanced course to be giving in the mid or late twenties. Nobody had ventured into that field yet. She had quite a collection of modern poetry: Stevens, Williams, Pound, Eliot. Already I had read that this T.S. Eliot was the most important poet writing to date—this being the twenties. I'm the kind of guy that if I'm convinced that this is authority, then it is up to me to *learn,* to find out why they consider him such a high-quality writer, why he's considered the most important—even though I don't understand a word the guy is saying. I've always done this. I don't know what intuition tells me, but it's almost unerring. It tells me what's the important and future thing. And then when I'm convinced of it, I make a virtual religious study; the book becomes my holy book. I read it over and over again. I remember doing this with "Prufrock" even. I know I did not understand what the hell "Prufrock" was all about. That was an indication of my level; I had never been exposed to much modern poetry. While visiting at Walton's with Lester Winter, I would look through these various books and finally I came to "The Waste Land," and again I didn't know what was going on. I must have reread that "Waste Land" until I memorized it. If you take a person whose mind as far as poetry is concerned is a kind of tabula rasa, and you pour into it Eliot's alienation, Eliot's ennui, his sense of the decay of western civilization, and combine this with an intuition that you have about reality, the reality of your own existence that you never formulated—*this* becomes its formulation. *This* takes on the meaning that you may have vaguely felt all along without, of course, putting it into words. Eliot became a tremendous influence on me. I realized there was an element of anti-Semitism, but I was willing to accept it. I thought, "He isn't saying too much I haven't already observed among Jews myself and disliked."

Interviewer: You thought it just referred to the *other* Jews.

Roth: Exactly. You thought it referred to the side of Judaism that you had come to dislike in first-generation Jews who had to subordinate everything in order to make an economic base for themselves. So, I would say that Eliot was the major influence on my life. I'm the kind of guy, too, who doesn't need endless examples. I take the one example and focus and contemplate every single aspect of it I'm capable of and, by implication, get very much of the rest without the details.

(Lyons, 1979, pp. 52–53)

O brothers, I said, who through a hundred thousand perils
Have arrived at the west . . .

—Inferno, XXVI. *Dante*

Itinerant Ithacan

Summer–Fall 1977

In "Kaddish," Roth spelled out the four "cloudy areas" that constitute the constant, near-obsessive nuclei of his emotional and intellectual concern. "Itinerant Ithacan," which is the longest of his published pieces since he has resumed writing, combines the first and the last of these nuclei: the crucial time in his youth when Roth became aware of his literary inclinations and his latter-day commitment to Israel.

Roth was to refer to "Itinerant Ithacan" as an "experimental piece." The experiment consisted of the juxtaposition of these two seemingly unrelated nuclei in a work that required sustained narrative tension and well-defined focal concentration. In this perspective, "Itinerant Ithacan" is to be seen as a most important stepping stone toward the conception of Mercy of a Rude Stream, the "memoir-form novel" that Roth has been working on for the past several years. An excerpt from Mercy of a Rude Stream was published in 1984 as "Weekends in New York—A Memoir."

Roth: [What I'm doing now is] essentially an account of the entrance of the young man into consciousness of a literary impulse, a desire to create great art. It brings to bear the peculiar, separate, and yet distinctly related world of the Jews in Harlem—that's the parental, Jewish world—and the world of Greenwich Village and the literary intellectuals. The individual about whom I'm writing is a young man who slowly becomes conscious of his literary tendencies. He is the nexus between the two worlds that never met. He simply carries it back and forth like a shuttle. Quite recently, I think that I've stumbled on this remarkable kind of an idea, a remarkable point of view or attitude. I hope the whole thing can live up to the point of view or attitude. So I shall finish this particular draft and then go back to it. And God knows what will happen.

(Lyons, 1976, p. 176)

Have been trying with M's help to finish a thirty or so page experimental piece for the local University of New Mexico (am deliberately addressing myself to university students, exploiting the name in a pie with a narrative filler and a crusty pro-Israel author writing it). This is an answer to a request, so it's just a question of whether I think it's good enough to release, in short serves the purpose. . . .

The idea [of going to Israel] is to prove whether there is a sequel to what I'm doing—or more than one.

(letter from Albuquerque, N.M.,
November 14, 1977)

Roth: I wouldn't be surprised if, before . . . I was too damn old, I might even transfer to Israel. . . . And this ties in with the thing that I've been writing. But it's a very peculiar thing, because it seems to turn its back, partly, on the only thing that I was any good at—the narrative, the narrative art. It seems to grope into fields that I wouldn't say were merely sociological but international as well: politics and a bunch of stuff that I have very little experience with. But nevertheless I don't hesitate to give my responses to these things. Nor do they limit me—that's the peculiar thing too. I seem to be able to go in large circles, and include within them personal past and experiences. It's a very funny type of writing. Largely, I think, it tends to run— there's no form to it whatever—but if there's any definition, it tends to run like a journal. I mean, one day this much is reflected on, and the next day another. Sometimes there is a connection, sometimes there's not. But I also have a scheme, and that is what I have yet to find out—if it will work. I have my doubts—that it can work, that I can work a narrative together with the author's quotidian. It remains to be seen.

This is what I'm wondering—whether one can use a narrative *and* my present attitude, my present feeling about Israel. In other words, can I yoke these two things together, do these two independently? I just don't feel that I can sit down and do a piece independent of my overpowering attachment for Israel, as if the reality of the writer did not exist, only the reality of the character. With world events so dramatic and also so fateful for all of us, not only for those who are Jews or oriented toward Israel, I don't think that you can actually separate—that you *should* separate, morally—the reality confronting the artist from the reality of his product. As I said, everyday he goes through experiences which are of first importance, and can't very well just say—as I once did, as I once was able to—"Well, they don't matter." And as Joyce did—let's see, it was in the middle of World War I, wasn't it, and he was able to block the whole thing off. . . .

Interviewer: And also the outbreak of World War II.

Roth: That's right. Not to mention the bitter struggle of his countrymen for independence from England. And all this, for the sake of something that he was writing . . .

Interviewer: These two masses of material, have you put them together?

Roth: No, I haven't. I have to go home and . . . try it. That's the whole thing in a nutshell. I don't know what I'll strike on, or if I'll strike on anything. It's conceivable, for example, that a writer writes a journal (I think Gide did something like this), writes a novel, and the two intertwine some way. If you look at some of the modern paintings, the painter doesn't seem to give a damn why he puts—in these abstracts—why he puts one element together with another. Well, I just ask myself, why do I have to accede to possibilities? If I like the thing, that's fine. One would have to be convinced, that's all.

Interviewer: You are actually asking yourself whether you can like something for which you don't have a model.

Roth: That's right.

Interviewer: You would have to *invent* the model.

Roth: Yes, I would have to invent the model. But then, of course, in the light of the tremendous struggles that are going on, can you stand the fable that you have created? In other words, can you accept its relative unimportance? It seems almost trivial. How can any fiction hold its own in comparison with the tremendous battles going on for survival, for life and death in the desert there?

(taped conversation,
New York, N.Y., October 23, 1973)

On Sunday, January 23, 1977, at ten o'clock of an overcast morning, bedraggled by a night of intermittent rain, the temperature for this time of year, a clement forty degrees Fahrenheit, R, having but yesterday returned from a series of visits to friends and kinfolk in the Southeast and Texas, and everywhere feted and lavishly entertained, and everywhere having swigged quantities of choice scotch, guzzled vintage wines, and with ill-concealed voracity gorged on such an abundance of rich food (in a mostly undernourished world), that in ten days of junketing he gained six pounds—R vowed as he gazed dourly out of his study window in the rear of the mobile home that was his residence to impose not only the most stringent diet upon himself, but to abstain from alcoholic beverages as well. At least for a while. Snow stretched in a braided causeway in the lee of the weedy north bank of the irrigation ditch on the other side of the narrow belt of neighboring property. As if bolted through massive clouds, a pale sunlight sifted down on damp elm tree branches.

But he had experienced something more serious during the trip than a gain in weight. Like the legendary dibbuk or incubus, a fierce and perverse resolution had taken hold of him—and perhaps was the cause of his immoderate eating and tippling and his boorishness toward his wife. They had just arrived at the bland Sarasota condominium of Iven, his last living college friend, having had supper on the way from the airport, and they were engaged in the shuttling and disjointed conversation of people who hadn't seen one another for a long time, chatting in separate pairs, R exuberantly with Iven's wife, and Iven in his serious way with M, when she tapped his arm, implying he wasn't listening to something important Iven was saying or was interfering with her listening. Tapped his arm so lightly, though firmly, that another time he would scarce have heeded the slight check, or if he had, altered his behavior accordingly. But not this time. So deeply did the trifling reproof rankle that in the privacy of their bedroom later, he all but exploded at his wife, his wrath scarcely contained by the awareness that his hosts were in the adjoining bedroom: he bared his dentures and swung his arm back in such graphic sideswipe at his wife that she flinched. And even though she tried to explain, and to placate him, he refused to be placated, he refused to be appeased. It was then and there that the savage resolve seized him, the resolve that had not relented since. He would travel to Israel without her; he would leave her behind in Albuquerque. Through the good offices of a distinguished Zionist and writer, Marie Syrkin, who had been here to give a lecture, he had been invited by Teddy Kollek, the mayor of Jerusalem, to stay for two months in a hospice set apart for creative individuals in the arts and humanities. His wife had been included in the invitation. But now he determined otherwise. He would go alone, alone and without her. She could stay home, mind the new car and the premises, pay the bills, and suffer the ignominy of the forsaken wife.

And yet, all the while, as he gloated over his retaliation, a strange pall began to enclose him, a dread, as if he were rehearsing not the satisfaction of a grudge, but his wife's widowhood; as though he were acting out a defunctive allegory that became more real the more willfully he clung to his resolution. So this was to be the end, after forty years of marriage.

That night during long periods of wakefulness, the devastating thought wracked him, that he no longer loved M, nor anyone else, no longer needed anyone's love. Immobilized he lay as if trussed by his own obsession, peering up at the tiny neon fang of the night light under the wall clock: neither loved the woman breathing beside him in the depths of slumber, the woman he had worshipped all his life; nor wanted to be loved. What then? What would happen now? Of his two sons, one had taken his father's former assimilationism seriously and had even moved further in the direction his parent pioneered, distancing himself into universalism—almost into a Gentile. He would be but little affected by anything that happened to the relapsing Jew, his father. But the other son had been less susceptible to precept; the lesson had been lost on him—or he had penetrated beyond the preachment to its hidden mystique. Out of the emotional straits the youth had been in, out of his existential dilemmas, he had converted to Judaism, and to Orthodox Judaism at that. Would his newly assumed faith sustain him in the event of his father's suicide?

Dear Marie:
    Thanks to you, it is now official! Mayor Teddy Kollek has invited me to stay at Mishkenot Sha'ananim (R squinted at the last word: had he accounted for all the letters 'a' correctly and in proper order in that now forgotten language?) as guests of the municipality of Jerusalem. It was a most cordial letter and was accompanied by a guest guide as tactful and courteous as the letter itself. If only I could command that same felicity in expressing my gratitude for the invitation! But then, how often does one have an occasion such as this in which to practice an appropriate reply? I did my fumbling best, a copy of which I enclose.
    I look forward to the experience with elation and pride—that I should be singled out for the honor of sojourning in Jerusalem as its guest. But also, I must admit, with a sense of apprehension (isn't that strange?), as

though I had been assigned some mission of immense moment, one upon which destiny pivoted. I reject teleology of course, still the heart remains somewhat dissident—as though better versed in matters pertaining to pre-destination. . . .

And once again he sat in Eda Lou's Greenwich Village apartment, below street level, sat there a CCNY undergraduate, in the late afternoon of a weekend at the close of the year; in her one-room apartment where palpable city dust drifted down ubiquitously on furnishings, windowsill, and mantle piece, dust scuffed up from hectic Eighth Street, just above the window. So near the scraps of conversation outdoors, guffaw and repartee, so near the scrape of shod feet in passing, clash of crosstown trolley, blast of auto horn, brought into the room along with the normal drone of the city; sat there for the nth time, conning T.S. Eliot's "Waste Land." While in the obscure alcove in the rear of the apartment, stretched out on the bed with its sable velour covering, Eda Lou tittered girlishly in the arms of her young lover, the handsome and talented Lester Winter, R's chum since high school days and now a sophomore at NYU.

Why was R invited along on these trysts? He could only guess. Because he could be trusted. Because he seemed unaffected by their lovemaking, almost indifferent. Because his presence dissembled the affair she was having with one of her students. Once or twice, she mentioned the stuffy, Victorian chairman of the English department, who would have a conniption, she said fetchingly, if he learned what she was doing. Once or twice, R did seem to play a buffer role when colleagues dropped in unannounced. So he explained matters to himself. Uncouth and slum reared, he felt privileged to be there in the proximity of refined romance. He went along. And there he sat, callow Tiresias, staring entranced at the bright page before him until he had virtually memorized it, until he felt hypnotized by the illumination of the floor lamp; and so quiet, the lovers at his back must have thought him drowsing, for he heard amatory scuffle, rubbing of clothing, and squeaky bussing, like bottle corks drawn. What the hell was the difference what they were doing? What could they be doing? The momentous thing now, the crucial thing, was what was happening to him. Like another Dr. Jekyll he had deliberately submitted his impressionable, pusillanimous, amorphous self to an entirely new experience, to a rapture of disenchantment, a rapture of alienation,—and like Dr. Jekyll, had become addicted. It was not as if he were unfamiliar with much of the poem's sordid and inane tenor. He lived in it. It was home. But now on the page it continually transformed itself into a kind of anodyne. Late last summer, only three months ago, Eda Lou had returned from a trip to Europe with a copy of Joyce's *Ulysses* which she had smuggled through customs. (And that too was something to note, that she could dimple with duplicity, decoy with her large brown eyes and genteel reserve; it was something to learn.) The last ten days before college opened, she and Lester had trysted in a place called Woodstock, in a quaint stone house made available to them by a colleague in the English department,—and again R had been invited to accompany them. Eda Lou had brought the *Ulysses* along for Lester to read. But after an hour or two, he put the novel aside remarking that it wasn't necessary for a writer to strain for such bizarre effects simply in order to prove his originality. So R fell heir to the book. And while the lovers dallied, or Eda Lou typed her lectures on a portable typewriter, or Lester in the evening, in the aura of candlelight to court the muse, sat at the table in the open hallway writing a lyric, R, unaccountably determined to exploit the opportunity, read the *Ulysses*. He read it doggedly, perplexedly, moiling through hundreds of close-printed and often baffling pages for a story. There was no story, and the meaning seemed to be the absence of meaning. It was like a junkyard world, stagnating, grimy and drab, in which nothing happened that wasn't a modulation of banality. One punch in the face of Stephen Dedalus by a British Tommy in a whorehouse; Bloom's wife routinely adulterous, heroics and lechery on a midden. What was there in that diurnal Dublin grubbiness different from his own dreary life in Harlem? If a one-eyed Irish jingo heaved a soap box after the fleeing Bloom, an Irish gamin spat on and smeared R's permanent record card while he waited his turn to register in P.S. 24. It was only the alchemy of language that transmuted the sludge into something noble, into a work of art. So that was how it was done? The tenement backyards of his neighborhood, the dingy cabbagey Fels Naptha soap mopped hallways, the battered brass letter boxes, qualified for alchemy—the myriad impressions he took for granted: the kids rolling dice under the shadow of the New York Central trestle, Petey Hunt humping Veronica under the stairs, the housewife setting out with black oilcloth shopping bag into the motes of slant morning sunlight, the ice man whistling Chimes of Italy in the cellar, or ponderous Mr. Perry, the street maintenance foreman, mounting the creaky stairs at the close of day. You didn't need to go to the South Sea Isles, didn't need to float down the Mississippi on a raft, or flounder through the snow of the Yukon. It was all here, right here. It was the language that made the difference, that transmuted meanness into literature. Jesus! What a discovery! Whole troves: Mr. Malloy seated in the sunshine before the wrought iron filigree of the cellar-way, smoking his stubby pipe with a baby bottle nipple at the end of the stem to protect his toothless gums. Purple crepe hung amid the graffiti at the side of the ravaged entrance door of the tenement. Yonnie Trury on bare-ass beach off the freight tracks of the Hudson River sporting a Bull Durham sack on his dink because he had the clap. Yossie Bayer's pimply baby brother in his high chair catching a cockroach in his chubby fist, and offering to throw it into his doting ne'er-do-well papa's glass of tea.

And having imparted these good tidings, the direct result of your intercession on my behalf, I hope you don't mind if I impose on your kindness further. What is the significance of these passages I have just read in the *Jerusalem Post* of January 18, 1977? The article is by Judy Siegal, and it is about a "PLAN TO SHAKE UP WORLD ZIONISM," as the headline has it. What is the meaning of the statement that "a team of independent professionals in Israel have proposed a four-year plan to the chairman of the Zionist executive . . . allocating decision-making powers to local and Zionist federations (I quote so fully because you may not have the newspaper handy); subordinating all types of emissary in each locality to a central *shuliah;* promoting settlement of immigrant and veteran Israelis and opening the Zionist movement to nonparty activists through democratic elections." These are "some of the far-reaching recommendations unveiled by Ra'anan Weitz, chairman of the WZO's settlement department and head of a twenty-six-member team at a meeting of the press in Jerusalem last week." God, I'm at sea! How I envy your undeviating, steady, and vertical accumulation of knowledge that so brilliantly buttresses your convictions. I need to be led by the hand, a belated and unschooled zealot. "Reducing the party influence in the Zionist movement abroad would inevitably, if gradually, weaken such influence at the top of the WZO—at the level of the executive and the various departments in Jerusalem." What on earth does that mean? Just as this article confuses me, a second one by Judy Siegal in the same issue of the *Jerusalem Post* is only too clear to me, alas. I say alas because nothing could be more dishearteningly true than the statements she attributes to Bar-on: "The Israeli who comes and sets up an *aliya* office in an American city is viewed as a stranger by the Jewish community. The most difficult bodies we will have to contend with are the Federations which collect funds and run various Jewish services. In the past they have shown an unfriendly passivity toward *aliya.*" Odd, isn't it? When I raised the question of actively promoting *aliya* in the Albuquerque pro-Israel committee at its monthly session, I was informed that one was apples and the other oranges, that pro-Israel activity and *aliya* were two separate things. One grumpy pundit invited me to set up my own *aliya* assistance committee, if I was so eager to promote emigration to Israel. Another solicitously advised me not to become involved, because it was all a can of worms. Fancy that.

By accident or by design of the immortal gods, as Caesar was wont to say, succinct and sapient Caesar, Lester in his first year at NYU enrolled in Eda Lou's course in freshman composition. He displayed such exceptional aptitude in fulfillment of his assignments, style so far beyond that of his pedestrian peers, the pre-meds and pre-dents, as he humorously adverted to his classmates, that Eda Lou invited him to membership in the University Literary Arts Club, sponsored by both herself and another English instructor. Poems began to flow from Lester's pen. On biblical themes first (for Lester had been a Sunday School teacher at fashionable Temple Emanuel on Fifth Avenue), dramatic monologues in the manner of Browning: of the herald coming to announce the death of Saul; of the Hebrew faker foisting on credulous Judean yokels the blood-stained stone that slew Goliath. From biblical themes he turned to romantic ones, love poems R thought— he wasn't sure—of dim water lilies swooning in cobalt pools; of a slight figure yawing in the wind of Washington Square Park; of brief and agate conversations in a corridor. In the delicious privacy of his own room, Lester read his poems aloud for R's benefit. R ransacked his wits for suitable comments, but rarely could extract more than an awed and lumpen: "Gee!" It was like assisting at an apotheosis to behold his high school chum visibly transfigured into a poet.

Soon after his admission to the Arts Club, Lester was nominated for the position of secretary and unanimously elected. How admirably his friend filled the new position R had early opportunity to observe. Lester seemed the very picture of lyric youth, as in cummerbund and open-collared shirt, poised and dazzling, he escorted faculty members and prominent guests to their seats about the candlelit tables of the tearoom. It was then that R was introduced to Eda Lou. She was dark, petite, and grave—and yet with ready smile of solicitude for his tongue-tied confusion. Lester's other secretarial duties entailed writing and addressing dozens of postcards to members and guests of the Arts Club announcing the place and time of the next meeting. Here R felt more at home; he cooperated eagerly in this minor drudgery, and the two friends sat about Lester's large study table in the evening exchanging witticisms to relieve the tedium of the task. As time passed, something peculiar began to happen. Momentarily, under his craggy copying of the model invitation set before him, R seemed to glimpse startling cajolings, inveiglings implicated in his own handwriting, as if the postcard were an imperfect palimpsest.

"I have something to tell you," Lester said one evening, a dull weekend evening muffled within the folds of autumn. His parents were away, his buxom, lively, hospitable mother, and his spare, close-cropped, taciturn father, retired textile merchant, away visiting their married daughters, Lester's older sisters. The family, with R now an inveterate guest, had dined on their usual Saturday night fare of lamb chops and creamed spinach, served by Serada, homeliest of pug-nosed Hungarian serving maids (who had retired to her room); and R had played excerpts of Schubert's *Unfinished Symphony* on one side of the gramophone record, and Caruso and Gigli singing the duet from *La Forza del Destino* on the other.

"Something to tell me?" R lolled luxuriantly in the billowy, black leather armchair.

"Yes, something I want to tell you in confidence."

R had never seen his friend so subdued and harried. It was true, as Lester's mother had remarked anxiously at supper: he looked peaked. His lips, whose fullness he was always trying to diminish by sucking them inward, were now parted and slack. He seemed exhausted by meditation, almost ascetic. His cheekbones stood out, deepening the sockets of his eyes. A stray lock had left his fine straight black hair and hovered over his brow. Slim and tall, he leaned on the gramophone cover, and with his toe fretted the pattern on the Turkish rug.

"If you don't want to—" R shifted in the armchair. "I mean it's all right if you don't— "

"No. I want to." Lester swayed in affirmation. "I stayed with Eda Lou last night."

Words so incredible they seemed without provenance, refractory in their own context. "You stayed with your instructor in English?"

"Yes."

An instructor at a university, soon to be elevated to assistant professor, so Lester had disclosed—someone in the empyrian of her Ph.D had . . . had . . . and he was only a freshman! How untrammeled the world seemed all at once, topsy-turvy, careening.

"I am in love with her," Lester was saying.

In love—the words spurned reality, the framed Corot reproductions on the wall, the green sofa with the antimacassars, the halos of the electric sconces on the gold wallpaper, the windows occluded by night. In love. The words boomed within R's skull as if he had uttered them at a late hour, and alone. If only his mind weren't forever groping in its phlegmatic murk—if only for once it would skip free into clarity. He shook his head.

"And she loves me," Lester said. "I want to marry her."

"Jesus, Lester, you're not telling me— I mean maybe I'm thick. When did all this happen?"

"I've been in love with her for a long time."

"All right. So?"

"I've been wanting to tell her since mid-terms. I want to take her away from that dumb bunch of pre-meds and pre-dents she has to lecture to, who don't give a damn, and don't understand any of it. They have no sensitivity. Nothing. Dumb wisecracks about her after class."

"Yeah, but I know—"

"I want to protect her. She's so fine. She's so gentle. I just want to hold her in my arms."

Mountainous incongruity piled up in the path of an engulfing ardor.

"How dear she is! So tiny, so dainty!" Lester's large hand curved toward its thumb in an all but closed circle. And above it, his ecstatic countenance in which tears gleamed unshed in his brown eyes.

"Jesus." R averted his gaze.

Lester snuffed, fidgeted for self-control. And silence masked itself in a deep hum, like the whirring of a sling.

"We met last night to set the date for the next Arts Club meeting," said Lester.

"Maybe you shouldn't tell me," R pleaded.

"Why not? You're my best friend. I know I can trust you."

"It isn't that. I feel as if I—I hardly know what."

"Please! You're the only one I can talk to."

"Well, I want to know. That isn't the reason."

"St. Marks on the Bowery is where she lives." Lester opened his eyes wide. "Cute apartment. White walls. Too long a walk from the university, she said."

"Well?"

"And we started to talk about my career. My—what do you call it? —promise as a poet. Musical sense. Depth. Maturity. It was about eleven o'clock." He shrugged slightly. "I happened to mention that John Warner encouraged my writing also. She knew it. It was obvious, she said, that Warner was bent on seducing me. She believed she ought to warn me—"

"You?" R sat up in the armchair. "He's a man!"

"I know," LW said impatiently. "I never bothered to tell you. He put his arm around me one summer night when Eda Lou was still in Europe and turned out the lights. But I had a Camel going. If he'd made a pass at my fly, I would have branded him. I told her I wasn't interested in homosexuals. I—I started to cry. I couldn't help it."

Time seemed like a distant rumor.

"I said she was the only one I was interested in. She was the only one I wanted. I loved her. Oh, I knew I was a freshman and she was an instructor. But that wasn't the way I felt about her. I felt that she was a woman and I loved her." He was close to tears again. "She came over and sat on the arm of my chair—she has those big wicker armchairs. She put her tiny hand on my shoulder, and suddenly the whole place went white, pure white, and I—" Lester's fingers moved spasmodically. "I called up home. I said I was staying with a friend."

Again R shook his head—strenuously.

"Why?"

"I feel like I'm butting in—where I don't belong."

"No, you're not. You're the only one I can talk to. You're the only one," Lester said with sudden vehemence, "without middle-class standards."

"Without what?" The question barely formed itself into speech, remained internalized: middle-class standards? Standards? What the hell did that mean?

"You know what my upbringing is." Lester held out the lapel of his fine English jacket. "I'm coddled, pampered. They know how I'm supposed to behave. Your parents don't, do they?"

"And that's middle class?"

"Of course it is. If I were to marry Eda Lou, I'd shock them out of their wits. An older woman. If I threw up my dental career, they'd curl up and die; not only my parents, my sisters, brothers-in-law. We're a tight-knit family. I'd have to break with them all. Reject them. Wound them! And I don't know whether I've got the strength of will. And yet that's what I've got to do. That's what I want to do."

"What?"

"Become like you."

R could feel drought encroach on his open mouth. "Like me!"

"Why not! I can work in the summer for my clothes, the way you do. Pot-wallop in a summer resort, help put on skits on the borscht circuit."

"But I'm from the dumps," said R. "How can you?"

"It's a matter of will." Lester insisted. "It's a matter of will. That's what the whole thing depends on."

"And you'll give up dentistry?"

"Give up dentistry. Quit NYU. Transfer to CCNY. Not ask my folks for a nickel. They won't throw me out I guess. And what if they do? Maybe that's what I need."

"Jesus."

"There's only one thing I'm afraid of."

"Only one?" R quipped weakly.

"They won't get her into trouble in her job at the university." Lester clasped hands prayerfully.

"Why?"

"I'm sure they suspect. I'm sure they'll ask *you*." He stared at R.

"Me?"

"Yes."

"What do I know about it?"

Lester nodded approvingly, "God, if only I saw myself with my B.A. Teach. Marry Eda Lou. Write. But it's such a damn long way still! And she said it would be folly if I did anything else."

"Like what?"

"Quit college. Get a job on a tramp steamer. Like O'Neill. Nobody has to know I'm Jewish. Or who my family is. Learn by hard knocks."

"You big galoot!" They chaffered at each other, giggling hilariously as they rode in the rush of fresh air on the platform of the clattering Eighth Avenue El—keeping clear of the low iron gates when the crabbed Irish trainman snapped them open at a station, his gloved hands grabbing the burnished steel lever handles. "That big galoot, third row, fourth seat, stand up! I was sure he meant me," Lester said.

They had sat next to each other, two in a single seat in the overcrowded classroom, because Miss Pickens (slim Pickens), teacher of Elocution 7, was absent, and Dr. Ackley, head of the Elocution department, had temporarily combined her class with his. And R, seeking a seat with only a single occupant, had steered toward the one in which the elegant Gentile youth was sitting. And jabbered with such abandon so long after the class had been called to order, intent on ingratiating himself with his new Gentile acquaintance, that gray-maned and thespian Dr. Ackley struck an outraged stance, and in stentorian tones declaimed: "That big galoot, third row, fourth seat, stand up." And to his everlasting credit, Lester had bravely begun to obey. "Not you!" Dr. Ackley thundered. "That big galoot beside you!" And red-faced and cringing, R had scrambled to his feet—and been immediately expelled from the class with the injunction that he return for condign punishment afterward. He just barely managed to beg off from the penalty that otherwise would have been meted out, that of bringing a parent to school. "He was so—" R gesticulated in humble apology; and out of desperation decided to risk the strange appeal. "I never met anybody Gentile who could be a friend until now. I got— I forgot myself. I'm sorry, Dr. Ackley." He could sense that the ruse had worked, if ruse it was. "You ever behave that way in a class of mine," Dr. Ackley shook a menacing finger—and dismissed R.

The classes were divided again, and the two youths separated, but a few days later they found each other, with gusto born of the common danger they had run. And after school they walked east toward transportation, R describing his narrow escape, to their common mirth. Just before they separated that afternoon—Lester for the Eighth Avenue line that would take him to the near Bronx, and R reluctantly toward the Broadway line a block further east that would take him to Lenox Avenue. "You're Jewish, aren't you?" Lester asked.

It was the question that R already anticipated with apprehension, the decisive question against which he had to brace; it was the question that would mean an alteration in their acquaintance, perhaps its end. "Yes." R tried to admit the stigma candidly. "I'm Jewish." But to his utter amazement: "So am I," said Lester.

"You're fooling," R tried to deflect the other's painful jest—with a kind of sympathetic appreciation that Lester was sidling out of an untenable situation.

"Of course I'm Jewish."

R wavered, yearning for the other's words to be true, for the unassailable interlocking of their condition. But how could his words be true? R gaped openly at his newfound friend: that regularity of features, oval face, that flawless, dappled sheen of skin, his irreproachable speech, easy and assured manner—and his clothes—the superb weave of the fawn-colored jacket and tweed knickers, the soft glow of brown brogans. He couldn't be Jewish. "Anh!" R scoffed.

"What do you mean? What do you think I am?"

"You're a Christian," said R.

"I'm Jewish. I'm Hungarian-Jewish. My folks belong to Temple Emanuel."

There was no rejecting his protestation. "Gee!" R breathed rapturously. "Boy! You are?" Lester Winter didn't act Jewish, didn't look Jewish, and even smoked a Dunhill pipe. What a wonderful friend!

And now they rode on the clattering Eighth Avenue El, R having gladly seized the chance to be with his friend a half hour longer, though the trip would mean ten minutes more of trudging home.

Windier than windy Troy it was, and as heady—intoxicating them with fresh air as they rode outdoors in the rolling coffins, their gray fedoras jammed down over their brows, jackets buttoned against the lash of the gale, and leather brief cases pressed like shields against their chests. And down below, the seedy storefronts slurred by, so sadly soon incandescent, in the secession of autumn light, in the shadow of the El— in contrast to the joy he felt. Pity stirred him for the humble and forlorn denizens of the passing facades who sat like chess pieces, flattened behind the window pane, as if in pocket chess cards. Pity stirred him at the prodigality of his heyday and the dearth of theirs, their lackluster vigils biding advents that would never arrive, their gross martyrdoms, like his mother's. But Lester seemed not to notice. "What are you going to major in when you get to college?" he shouted above the racket of the train.

"Huh?"

"What are you going to take up in college?"

"Oh. I'm going to be a biology teacher."

"In high school?"

"Yes."

"They don't earn very much, do they?"

"Compared to *my* jobs?" R tried to force an inconsequential, comic note into his answer. He had earlier regaled Lester with accounts of his menial jobs—his Park and Tilford delivery boy job, cleaning out the miry elevator pit in his best blue suit, his chore boy job mopping the tiled floor of Bylos's corner drugstore, where he had first learned the expression *elbow grease,* his job at the Polo Grounds hustling soda.

"But not as a career," Lester reproved. "High school teaching doesn't pay very well."

"No," R agreed faltering, feeling a vague sense of disappointment. His friend's insistence on common sense, on the practical, the prudent, marred the elation of the present, marred the incalculable future of their nascent friendship. Only yesterday, when in new-minted acquaintance, they had sauntered east along motley Fifty-Ninth Street, the tenements alternating with medical schools, Lester had sung snatches of the *Pirates of Penzance* in which he had played a part last year. He had such a true rollicking voice, unerring and blithe. "A pair of socks, a pair of socks, a most ingenious pair of socks." And he had dwelled on poetry, had spoken of modern verse, with which he was serenely at home, audacious, unsanctioned modern verse, too contemporary for school assignment: of Untermeyer's *Anthology*—had R read it? No.

Lester actually owned a copy: "What Thomas said in a Pub," by James Stephens. *"I saw God! Do you doubt it? Do you dare to doubt it?"* recited with such airy, unconstrained gesture that in the dilapidated doorway of a tenement, tattered black youngsters, like stamens surrounding a gangling adolescent girl, squirmed and giggled at the sight, and the crippled adult on the stoop pivoted on the rude staff of his homemade crutch, and glistened with mirth. And Edna Millay's poetry—Lester owned copies of her books too; he would be happy to lend R any of them. *"My candle burns at both its ends, it will not last the night. . . . We were very tired, we were very merry. . . ."* And all so perceptive, so intimate, with such authority, as if their domain were his. Of Sandburg's deceptive simplicity: *"The fog came on little cat feet. . . ."* Of Vachel Lindsay's elemental rhythms: *"Fat black bucks in a wine-barrel room."* And R himself beginning to feel giddy, the street opening like a trumpet, and buildings skewing about in fabulous surmise, and all the humdrum perspectives of dinginess plying a new latency, an awakening.

But that was yesterday. Today Lester was talking about income, about earnings, about careers and decent livings. R felt a sudden secret lift, as if his very improvidence harbored something precious, some uncompromised latitude. How explain it? He couldn't. "I'm a *malamut*," he decoyed whimsically. Lester laughed, as he would at every new Yiddish fragment he heard; he knew so few "What's that? An Alaskan husky?"

"Oh no. He's the old guy who slaps you around in the cheder—the little dump where you learn Hebrew. You never went to one?"

"I went to Sunday School in Temple Emanuel. In Bermuda I didn't go anywhere."

"Sunday School?" R marveled. Cross streets slashed into the continuum of tenement masonry, nondescript vistas of populated sidewalks and untidy fire escapes, swiftly swallowed up by tenement masonry.

"I thought only Gentiles went to Sunday School."

"Oh no. I'm teaching a class of children there myself."

"Oh. So what are *you* going to take up in college?"

"Dentistry." A trace of preening inflected his voice.

"Dentistry!"

"My brother-in-law Sheldon, who's a dentist, thinks I'd make a very good one. I have good hands, and I like using them. I'm sure Sheldon would make room for me in his office as soon as I got my D.D.S."

And once again in the muted rumble pervading the apartment, the book in his lap, and slumped, R listened incuriously to the lovers, listened and ignored. How the hell could they? What could they? Too tenuous for him, true love and its delicate caress, too remote from his own hasty and carnal snatching. Never mind. Never mind. A crowd flowed over Eighth Street pavement, so many— And day by day, he was more certain of it than ever; he was never going to be a biology teacher, a high school teacher, never, never. He had already told Mom, to her anguished consternation: "*Gott soll mir helfen!* For this I've slaved? For this I endured *him?* Ah, that you ever attached yourself to that wealthy, high-flown Lester Winter! He's undone you." I'm sorry, Mom, I don't want to hurt you. It's gone dead, Mom, the whole subject. I have no mood for it. "Then other studies, another career. What?" And at the shake of his head, she became incensed. "You'll be as nothing, dregs! Who will support you, tell me? Lunatic though he is, can anyone blame him, wanting to be rid of you, with his narrow shoulders and meager strength, a noodle-porter all these years, nurturing you on ten-cent gratuities. He'll throw you out. Go wallow in that Village sty. What will become of you?" And there now was his answer—how pitilessly it forced its way into R's mind, how impersonally it preempted all sentiment: *On that divan or bed.* I can't tell you right now, Mom, words formed behind his lips; I can't tell you right now, but I know.

What in hell was I to do? R leaned back from the typewriter in scowling introspection. What? Wrenched away, and quite haphazardly from the ghetto's spontaneity, the ghetto's conformity—and security—where you were Abie or Izzy or Mendel, unaware of distinction, almost indistinguishable in the homogeneity of cheder and street, wrenched away from all this, and dumped into tough Irish Harlem, where you were suddenly—and sullenly—Jewboy. Isolated intruder into the savage sunlight of summer, all unadroit at baseball or handball or marbles or tops, unknown and goyish competences in the ambience you had left: a ham at everything. So one got a sense of twisting about from old to new dispensations: Jess Willard was Irish, Mayor Walker was Irish, the New York Giants were Irish. "Every virago with only a single tusk in her head boasts she is Oirish," Mom mimicked them. Lords of the world. So one abandoned the old, in precarious ingratiation with the new; and alien even among the few Jewish adolescents in the street, who quit school early, got their working papers, and began their singleminded pursuit of fortune, he conjured up a world elsewhere,

elsewhere—the kid with the library books under his arm crossing Mount Morris Park at dusk, the kid who had learned the knack of trying to match words that would vie with the pale star in the limpid sky above the rocky monadnock to the right, with its unused fire-warning bell tower on top, words as limpid and holy as the scene. Strange. The second novel that had continually peeped through his writing of the first, that had recommended itself as a natural successor to the first—and was never written because Marxism or Communism fell like a giant shunt across his career, that second novel would have treated of just that theme: the youth's search for the world elsewhere: how the immigrant urchin who had lost the primacy of his ghetto haven and jettisoned faith and precept in the turbulence of Harlem, won another haven, a superior one, he thought, a permanent and inviolable one, in the world of letters, in the world of art. Not to be. Shortcircuited. Aborted. One scene only remained in his mind, because he had already written it, vivid as the reality itself: of his helping Mom in the bare kitchen of their new Harlem flat empty the sugar barrel in which their crockery came packed, wrapped in Yiddish newsprint. No further.

For now it is February, he told himself, and the wild sunflowers, so rank and saucy in their prime, have shrunk to rusty, brittle buttons, foraged clean by migrant birds. It is February, and the snow lingers daubed like waste plaster in last year's undergrowth. That time when elm tree branches, bare bough and twig, hibernate in smoky immobility. It is 1977, not 1925. Oh, if only I could find that note once I jotted down seated on a bus-stop bench opposite the University of New Mexico on a Sunday afternoon when no human was visible on Central Avenue not enclosed in the glass and metal of an automobile—and my arthritis gave me pause, but more than that, the sudden insight into my youthful prospects breached memory, became the present where I sat between the campus and Sandias: impoverished, dreary and hopeless youth. Ah, could I but find that entry—he clawed at his elbow's itch. But what's the odds? Only she could save me, salvage the splintered debris I called a person. . . .

Yes, I do ask, dear Marie, and, please, will somebody tell us, lead us by the hand, we who cling to Zion for renewal, we who are for Israel, we prodigals returning from debacle, we who are sated with negation. . . .

Eda Lou sat up first. "Sometimes you look like an ancient Hebrew prophet."

"I?" R grinned. "Raven never flitting."

"You missed your vocation." She smoothed silk stockings on trim calves.

"My rabbi came to the house to tell my mother I was going to be a great rabbi someday. So Mom gave him a glass of seltzer."

"Seltzer?"

"Fizz water."

"Oh, soda water."

"Yes. Out of a glass siphon. I used to pity the poor delivery man who climbed groaning up four flights of stairs with a full case of bottles."

"You two have such utterly different recollections." She looked down fondly at Lester.

"Don't we though?" He had been listening indolently and now rose from the couch.

"Yes, you remember Bermuda and darkies singing World War I songs, just as clearly as R remembers soda water siphons."

"I guess that's what makes us such great friends." Lester buttoned his collar and pulled up his tie. "It's getting to be two years since old man Ackley bawled you out in Elocution 7 for whispering to me." He came over to R and rumpled his hair affectionately. "Raven never flitting." And looking down at the book in R's lap, Lester wailed in mock anguish. "It's an *idée fixe*. What's got into you? Eda Lou, he's reading 'The Waste Land' again."

Eda Lou tugged prettily at the tassles of her brown dress. "Let's buy him a copy." She addressed her reflection in the mirror.

"Oh no," R protested. "Waste of money, gee. I've practically memorized it."

"Why don't you try other poets?" Lester's long arm swept out toward the bookcase. "Taggard, Frost, Aiken, Teasdale—Eda Lou has a whole shelf full."

"I don't learn that way," R said stubbornly.

"Learn? You're supposed to enjoy."

"For Christ sake, how am I going to enjoy when the guy's suffering? He's in plight. Excuse me, Eda Lou," R added. "I didn't know that before about poetry."

"Oh, that's all right." She smiled. "How do you know it now?"

"The gas house," R ticked the items on his fingers. "Like the one on East Fourteenth Street. That's how I felt. Scared. The tar on the river when you're alone on the dock. The dull canal—the language itself tells you."

"Oh, yes."

"I think we'd better clear out," said Lester. "You've got all the Sitwells to prepare."

"Oh no. Please join me. I'm going to make some raisin toast and coffee. Does anyone like cinnamon and brown sugar?"

"I'll just have cinnamon," said Lester. "Just a bite. I have a party tonight."

"You, R?"

"I never heard of such a thing. But I'll try it. When I told my mother I drank black coffee here—without chicory or milk—she said I'd go crazy."

Eda Lou laughed. "I'll get everything ready."

"May I help?" Lester offered.

"Oh no. Thanks."

Lester dropped into a chair and shook his head uncomprehendingly. "One poet, one poem."

"No, I got plenty of time. I read the 'Love Song of Prufrock' too," R countered. "Why does he construct out of rags and patches, as you always say? A crazy quilt. Because that's how life looks to him."

"Well, that's obvious enough," Lester countered with a certain asperity. "I never demanded paraphrasable poems. And I'm not saying it's a hoax, like the Bynner-Ficke stunt. All right, disillusionment. But the poem lacks a center, any kind of syntheses. It's a mosaic, and not even his own mosaic."

"Yeah, because it's out of control," said R.

"What's out of control?" Lester asked.

"Life. Everything. It's like a cracked insulator."

"I don't think I ever heard it put that way before." Eda Lou gravely began filling the urn-shaped electric percolator under the faucet.

Her encouragement daunted him. "I mean if it was all coherent," R fumbled, "fused together into a whole, it almost would have been contradictory to what he was trying to say."

"Well, how many times can you read 'London Bridge is falling down'?" Lester demanded satirically. "Rats! He's promoting the idea that all meaning is gone out of life, and I resent it. He's trying to impale romanticism, and he's really impaling all beauty, just as he does in Prufrock. If he has his way the youthful romantic poet is never going to get a chance to develop. That's what I object to. I can feel it in the lapse of my own writing—whenever I try to write a lyric nowadays, it's choked off."

"That's not entirely Eliot's fault." Eda Lou finished leaning pieces of toast around the dark frustrum of the toaster and stood licking a dainty finger tip. "Yeats said he stopped writing a poem in the middle, as soon as he read 'The Waste Land.' "

"Because he started a fad, and it's all over the place."

"It's the other way round," R maintained. "You mean Eliot?"

"I scarcely think it's a fad," Eda Lou said soberly.

"All right then, I'm jealous. Incidentally, he's none too complimentary about Jews," he addressed R.

"Neither am I."

"That's a joke?"

"No, I'm serious."

"I always have to explain that to my classes," Eda Lou moderated, as she turned the toast. "He loathes cities, he loathes modernity, progress. And the Jew has become a symbol for all of it." She laughed lightly. "I don't think he likes women either."

There was a mollified silence.

"Is everyone ready?" she asked.

"Excuse me a minute." Lester stood up and walked briskly toward the bathroom.

"Your face always lights up when you speak about your mother," Eda Lou arranged the toast on a plate, placed fresh slices about the toaster. "I'd like to meet her."

"Huh?"

"She must be a remarkable woman."

"Well—" R hung his head. "She doesn't know how to speak English."

"Oh, I think we'd understand each other." She left the toaster and took a few steps toward him. "I wish you'd feel free to come here on your own. I know it's an awkward time to say it. You don't have to depend on Lester."

"I—" He stared up at her.

"Yes. Obviously I don't want to hurt Lester. But I know I can rely on your discretion." She tilted her head in bird-like admonition: "Child," she said. "You have so much to offer." Then she walked back to the kitchenette. "Have you ever tried to teach your mother to speak English?"

"No," R said slowly. "I never thought of it. We always spoke Yiddish. We live in a small world. So—"

She shook her head and turned the toast.

Lester came out of the bathroom. "Mmm, that smells good. Too good. I've got that party tonight. My oldest niece's birthday. Sure you don't need any help?"

"No. Just sit down anywhere. I'll play hostess."

Lester sat down. "I was just thinking. I still don't understand why you're so interested in 'The Waste Land.'"

"I've already told you."

"But you haven't. When?"

"Please, no more discussion of T.S. Eliot." Eda Lou brought the tray to Lester, who helped himself with his usual adroitness.

"Suits me. But may I ask why 'The Waste Land' should be important to a prospective biology teacher. Is that within bounds?"

Simultaneously she turned toward R, tray in hand. "The sugared toast is on the right," she smiled.

"Oh boy!" R helped himself. "Gee, there I go again. I said I'd cut out saying *gee* and *oh boy*, and I keep saying it."

Lester took a bite of toast, munched, and dabbed at his lips. "Well?"

"Well, what?"

"What's it got to do with biology?"

"Biology?" R proffered perplexity by a display of bitten, brown-sugared toast. "You mean my saying *gee* and *oh boy?* You told me yourself. And I smack my lips all the time."

Eda Lou laughed outright.

"No, no!" Lester sipped his coffee hastily. "I was talking about—" He indicated the black-bound volume on the sidetable. "That and biology."

"We agreed not to talk about that anymore," R complained.

"Yes, we did," Eda Lou corroborated.

"All right. Skip it."

"Beside, I'm not going to be a biology teacher."

"You're not? Since when?"

R shrugged.

"What happens to your B.S. degree?"

"In shambles, I guess."

"That *is* news," said Eda Lou.

"T.S. Eliot have anything to do with that?" Lester asked.

"Oh, for Christ sake!" R burst out. "All I've gotten is a flock of Cs and Ds. I'm failing my conditional in trig. I won't see a bio course in a year. Listen, what are you harping on this for? You don't like Eliot, OK. But that's how the world seems to me."

"Because you have no standards."

"So *you* have. And what can you do with them?"

"I really don't see what all the fuss is about," Eda Lou intervened. "Do either of you know what you're arguing about?"

They were both silent. "I'm a disgruntled romantic," said Lester.

"No, you're not." Eda Lou came over and put her arm about his shoulder. "You're a sweet, sensitive, gentle lad. And I don't like to see you upset because of some transient literary crisis. We all go through them."

"I'm not upset. And I'm not going through a literary crisis, transient or otherwise."

"You're sure?"

"Not in the least. I haven't staked my life on being a poet." He slipped into his jacket. "I was just looking at a Brancusi the other day. And thinking. There are other things I can do—Ready, R?"

"Oh, sure." He licked cinnamon sugar crumbs from his mouth.

"You've hardly eaten your toast, either of you."

"Oh, I have that party. Want us to help clean up?"

"Oh, no, no."

They got into their overcoats. Arching her neck winsomely, she surveyed herself in the mirror.

"Good night, honey," Lester bent over her tenderly.

"Good night, lad," she kissed his lips. "Enjoy yourself at the party."

"Oh," he deprecated. "It's a tutti-frutti skitsoid." His pun amused him. "Some people like banana splits and other things," he half-sang, half-intoned, "But I like my chocolate soda. Ice cream parlor operetta with an assist from uncle."

Her forced smile darkened her features. "Good night, R."

"Good night, Eda Lou."

She ushered them through the hall to the outer door, shrank back involuntarily as she opened the door on the cold and towering stridor of Eighth Street.

Tuesday. February 8, 1977 (his seventy-first birthday, deliberately suppressed). The weather fair, the temperature seasonable, the mercury rising celeritously from twenty degrees at 7:00 A.M. to fifty-five degrees by mid-afternoon.

Dinner at the Sandys'.

Now then, when he and M arrived at the apartment complex in

which the Sandys lived, the security guard at the entrance to the courtyard directed them to turn to the left where they would find visitors' parking space. "But don't go any further than the garbage bin," he instructed. "That's private."

R drove in the direction the other indicated—and found only a long row of numbered spaces, no garbage bin of any sort, and no parking provisions for visitors. In a fury, he spun the car about and drove back to the entrance gate to demand an explanation. Almost at the same time that he reached the gate and was calling to the guard in his cubicle, cheerful Dan Sandy arrived. "There are vacant parking slots over there," he pointed toward a whitewashed fence at the opposite end of the court. The better to help guide R to the place, Dan got into the car, remarking mildly that the guard was a newcomer to the job, and hadn't familiarized himself with the layout of the courtyard. After R parked the car, and with Dan leading the way, the three walked back in the direction of the entrance; close to it was a flight of stairs leading up to a block of second-story apartments, and at the top of the stairs stood their hostess, Vicky Sandy, greeting them as they climbed. Moments later they entered the apartment, were introduced to the other guests, and served refreshments, scotch and soda for him, for M, vodka and tonic. Conversation followed.

Once more R encountered Dan's sanguine belief in the indefinite duration of the Diaspora. He granted that Judaism would be modified in the years to come, but nevertheless, the Diaspora would endure, he insisted. The contrary would be true, R maintained, and brought to bear what to him were irrefutable proofs of his contention: the virtual disappearance of Yiddish as the common language of Jewry in the Diaspora; the waning of the religious sanction that had once bonded Judaism together, the waning of a belief in God; the Nazi liquidation of the great Jewish centers in Eastern Europe, once an inexhaustible reservoir of orthodoxy; the exodus of Jews from the lands of their Diaspora to Israel; the ever-increasing tendency of Jews to assimilate into their non-Jewish social environment, as evidenced by the fifty percent rate of intermarriage among Jewish college youth—and ninety percent of Jewish youth attended college; the declining birthrate of the Jewish population, even below replacement levels. So what was to prevent the Diaspora's disintegration, R demanded. Certainly not those freakish sects with their earcurls and fur hats and fantastic observances. How could anyone persist in believing that the Diaspora had a viable future, or would even be extant a century hence?

"Oh, no, we have had assimilation in every epoch, and we are still here." Dan asserted. "It is Israel that has no viable future. I take a dim view of Israel's future."

"A dim view!" R expostulated, allowing the argument to shift ground. "You mean you disapprove of Israel's existence?"

"No," Dan rejoined warmly. He still spoke with the slight furriness of a residual foreign accent. "I mean I have little hope for the future of Israel."

"Oh, that's different," said R. "Dim view has an overtone of disapproval to me."

"I didn't mean it that way. I meant that I was afraid of another holocaust of Jews in Israel."

"That's always a possibility," R conceded. "I don't think it will happen."

"But the corruption in high places in Israel is frightening," Dan urged. "The cynicism among the rank and file in Israel is growing—you can see it in the emigration from Israel. It more than balances the immigration. And the strikes. Every day a new union walkout. And every day Arab military strength grows with Arab petro-dollars. How is Israel going to survive?"

"As it did before," R clung stubbornly to his view. "By its own valor and superior technology, and because of Arab disunity. And Arab rivalries."

"But on Israel they always agree."

"That's always been true. But despite that—"

"You see, there are only three million Jews in Israel. And in the rest of the world there are more than ten million Jews in Diaspora. We don't put all our eggs in one basket. That's where you should look for the Jewish future."

"And I don't," R retorted brusquely.

Worth meditating on, R reflected, his attention drawn to a flock of crows parading over the bare sienna patches of the adjoining property outside his study window. How the light gleamed on their ebony plumage, on the feathers of that raucous sentinel perched on the fence post, and stretching his full length to caw. *That time of year thou mayest in me behold. . . ."* The question was, R asked himself: did he really want the Diaspora to survive? To survive beyond its role of sustaining the young, beleaguered state of Israel until it had at least won for itself a secure niche in the Middle East? He wasn't sure. He really didn't care. Too long had he been antagonized by his own people, too long severed from them, too long disdainful of their pursuits, their exile traits, their senseless observances. Or was he still galled by his detestation of his father, plagued by Freudian canker? Or just the sight of Pop pinching Mom's arm black and blue because of the inelegant way she sliced salami in that little delicatessen on 116th Street that Pop owned—and failed at. R had reunited, realigned himself, rather, with Diaspora Jewry solely for the sake of Israel. On the state of Israel alone were his loyalties fixed, his loyalties locked. He felt none of the sorrow and alarm of his fellow Jews at the likely disap- pearance of the Diaspora. They couldn't have both ends and the middle. They had a country, to which they were at liberty to return: Israel. And if they chose not to—farewell! Might the transition from exile to adopted homeland be without travail, without ordeal.

At all events, by the time the party ended, mollified and diverted by cordiality, good food, wine, and animated exchange of opinion, R fancied that M too had been rendered equally mellow. And with Dan benevolently escorting them back to their parking place, all three got into the car—the engine balky still at backing when cold, and R uneasy because his new contact lens caused glittering rowels to spring from every street lamp and headlight, and hence a little inept at handling the vehicle—. Soothed by Dan, R finally managed to get the car under control, and drove as far as the gate. There he bade his genial host a grateful good night.

"How do you feel?" R made stock conjugal inquiry after safely negotiating the left turn around the median strip on Menaul.

"Well . . ." Her tone of voice was disconcertingly level.

"Well what?"

"How should I feel when I'm yelled at and told to shut up?"

"When was that?" He found a new place to grasp the steering wheel.

"This evening."

"This evening?" He repeated with staunch incredulity. "When did I tell you to shut up?"

"When you turned around and drove back to talk to the guard."

"*I* did?"

"Yes. I tried to tell you I just saw the garbage bin."

He drove on for several blocks silently.

"That's pretty brutal treatment to get from your own husband," she resumed. "It's a kind of battering without physical contact. I don't see why I deserve it."

"You don't." He eased up on the throttle, slowed the car down in order the better to concentrate his attention on his thoughts. "I don't recall saying it—which is even worse than if I did."

"I don't know what to make of it."

"I don't either. I've been feeling myself becoming more obdurate, more brutal, as you say, with every passing day. I wonder why."

"I do too. And I'm tired of being the target of it."

Once back in their mobile home, M ensconced herself resolutely on the black vinyl sofa beside the alabaster reading lamp. And with her long legs in their speckled slacks raised to mid-rung of the antique mahogany step ladder (Berger exercises, she called them, to counteract her varicosity), the *University of Chicago Magazine* in her lap, she began reading. Light from the lamp shone on her features, aging, but no less refined and distinguished than the first day he had seen her at the piano long ago in the artists' colony of Yaddo, no less patrician. (She had been fretting lately about the increasing height of her brow caused by her thinning hair and wondering if extra large goggles might mitigate the growing expanse of forehead.) Her hair, blond-gray or gray-blond, evaded description, no matter how long he gazed at it; it remained ambiguous in hue, something like the underside of a falcon's wing in flight.

He felt agitated and deeply perturbed, at once fierce and resistive. "I seem to be in a crisis," he finally said, speaking as if he were enclosed in a peculiarly hard and frigid aura that made it almost impossible for him to reach outward. "Either *I* am in a crisis, or *we* are in a crisis. I've never felt this way about our relationship before. It almost seems possible that we would be best off if we separated."

"I don't see how we can avoid it, as long as you keep up this way."

"Nor do I. Jesus!" he exclaimed, and he seemed to shrivel within the silence that followed. "I can't believe it could happen after forty years."

"I wish I could help." She lowered the magazine to rest on her thighs. "But I just don't know what's bothering you."

"No."

"The way you've been behaving seems crazy."

"I agree with you."

"But I don't know what I can do about it. Overlook it, I suppose. I think the Israel trip may have a great deal to do with it."

"I think so too."

"You're afraid to go, but you're committed to going. Is that the trouble? You don't have to go, you know. You're under no obligation. You can call the whole thing off."

"No, I want to go. I have to go. I feel as if my—as if the next stage of my development, of whatever is left to develop, personally, creatively, my fulfillment depends on my going. On the contrary, I have a sense of urgency about going that overcomes any—" he groped for the right word—"any anxiety about going. I'm not afraid to go."

"Then do you know what it is? What *is* bothering you?"

"I think the trouble is I decided to go to Israel without you—as I told you." His eyes lifted to the ceiling where each chromed Phillips screw-head winked down at him from the centers of the rows of plastic daisies that supported the white fiber board. "A kind of Ulysses urge." And then he muttered under his breath, "Jewlysses."

"Oh, I'm not going to pine," she had evidently not caught his abominable pun. "I've already made plans to stay. I have things to do, friends to see. I have adjusted to the idea, if that's all that's bothering you."

"No. What's bothering me is my decision. It's boomeranged."

"That's not my fault."

"I realize that. I would like to revoke it."

"Oh you would? Then you think I'm at your beck and call?" Her composure remained feminine but strict. "The other day I was told I was not to go. Tonight I am. I'll have to think about it. You can't reverse my life that casually."

"Aw, come on," he pleaded. Humility became him poorly he knew. "I can't go there without you. It's just been some futile stab at being doughty and independent. Carried away by a burst of rampant Judaism. But it's completely illusory."

"I thought you were being rather extreme about it—and romantic too."

"Maybe. But you *will* go?"

"You really mean it this time? You're really sure?"

"Yes. Because I can't mean anything else. I can't do otherwise."

"That's very flattering."

"It is too! To confess your utter need to someone you love? What higher compliment can you pay your wife after forty years? You said yes, didn't you?"

"You know very well I'm dying to go."

"That's fine. We'll go together."

"Do you know what set you off?" she asked.

"Oh, sure."

"Aren't you going to tell me?"

"In time. You're my amanuensis, aren't you?"

She picked up her magazine. "I'll have to begin calling travel agencies. I might as well begin making inquiries right now. I doubt whether there are any package deals for two months to Israel."

Quiet of a late hour. A planet boring its way through space and time, a planet spawned out of eternal magma, swarming with existential dreamers. The mustard gold carpet between himself and his wife, the dark Steinway on the left, the buff drapes drawn, like a background behind her, all were chimeric, yet all were essential. Devoid of consolation, transitory all of it, even her wonderful constancy and tenderness—it was all limned upon oblivion. Only one thing remained incontrovertible, as incontrovertible as it was immaterial, and that was the uniqueness of the event.

Dear Mr. Kollek:

The living arrangements in the retreat at Mishkenot Sha'ananim which you are placing at our disposal, the combination of marvelous view, the tranquillity, and yet easy accessibility to Jerusalem old and new exceed anything we could have hoped for. We are both happy and excited by your generous invitation.

You mention the possibility of my meeting other people in the field of literature and sharing my knowledge and experience with them in lectures or discussion groups. I should be glad to do so, although, alas, I fear I have little to offer in this connection except observations on the vicissitudes of one who has suffered a forty-year block in his writing. Nevertheless whatever I can contribute I am eager to.

If scheduling allows, I should like my stay to begin the first of August and extend to the end of September. I trust you will notify me whether that is feasible.

Once again, please be assured of my profound gratitude. The invitation is a great honor, and a trust as well. I hope I can show that I merit it.

From my wife and me, our best wishes.

Shalom.

Report from Mishkenot Sha'ananim

October 1977

The last two pieces published by Roth in 1977, "Report from Mish-kenot Sha'ananim" and "Vale Atque Ave," were written in Israel in August and September, respectively—that is to say, at the beginning and at the end of the Roths' two-month stay as guests of the Israeli government.

As these "twin" pieces make clear, Roth at the time was entertaining the idea of "making aliya," of moving to Israel permanently. The plan never materialized, for reasons that Roth explains in one of the interviews to follow. His commitment to Israel, however, was unaffected by his decision to choose galut over aliya. It was, in fact, ill health that compelled him at the last moment to cancel advanced plans for a second, and longer, stay in Israel in the latter part of 1978.

The Roths have been invited by the government of Israel to spend August and September in Jerusalem, same place Bellow stayed in and came home with glittering chitchat. So off we go.

(letter from Albuquerque, N.M.,
May 24, 1977)

To return to an interview, catching me immediately after my leaving Israel might yield stimulating report; I would hope so and would hope too, though but scantily endowed with wit (and power of analysis), that it would prove polar opposite of Mr. Bellow. Ancient Hebrew on a sewer cover in an area where Jesus may have walked and Mary wept intrigues me much more than adroit dissection of opinions of eminent personages.

(letter from Albuquerque, N.M.,
July 6, 1977)

We were met at the airport by a car with driver who took us from Ben Gurion to Mishkenot Sha'ananim. My most salient impression in that first blur of our journey from Tel Aviv to Jerusalem—following about ten hours aboard El Al—was of the number and furious pace of vehicles on the highways. Everyone drove with what I could only describe as a kind of ferocity. It couldn't be due to the fact that gasoline costs more than two dollars a gallon here, because slower driving would certainly conserve more gas. So I don't know what the reason is. Maybe it's the ever-present danger confronting every Israeli that makes the drivers so aggressive, and yet they are skillful too.

We were cordially greeted at Mishkenot by the tall, slender director, evidently of English extraction, and by the cheerful head housekeeper. Perfectly at home in English, she showed us our new quarters. We were tactfully reminded of necessary precautions that had to be taken for our own protection, such as double locking the outside door and not leaving valuables next to open windows on that same public side. The young director advised us in crisp English that on this first day in Israel we ought to take a shower and a nap to rest up, and then at about eight o'clock in the evening (which would be noon in Albuquerque) patronize the charming restaurant nearby, actually within a few steps of our door, and have our dinner there, even though—as he understated—the prices were a bit high. A bit high they certainly were, though the service and the ambience of the place were superb. The windows next to which we sat afforded a nighttime silhouette of Mount Zion and a view of car headlights slipping like beads down the curving road. Nevertheless, the price for an omelette—and eggs we were assured are so plentiful in Israel that they are frequently exported at cost—the omelette, with special discount for guests of Mishkenot, was three dollars a throw. Two of those, plus a bottle of Israeli wine purchasable for about a dollar at the Supersol, plus the tax added, somehow brought the bill up to thirteen dollars. It was all very enjoyable and saved washing dishes, but once was enough. The next day, you may be sure, M and I went on a grocery shopping spree at the local Supersol to the tune of forty dollars, the first time in our married lives we had ever spent that much on groceries at once. Prices are high, except for local produce.

What is Mishkenot Sha'ananim? It is a center developed by the city of Jerusalem, through the efforts of Teddy Kollek, a center to which people are invited from all parts of the world, Jews and non-Jews—interesting and creative people—who it is hoped will contribute their insights to the cultural life of the city. The buildings are essentially those from the 1860 settlement that Montefiore with the aid of funds from Touro, a New Orleans magnate, started outside the walls of the old city. It was the first such settlement for Jews outside the walls, and in order to lower the price of flour for these impoverished Jewish residents, Montefiore ordered a windmill built which would grind grain. It worked for a couple of years before going out of kilter. It now serves as a historical landmark and miniature museum. The buildings from the 1860 settlement have now been beautifully renovated, after the decline of the area when it was on the border between Jordan and Israel between 1948 and 1967. There is a music center and a small building nearby that serves for lectures. This summer most of the nine apartments into which the original eighteen have been converted house literary people: writers, scholars, translators, journalists.

But this tells you almost nothing of what a joy it is to live in this place, a joy to the senses and a joy to common sense. Our combined living room and dining room is palatial and lofty, with a vaulted ceiling and white walls decorated here and there with an ancient plate, a painting, a small etching of a synagogue. Underfoot the floor is Jerusalem limestone, stippled for better traction, and utterly squeakless, which is a help when tiptoeing around in the morning while your wife is asleep. The furnishings are tasteful and of fine workmanship. Everything is imbued with quiet dignity, the cane chairs, the chests, the lamp stands of massive pottery, the occasional rugs. The master bedroom is provided with twin beds and a sufficiency of closets and bureaus. The smaller bedroom makes an appealing study or children's den. The kitchenette with its supply of substantial Farberware, made in Israel of course, meets the standards of the most exacting housewife. I love the old-fashioned hat tree in the entryway with knobs protruding at all angles. And as if all this were not generous enough, there is an upstairs studio as well, offering maximum seclusion to the writer. This of course has become my study.

I can't tell you how exciting it is to wake up in the morning and look out across the lush green bottom of the Hinnom Valley, at the walls of the Old City—gray in hue like that of Laguna Pueblo seen from the road to Grants—at the ancient religious edifices and the green groves on the slope of Mount Zion. On *erev* Shabbos and Shabbos morning, scores of youths of both sexes with *siddur* in hand walk swiftly down the valley, cross the causeway to the other side, and climb Mount Zion. In a few minutes they disappear within the Old City on their way to prayers at the Western Wall. I confess I admire the resilience with which their legs stride along as much as I do their piety.

We have already made several friends, not only among the guests, but "outside" friends as well. We were invited to the home of Bill D., Professor of English Literature at the Hebrew University. Originally from South Africa, he had fought in the 1948 War for Independence without knowing any Hebrew, having to guess at the meaning of commands by the officer's tone of voice. Together with his wife, Shirley K., a poet, we drove around the entire periphery of Jerusalem. Our hosts showed us how incredibly the new city had grown since the 1967 war, how much it had developed, with the Hilton Hotel rising like an axis in the center. They showed us also the dividing line of the city before the 1967 war and how completely obliterated the former border is by new constructions. Then Bill drove us to Bethlehem, where from the height of a former Jordanian artillery emplacement we were treated to a magnificent view of the stark heights and depths of Jerusalem with its numerous points of interest.

Other friends we have made are Betty and Burt E. Having sold their summer and winter homes, as they said, and their thriving clothing business in San Francisco, this young, middle-aged, intelligent, and sophisticated couple decided a year ago to settle in Israel. As I looked out the windows of their apartment, temporarily loaned by a friend, and saw in the east the scattered lights of Mount Zion and the Old City, I was reminded oddly enough of the same kind of scene in Florida where I had recently visited one of my last living college friends. Why were these people not in Israel also; why were they there? That question bred a lively discussion.

A number of suggestions were advanced by the various guests: people came here for religious reasons, or to escape personal maladjustments; some came here to atone for or forget a shady past. However, it was a *sabra,* a wholesome, strong young woman from a kibbutz, who advanced what to me was the most compelling and prevalent reason why people came here from the U.S. and western countries. "I have no feeling of ambivalence," she said. "I am not ambivalent in my feelings about my country. Jews in the Diaspora are. It is the universal soul sickness of Diaspora Jews. You participate in the countries of your asylum only up to a certain point, and because of that, you have a feeling of guilt, because you harbor within yourself an irreducible reserve, that of being a Jew, with a Jew's consciousness and a Jew's state of mind, which makes him different from his fellow citizens. What it comes down to is that those who can tolerate this guilt or ambivalence, and most of the Diaspora are hardened to it, they remain in Diaspora. Those who feel it too keenly are the ones who make *aliya."*

One thing is certainly true, now that we are here. Like most retired Jews, I believe I unconsciously keep an eye open for some colossal bargain in the way of a quiet flat or house suitable for an aging couple without children or pets, where the sound of a piano or the tattoo of a typewriter wouldn't be too objectionable to neighbors. M, who foresees everything, has already bought a little book whose first lesson is devoted to the letter *gimmel;* she has now learned the word *gahg, gimmel-gimmel,* meaning "roof," which elicited from this inveterate and insupportable Joycean the remark that she was now a genuine *gahgoyl.*

On King David Street yesterday, close to Sir Moses Montefiore's windmill, as I was looking over the pleasant valley of Hinnom, at the dark cone of the Church of the Dormition, where tradition has it that Mary slept her last sleep, and next to it at the minaret-like structure of the Church of the Coenaculum, reputed site of the Last Supper, I heard two balding Jews bidding each other farewell. They spoke English, so I understood what they were saying. "Well, goodbye," one offered his hand to the other. "My trip is over. I'm going back home."

"Goodbye," said the other. "But home you're not going. You're going back into *galut."*

> *Roth:* I feel no cultural affinity for Austria, though I was born there, nor for Israel, though I'm a Jew.
>
> (Howard, 1965, p. 75)

> *Roth:* I could be perfectly happy in Albuquerque, but the logic of my literary development seems to require that I live in Israel.
>
> (Pomerantz, 1977)

Vale Atque Ave

October 14, 1977

The sun that rose over the southern slope of the dark cone of the Church of the Dormition when R and his wife M first took up residence at Mishkenot Sha'ananim, now rose over the Diaspora Yeshiva to the south.

The hour was fast approaching for their departure. Five days hence they would have to pack, which meant only four days free, and of these, much time would have to be spent in preparation for departure: in the purchase of trinkets for Gentile neighbors in Albuquerque; in obtaining enough lirot to leave the country—and bestow small gratuities on the domestic help; in sending off via surface mail books and periodicals they had acquired; in arranging to ship their luggage beforehand at the local El Al office; in settling accounts at Mishkenot Sha'ananim for two months of the *Jerusalem Post,* mailing charges, use of telephone, and excess breakage. And, of course, much time would have to be spent bidding farewell to the warm and generous friends that he and M had so readily made here.

Now that he had declared his intention to return to Israel—and despite the wry objections of his friends, all loyal Jerusalemites—to settle in the Tel Aviv area, he had two separate teams of acquaintances scouting for a suitable place to live in next fall. He trusted in their loyalty and their expertise. They understood his need for quiet living quarters in which to write. They understood his need to be reasonably close to the heart of the one city in Israel where he could still discern the vestiges of his boyhood. It was the one city that paralleled and evoked the East Side. For him, the keyword was not *roots;* the keyword was *continuity.*

And yet it would not be merely the East Side as he had known it that he would be returning to; it would be the East Side suddenly expanded, suddenly diversified, suddenly a metropolis, as if all of New York had become the East Side. It was there that he hoped to find himself again. It was there that he hoped to force the connection between the East Side experiences of his boyhood, the evolution of the slum youth into literary awareness, and the old man's acceptance of his people for what they were.

That much was clear in his mind, however askew his plans might go. But what would he say to his friends in Albuquerque about his future plans; and, especially, what would he say to his Jewish friends, those with whom he had only lately begun to associate on pro-Israel committees and Diaspora-strengthening educational boards? What should be his attitude toward them? He couldn't decide. He had made his choice to cast his lot with Israel; they still vacillated, they lingered in the Diaspora. He felt as if he had gone beyond them.

Clear sky . . . late September . . . the Sabbath. Through the lozenges of the window beside his desk he could see the flutter of leaves in a light breeze and farther off the steady cypresses like sentinels. He stood up.

And he walked out through the back door that once had been the front door of the Mishkenot Sha'ananim into the suddenly increased medley of traffic noises on the Hebron Road across the lush Valley of the Hinnom. A gaunt cat scaled the low buttressing wall and disappeared among the shrubs. The long and lonely colonnade of venerable pillars of Ramsgate origin that supported the roof divided into separate frames the panorama before him: the white cross of St. Andrew on the blue flag flying above the Scottish Hospice, the Arab villages in the distance on ashy hilltops, into which Israeli afforestation intruded, the road winding quaintly about the groves of Mount Zion, the Diaspora Yeshiva, the Church of the Coenaculum, the Church of the Dormition, the Old City wall, weathered above and stained below where it had met the soil. David's Tower honed to a point against the turning sky; and near at hand the renovated buildings on whose tawny and rose limestone blocks the sunlight clung like a lacquer.

And so farewell, he thought, turning back to the comfortable apartment that Jerusalem had placed at his disposal the past two months. How did the Romans say it? *Ave atque vale*. He would reverse the order: *Vale atque ave*.

In February 1978, Roth made a trip to Tel Aviv in preparation for the longer stay he had been planning. The following is an excerpt from a letter to a friend in Israel, written soon after his return to the United States.

The essence of Tel Aviv has worn off after these almost three weeks, which is just as well I think because, being there alone, without Muriel to fend for me, as she does ever and unwittingly (and as I am only too happy to have done for me), alone among my own, and without the language, and with naked sensibility, was at times traumatic—at least so I felt the first few days after I returned, as if I hadn't known what I'd been through. I forced the issue, as it were. I had to (nurtured in the Romantic tradition) go through the transition into Israeli reality. That's what the literature would be all about if I'm capable of capturing it, or endure long enough.

(letter to Bill Daleski
from Albuquerque, N.M.,
April 4, 1978)

Roth: I do not know Hebrew. I don't have many illusions about the future of Israel. I have very strong reservations about the Israeli politicians. But in Israel I see a Jewish cop running after a Jewish thief, and I see that both are at home there. This is what I mean by "continuity." Because in America the Jew is not at home. He's always the outsider. . . . Even the East Side was not a world created by the Jews, but a world *left* to the Jews. Continuity, there, was with the Diaspora—a historical phase that the creation of Israel made anachronistic. I realized this after the 1967 war.

(Materassi, 1983, pp. 53–54)

Interviewer: What was your life like in Israel? What kind of emotions did you experience?

Roth: I realize fully what your question implies, and what it really means is that I have to almost project backwards into states of mind while I was there. I felt, essentially, like a foreigner. I mean, here's the land I espoused, here's the land I identified with, here's the people and so forth—but, as an individual, as a person, I'm a *foreigner* here. It's not merely the language. It's the landscape, you know? And I realized that if I were to make this transition—*aliya,* as it's called—I would have to go through a thorough process of acclimatizing myself to a new land, even though it is the land of the Jews. It is not the land, it is not the culture, for that matter, quite apart from the language, it is not that profound, that wonderful, deep culture that the English language, that English literature, has given me. And there's nothing for me to build onto their existence. It's very real, they have very serious problems of all kinds—you see it on the face of everyone there: care, anxiety, and such a deep seriousness that amounts often to rudeness. But, as I speak now and I think back on it, it's something that would almost be in a sphere by itself, separate from the great tradition in which I was raised.

Interviewer: Is this something that you discovered there, or did you discover it after coming back?

Roth: The question that you ask me is a searching question, and to answer it, I am now trying to formulate what I felt then and *didn't* formulate. I think I went there under the illusion that somehow or other I, as a Jew, . . . it would be as if you went back after a long stay in New York—but no, it's not the same thing: you went back to Italy: that's *home.* But [Israel] is not home for *me.* I mean, it's a great historic tradition, and if you take me to some place or other where possibly some biblical figure whom I'm probably related to fought, lived, died, suffered, what have you, then I feel it, I feel it immensely. But I feel it as a literary thing, as a cultural thing. I feel it, too, I suppose, as an emotional thing that I'm touched by. But to be confronted with the actual living, the *here and now,* I am not prepared to. And it would take me some years to be. And when one looks at one's age and says, "Oh, you're not going to be . . . ," that's the most you can do, and that's it. Now you have the "Report from Mishkenot Sha'ananim." The most you can do is to give the landscape and give vignettes, which is something you are doing from the outside—if not as a journalist, you're doing it almost as a traveler.

Interviewer: So, actually, you chose *galut* over *aliya* because of language.

Roth: Yes, because of language and because of culture, especially because of culture. I realized that although my emotional and political identification with the Israelis had taken me to their land, I had to come back to America. However, the very fact of having gone to Israel gave me a new base in this land and this culture. It's too late for anything else.

That is a very good point. I'm glad you asked me. It's also

ambiguous: here I am criticizing Joyce for not going back to a new Ireland, right? On further thought, I feel justified in doing so because at least he was an Irishman, he would have gone back to an Ireland which would have had new features, undoubtedly, but he certainly would have recognized his Ireland, he would have recognized his Dublin, wouldn't he? No matter what the changes were. He would have recognized the countryside and certainly the tongue. But for me Israel is a new land. So it isn't quite analogous. . . . This is not my soil. But, again, one has to remember this is a Jew speaking, a Diaspora Jew. And that the only time he ever felt a sense of belonging to both a place and a people was during the short period when he lived in a Jewish mini-state, and he didn't know it. . . .

Interviewer: On the East Side, you mean.

Roth: Yes, on the East Side. Now, it's very likely—this is an aside, if you want it—that, had I stayed there, I could have become a rabbi. But I didn't.

(taped conversation,
Albuquerque, N.M.,
February 10, 1986)

Segments

Spring 1979

In 1979, Studies in American Jewish Literature *paid Henry Roth a significant tribute by devoting its spring issue to him. Bonnie Lyons, the author of* Henry Roth: The Man and His Work, *was the guest editor.*

Roth contributed two unpublished entries from a 1978 journal, giving them the collective title of "Segments." Both entries concern Roth's rather sharp disagreement with Saul Bellow's position on galut, on aliya, and, more broadly, on what it means to be an American Jew—or, as Roth would have it, to be Jewish-American.

Wednesday. August 30, 1978. Unusually cool morning for this time of year: fifty degrees. Clear. (After a restful night, whose somnolent milestones were two Bufferin tablets at 1:00 A.M., followed by a Dalmane capsule three hours later.)

I don't do much reading these days. I read much too slowly and laboriously (with one lens plastic), and what I do read, especially of modern writing, generally concerns Israel—the *Jerusalem Post, Mid-stream,* and the like. Modern novels I almost never read. Were they like the great seminal or classical novels of my youth I might still read them, but they aren't, not for me at any rate—though I have recently gorged the hook of a single sentence of a work by Gabriel Marquez. So I have never read a novel by Saul Bellow. The reviews themselves give me some guide as to what his novels are about—and what they're about hasn't interested me. They didn't seem to address themselves to my own collection of spiritual quandaries. I would be the first to admit this is scarcely a valid reason either to read or to eschew a man's work. Still since the time at my disposal is short, I'm chary how I expend it: I can't be bothered, except by the greatest relevance.

However, to make up for this failure or inability to cover a great deal of ground in a short time, I do have a peculiar propensity for concentrating on some very short piece—a dedicatory speech, say, or an address delivered on the occasion of receiving an award—and subjecting it to my very limited intellectual and analytical faculties—something in the nature of a laser beam, I fancy, that lines up modest radiation into a single wave length. The occasion to exercise this propensity was offered me by Saul Bellow's address to the Anti-Defamation League on his receiving its American Democratic Legacy Award (Reprinted in the *ADL Bulletin,* December 1976).

I confess I found myself at odds with Bellow from the very outset of his address to the ADL—even from title and subtitle. "I Took Myself as I Was," the title reads, and under it, the subtitle, "The only life I can love, or hate, is . . . this American life of the twentieth century, the life of Americans who are also Jews." He took himself as he was? Further, is that all it behooves a man to do who feels the need for a better world? To take himself as he was? Or isn't it incumbent upon him to reject the plaudits, his successes in a mercenary and decaying world, and reexamine his position in relation to that world and where it is going? To take himself as he was, as Bellow put it, implies complacency, has a taint of arrogance. In the light of his worldwide renown and Nobel prize, to take himself as he was means, in the vernacular, that he picked a winner: his choice was a good one, and he's content with it. Why jeopardize it by reexamination—and possible repudiation? And yet to me, in my simplicity, true greatness, true nobility would demand just that: that he risk his laurels by regeneration, even though his failure by "contemporary" standards was a foregone conclusion.

The view that he met in Israel—and which he rejected outright—was that life in the Diaspora was "inauthentic" (the quotes are his own). "Only as a Jew in Israel . . ." he was told, "could I enter history again and prove the necessity and authenticity of my existence." And he adds below, "That would wipe me out totally." Would it—necessarily?

The radical change of commitment of a Saint Augustine, successful and prominent rhetorician and Manichean, into a Catholic neophyte, after much anguished soul searching, did not wipe him out totally. The negation of his former self transformed him into one of the greatest figures of Christianity, second only to Paul himself. (And what of Paul, that successful former rabbi Saul?) Bellow manifests a narrow, even petty, protectionism, jealously guarding the precincts of his Diaspora success. Little wonder that Cecil Brown, black playwright, in an essay by Alvin Rosenfeld in *Partisan Review* (December 1977), charges Bellow with possessing "an invested interest in a reactionary vision."

Even more ignoble to me than his apologia pro vita sua in his ADL address is his eagerness to vindicate the Diaspora in its obvious intention to remain in exile (and in affluence). Mischievous is the mildest way I can describe his denigration, or implied condemnation, of *aliya,* that corollary of exile's end. Here he exhibits a blindness to the meaning of Israel to Jews the world over, whether they go on *aliya* or not, as well as downright meretriciousness in argument.

Thursday. August 31, 1978. Sunny, cool morning. Lovely weather for the hale and active. As for myself, am hobbling about with the aid of a cane, my arthritic ankles wincing at every step. Having foresworn Indocin, because, rightly, or—more likely—wrongly, I attributed last night's sleeplessness to the drug, in the belief that it was overstimulating me, I'm now trying a combination of two Ecotrin, a candy-coated aspirin, and a half tablet of Percodan, a powerful analgesic, which together enable me to sit at my desk and scribble while I groan.

I can hear myself sigh in gratitude for the Percodan as the pain abates in my aching articulations. . . . At the other end of our mobile home, my beloved is at the piano riding the glorious tempest of a Beethoven sonata; while before me, out of my study window, which opens on the south, the new occupants of the narrow strip of property between the mobile home court and the irrigation ditch, the Duke City Landscaping Company, has by dint of forklift, bulldozer, and truck at least cleaned up its yards, scraping it down to pristine adobe dirt— and at the same time removed a mountain of trash, unimaginable fire hazard, from the vicinity of our common fence. Some semblance of order has been imposed. Under the late-summer sunlight, the water drums are herded here, the lumber piled there, the manure next, followed by gravel and sand—with only a dust-blue sedan that has been parked on one side of the property for days, almost as if abandoned, to impart just that right touch of junkyard to make us feel at home.

Praise God for Percodan. To echo Hopkins: *"He fathers forth"* (together with the pharmaceutical industry) *"whose beauty is past change."* But who in hell fathered forth my arthritis?

I realized at the close of yesterday's mini-critique of Bellow that I had omitted mention of my objection to the subtitle of Bellow's address to the ADL on the occasion of his receiving its American Democratic Legacy Award, namely: "The only life I can love, or hate, is . . . this American life of the twentieth century, the life of Americans who are also Jews." Now here we have an equation (he repeats it identically later): "Americans who are also Jews." But it is different from an apparently similar equation: Jews who are also Americans. The first states that we are Americans first, and then Jews; the second, that we are Jews first, and then Americans. And probably this is precisely where I diverge from Bellow. A minor matter. Of greater consequence is that this is Bellow's point of departure. It is on his being an American first, and a Jew second, that the bulk of his thesis rests. But is that a tenable presumption? In my opinion it is not. Anyone who admits to being a Jew anywhere in the world, except Israel, is a Jew in the mind of the non-Jewish auditor first, and a citizen of that country second. Any Jew anywhere who admits to being a Jew implies his exile. (It's an interesting social phenomenon—whether it's a contribution to the argument or not: a Pole immigrating to America becomes a Polish-American, an Italian, an Italian-American; a Jew coming from those countries becomes an American Jew. What happened to the other half of the hyphen? Few indeed are Polish-American-Jews, Italian-American-Jews, or the like; whereas, may I be forgiven the levity, there is no shortage of Galitzianer Jews or Litvaks.) The point I'm driving at is that Jew dominated the equation in the country of origin, and Jew still dominates it in America, Canada, Australia, or other *freieh medina*. Hence the tenure of Diaspora anywhere is bound to be precarious, Bellow's assurances to the contrary notwithstanding.

He says in the concluding paragraph of his "I Took Myself as I Was" that the assumption (of his Israeli interlocutors) underlying the position he rejected, was "that America is bound to go the way of other Christian countries and expel or destroy its Jewish population." And he counters by way of refutation: "But is it a Christian country like the others?" He is now beginning to perform a sleight of hand, which he completes in his next sentence: "—this nation is not in the European

234 *Segments*

sense a recognizably Christian country." We're distracted by certain contraband qualifications: "like the others," "European sense," "recognizably": true legerdemain here, and for what purpose? To leave us with the alluring and utterly false inference (from which he cleverly steps away), that because America is not a Christian country, we need have little fear of destruction or expulsion. As if Moslems had never persecuted us, nor professedly atheistic nations, nor above all the Neopagan Nazis!

"But one need not hold long arguments with views that are so obviously wrong," to quote Mr. Bellow. And I would make an end, except that Bellow himself simply won't allow it. He has to clinch the untenable with the denigrating. Sigmund Freud, he recalls reading, "once observed that America was an interesting experiment, but that he didn't believe it would succeed. Well, maybe not. *But it would be base to abandon it.*" (Italics mine.) Is this, or is it not tantamount to saying that making *aliya* to Israel is a base act? The Jew who does so, abandons America, and hence is base. Bellow undoubtedly would protest that this was not the intent of his statement, and I trust it was not; nevertheless, it is difficult to draw any other inference. To stay here, to remain here in Diaspora, is commendable.

Have I said enough? I think I have. The core of Bellow's argument in favor of continued Diaspora stems from the anti-Zionist Morris Cohen's quotation of Santayana's definition of piety, a word that Bellow seeks to rehabilitate. Piety, says Santayana, is "reverence for the sources of one's being." To me the definition is open to question, or misconstruction. Are these *selected* sources of one's being, or all the sources? "Ich hatte einst ein schones Vaterland," wrote Heine. "Es war ein traum." (I'm relying on memory, and both it and my German may be in error.) Did Heine, who foresaw the monstrosity that German nationalism would one day beget, reverence the cult of German nationalism too as part of the sources of his being? A German death camp victim on the threshold of a gas chamber reverence the German culture that had brought him or her to this horror? A Black reverence the deprivation and depravity that ghetto life imposed and white domination maintained? What if the sources of one's being are both attractive and repulsive, the camaraderie and homogeneity and freedom of the East Side ghetto, and the searing taunt of "sheeny" heard there for the first time. Isn't that exactly the plight of the Jew in Diaspora? He's *deprived* of reverence in any whole sense for the sources of his being. (The same holds true of the Black.)

To conclude: "And if Cohen is right," says Bellow, "and the future of liberal civilization is bound up with America's survival, the damage (caused by our abandoning America) would be universal and irreparable." Does the *oleh* who quits America to settle in Israel join the enemy camp, like Coriolanus? Though his motives in emigrating to Israel may be to terminate his millennial exile and reunite with the country from which his ancestors were dispossessed centuries ago, nevertheless Israel, beleaguered Israel, is an outpost of that very civilization whose values Mr. Bellow and Professor Cohen hold dear. *At the gates of Rome is Carthage defended.* Contrary to Bellow, it is the going and not the staying that is an act of piety and valor.

Interviewer: Has your position vis-à-vis Bellow changed since you published "Segment"?

Roth: No, it hasn't, really. And part of the reason it hasn't is that I haven't read the whole book. Which is very unfair to Bellow. And I think I stated that. . . .

Interviewer: So why don't you like him?

Roth: I don't know. I suppose I've become offended by his intellectual arrogance? Or intellectuality that I don't possess myself . . . ? I don't know. But I suppose I demand of any person of any stature a degree of humility, and I guess I don't feel it in Bellow. . . . And in this piece, which became for me a little specimen, I was confirmed in my feeling about him. I felt here was somebody a little bit pretentious, calling upon the philosopher, Morris Raphael Cohen, who was bitterly anti-Zionist, by the way, and therefore was not a fair choice on the part of Bellow. I feel he might have called upon other people who are philosophers on a par with Professor Cohen—after all, he was among the great *teachers* in his time, but as far as, I think, his philosophic contributions are concerned, they are not seminal, and they are not of any great magnitude—like Einstein's, for example, who *was* a Zionist. That's one. And as far as the aesthete, Santayana, is concerned, again, that seems to me really dragged in by the ear, after all, except insofar as Cohen quotes Santayana about reverence. And piety, yes. Reverence to roots. And then this brings up to my mind the whole business of what one's roots are.

Interviewer: One of the things that you seem to hold against Bellow is the fact that he went back to Diaspora.

Roth: It is not only that he went back, but that he makes a defense of it. And not only a defense, but you feel as if there's a rationalization there. I was going back to Diaspora—but he rationalizes his decision. I didn't feel an inevitability about this going back. I would have said candidly, "This is where I live, I can't function anywhere else, and I feel guilty." That would have been my reaction—that *is* my reaction. Were I a man as young as Bellow is, I probably would have said, I probably belong here, but I can't take it. So, to sum up in just two words what I feel about the Bellow piece, I feel as if it were a mixture, of *pique*—you know what I mean—pique and sophistry.

(taped conversation,
Albuquerque, N.M.,
February 10, 1986)

The Wrong Place

1978

The first outcome of Roth's six-month stay in Spain, between 1965 and 1966, was "The Surveyor." Twelve years later, he went back to the wealth of comments and observations he had stored away during that trip and wrote "The Wrong Place." In this piece, which incorporates some of the material out of which "The Surveyor" evolved, Roth illustrated his becoming aware of a latent urge within himself to reunite with Judaism.

The largest portion of "The Wrong Place" is an excerpt from a very long letter that Roth sent his high school and college friend, Iven Hurlinger, entitled "Letter to Iven." In view of publication, Roth made some changes in the original version. For the most part, these are minor alterations concerning diction and construction. The major change consists of a totally different ending. Quite apart from its literary value, the original ending is particularly interesting for its presentation of what could be termed a fleeting ideological "temptation" in the direction of Catholicism. Accordingly, the ending of "Letter to Iven" is included here.

"The Wrong Place" was originally published with the subtitle "From English for Foreigners." This has since been altered. Roth

intends to give his work in progress, Mercy of a Rude Stream, *the subtitle "Advanced English for Foreigners" (see later).*

To get down to the business—of symbiosis, I was about to say—of what I've accomplished, or is in the works so far, there is, first, the study by Bonnie Lyons, together with the "Kaddish." . . . Also, the piece to appear in (Loyola) *New Orleans Review,* placed there through Bonnie's good offices. After you've read it, you might find the *second* part worth translating. The site is again Seville; the material is different, and the commitment definite. Appearance not due until fall semester, I imagine.

(letter from Albuquerque, N.M.,
July 6, 1977)

*A*fter a week spent in a Seville pension, a kind of boarding house—described by the Office of Tourism as *de lujo,* and anything but *de lujo* as far as we were concerned: dismal, cramped, cleaned in a slovenly fashion, the fare skimpy and rank with inferior olive oil (a very nice proprietor though, very affable; I almost think the poor chap grieved over the deal he was giving us)—we are now ensconced in our own *piso,* an apartment. It is furnished, has four rooms and kitchenette, a private bathroom in which there are two different types of flush toilets, one male and one female. Unfortunately, you can't get by one to get to the other, so close together are they, and you're always turning something when you should be pulling something. Only thing to be said in their favor—broadly speaking—is that one of them can always serve as an ashtray while you're using the other. The building is clean and has an elevator. From the back of the apartment the windows overlook a lovely conglomerate of white-washed dwellings; from the balcony in front of the apartment the view includes the Giralda, minaret of twelfth-century construction, now surmounted by a belfry and a statue of Faith (la Santa Fe). The rent for the apartment is four thousand pesetas per month, paid three months in advance, and before you gasp at the magnitude of the sum, remember they're only pesetas, and divide them sixty to the buck. I understand it's not bad for what we're getting. Gas and current are extra, and we had to invest in a door mat, a few sheets, and a couple of additional cooking utensils.

Physically, then, we feel well situated. Neighbors are friendly, not at all noisy—or nosey—which is a blessing. Walls here are the kind that send you answering the door when someone else's door bell is buzzing. We're close to a shopping center, close to one of the better cinemas in town; the bus stops right in front of the house. Street noises there are in plenty, especially those caused by the droves of motorcycles, scooters, and queer three-wheeled vans that course along Avenida Eduardo Dato. Fortunately we can retreat to the other side of the apartment when the din becomes unbearable. I have established my study on that side. One of the minor disadvantages of the place, as of Seville generally, is that I can't hold a conversation with the natives: they speak a rapid-fire dialect called Andalusian, in which the letter "s" virtually disappears, and I speak only a limpid Castillian—it limps—so we never progress beyond a few deprecating head scratchings, si-sis, and handshakes. M is more practical than I am. Instead of trying to learn the vernacular by head-on encounters, she has hired the services of a tutor, a young bank employee who has spent some time in England. I may have to sidle in on a few sessions.

We had some difficulty with the hot water supply at first. It just wasn't hot. It seems that all those appliances one takes for granted in the U.S. are what is called "particular" here, that is, private; and the hot water heater was particular, very. So we got in touch with the renting agent over the phone about the matter, and the next day a quizzical middle-aged gentleman with a screw driver came in to examine the appliance. He removed the lower cover, toyed with the wires a few minutes, then screwed the cover back in place. I think he said he would come back the next day with a mechanic. I caught the word *mañana,* and I caught the word *técnico.* I think I even heard him say, *"No vale mucho,"* meaning the appliance wasn't worth much. He appeared the next day, but without a *técnico.* Once again I thought he said the *técnico* would come tomorrow. But the morrow came, and no *técnico.* By now we had been three days without running hot water. So I called on the renting agent in person and asked him to do something soon. He promised the *técnico* would be at the apartment tomorrow—in Castillian this time, not Andalusian. But again the morrow came—and went—and still no *técnico.* So I called again on the renting agent, and this time I was emphatic: would I have to complain to the American Consul that I had been cheated, I protested. I had paid three months' rent in advance for an apartment with hot water. He seemed deeply disturbed and immediately telephoned the señorita who owned the piso. There ensued a polite harangue in Andalusian, and when it terminated, the agent turned to me triumphantly: in view of the inconvenience caused me by the lack of hot water, the lady would remit five hundred pesetas; the middle-aged gentleman would bring it tomorrow. "That's fine," I said. "I'll remit an equal amount if somebody will fix the hot water heater." *Técnicos*, the agent explained, were hard to come by. They had migrated to Germany where the wages were higher. *"Dios!"* I said. "Will my wife and I have to do the same in order to take a bath?" No, no, he assured me. That wouldn't be necessary. The *técnico* would certainly be out to our place tomorrow. He personally guaranteed it. This time he was right, but just. The *técnico* and his assistant arrived the next day, at 7 P.M., better than a week after we had first complained. It took him about fifteen minutes to install a new element in the heater. Then I suppose he went back to Germany. . . .

About Seville, my impressions are, to say the least, chaotic, and I'm afraid are apt to remain so for some time. The place is chaotic. Whoever heard of a city with a half-million population, and bursting with modernity on the outskirts, with radial cranes wheeling in all directions, but whose center has streets only two yards wide, or less? (I turned my head in time to see a native laughing at me as I stretched my arms out from wall to wall.) Not only that, but every street changes its name at least a half dozen times—every time it crosses a plaza. Some streets can be covered by a running broad jump—not in width, in length! When I recalled what I had read of Cortes's escapades with the señoras, about his scaling walls to reach balconies, and thus get at other men's wives, I thought, shucks, it isn't all that much of an exploit. Given the bravado, or the folly, the leg work can be readily mastered. All one would have to do is stretch out across the street, and work upward with legs and shoulders. Picturesque streets they're called, and the way vehicles squirm through them is picturesque too. As for the pedestrians, progress is a series of balancing acts done on the curbstone next to the wall: there is no sidewalk—that's in the house. Old Bernal Diaz put it succinctly when he remarked in another connection that you can't take five steps here without draping your beard over your shoulder. You had better.

The sights? We have seen a number of the heralded ones: the Giralda, the Cathedral of course, the Ruinas Itálicas, part of the Maria Luisa Gardens, the Church of San Gil, the Torre del Oro on the Guadalquivir, the vast Tobacco Factory (where Carmen had her fling) now housing the University of Seville—to mention just a few. But here again, my impressions are much too raw—or too roily—to be worth much. The Giralda is my favorite. For five pesetas you may climb the inner ramps of this justly famous Moorish tower. (The sign says in genial encouragement, NO STAIRS, omitting mention of the thirty-odd ramps, but they're easy.) You may trudge upward over a brickwork floor in lozenge pattern, worn hollow—the heart aches at the thought of the myriads of tourists and visitors the floors have borne. The ramps are dark, until you reach the balconies where light comes through the archways. And then what I do is pause at each balcony for breath and for the view. Because the building's cross-section is square, there are four balconies for each full turn. From two of them you can see "modern Seville," that is, Seville since Christopher Columbus: the fountain in the middle of the plaza with its satyr-like heads spouting water, the rusty archbishop's palace on the left, a dazzling white church on the right, the guides down below waiting to pick up a tourist. From the other two balconies you get an intimate view of the Cathedral façade—begun sometime before Christopher Columbus (the Giralda was incorporated into the Cathedral). As you climb and pause at each balcony of the ascent, wider views of Seville alternate with higher levels of the Cathedral, the modern continually contrasting with the medieval; you see the lower elaborations of stone, then stone cauliflowers around the first pinnacles, and again, after a fresh view of Seville, the work done higher still, perhaps a stained-glass window, perhaps an inner buttress. Soon you're face to face with a grimacing gargoyle, and for the first time you can actually see the channels in the upper ridges of the buttresses that convey the rain water to the gargoyles. And once more, after another survey of Seville—the tiled rooftops stretching away, the green meadows across the river—the entire design of the buttress is presented to you: how it takes the thrust from the Cathedral's walls and transmits it three times from one buttress to another—and distributes it to another system at right angles. A marvelous sight! The roof you see below you is groined, but not as seen from within the Cathedral, when the roof is above you, no, convex now, billowing—if you gaze long enough it heaves. This is the Cathedral of which one of its founders said: "Let us build one so huge, posterity will think us mad." As far as I'm concerned they succeeded. But what a tribute to man's skill in the arts of peace, his faith, and his vision! There are few monuments to match it. In an obscure corner next to one of the Cathedral entrances there is a small marble headstone, and if I have made out the inscription aright, it says three *peones* lie buried here, three hodcarriers who lost their lives in the construction of the sacred edifice. I do them reverence.

Ruinas Itálicas: a six-peseta bus ride—about twenty minutes in duration—will take you out there, and ten pesetas will admit you to an amphitheater built in the third century A.D. The way the tiers rise up before you, it's like receiving an ovation in stone when you enter— we were alone, M and I—or were the seats empty because the spectators had risen? Much of the place has decayed, much of it tumbled down, but the shape is there, and the people once were. Dens are still fairly intact, and a few arches are still standing; the portals are discernible where the fans rushed in. You are they, and they are you, and someone else will mark the lizard on the wall that you mark, and someone has. For a moment you extend both ways, like the waist of an hourglass.

Or you can stroll—free of charge this time—along what's left of the city wall, first built by the Moors about 1100. Square towers, gates, and overhead a ratchet of battlements (I think they're called), each topped with a pyramidal cap. If you go around to the other side of the wall, on shabby Macarena Street, you'll see kids poking holes in the handiwork of their forefathers and adding the sand they dig out to the mud pies they're making beside the curb. Close by—in fact, at one end of the wall—is the famed church of San Gil. This is the one presided over by the (notorious I was about to say) Virgin of the Macarena, the often-styled "sweetheart of Seville," and you can believe it. I'm sure that many a wight has confessed to wet dreams about her, to a priest who undoubtedly understood why. She's a ravishing brunette, simultaneously grieving and inviting. Teardrops in three dimensions are limned on her cheek, her face and body are arrayed in jewels, brocade, and seductive lace. Her headdress, a sunburst of wrought gold, crowns the carnal with opulence. I don't get it. How can this be the humble mother of a thirty-year-old crucified son? My palate cloys as I look at her, as though I had stuffed a whole eclair into my mouth.

And there's more, much more. I'll never reach the end, so I'll have to abridge the rest into a few tokens: the wall around the Alcázar rears up like a wall in fairyland, huge, tawny, blocks of stone stem contemporaneity, the bustle of traffic, the flow of time. And inside the same Alcázar, which you can visit for twenty pesetas, endless tracery, endless inlay, endless arabesque. The eye becomes glutted with filigree; it balks at another look. Near at hand is the Juderia, behind a gate locked at night by the Jews who lived there centuries ago, and now as quaint and charming a street of small private houses as you've ever seen, choice as Greenwich Village Mews, and probably as expensive. And there's the Cathedral interior, of such awesome grandeur, the space enclosed has become a presence; you can stand in sanctified gloom under the bier of Columbus, borne aloft by four noble figures near a wall, stand under the ashes of 1492 that separate two eras, the medieval and the modern, and two worlds, the old and the new—and wonder.

From where we live it's a short bus ride to the center of town. I get a great deal of pleasure in taking the bus early in the morning before breakfast and then rambling about town while everything is quiet. I dip into courtyards, read the inscriptions on plaques, peer into a patio, and pause before a fountain. Invariably my excursion leads to the Cathedral. For one thing, it's a very prominent landmark—or sky-mark, provided there's enough room in the narrow streets to descry it. It helps orient the stranger. Principally, though, the place holds a real fascination for me. (Admission is free, incidentally, from seven to ten in the morning.) So I stand before one of the huge doors and study the saints on the pedestals around and above the lintels, and I try to surmise whom the effigies represent. Or I gaze through the door for a while at the opposite door, open also, about a city block away, past which the far pedestrian appears close at hand, but as through a telescope reversed; at least, he might be close at hand if it weren't for the hallowed gloom intervening. Then I usually go in. You can wander there at will at this hour; you can watch the priests conducting services at different altars (the place is equivalent to a half score of churches in one). You can hear litanies intoned, masses said; you can observe worshippers offering prayers at different shrines, kneeling before this altar, genuflecting before the other, crossing themselves before high, wan crucifixes.

Or you can stand below the stained-glass windows, some dating from the sixteenth century, and revel in the gem-like glow that radiates from the touching yet strangely tranquil scenes they depict. I find myself in fancy adopting the state of mind of the Marrano youth whose background I came here to find—for the purpose of writing a novel—the crypto-Jew who, contrary to edict, managed to slip through the Inquisition's net and land with the conquistadores in the New World. It's easy, I muse, as I stand there raptly gazing up at the stained-glass windows that shine like ethereal retablos, it's easy to accept Catholicism. It's beautiful. If only my mother and father would cut out their clandestine observances, I'd forget about Judaism. But no, they've got to persist in their stealthy matzo baking before the Passover, their stealthy candle lighting behind closed shutters on Friday evenings, their dissembled Yom Kippur fasts, casually twiddling a toothpick in public. Why don't they let me alone, desist from these vestiges of the past, why do they cling to this exile within exile—Jews driven from Eretz Israel, suspect Catholics within fanatic Spain? Enough is enough. But then, Sh'ma Yisroel rises in the throat in stubborn counterpoint to what the eyes rest on. *God on high, on this earth how many nations! The Romans, the Persians, the Babylonians*—lamenting with the Rabbi of Berdichev, Paul Robeson's sonorities override the chant of the nearby choir—*the Romans, the Persians, the Babylonians . . . the Germans*. It's impossible to throw off that heritage. I am aware of myself in dispute: protest all you like that you're a Catholic or a Christian, my Marrano friend, consume pork ostentatiously, or the wafer; but unless, unless polarities are truly reversed and faith replaces, nay, displaces faith—as Captain Ahab knew, striking the slender rod in the magnetic field of the disoriented compass—unless the change takes place within the soul almost allotropically (and it's happened even to rabbis), so that you're alien to the being you were, then you remain what you are, and the other man's beatitudes and epiphanies roll off you like surf off a rock.

I walk on. A short distance away tapers are burning. They burn before a small shrine so inconspicuous it seems tucked away within the flutings of a vast column, and a woman worshipper kneels there: an image of the infant Jesus lit up by the candles points like a doll and like a doll holds a cross aloft. I retreat into the shadow behind the woman and stand and watch with appropriate reverence. After she has arisen and left, I move forward and stand there even more reverentially. Not bad, I meditate, not bad at all, not onerous in the least. Well, how would you pray, I ask myself, if you were to convert, or if you prayed. Good fortune, I think, send me good fortune, Babe, happiness for today. And yes, while I'm at it, why not pray for that novel about a Marrano that I shall probably never write, pray I might write it. I am aware of a sense of surrender, a sense of religious commitment. I can glimpse Eliot's distress, Eliot's necessity, Eliot's compulsion—without being persuaded. Turning away and walking a few steps further I notice a man in the gloom dropping something behind the bars that fence in an unlit altar. After he passes, I approach. There is a box in the darkness, and some words written on it that become legible: *Limosna para culto de Nuestra Señora*. I hunt among my coins and find a ten centimo piece—tin dimes I call them—and drop one into the slot. My God! I've gone all the way, I think, even unto giving alms for Mary's sake. Let's see if it helps. The act sets in motion a train of waves, a sort of alteration of frames of mind, of tentatively accepting and of not quite rejecting, and of further accepting again, something like a theoretically infinite resilience. Will I have to become religious, I ponder, in order to write about a Marrano, consider admitting the Holy Ghost, whoever he is. . . . It's an interesting experience. One thing I haven't done yet but intend to, and that is to cross myself before one of these fanes. I haven't done so, partly because I'm stiff necked, I suppose, but also because I'm a little afraid of being awkward, hence conspicuous. I intend to practice a little. I recall reading that during the Inquisition, one way of telling recent converts apart from old believers was the way in which they crossed themselves: the old believers were more neat about it. I watch a statuesque young blonde, a tourist probably, cross herself before a crucifix. She crosses the whole of herself in large airy sweeps. I'm not up to that. I'd like to make a small unobtrusive transit, a modest little cross, but convincing.

By the time I emerge from the Cathedral, broad daylight has unfurled over Seville. It shines on the sober Sevillanos waiting in queues before the bus stops, gleams on the espresso machines in the cafés, on the buzzing scooters and cycles, and glares from a traffic policeman's white helmet. It leans on the old buildings and steeples and illuminates the black iron chains that hang in their massive curves between the stone posts in front of the Cathedral.

What do I believe now? I question myself as I join the queue waiting for the No. 9 bus that will take me back to the apartment, my wife, and coffee. The resonance of the experience continues. I scoff, but with my fingers crossed. Have I left the door ajar to my well-guarded atheism? What if I left it wide open, would I write again? I'd be following in Eliot's steps then, along the sacred path, the Christian path. This is going to be interesting.

With the same belief, the conquistadores—I move along in the queue toward the bus steps—could tear down a whole civilization, and without compunction loot, torture, and enslave, their deeds sanctioned by their belief, and their misdeeds absolved. And then I hesitate at the very bus door: somewhere around here they used to burn us.

And I change my mind. Yesterday, while researching the background of the Marrano youth, my prospective central character, at the Seville library, I came across the first really accurate survey of the city, done in 1780 by British engineers engaged for the purpose. It was a quaint map; prominent landmarks and buildings were colored and in cameo, like a frieze, or compromise third dimension. A legend in the upper lefthand corner named and assigned a number to historic structures in the city and its environs—and one of those named and numbered was the *Quemadero,* the place of burning. But no one knew where it was. Obliterated. No tourist guidebook mentioned it. Near El Prado de San Sebastian, said the gaunt librarian, and regarded me curiously; it was outside the city walls—which had long ago been razed, he added. So with strips of paper as makeshift compass (in lieu of dividers), and wooden metric rule which the librarian loaned me, I located the place with a fair degree of precision, juggling meters and *varas* and yards. And now I drew out of my pocket a map of the modern city of Seville, on which I had marked the spot once occupied by the *Quemadero.* It would require a brisk walk to get there, but . . . I relinquished my place in the line and struck out in a southeasterly direction, as indicated by my bearing on the map (I had used the Cathedral, incidentally, as a fiduciary when triangulating to the *Quemadero*). Avenida del Cid was the place I sought; only I would have to stride along at a good clip if I wasn't going to worry M by my overly prolonged absence. Past the orange trees that lined the sidewalk, by the travel agencies, and the little storefronts displaying their tourist wares: berets and antiques, silver torah pointers and dice boxes . . . and now and then a framed and stern Francisco Franco. Over paved lanes in swart greenery across a corner of the Jardines de Murillo, by rows of sycamores and by trees I didn't know, breathless I arrived. There was El Cid, El Cid Campeador, semilegendary hero of eleventh-century Spain, symbol of the Christian reconquest of the Iberian peninsula from the Moors. Of heroic mold, elevated on a pedestal, bronze champion bestrode bronze charger. He stood up in his stirrups brandishing his pennanted spear, and he loomed above the little park, above the lawn and the flower beds swarming with scarlet calla lillies. *(Ya don Raquel e Vidas—en vuestras manos son las arcas. . . .*) Here it was! Here the youth's parents had been burned—judaizing heretics. And slowly, as I approached the site, I began to doubt that I would ever write that story, that I would ever chart the course of the youthful crypto-Jew who became a conquistador. Why had I come to Spain? Ostensibly to familiarize myself with the background of my Marrano

* "In your hands are the chests, Messers Raquel and Vidas." With these words (from *El Poema del Cid*), El Cid's "expediter" tricks two Jewish moneylenders into lending El Cid a large sum of money, collateral for which is locked up in a couple of fancy chests, *arcas.* Instead of the fine gold the chests are alleged to contain, they contain sand.

central character. But that wasn't the reason I had come here. It was evident now, though all this while I had concealed it from myself. I had come to Spain to reunite with Judaism—via a side door! I wouldn't admit it until now, but that was the reason. Still, all other doors were closed to me—I stood there, in the shadow of El Cid, conscious that I was treading on the ashes of martyrs—I had closed the doors myself: on the business Diaspora, the acquisitive Diaspora, the observing Diaspora. What door was open? Idiot, I thought: the same door that was open to those Marranos' descendants who but yesterday fled from Arab persecution: Israel! The newspapers reported it. My God, what a detour I've made—stupendous—and paid three months' rent in advance!

One suffers at length a kind of reaction to it all, to the overpowering religiosity that surrounds one—at any rate I did. I awoke Monday morning with a terrible feeling of despair. It seemed to me there was no escape from the fearful conformity of Catholicism. It pervaded everything. I felt as though having dabbled in Catholicism, I had brought upon myself a violent attack of heresy, or having dabbled in Christianity I had contracted a furious apostasy. The week before had been the time of the Domund, when the Church collects funds for its missionary work all over the world. We had been pestered in the house and out on the street by swarms of kids with plastic containers, something like the *pishkehs* the old Jews used to jingle on the East Side. It wasn't enough that we had donated once. We were expected to donate every time a kid proffered his canister. We already had pinned to our lapels the little slip of paper that attested to our having contributed, but that didn't seem to make any difference. At first I tried to protest—to no avail. As a matter of fact giving or not giving didn't make much difference. I felt conspicuous either way: a *tourista,* a Black Protestant, or perhaps they even surmised I was a Jew. This ubiquitous tag day may have contributed to my despair. I felt trapped. If I hadn't advanced three months' rent on the apartment, I might have begun to pack, but you know my frugal soul. And then I began thinking: look here, you came to Spain to get an idea of what it was like to be a Marrano, to be subjected to the ruthless conformity of a single creed. And a creed you loathed beside. You are now getting that experience, and you've got to be disciplined about it. I began to feel better. What cowardice to run away at the first unpleasantness. Had I no faith in rationality, in science? Of course I had. And now I felt even better. Who were they to make me run? I could outlast a million such Domunds, visit a million churches, see a million crucifixes, hear a million Hail Marys. I was still myself and I lived in the twentieth century, not in the dark ages of their obscurantism. By evening I had completely recovered my cheerful self, my equilibrium, such as it is. Evidently I was still a Marrano, a latter-day one without the *shema*.

(from "Letter to Iven,"
Winter 1965)

We were just arriving at the house on Eduardo Dato when the delivery boy came down the stairs with a telegram. I immediately surmised it must be from you when he asked my name, and it was. Oddly enough, we were returning from the great Cathedral in Seville where we had gone to hear "los Seises" (the Sixes), a group of kids all dressed in medieval costume of white and blue striped tunics and plumes who do a kind of ritual dance before the main altar at this time of the year (Purisima?). Though I stood while others kneeled, finally toward the end a little bell tinkled off somewhere, and everyone dropped to his knees, even those two or three others standing, and so I had to do likewise. Your telegram then is the payoff, divine recompense for my obeisance.

(letter from Seville, Spain,
December 14, 1965)

I could say much about Spain, but nothing important. . . . The Spanish are trying very hard, and who isn't, to imitate the U.S.; stores are full of our, or Spanish gimmicks, and throngs before them hungrily absorb the sheen and the form of TV and electric coffee pot. On the other hand there's a cross about everywhere you go, a priest or a monk about every other where, and a nun in the intervals. Tile pictures of Aunt Mary and cousin Jesus appear in the most unexpected places, even on diesel locomotives. Mother and I have tried kneeling at one of the recent religious functions we attended—a little bell sounds, and I guess the Holy Ghost pops out of a void, and everyone genuflects. It's not the most comfortable of attitudes. I'm dying to try a bit of that wafer they all line up for in front of the altar with open mouths. (What, no marmalade!) It's called Holy Commun-ion. . . . Francisco F. is also about every other otherwhere, including the stalactite grottos we visited in Aracena; there the plaque said Franco Franco Franco. . . . Right now, speaking of Seville, the picture is one of a city straining after the modern Seatos (Spanish Fiat), and building innumerable viviendas, government-sponsored housing proj-ects, or really apartments that you buy, don't rent, tens of thousands of units. But clearing up the rubble afterwards are trains of little donkeys that carry the broken brick and sand in panniers on either side across the noisy traffic lanes of Eduardo Dato, a scene Cervantes would easily have recognized.

(letter to Jeremy Roth
from Seville, Spain,
December 17, 1965)

Seville, well . . . It's quite an experience to live in a country where Catholicism is going on all the time, where the bystander is more or less bathed in, or I should say massaged with all the attributes of Christian religiosity. It gets tiresome, or worse, especially to active nonreceptives like your pa. Beside it's too glorified; they insulate almost everything with gold, and I never did take to the stuff as you know, nor ever equated glory with gilt. It was a relief to go to Morocco for a while and see something else beside the Holy Family. Incidentally, for your information, the man with the beard standing by at the birth of Jesus is not the family physician; he's St. Joseph. Poor guy had nothing to do, had nothing to do with, and had nothing to do with it.

(letter to Hugh Roth
from Seville, Spain,
December 18, 1965)

Interviewer: Earlier you mentioned that you became an atheist at fourteen and that your only subsequent identification with Judaism many years later extended only to Israel. Do you find yourself returning to religion lately? I thought I heard strains of something new in your recent pieces.

Roth: In a new piece ["Kaddish"] I quote a rabbi who began his *Kaddish* by saying, "Good morning to you Lord God Almighty," which is one of the most remarkable statements I've ever heard. Here is the creator of everything and one of his infinitely little creatures bidding Him good morning. I have been profoundly moved by the religious current or theme, though I can't believe it. Nevertheless, I am profoundly moved by it, so I found no reason why I couldn't use it. Why should I block it off when it is one of the great moving currents in my own creativity?

(Lyons, 1979, p. 57)

Nature's first green is gold,
   Her hardest hue to hold . . .

                         —Robert Frost

Nature's First Green

1979

Although very short, consisting as it does of barely four printed pages, Nature's First Green *was Roth's first "book" after* Call It Sleep. *It signaled the beginning of a new phase in the writer's life —one devoted to disciplined, precisely focused writing.*

A beautifully printed volume, Nature's First Green *was the first in the series of limited signed editions put forth by Targ Editions. Bill Targ, formerly editor-in-chief at Putnam, wanted "something very special as an opening" for his series. Accordingly, he turned to Henry Roth. One of Roth's letters to him became the nucleus of* Nature's First Green, *although, as Targ writes, "his letter is of course not entirely the book I published."*

As Roth has repeatedly pointed out, it was thanks to Bill Targ's timely encouragement and support that he resumed writing with the steadfast determination he had lost in the forty odd years that followed Call It Sleep.

*P*robably there are lots of reasons I won't write my memoirs, but chief I think is that I simply don't remember well enough. Secondly, everything I do remember is enveloped in such a parochial and constricted illumination that the event hovers like a tableau in the midst of a vignette in the void. Transitions are absent. It's all a great sieve, and just why I choose to relate this particular anecdote I don't know, except that it seems to suggest, though remotely, what I'm trying to say: about my own recall, about the past, about the experience of reality, maybe. (Incidentally, since I'm such a poor hand or head at remembering what actually did happen, the agonizing choice of whether to conceal or reveal never presents itself. It's all welcome, grist for the mill and damn little of that.)

At age fourteen ("Nature's first green is gold") in the seminal summer, I wandered through motley Fourteenth Street, seeking, and also shrinking from, the casual work kids do during summer vacation. When lo, a man came sweating by, lugging two metal canisters of movie film . . . heading for the Fox Theatre a couple of blocks beyond. He hired the idler on the spot. Soon I was fetching film from the distributors uptown, film heavier than mill wheels. Between times, in the projection booth on the unused third balcony, I mended the celluloid when parted, rewound the film, and learned to direct a spotlight on the straw-hatted hoofers in their capers on the stage and the lovely soubrettes with functioning window shades cleverly built into their skirts. Freed from his duties, the personable young projectionist sat in his undershirt in the balcony window and flirted with girls in the open windows of the upper stories of the Hammacher & Schlemmer hardware mart across the street.

And I became the reigning comedian of 119th Street in East Harlem.

I, who had lacked all popularity, all charisma, and all aptitudes at marbles and baseball, at pitching pennies or matching pennies, and all the shifty and valuable wiles of the slums, became the idol of the mixed group of Irish, Jewish, and Italian gamins of the street. Sitting out the sultry nights on the stoops of neighboring tenements, they would come crowding around me when I returned home from work pleading for me to repeat the latest numbers I had heard or seen on the other side of the footlights. And I obliged them: "So I hung up my coat, and I said, hang there, you hundred-and-fifty-dollar fur coat, and I leaned my cane against the wall, and I said, lean there, you fifty-dollar gold-headed cane, and I tossed my hat on the table, and I said, stay there, you twenty-five-dollar Stetson. And her father came out of the parlor, and he grabbed me by the seat of my pants and threw me out on my ear. And he said, lay there, you ten-cent bum!" And the three clowns who by pratfall after pratfall demolished the house that was all but built, when this one dropped a hod of bricks on that one, who fell atop a plank that seesawed the third aloft to begin a chain of calamity that went on and on until all that was left of the structure was rubble, and all that was left of me was a squeal—and that was all that was left of the kids too, after I was done.

"Hey, tell us what you seen tonight," they trooped around me under the street light. "Hey, come on, tell us again what they done." And I was popular for the first time in my life, and no longer called Cockeyes because I wore glasses, or Fat the Water Rat because I was pudgy, but honored with my own name, the purveyor of hilarious skits and ditties:

> *Oh, I got a bimbo down on the bamboo isle.*
> *She's waiting there for me*
> *Beneath the bamboo tree.*
> *She had all the other little bimbos beat a mile.*
> *She dances daily, gaily*
> *She'd make a hit with Barnum and Bailey*
> *And when I go again I'll stay awhile . . .*

My fourteenth summer was green: earning wages of laughter, paid to watch movies and attend vaudeville shows, and then come home to play a stellar role in the simmering Harlem street at night. Even Pop relented in his aloofness and became friendly when I entered the kitchen, still giggling over the hula-hula dancer billed as Madam Kishka, Madam Guts, swaying to the strains of, "Yacka hula wickie doolah, Moishe lyeh mir finif toolah . . ." He laughed when I told him about the Jewish comic who said all his relatives hurt him: his hants hurt him, his knieces hurt him, his oncles hurt him. Even Pop relaxed, because I lightened the burden on his narrow shoulders with my eight dollars per week. And Mom beamed when I crooned Dvorak's *Humoresque,* though she didn't know the English words to the tune, and I didn't know it was Dvorak's *Humoresque:* "Woman is a puzzle that is bound to put a muzzle on the man that makes a fuzzle of romance." Oh, the summer of my fourteenth year was flourishing green.

Came a certain frog act. The batrachian, a contortionist in green costume, lolled on a green baize dais or podium under an equivocal spotlight of aquamarine. It was an unusually hot day, sweltering, beside the hissing carbon arcs. My spectacles fogged, and the spectacle too; the amphibian dissolved into the green murk on the green baize in his green togs. And suddenly where the hell was he? Caught him! And suddenly he flopped elsewhere, slithered off into penumbra out of ken of the scurrying spot that shamrocked after him in pursuit. Well, he and I chased each other the length of the proscenium a good long spell, a good long spell. And below, the audience hooted and guffawed. At the sopping end, when the prosaic footlights came on, the phone rang, and the projectionist raced back from the window to answer it. Distinctly in the receiver came an outraged, "What the hell's goin' on up there?" He made a stammered reply: "I had a hurry call, I was caught short. The kid..." And after he hung up, glowering, he turned to me: "What the hell happened?"

I ask that to this day.

Roth: Whatever merit the piece has, it will always remain in my mind as the pump primer, provided by Bill Targ. And contrary to the author's statement it did at last initiate an actual stream of serious, continual, regular writing. The veritable kind of writing that a professional does. As Gerard Manley Hopkins said, "Sheer plod makes plow down sillion shine"—it's the plod, it's the sheer plod, that makes the plow so brilliant, so shiny.

Interviewer: When you said, "contrary to the author's statement," you were referring to the initial paragraph, weren't you?

Roth: For the author, his whole past—the frog, the green light on the green stage and so forth—everything was just a blur. It represented in my mind such an overlapping, such a blur of events, that I couldn't discriminate, I couldn't separate them. So this is what Bill suggested that I write. Having done that, "contrary to the author's statement" (in other words, it didn't seem to me I could ever separate these elements), the writing ultimately became pervaded with an unquestioning purpose that could not be deflected. This is what really serious writing is, isn't it? You finally become so *imbued* with that kind of purpose, that nothing can throw you—a week in the hospital, *two* weeks in the hospital, somebody terrible that pesters you, or what have you. That's the way I was with *Call It Sleep*—after all, it took four years to finish the damn thing. You can imagine what happens to a guy in four years. And when the first draft of my present writing *Mercy of a Rude Stream,* was completed, when I said, I have done as much of the damn thing as I want to, *it was 1983!* And when I joined that first draft to this marvel of modern technology, the computer, or word processor—which is really a quantum leap from the typewriter—it seemed at last I had at my fingertips what I needed for this peculiarly complex, contradictory mind.

(taped conversation,
Albuquerque, N.M.,
February 8, 1986)

Roth: [Bill] said, "In one of the letters you wrote me, you mentioned that life to you, when you look back at it, was like the time you were an assistant to a projectionist in a movie theater, and the frog act came on and you sweated all over, and it all became a big blur! So why don't you develop this further?" And I did. This was the developing further. And in fact I got a letter back from him saying, "It's very good, I would like some more." So I thought to myself, what the hell have I got here to develop, it's only this very, very tiny little episode in the life of a fourteen-year-old kid. But when I sat down to it I managed to squeeze out, you might say, these various other things. Because, you see, in those days, when they were first introducing the movies, and vaudeville was being phased out, they would have a five-reel movie, and then they would have several vaudeville acts, usually one juggler, a contortionist or something like that, then a couple of what they called hoofers—those were the guys with the canes and the straw hats—and then maybe a monologist, I guess it's the word for it, where the guy does the stand-up funny stories, and maybe dancing, and so forth. So I would see them two or three times . . . and being young and impressionable, it didn't take any great effort for me to memorize the whole act, or the whole speech. And then when I came back to the street, it was the only time I *ever* had any popularity among my peers, because I could repeat these gags!

All of this I eked out, and that's the basis for *Nature's First Green.* I kind of forced myself back into the role of the writer, then it built up a little bit of momentum, you know? And I went on from there. But I was up against a peculiar . . . not a block, anymore . . . but a peculiar barrier: I'd already done the childhood, or I had already done an *interpretation* of that childhood. It was not right, because that childhood had nowhere to go. It was right in one sense, and wrong in another sense. It was right in the sense that it really represented the writer of the thirties, without my knowing it. He had nowhere to go either. Once he left his source, once Thomas Wolfe left the North Carolina that fed him, that gave him vitality, the metropolitan or cosmopolitan world into which he went—Greenwich Village, or you name it—that didn't feed him. That was a world that fed on itself, you might almost say. It brought *them* nowhere, it brought *me* no light. . . .

And, to come back now after this long circle, having got myself started, I then went on to reconsider, what should I do? I couldn't start from the beginning anymore. What was I going to do? And so I thought, well, let the beginning take care of itself. Begin in Harlem—that's where you are now. Begin in 1914. Begin with the arrival of your homely relatives from Galitzia. . . . Fortunately, unfortunately, they arrived. Fortunately, because they impressed on me what life must have been like on the other side—in other words, what they gave me were samples of that life. And it was awful. Also, I had a grandfather who was very orthodox, and he gave me a beautiful example of what orthodoxy was—that is to say, the orthodoxy of that time. He was a tremendously self-centered individual—and no exception either: that was the patriarchal Jew.

They offered me something that I could use, later, novelistically. But on the other hand, by coming to Harlem to live, we pulled out of the East Side and pulled away from the roots, if you want to put it that simplistically. And therefore there was no place for me to go. Only when I did this piece did the idea occur to me that I was practically an entirely different individual now from the one who had written *Call It Sleep;* I approached life now on a different basis, entirely. Not on the basis of reviving, revitalizing the childhood sources that had given birth to that book, but rather now facing adult problems the child didn't have to face. I mean, if you are dealing with a child you have to make allowances, you have to conform to his world. Now, as an adult, people don't conform to your world—they have their own, right? It's a give-and-take proposition. And I think that's where a good deal of growing up, *my* growing up, was interrupted. The growing up was warped by the fact that while I became an adult, I didn't have any experience in this give-and-take world. Had I grown up on the East Side, I would naturally have evolved into a young adult in a Jewish environment in a connected fashion. Here, there's a sudden break—I'm now in the goyish world. They are not going to conform to my Jewish world, or in any way accept me. Nor in any way could I grow up in their world. It's a terrible truncation.

(taped conversation,
Albuquerque, N.M.,
February 7, 1986)

Roth: It has taken me a whole lifetime to begin to write again. I didn't begin to write until I was seventy-three. I'm seventy-seven now.

Interviewer: What do you think was responsible for making you write again?

Roth: Apparently one factor that was needed was the crystal. There's such a thing as a supersaturated solution which needs only one crystal to cause the whole to crystallize. The crystal was Bill Targ, who got me started. Evidently the change had taken place— after almost fifty years had elapsed. . . . I think that apart from being an expressive individual anyway, the question almost should be, why did I stop writing? I don't know what stopped me really. There was a tremendous block. I couldn't write because nothing seemed to me to be pertaining enough, close enough for me to want to write on a long-term basis. And finally the time came when it was; why it came when it did is, again, something that's very complex. But I think what happened was that I finally reached a new plateau where I achieved a kind of inner stability from which I viewed the events of my own life without everything turning to jelly, everything turning fluid, as it always happened before. Always before there had been so many moral alternatives, choices according to the way you looked at things. Now that didn't seem to happen anymore. Also I no longer felt that horrendous indecision immobilizing me. I found I could write, and finding I could write, I did. I know it sounds simple, but that's about the size of it.

Interviewer: How long ago did it happen that you finally found you could write?

Roth: Let's see, about three or four years ago. When I wrote Bill [Targ] saying I'd like to send him my stuff.

Interviewer: How do you feel about the work that you're now writing?

Roth: It's a necessity for me. I tried to indicate before that I never succeeded in becoming a professional writer. The pro doesn't write because of an inner necessity. A good pro does it because this is the way you make a living. It may be true that things are combined in many a professional, but in me they are not combined. In other words, the feeling of the need to make a living was never strong enough to compel the writing. So in connection with what you asked about, the answer is that probably the most important change that took place in me was the reconciliation with a new self.

Interviewer: So it has taken you fifty years to reconcile?

Roth: That's how long it took my kind of guy finally to accept himself. . . . This has other implications, stemming from the acceptance of self—and here again is a repudiation of Joyce: the acceptance of history. Remember, I told you that in trying to write a prologue to my second novel, I found myself completely polarized by history, could scarcely prefer one cause over another. I'm no longer troubled by that. I know where I stand. Reconciliation with one's own excesses seems to include reconciliation with those of humanity. This in turn, in my case, paved the way for reunion with my people. It was something Joyce never allowed himself, refused to do; and so for him history remained a nightmare from which he couldn't wake. The result was *Finnegans Wake*. If the *Ulysses* was the "Event Horizon," *Finnegans Wake* is the "Black Hole" of English literature.*

(Goldsmith, 1983)

* The "Event Horizon" is the region in the vicinity of a "Black Hole" in which change may be perceived and from which the space voyager may escape. The "Black Hole," on the other hand, is so dense that events become fossilized, and not even light can escape, let alone the space voyager.

Weekends in New York—
A Memoir

September 1984

The five years between the publication of Nature's First Green *and that of "Weekends in New York—A Memoir" were very productive for Roth. Although new pieces did not appear in print during this period, he completed a first draft of four autobiographical volumes that became the guide for* Mercy of a Rude Stream, *described by the author as a "memoir-form novel."*

"Weekends in New York—A Memoir" is an excerpt from this work in progress, which the author does not intend to release for publication in his lifetime in its complete form.

Oddly enough, mind seems unaffected [by illness], better, more settled in some ways, so I am writing, better described as suborning an autobiography to my whim. . . . Have a whole damned lifetime to manipulate in the narrow span of what's left.

(letter from Albuquerque, N.M.,
May 27, 1980)

Very, very strange phenomenon relative to a man my age, have been writing for the past year and a half, or so, and quite vigorously. . . . As of today I've finished a first draft of Book Two. . . . Head and maturity seem to have improved in inverse proportion to carcass.

(letter from Albuquerque, N.M.,
February 8, 1981)

What I have in mind is to portray the evolution of the insufferably self-centered, immature, in many ways parasitic and contemptible autodidactic literary youth into approximate adulthood, approximate regeneration, his reconciliation with self and with the necessity of change.

(letter from Albuquerque, N.M.,
April 21, 1981)

I'm well on the way to Volume Two of my fictionalized and debased past, and hope with the token of rejuvenation of moving to more favorable, or at least different surroundings, to go on from there. Chief aim, given the necessary forces to complete this long-drawn-out job (dubious), is to portray a groping, approximate regeneration, achievement of adulthood as a reciprocal result of Muriel's affection, and some kind of blind, stubborn determination to realize the best traditions.

(letter from Albuquerque, N.M.,
November 2, 1981)

When I've completed Book Three, which I envisage as taking the narrative full circle, I would then have the advantage of a unity that might raise the quality of the work. . . . As to quality I am no longer sure of myself. . . . The quality at best is what might be expected from the declining and aged practitioner. But so far, I keep at it, through the physical ordeal of this unspeakable disorder.

I said that I was no longer sure of myself—that's been true for a long time. What I mean more specifically is that I am conscious in the relation between author and product of a "maturing" that is not only belated, perhaps the most of any scrivener known, but a maturing in the sense of an almost fierce negation of the individual who fathered *CIS*. . . . The negation in the first place takes the form of a violent negation of Joyce, not of all that he contributed, his virtuosities and innovations, but of what he stood for, or more precisely the direction he faced, what proceeded from his monstrous detachment and artistic autonomy. I move uncertainly in a new reality.

(letter from Albuquerque, N.M.,
April 20, 1982)

Writing continues to be the chief "discipline" of my life. Because in so many ways the mind of the author has changed since those flourishing and unregenerate days of his first novel, the treatment of the fiction is quite different—I fancy—with less of the no longer attainable lyricism, and more reflection. . . . This particular [third] volume may or may not be of interest for at least two reasons: it deals with the personal crisis in the author's life, separation from the older woman, his more than sponsor, and also tries to account for, or at least treat of, the breakdown in identity leading to a breakdown in creative productivity. . . . It contains, I believe, two singular elements: one is the zaniest and correspondingly sad separation from a woman on whom one depended in unheard of immaturity; the other is my separation from the erstwhile central character of my novel, Bill Clay, the proletarian turned tyrant. Fortunately, a few notes of a journal kept during the period 1937–39 survive, giving the writing a certain sense of substantiality. It will undoubtedly be many months before a reworkable draft is even completed. . . . By the way, of its own accord seemingly, after the opening thirty or so pages, the work shifted gears, as it were, and went from first person to third person.

(letter from Albuquerque, N.M.,
January 18, 1983)

At the outset of the present writing, call it Volume Three, I did feel a high degree of uncertainty. But now that the work has progressed, and I hope will continue to, the uncertainty has been reduced (though I may hit a snag tomorrow that proves insuperable; the writing is a day-by-day hazard). The conviction emerges that both treatment and content provide something unique. And moreover, being the kind of guy who can only grow, it would seem, by dint of his own creating, I have the feeling that exactly this is at last taking place. This growth, as it were, resonates against the work itself. I am more than a little astonished that after all these years, and almost at the end of them, the writer should have succeeded, quite against probability, in having executed a 180-degree turn in attitude. And not even know he had done so until well into the routine of daily work. It is a little like finding out what you were looking for after you have found it. Anyway that seems to be the case, to have made the preoccupation with self a stepping stone to the preoccupations of others. (For me, I might almost say, though I would dearly wish the results to be notable, whether they be good, bad or indifferent, they would represent a triumph.)

(letter from Albuquerque, N.M.,
April 10, 1983)

There's much else. The most significant thing that has happened to me, or to my writing, most significant and as yet unappraised as to value, are these two "last" volumes, the latter of the two which I'm near to completing, and thus a first draft for all four. A couple of journals and a few small notebooks, which were withheld from the general bonfire of papers in Maine (and which deal with the agonizing separation from Eda Lou Walton, and the other, my exile in L.A. under the domination of my Communist Party mentor, constitute the basis of the work and inform with particularity something which in retrospect had been an agonized blur. . . . Anyway to me it represents a return to the quotidian, and away from the haunted interiors, all of which is welcome and a private triumph—what it will mean to others is moot and pending. I'll add just one more thing, not to be enigmatic, only a little reserved, that here I finally broke through imponderable barriers in myself—and the previous reluctance to do so becomes a graphic or novelistic element. . . .

And I say this without fake modesty, because its treatment of narrative, or I should say, its narrative method is so seemingly haphazard, *is* haphazard, that if somebody said considerately, "Oh, no, this is impossible," I might feel chagrined, but resigned. (More likely: "Oh, no, how pathetic.")

(letter from Albuquerque, N.M.,
September 24, 1983)

I've reached that peculiar stage where existence is inseparable from a sense of the end. . . . Let me tell you my thinking re this W[ork] I[n] P[rogress] at the moment. I've given myself a short vacation after reading four "volumes" (horrors!) of my serious scrivening since 1979 (I may have told you: I had no idea almost five years had passed). Quality apart concerning all of it, Volume Three interests me most of all, being the most variegated and imbued with a sense of life and change. Also it epitomizes the main thrust of the writing as a whole; and that is, as nearly as I can formulate it, to convey the degenerative effect on the sensibility of the immigrant, stripped of his original support, by his U.S. environment. And the redeeming quality of that selfsame environment, or should one say, its fundamental ethos. So in one sense it's a shocking negation of the child in *CIS* and an affirmation following that. The subject has been treated before, but not of or about the artist or writer himself.

To conclude, I'd like to get a word processor and try to achieve something approximately finished in Volume Three, which I would publish first (and the others as indicated or expedient, or appropriate).

(letter from Albuquerque, N.M.,
February 26, 1984)

Interviewer: What are you working on: is this the journal, or is this a novel?

Roth: Oh no, it's a novel, but I use journals that escaped the conflagration that was the fate of my other writings. In Maine I'd decided, hell, I'm through writing, there's no use keeping any of this. Joe McCarthy might get hold of it—that was in the forties—and I'll just be in the jam, a Red jam, so to speak. I might as well burn it up, because my literary career is finished. But these three journals of the late thirties—1938, 1939, just before World War II—were stuck away somewhere, some cupboard or other in the farmhouse; I didn't see them, I guess. And when I did find them, I decided I couldn't burn them. I valued them too much. They were of a critical period in my life, and in Muriel's too.

I draw on them now to create some sort of a particularity in what otherwise, after forty-five years, would be a generalized blur. I use the journals sometimes verbatim, but sometimes I only alter the entry when I feel it's appropriate to do so.

(Goldsmith, 1983)

My writing has entered a new phase, or perhaps I should say, *I* have: from artist, God help us, to practitioner—all this with the aid of an industrial consultant, seriously (though I won't go into details)! He's provided me with a typist, who rips off the keys like a machine gun, which has proved a great boon. I have to have copy ready for her. Result has been that she has already done some sixty pages (with genuine enjoyment, a good sign), what amounts to two excerpts, which I plan to send to *Commentary* tomorrow for proof of the pudding. In any case, I'm proceeding from there, quite stimulated and at times almost exuberant, discounting the aches and pains. I have now gotten some sixty or seventy pages ready for her, and I just hope we can keep this thing rolling. It's quite scandalous by the way, but I've finally gotten over reticence about that; and another thing, the narrative time line, though not exactly thrown to the winds, is not adhered to. Total length, judging from my rough typed draft, should come to (I wince) close to a thousand pages. Here I am, talking about all this, and tomorrow may see it collapse. Or me.

(letter from Albuquerque, N.M.
April 29, 1984)

April 1939, Saturday night

I walked east to Central Park West, and there, across from the park, turned south. It was now 8:30 P.M. I hadn't realized that the many-storied apartment houses along the way were occupied by well-to-do Jews, until I saw a car backing up before one of them, and backing up too hard, so hard it struck the front bumpers of the parked sedan behind quite forcibly. The uniformed doorman came out and said jocularly: "Boy, are they gonna sue you, are they gonna sue you, Dr. Gottlieb." Unperturbed and smiling, Dr. Gottlieb got out of the vehicle. And I, looking about, saw that most of the people on the avenue appeared to be also Jewish, and, as far as I could judge, affluent.

At Fifty-seventh Street I turned east, aimlessly, gaze sliding from face to face in the passing crowd. When I reached Broadway, my attention was drawn to quite a large group of people on the northeast corner in front of Weber & Heilbroner's men's furnishings. I crossed the street and drifted over and found a comfortable prop to lean against: the parcel drop of the U.S. mail. The crowd had gathered about a cluster of five women and two men. The women wore headdresses made of white muslin or linen, trailing behind their shoulders, like that worn by members of the Red Cross. The men wore street clothes. One, a tall, cadaverous, aging man, with faded rusty hair, carried a Bible; the other, short, wiry, with dark eyes snapping and intense, carried a briefcase as well as a Bible. The women, for all their white headdresses, were unmistakably plebeian. One was a large, Scottish-looking woman with strawy eyelashes, almost colorless, who shut her eyes when she sang; another, with pinched lips and sharp nose, looked Polish; another, a matron and stout, with graying hair, reminded me vaguely of a chambermaid I had seen in a hotel. The fourth, who bore a tambourine, was a Negro woman with very taut, fine brown skin like polished briar. The fifth, a brunette, was quite pretty—and petite. Their backs were turned to me, for they were facing the street, but I saw their faces from time to time as their heads swayed in song.

The usual New York crowd had collected, and they stood about amused and nudging one another. I couldn't make out what the evangelists were singing, except that the words God and Jesus resounded again and again from the music of the hymn, the music of some popular tune. The Negro woman led the choir, and her rhythms and husky voice were enough to hold anyone's attention. I thought of my old friend Bill Loem, those months ago—years ago, they seemed now—when we stood in the park in Cincinnati, and listened to that same kind of religious meeting, and his voice had become blurred and harsh when we turned away, and he wept, stalwart of the Communist Party, steeled in the struggle, wept out of sheer nostalgia—and never forgave me for having witnessed his tears and his grief, and his betrayal of weakness.

I looked about. Behind the revivalists, in the Weber & Heilbroner show window, gray suits and gray felt hats with braided leather hatbands were on display, and red socks. To the south, across the street, burned the orange neon sign of an auto salesroom: NASH. Cafés and drugstores glared on the crowd. The huge Coca-Cola ad aloft bubbled and glowed. Dimmed headlights of cars passed. All about droned New York's dense, intricate din. A circus wagon, horse-drawn, clattered by. The ceaseless Saturday night throng streamed in both directions toward the group that had gathered on the sidewalk, like a solid eddy about the little cluster, some filtering through, some skirting, some tarrying out of curiosity, augmenting the bystanders. Two thousand years ago, I mused, that little knot of evangelists might have been enrolled among the martyrs, might have been the founders of the church. But now, what? Fanatics, forlorn fanatics. Still, it was interesting to wonder what that gilded lady would have looked like—she wore a black hat with the high white peak like an ice-cream sundae and was wrathfully elbowing the little troupe of hymn singers out of her way as she tried to get through—what she would have looked like, elbowing the sainted apostles on the streets of Jerusalem.

Poor nuts, I thought, some new sect, and decided to move on; but then I remembered I had nowhere to go and so changed my mind and stayed. Strange, how I disliked watching this kind of spectacle. It embarrassed me terribly: humanity exhibiting its pathetic manias in public. I forced myself to stay on. I thought: well, see it through. The crowd was so scornful and cynical, something might happen; something might happen that would bring grist to my mill; it was my duty to stay on and see it happen. Besides, there was a certain tension in the air. Blasé New Yorkers usually ignored this sort of thing, but this crowd was hostile, had deliberately stopped to jeer. I could feel my own quickening pulse responding to the latent resistance of the onlookers.

Presently, the singing came to a close, and the large Scottish-looking woman came to the center of the circle and began to preach. She quoted from the Gospels, proclaimed the imminence of Christ's second coming and the end of the world. Her delivery was poor, her voice without control; she stopped frequently in the midst of dire prophecy to fumble for words, alternating between hysteria and the uncertain speech of a woman of humble background. And now entered the spoiler—pushed his way toward the center of the semicircle and began his antics. Sober, he might have been a tractable enough grocery clerk for the A & P. Drunk, he was the irrepressible clown: an Irishman, if the brogue that cropped up in his speech was any indication.

[Ireland (I muse, sit back today and muse) once fighting a savage, sanguinary war for its freedom—let's call it "freedom" in quotes—for its independence from England, for its sovereignty—leave out all the emotional shibboleths and griefs (for its sovereignty, and not one that would entail the annihilation of England, as the PLO is pledged by covenant to win at the expense of Israel)—leave out all the highly charged wrongs and enmity, Ireland fighting for its right to a distinct entity (the South fighting for its right to secede, with its institutions, from the Union). Place the whole thing in a perspective of economics: Ireland fighting to rid itself of the British investor, the British landowner, businessman, industrialist, banker, in order to keep its wealth and resources from flowing out of the country, and in the hands of its own landowners, investors, bankers, and industrialists. Whatever. How could Joyce so separate himself from the fierce struggle of his country-men for their independence—and focus his attention on a single day in June 1904, and exclude, while writing about it, all the bloodshed and turmoil between the inception of his work and its completion. What specious claptrap is this silence, exile, cunning (borrowed without acknowledgment—was it from some religious order?). What a fraud, what a cover-up! Ah, but friend (I now continue to myself), didn't you do the same thing? Fled, deserted the struggle of your people, more afflicted than the Irish ever were, for a land of their own, their own land. Indifferent, averse, scornful, opposed on principle, adherent of Marxist internationalism, you thought. How can you take Joyce to task? In what way were you different? Until June '67, when all the diffuse fears of the fate of the Jews, the scarce-credible rumors of a new Holocaust, condensed, sublimated into terrible dread, a terrible woe. Until then, you had been a Party-line purveyor, maybe an increasingly uneasy one, but still a Party-line servitor. How were you different (cringing henchman of a paranoid), seeking to dissociate yourself from fellow-Jews, but instead were a fervent defender of "the oppressed and dispossessed and inoffensive" Arabs, the anti-nationalist internation-alist—as Joyce, the universalist, quit Ireland (and never wrote about anything else). You found a haven for your alienation from your people in Marxist doctrine, as Joyce in universal culture, and both

proved sterile. I seem to feel a difference between us and yet can't put my finger on it: why did I eventually become partisan, not of the Diaspora I shunned, but of Judaism's rebirth in Israel: while he never reunited with a new Ireland? Perhaps it was because I came later in the day, or because I could never create so coruscating a blind alley as he, with his dazzling virtuosity, a mausoleum to lie in. No, my fate was more like Pound's; to live long enough so that the warp of time became manifest, so inexorably contrary to one's views one had to repudiate them—even repudiate the self, though grown old, testify to the truth though grown old. I am only furious at myself for having taken so long, so ponderously long to have effected the change—to the degree that I have, however inept, inadequate. One Israeli lad, ambushed and slain in Lebanon, is one of my kin, a surrogate son, ambushed and killed in Lebanon—and the same holds true for the way my beloved M feels, distressed and sorrowing at the news. Oh, I know the question that will be asked: What are we doing in Lebanon? What about the claims of the PLO to an independent state? What about Israel? Her security, her existence. Who is going to ride above this battle, look down at the warring sides with Olympian detachment?—only Olympians. That sort of detachment spells paralysis; has spelled it for me these four decades and more; compels me now to intrude upon my own work, disrupt its unity for lack of time—for I know I shall never have time to set forth my views later, in their due place, neither the time nor the strength, perhaps not even the faculties. . . .]

"What're you doin' here?" the drunk heckled the Scottish-looking woman as she preached. "Will you tell us: what do you think you're doin'? Thish no church." And when she refused to heed him, he alternated ogling her with gapings of mock solemnity, lolling his head. She closed her eyes to blot him out. He grinned in triumph, turned to the crowd, and brayed like a donkey. The crowd guffawed. Encouraged, he went the rounds of the little group, trying out his big grin, and feigning fright at each stony response. He winked broadly at the pretty brunette and said: "You don't want to be here. No-o-o." He rocked back with besotted earnestness. The little man with the briefcase and Bible gave him a shove. And ugly in an instant, the drunk turned on the other: "Whatsa matter with you?" But before the confrontation could develop further, the Negro woman struck her tambourine, and the group began to sing. Song cemented them, and the drunk wandered back to the inner ring of spectators.

And now the little man, with a swift movement, set his briefcase against the base of the lamppost and strode out to the middle of the circle. He had been a sinner, he declared, but through the holy power of Christ Jesus he had been saved. He spoke with an accent, something middle-European, but an accent I couldn't identify. Once again the drunk stepped out of the audience into the open center. With a Yiddish accent he mimicked the preacher: "You read the Bible, Mister? Oy, he reads the Bible. You gotta Bible, Abie?" He flapped upturned palms. The crowd laughed. Individuals turned completely around in transports of mirth and stamped their feet.

"Bombs will rain from the air," shouted the little man. "Airplanes will drop bombs from the air, and whole cities will be laid waste, as it is written: the world will be destroyed before the coming of Christ!"

"Whadda ya know?" said the drunk. "Abie knows all about it."

"The hand of God will take care of him," said the Negro woman.

"Is he your boyfriend?" the drunk leered at her.

She turned her head away. He lurched toward the pretty brunette: "Is he your boyfriend?"

"Don't pay him no heed, Sister," the Negro woman admonished.

"Who is it doesn't feel in his heart the coming of the last days?" the preacher shouted. "Daily, daily the end approaches. Armageddon draws nigh, the doom is made ready—will you be ready for that day? Come now to Christ Jesus. Tomorrow will be too late! I implore, I implore—" he brandished the Bible: "Heed the words of Revelation! Seek Christ Jesus for your soul's sake!"

"He's your boyfriend," the drunk reeled toward the woman with the pinched lips and sharp nose, the woman I thought was Polish. And suddenly she uncoiled, so suddenly only the sound gave proof of the act; she slapped him.

He staggered away toward the curb. The Polish woman followed. And slap! "You win," he grinned, whined comically, ducked. "You win, lady." And slap! And again. "I'll take it from a woman," he took shelter behind fending arms. "I'll take it from a woman."

"I'll show you!" the Polish woman swung again.

"That's enough, Sister Mary!" the Negro woman cried out. "Leave him alone."

But Sister Mary had tasted blood. White headdress flying, she pursued the retreating drunk, who still repeated with each blow: "I'll take it from you because you're a woman."

"Sister Mary!" the other women cried. "Sister Mary, come back!"

"I'll show him!"

"Leave him alone, Sister Mary," the Negro woman followed her sister revivalist. "Leave him alone. He's troubled in spirit."

Reluctantly, Sister Mary desisted.

"I took it because she was a woman," said the drunk.

"This man claims to be a Roman Catholic!" the little man shouted. "And yet he mocks prophecy, the clear prophecy of the Bible foretelling the ruin of the world and the end of days. He claims to be a Roman Catholic, and yet he blasphemes the name of God. What does this show? It shows that salvation lies neither in Catholicism, nor Protestantism, nor Judaism, but in Christ Jesus alone. Now! Seek salvation! Now! Before the coming of the Almighty's wrath!"

A well-spoken refined-looking woman, with hennaed hair and wearing glasses, had come over to the drunk: "You look like a decent man," she addressed him. "Why don't you leave them alone? I don't believe in what they say any more than you do. They're poor, troubled people, but they're perfectly harmless and should be left alone."

"I took it, didn't I, lady?"

"Yes, but now you ought to go on and leave them to preach their message."

"Yes, you have no right to disturb them," seconded a portly man with a neat mustache. "They're just trying to tell in their way they feel something's wrong. It would do you good to listen."

"Who're you to tell me I've got no right?" the drunk demanded truculently. "I'll take it from a woman. I won't take it from a man."

"I'm not asking you to take anything," argued the man with the neat mustache. "I'm just asking you to grant these people their rights of free speech and not to disturb them."

"Please, be quiet!" the little man rushed over.

"I got as much right to be here as you got," the drunk edged closer to the man with the neat mustache.

"Certainly. It's a free country."

"Well, who the hell're you to tell me what to do?"

"I'm just trying to be your friend."

"I don't want you for a friend—there!"

"All right, but don't disturb these people."

"Will you please be quiet!" the little man shouted at the top of his voice. And other voices in the crowd joined in: "Leave them alone, you! Go on, beat it!"

"Try to stop me," the drunk defied with surly self-assurance.

"I won't try to stop you," said the man with the neat mustache. "I'll get a cop."

"Yeah?"

"Yes, I will."

The drunk rocked on his heels for a space. "I'll show you I'm a sport." He drew from his pocket a handful of small change. "I'll show I'm a sport." He sorted out the nickels and pocketed the rest and stepped into the center of the circle again. "I wanna make a contribution," he said to the little man, whose voice had become hoarse with preaching. "A goodwill offer." The little man avoided him. The drunk swayed after the other. "I wanna make a little contribution—"

"In the name of Jesus, go away!" the little man struck at the proffering hand, sending the coins flying to the sidewalk.

"Where's my nickels?" the drunk wagged his head. "All right, here's a dime."

And now, *deus ex machina* in blue, the cop arrived: a sergeant, a huge man who hulked above everyone else. He stretched out his arms and seemed to encompass everyone there. "What's goin' on here?" he asked. "What's the meanin' o' this?" He seemed as pained as he was perplexed.

"We are preaching here to save our fellow man before the coming of the end," said the little man, who scarcely reached the sergeant's chest. "We are preaching the warning of Revelation. We are preaching the Gospel," and he added quietly, "the word of God."

"Sure, I've nothing against the word of God," said the sergeant, "but it's an inconvenience to traffic."

"We have a right to stand here," said the Negro woman.

"That you have," said the sergeant. "But you've no right to obstruct the sidewalk."

"It ain't us; it's him," the Polish woman pointed at the drunk. "That one."

"Well, go over to Columbus Circle," the sergeant stretched his arms even wider. "There's more room there."

None of the revivalists would budge.

"Please!" the sergeant beseeched the little man.

He wavered.

"Please!" the sergeant repeated. "I know it's important for your message to reach the people, but this ain't the place to do it on the sidewalk in front of Weber & Heilbroner."

The little man nodded, took a firmer grip of his Bible, and prepared to leave. "Mister, is that your briefcase?" I asked. He regarded me wordlessly, picked up his briefcase.

With the sergeant in the rear, herding them south toward Columbus Circle, they made their departure, the drunk trailing them, grinning happily.

June 1939, Saturday night

To begin at the beginning—more or less—I had a note from M informing me that her father had said he would take us all out to dinner (instead of our having dinner at her sister B's, as she had planned) and would I call for her at six o'clock. We would then go to B and her husband J's at 6:15 for a snifter, and the parents would come at seven o'clock. I quit writing at 4:45. (An outline of a sketch, this time perhaps salable, of an incident connected with my swimming with the Irish toughies of 119th Street off bareass beach in the Harlem River. Interesting, the kind of coexistence I'd established with my demon— my obsessive anxiety—provided I didn't strain too hard—or too close to the self.) I bathed—and shaved with a new blade. Then with necktie in my pocket, and not yet daring to risk putting on a clean shirt, but dressed in my faded, blue polo shirt, blue slacks (Macy's basement bargain) and the Wanamaker English jacket of gray plaid—of my old benefactor Edith's bounty—my tan shoes, none too sturdy in appearance any longer, and my gray, weathered felt hat, in want of cleaning and blocking, and with small vent-hole at the crimp, I sallied forth. At the last moment I remembered that M's note instructed me to bring pipe. So I pocketed pipe, and in typical, absent fashion, deciding not to take the Bull Durham cigarette tobacco along, left the pipe in my room instead, and had to return and fetch it. I bought a small tin of more expensive pipe tobacco, Revelation, eighteen cents out of the $1.40 I had left until my next Home Relief check a week or more hence. Then I knocked at M's window.

She wore a print, completely sleeveless. She had cut the half-sleeves away when they tore at the seams under the armpit. The material was of some cottony stuff printed with a design of little brown and black circles. She smiled at me from the other side of the open steel door; I looked at her questioningly and indicated her room. She said: "It's safe." We went in and she clung to me and told me the day's news: J and B had been there, also Mr. and Mrs P, her parents. They had all had a light lunch there, Swiss cheese and Jewish rye bread, and liked it. She had been copying music before I arrived, and one of the sheets was still wet, and I almost touched it—lying on the table under the gooseneck lamp—but she said just in time: "It's still wet, darling." It looked beautiful, though (her cantata which she was preparing to have blueprinted), the black India ink notes contrasting strongly with the thin white paper. She remarked on the three-pointed pen she used, its tendency to clot: the ink coated the pen like a paint. I suggested that the musical notation would make a fetching design for a cloth. She thought she could make a million dollars on the idea. "I have a shirt here," I said, producing my necktie. She got the shirt out of the drawer, and I matched it with the tie. "How do you think it will look?" The shirt was gray (also of Edith's provenance), the tie blue.

"It's better than what you have on," she said.

"Oh, I wasn't going to wear that," I said.

"I know, darling."

I doubted that shirt and tie matched, but she thought they would do, saying my best colors were gray and blue. I said I'd go out for a walk until six o'clock, and she said she'd dress meanwhile. She clung to me and shed a tear. I shook her and told her not to be silly. She promised to behave when I came back. And before I left showed me a letter from the head of her department, in which she described the consternation of the girls at W College on learning that M would not be teaching there next fall.

I walked west to Lexington Avenue and loitered before the antique shops, the chinaware, and chairs, and ruminated on my writing: whether I had recovered enough equanimity to tackle the sketch— *Broker* (how apt the subliminal self was)—that had sent me into the night on the verge of hysteria, or whether to elaborate the Harlem River incident. I mused, trying to find graphic analogies for my state— if I ever had to describe it to someone: short circuit, but not the apocalyptic one of my novel. A kind of hairline crack, say, in the distributor of a car, or perhaps a spark plug, that diverted just enough mental current from its destination to impair performance; something of the sort. It was always there, deflecting the mind, draining it, depriving it of its natural élan. It would never allow again any long, integrated literary work, never could sustain one. And I would have to live with it now and from now on . . . live with it, become inured to it, become resigned. . . .

I returned to M's room a few minutes after six. She was dressed in her homemade hopsacking suit out of oaten-colored cloth that I had helped her fit, or hang, crawling around her ankles with foot rule and pins. And on her head, canted pertly and with a black ribbon trailing in the back, she wore her little brown postage stamp of a tam. I washed my face and neck again to insure as cool an appearance as possible and slipped into my newly laundered gray shirt. She buttoned the back of the collar after my tie was properly adjusted and we sat down to compose ourselves before setting out.

We decided not to imbibe any alcoholic beverages at J and B's in order to stay cool, and neither of us felt we needed any.

"Why is B so nervous about their coming here?" I asked. I knew there had been considerable parental resistance to her marriage to J, but I thought that was all over with—that he was accepted now, a successful free-lance photographer.

"No," M said. "There's always been that antagonism between the two: B gets like that"—M clenched her fist—"whenever she sees Mother. Mother has a strong tendency to be masterful, and B has resisted her all the way. There were some awful scenes at home." We stood up and prepared to leave.

"What about you?" I asked. "Did you get along?"

"Oh, yes, she approved of me. I did all the things she wanted me to, or almost." We walked out into the fine late afternoon. "Got top grades in school. Phi Beta Kappa in my junior year."

"And now you're about to do something more outrageously un-conventional than all your—your siblings." We entered the shadow of the covered way under the new construction, and she took my hand.

"This is one block where I'm sure your collar won't wilt," she said.

"That's right. I ought to be grateful for Vermont covered bridges on New York sidewalks. You know something? You don't burp any more."

"Yes, J's noticed that too."

"What's its miraculous disappearance due to?"

"I don't know. You're going to say it's you, smarty-pants."

"Of course, the only new thing in the picture is my taking you to bed."

"But that's no longer new, darling," she said silkily.

We laughed. I admired—and envied without covetousness—the easy, unruffled flow of her thought, the tranquillity of her riposte that still served its purpose without heat or satiric barb. Ah, to have been bred that way, been brought up that way. It wouldn't have done me any good to have run away from home at an early age. As the seedling was bent—or however that maxim phrased it. God, there was so much to think about when I was with her, so much that reflected itself back to myself in the glass of her constancy, revealing about me that which made me shake my head in gloomy distaste again and again.

We went into the elevator, and up two flights, and rang the doorbell. B looked pretty, tip-tilted nose and blonde hair, and comely in a kind of postcard-pale yellow dress made of something rayony and topped by a small jacket that for some reason seemed to go with the word *bolero*. And J wore a brown suit of gabardine and a chocolate-brown shirt with a bold plaid McCrossen tie. I was relieved to note that he was not wearing a white shirt (a white shirt was something Mother favored—that and tobacco pipes). His shirt was open, necktie loose. Their phonograph was playing as we came into the living room the "Beer Barrel Polka," J's favorite for the week. Their living room was large, nicely furnished, semi-*moderne,* plate-glass coffee table on wrought iron legs and Scandinavian chairs. J's photographic equipment was discreetly spaced about and on the white walls his commercial photographs: a game-hunting arrow with broad-headed tip hanging down, which he had photographed for an insurance company over the caption of their always hitting the mark: a row of test tubes in a rack, a photo done for Consumers Union analyzing the ingredients of a candy bar. He had also taken and enlarged, for his own enjoyment, several pictures of the Lower East Side, teeming as ever with pedestrians halted or in passage beside pushcarts. I studied them nostalgically, and in one I thought I could make out the word *Mohel* in Hebrew lettering on a sign above the doorway of a tenement.

"There are an awful lot of people born in New York. Were you?" J asked.

"No, I was born in Austria-Hungary, but some years ago, after the war, I was born again in Poland." They laughed.

"What's the name of the town?" J asked.

"Too many z's in it to pronounce," I said.

B recalled crossing over the border into Canada with a party of social service workers. The rest of the people were born in New York. But she had said proudly: "Portland, Oregon."

"That's when Father was a minister in the logging camps," said J.

"But you weren't born there?" he addressed M.

"Oh, no, I'm a true Brahmin," said M. "Somerville, Boston."

"And you?" I asked J.

"In Suburbia, New Jersey."

Our levity and small talk seemed to accentuate our nervous anticipation, like tics of uneasiness. What did we want to drink? J asked. We couldn't decide between vermouth and abstaining, and the question languished there. B told M she had done an elegant job in making her dress.

"Does the pattern call for a belt?" she asked.

"No, it was optional," said M. "Would you like it without?"

B thought she would: "Either that, or a little tighter."

"Yes," said M. And with a whole body's affirmation pulled in the cloth belt a grommet or two more snugly about her narrow waist. Again the question of drinks came up, and we still couldn't decide. J gave up. I thought M would benefit by having a vermouth cocktail, and she agreed. With J's permission I made her one, and served it, but had none myself. To J's nervous garrulity on the propriety of having drinks before the main guests arrived, I said that nothing in my tradition dictated either, only that a *shicker* was a *goy*, and translated that for their benefit; but more to the point, if ever I had an obligation to my shirt collar, this was the evening. I drew out my pipe.

"Oh, yes, that's right," said J, and immediately followed suit. His smoking tobacco looked at first like the brand known as Model, and I lamented my extravagance at splurging eighteen cents for my can of Revelation, while his cost only a nickel. But it wasn't Model.

"Let's play rummy," said B. The "Beer Barrel Polka" was set spinning again. J caviling that the music was too low—tinny—but no one moved to remedy the sound, so on it churned: "Roll out the barrel; we'll have a barrel of fun." Then came the business about the window shades. Sunlight of late afternoon sloped into the room, and B said she was too warm—and pulled the shades down. But J objected—and raised them again.

"They're better down," M suggested. "The window panes are simply filthy."

"They still let in some light," said J. "Oh, you lived in a brown house," he chaffed, "with brown insides, and you wore a brown dress."

"M still shuns light," I joined ungallantly in the banter. (J, the photographer, loved light, and at night wanted all the electric lamps on at once.)

M pulled the shades down once more, but up they went again, thanks to J. Everyone wandered about, or sat uneasily, as I did, nursing the spruceness of my shirt collar. I had taken my English jacket off when I came into the apartment, as a primary means for keeping cool; but as time approached for the guests to arrive, I fetched it again and put it on.

"Do you really want to wear your jacket?" asked J.

"No," I said, "but they'll soon be here."

"Don't be silly," B admonished. "Here give it to me. I'll hang it up." I surrendered the garment.

"The P's are human, you know," J reassured me.

"Well, I'm trying to accept the rules of the game and behave accordingly." And just then the door buzzer strummed.

I remember a woman, sharp-featured, spare, and quick—she seemed sharp-eyed too—cleaving into the room; attired in a red hat and a blue and white vertically striped shirtwaist, she carried a red handkerchief, and her lips were rouged the same color—carmine. I don't remember the color of her skirt. She greeted her daughters with a kiss, and her voice was light and sweetly cordial and completely stylized. Followed a man, heavy shouldered, bulky and big, clad in a gray suit of thin weave. He had a sunburned bald head surrounded by a fringe of gray hair and a bulbous socratic nose. Compared to him, in almost all respects, features and figure and grace of bearing, his wife epitomized aristocracy. He was deliberate in his movements, as befitted his ponderous physique. I shook hands with the one and with the other. After that, events, though not blurred, became episodic, and I am no longer certain of their proper sequence.

Father sat down in the easy chair before the window in contention, settled himself comfortably and drew out his heavy briar pipe. Mother began talking rapidly and brightly about their lovely boat trip from Boston to New York and the perfectly glorious weather we were blessed with. B, who had been in Buffalo recently for a social workers' convention, said that the weather there had been positively cold. Had she looked up so-and-so while she was there? Mother asked. No, she hadn't had a chance to. Some talk of Niagara Falls and their beauty on the Canadian side.

"A big piece fell off the American side," J remarked.

"Oh, yes," we all agreed, with Mother adding: "Wasn't it too bad? The Cave of the Winds is gone."

"Is that so?" I was genuinely surprised. "A friend and I visited it in 1924, after high school graduation."

"The king and queen of England were there when we were," said Mother.

"We could have come within ten feet of them, if we had wanted to," said Father. The royal pair, he went on, were staying at the Regency, and had he chosen to go to some sort of Kiwanis International reception there, he and Mother could have been near to British sovereignty itself. Mother had declined to go.

"I'm too much of a democrat to think it's worth the trouble," she said. "A democrat with a small d of course."

J brought out pictures he had taken of the monarchs at the World's Fair, which showed them in the same limousine as Governor Lehman and Mayor La Guardia. "The bouncy little man," he explained, "is La Guardia."

There followed talk about conventions, with Father chaffing B about belonging to a social workers' organization, a kind of a union, heaven help us. He had a hearty laugh with a deep jolly ratchety timbre about it. They spoke of conventions in general—and the way the Legionnaires behaved. Everything had to be chained down or removed, especially in the hotels they occupied, because anything was apt to be heaved out of the window. They were a wild bunch, but taming down a bit, said Father.

"They're growing older," J offered the opinion.

"Oh, no," Father differed, masculine and forceful. "The hotels demand a bond before they'll accept the Legionnaires as guests. That's what's taming them down." He went on to recount the difficulty he had had in getting a certain suite of rooms for his offices in one of the better-class hotels in the Midwest. The American Legion had held its convention there the week before and wrecked the place; and the manager adamantly refused to let him have the suite. "But this is a different kind of organization," Father had tried to convince the other. "This is the Kiwanis, not the Legion." The manager had listened politely, and a little knowingly, but still refused as adamantly as before. "I'm going to have that suite," said Father (and once again the timbre of his voice summoned up the essence of administrative, of executive America). "And since you won't give it to me, I'll have to go over your head." He had called up B, a large stockholder in the hotel, and B had called the manager, advising him he had made a mistake (at which we all duly laughed). "Well, you never saw a man so humble before," said Father. "By the time we were ready to leave, he went out of his way to tell us how very wrong he had been in his estimation of our organization."

Other conventions were discussed, the entire spectrum of conventions: the Retail Liquor Dealers, who went about plastered drunk for three days, said Mother. The Lumbermen's convention, whose members went about sporting canes and wearing a stick in their lapels. The Canners, Mother thought, were the worst.

"The canners?" I said in surprise. "They sound so innocuous."

"Oh, they're anything but," Mother assured me. "They really behave dreadfully." Then the Shriners were brought up for consideration. I have forgotten now whether it was the Shriners or Legionnaires who sprayed acetate on women's legs, which made them feel as if wading through water. J recalled how on one rainy day, a group of Shriners bought fishing poles and settled on a curbstone and fished.

"How much did you get paid for that?" Mother stood up while J was still talking and was inspecting a photograph he had taken for *Field and Stream:* a camping scene, a tent pitched by a stream with a canoe on its bank.

"Must you know?" J parried.

"Yes. It's very pretty. Now don't be coy, J. It's all in the family."

"For your benefit, G," he addressed her by her first name, "I was paid fifty dollars."

"That's a tidy sum." And now her quick eye came to rest on the window. "Why, J, what a window!"

"I just didn't have a chance," said J. "The day the window cleaner was here, I forgot to tell him, and when I was he wasn't."

"B," Mother advised. "You could easily train ivy to go up the window."

B didn't seem interested. . . .

[I feel quite depressed as I transcribe from journal to typewriter. What does it come to?—this mounting up, piling up, even in recollection, of allusions to a world of which I shared not the remotest part, cared nothing for, either, though that's beside the point—maybe—could only sit, feigning alertness, and keeping fingers unlocked in my lap because they stuck together. I try to recall, but it is beyond recall, whether I sought M's eyes or not, M's smile of encouragement or sympathy. In later days publicists and sociologists would speak of a generation gap. There was no such term then; it was taken for granted that American parents, in general, those of the middle class (not my own immigrant ones, of course), expressed attitudes no longer in vogue—nothing wrong with them, only at variance, because taken up with traditional concerns, positive concerns, American business, American drive, the overcoming of obstacles, forging ahead of competition: success. There it was again. And perhaps it was that, in this unfamiliar setting, without realizing it then—but only now—that tenuous sorrow, scarcely at sentient level, that I felt in the sacrifice of my own estranged kin, I also felt here. Without knowing it, just feeling it: the no-longer creative sacrifice of personality for no-longer affirmative, no-longer stirring aspirations. Other men and women, better equipped intellectually and by training, have said all this long before, and with a trenchancy far beyond me.

Different, though, were the ways of analysis and the ways of feeling. M's father, the idealistic clergyman with a mission to Far Western logging camps, a mission of salvation, become the executive secretary; a kind of spiritual gloss mitigating the crassness of conservative American businessmen. If I could only have formulated his role then, as M did, as M perceived it, and as I have now barely learned to do, I think I could somehow have buffered the nameless, blind wave of hopelessness and of isolation I felt. On top of everything else that I was, and detested being, I had to enact this that I wasn't. Only that tall girl dressed in her homespun hopsacking suit, who sat across the room, was my nexus here. She was my future: I had no other: she was my need. But what was I on the scale of her need? Home Relief pauper, dubious scrivener, Jewish neurotic.]

July 1939, Friday night

I took M home Friday evening for the Sabbath supper. She had gotten over her apprehension about going to my parents' home; and on my part, it was a deliberate decision to go there Friday evening, when Pop was sure to be home, and we could, as it were, keep the reconciliation thriving.

It was dusk when we got off the Brooklyn train. We passed the hovels where the Negroes lived. Perhaps it was just such unmitigated squalor, I thought, about which I had tried to make a superficial story that now lay in my bureau drawer, exacting such retribution. It could be made to seem so, though it probably had nothing to do with the case, an afterthought. I slipped M's hand through the crook of my arm. Around the corner, in houses adjoining Mom's, lived the Gypsies; we saw flounce of gaudy skirt, drab men sitting on the porches. Mom said, always observing life with such utter absence of self that her very recounting was fraught with the sublimity of primitive generalization, how enviable: the young Gypsy woman who had lost her husband screamed her grief incessantly hour after hour, unconsolably—until the day he was buried. And then, said Mom, it was as though the young widow had wiped the slate clean. You would never have known that yesterday she was howling in bereavement. Wiped away and over.

Mom welcomed us—at the door, Pop as usual lurked in embarrassment in the front room, until he had mustered up the necessary social self-possession to come out and say hello. We had brought back several empty jars—to replenish Mom's supply—jars that had been full of homemade jelly she had given us when we were last there.

The table was covered with a white tablecloth embroidered with white figures and set with new silverware—and with all the professional skill of Pop's calling as a waiter. As we stood talking, Mom's ancient poodle decrepitly crept in—newly shorn of its scraggly curls—and I quipped that it looked like a clam without its shell. "That's my friend," said Mom staunchly and laughed. For once she refrained from adding, "That's my best friend," to Pop's annoyance.

There was, as always when my father entertained guests, guests whom he had been expecting, and in expectation accumulated a degree of tension, that nervous abrupt air about everything he said and did. It was at such times, when he was close to being overwrought—and most apt to fly off the handle at a trifle—that Mom seemed to insist on doing things her own way, with an obduracy nothing short of deliberate provocation. It was an ancient, grievous story. First, contrary to his expressed wish, she broke off irregular chunks of the braided *challah,* instead of cutting neat slices, as he urged. With company present, Pop always concealed his anxiety (I suspect anxiety over his volatility, fear of the imminence of his uncontrollable eruption) by adopting a su-permild tone of voice. It purred with humility and inoffensiveness. The poor man evidently thought, if he thought about it at all, that his unctuousness created an image of himself that he would give anything to be: the calm, polite, and self-possessed individual. Instead, his show of cordiality had an air of unreality about it; one sensed another person behind the feebleness of the wheedling, good-humored front. Especially was this true to anyone who knew him, knew how fantastically at variance this deportment was with his customary behavior—which showed itself when Mom insisted on tearing off hunks of *challah* (more picturesque actually than sliced, I think, and more tempting in its homey honesty). His voice shifted momentarily to the harsh, rancorous sound I had known so many years. He glared at her, the meek, benign, countenance becoming leathery with hate and exasperation.

Again, he urged her not to place all the "appetizer" dishes on the table at once: the small meatballs in jellied gravy, the gefilte fish in its clotted and spiced aspic, the chopped eggs in rendered chicken fat, the cucumber salad. He pleaded that she bring on only one or two at a time. She refused to heed. They were all brought to the table at once. Again that glare: of volcanic fury pent beyond endurance. Tortured spirit, and my mother too, both of them wrecked lives, wrecked in different ways. M, dear girl, sensed it all and sat there quietly, her tender brown eyes toward me. The pity of it all. My father's lower teeth were almost all gone by now, and his cheeks had the toothless sag of old age.

We talked about the World's Fair. I had been there and Mom, too, but my father and M had not. We discussed the exhibits, and Pop said he had heard that the Fair authorities contemplated lowering the admission prices.

"What about those who've bought books of tickets?" M asked.

"That's what they're waiting for—till they use them, so there shouldn't be no squawk. And you, you're going when your father and mother come again?" he asked. M said she was. "The trouble is," said Pop, "I only have Saturdays off."

"Yes, it's crowded weekends," I sympathized.

"I think I'll go there and spend the whole day," said Pop.

"You'll have to. But even then I don't know whether your legs will hold out."

"As much as I'll see, I'll see. I know I won't see half of it. But I'll spend the day."

"Good," said Mom, in Yiddish. "Even two days. I won't miss you." Pop's face darkened, but he made no reply. "I'll be rid of you for a day," Mom pressed on. It seemed so gratuitously cruel, so unnecessary (so unnecessary, and yet with what horrible necessity) that I snapped at her in Yiddish:

"Why do you have to say that!"

She laughed, and with blatant mockery: "What did I say?"

"Oh, you're always starting these things," I said. "Why do you irritate him?"

"Ah, you're being a fool!" said Mom.

"You don't have to torment him," I growled—and was glad M didn't understand.

"You're also a distraught one," Mom retorted. "The way he is, you are. You kindle at a single word."

I thought it better to hold my peace.

"Well, I think I'll spend a day there," Pop resumed. And to M: "Later in the season, we'll all go there, hanh?"

"That would be nice," she said.

Later, talk turned to our cousin Stella's house party. My mother found fault with the spread; not too bountiful a showing, but she liked the rooms. My father remarked that there were too many guests and it was too hot; so he had left early. I commented on Shirl's loss of weight, that she had acquired a slimmer figure. His face softened and he chuckled: "Yes, she's getting a *shapeleh*. She took off eighteen pounds already. She's going to lose twenty more. She was too heavy."

"What did she weigh?"

"I think a hundred eighty pounds," he said. "She has big bones. Like her father. He had big bones."

"It wasn't all diet, was it? I think she said something about injections."

"No, she gets a needle," said Pop.

"That's what I mean." And to M: "We're talking about a cousin of mine who was at the house party," I explained.

"Yes," Pop warmed to the subject. "Dr. W used to give her a needle in the arm; but her arm got so sore, now he gives her a needle in her back—on her *tokhes,*" he said to me in Yiddish and smiled.

Said Mom satirically: "She's become his private secretary and bookkeeper."

"*Azoi?*" I made light of her remark.

"Ask him," she advised.

I didn't. But thought at such times became too condensed for separation, streaked like a livid thread through the mind: of what *he* was, plied with inferences of Mom's adamant spite—and with what *I* was. And there across the table sat the tall, rangy girl with her patrician features and dark blonde hair. Her attachment was so wholly unfaltering; she had no need to dissemble that she knew as well as I the least tremor of dismay would undo me, no need to pretend that she had given herself completely. Outside, Gypsies were singing. They sat on the running boards of parked cars (they always have such fine machines, said Mom) and sang something I thought vaguely familiar, some currently popular song, but sang it with typical throaty Gypsy quaver.

We got up from the table, and went into the front room, where we sat and talked a while. Pop wanted Mom to let the dishes go, but she insisted on doing them. "I must make exercise," she said in English, and M laughed. We were thirsty, all of us, and Mom proposed we quench our thirst in seltzer water. I offered to fetch a pitcherful—but with no great show of alacrity. No, she would go, said Mom, and I acquiesced. M looked at me in surprise. "My mother'll get more," I excused myself sheepishly. My father said that seltzer left a bitter aftertaste in his mouth; so did ice cream. I recalled Saratoga Springs, the summer mornings only a year ago when M and I had driven from Yaddo, the artist's colony, in the Model A to the free sulfurous seltzer burbling in spurts out of the pipes of the public founts.

Then some talk of the stock market. I tried to convey the full import of what another cousin's fireman husband had stressed was the fate of the small speculator. Pop's reply was to admit that he had lost money in the stock market the past several years, but now he had learned the game and was confident his luck would change: things would be different. (Which explained in large part where his money went during all those years, as well as justifying Mom's contention that she was sure he was making money, but she didn't know where it went. Her choler, inflamed by decades of Pop's niggardliness, went so far as to accuse him—to me—of supporting another household some-where: it couldn't be otherwise than that he was keeping a mistress and bastard somewhere.)

Followed some further talk about my refugee cousins whose exodus from Czechoslovakia Pop was sponsoring: Raphael, the head of the family, had earned his living selling goods on the installment plan. In his letters he hinted that he would appreciate Pop's help in estab-lishing a *mikveh* in New York—a ritual bath, I explained to M—but Pop had other ideas: he proposed going into partnership with Raphael in the running of a bowling alley. "Bizarre man," said Mom laconically, and to me, "His cousin will soon see he has a screw loose."

Came time to take our leave. At ease at last, Pop saw us to the outer gate. It was night. He shook hands with both of us and told us to take care of ourselves. I knew he was watching us as we walked to the streetlight on the corner.

Back at M's room at about 10:30 P.M. It was the hour for my departure—according to house rules. I lingered. And presently, as I embraced her, we heard the landlord leave. He and his wife kept to a set schedule—for reasons of their own. He left at 10:30 P.M., and she returned for a final inspection and to spend the night at 12:30 to 1:00.

"He's gone," I said.

"I'm tired," said M.

"Are you? Then I'd better go." But she didn't want me to. She wished I could stay with her. "Where?"

"On my couch."

Someone else had stayed there one night, a woman friend. Ir-resolute, I tarried a little longer—and then decided to stay on. She said she was afraid of loving me so much.

Afterward, the landlady returned prematurely, and there was no way for me to slip out. Fortunately, I hadn't taken the shower I had contemplated, for if I had, I might very well have run into her.

"It seems so silly to have to do this," said M.

And I: "It's better to do it, and be silly, than not to do it."

And I thought as I looked at her in the dark, the swirling brown crepuscule of the city in which light from somewhere was held in suspension like a sediment, that her features wavered so that, though she slept, she seemed to be smiling. Brown swirling night that made her tall, small-breasted figure like something carved out of speckled limestone. I thought of my parents, of their abysmal unhappiness—that yet did not deter me from seeking love. Or was it because of their disastrous lives that I did seek love? I cannot seem to recapture—now as I write—the beauty of the moment of our intimacy, the ancient enchantment of it that imbued everything and made it rare: from the moment when she said I'd catch cold without pajamas, and she ought to have a pair on hand to offer me—to the final kiss. I felt as if I had indeed found peace within myself. And hearing the passing of automobiles, crackle of voices, and footsteps on the pavement outside her open window, I thought as I lay beside her of Ulysses' exclamation in *The Divine Comedy* of having reached the West through a hundred thousand perils.

It was a defiance of fate, really, to come away from such grievous unhappiness at home there in Brooklyn and to reflect that it was within the realm of the possible for ourselves to end that way, and without a shadow of a doubt to end old and doddering merely on account of living long enough—and yet to venture. But it was incomparably worse not to venture. Fortunately for me, I only *seemed* to have a choice; in actuality—I had none.

Present plan is to complete this memoir-form novel, of which I'm sending a sample (necessarily, though not greatly, modified for the sake of acceptability). Aim is complex for me and, I fear, fuzzy too. If susceptible to formulation: to strip away from the "artist" his claims to immunity—if not claims, then aura—and show him even more subject, almost inevitably, to the degenerative forces within a society. Maybe I'll say it differently or better another time, but that's the general intent: to take the ground from under the innocent victim of *CIS*—as I may have remarked before, show him victimizer, but more to the point, all of us as victims—in a degenerative society. Only thing that retrieves it from *Portnoy's Complaint,* there is regeneration, of a sort, there *is* love.

(letter from Albuquerque, N.M.,
September 18, 1984)

It sounds as if you're banking on *Mercy of a Rude Stream* (hereinafter referred to as Mors (!) o mors aeterna). What a responsibility, son, if I read aright. All you should say about it is what S. Johnson said about the dancing bear: not that he dances well, but that he dances at all.

(letter from Albuquerque, N.M.,
November 11, 1984)

Am suffering a sort of letdown after finishing a draft of what might pass as Volume One of a multivolumed work, much of it in rough typescript. As I look at what awaits me on the shelf, about six big manila envelopes, my flagging spirits just plain flop. The thought of trying to refine something worthwhile out of that hill of prolixity, tailings, and slag of banality—well, you can tell by the choice of fancy metaphors I'm looking for an exit. Finding one might be best for everyone concerned.

(letter from Albuquerque, N.M.,
May 12, 1985)

Roth: [My] writing now flouts the novel form, if you wish. It has a story to tell, which is more or less autobiographical—more or less: I stress that. Because it goes off into an imaginative re-creation, or it departs entirely from the reality itself and becomes what we would have called, formerly, fiction. Or, it reverts to the present. You saw that . . . the one in *Commentary.* It slashes right across something that was written way back in 1939. The individual comes back to himself.

Interviewer: The journal goes back to that time?

Roth: Yes. Especially because I no longer felt I could write anymore, anything. So I reverted to a journal, just to keep going. Fortunately I did, because some of those things have interest for me, if not for anybody else apparently they did for *Commentary.* So I took those pieces out of it; then I thought perhaps this makes a kind of unity here—Doomsday coming on with this prophet, the street preacher. . . . And he was right, too, foretelling the devastation of cities and all that. And then somebody said, "Abie's Irish Rose," I mean, there was a play way, way back, where the Jewish protagonist marries an Irish girl, and there's the usual humorous situation of this intermarrying. So, the meeting with her parents, and her meeting with my parents—and then a kind of an affirmation that life, that love, that, no matter whether Doomsday was tomorrow, if this is love and this is what you actually are, then you go with it. That it's worth it, nevertheless. I mean, that was in the back of my mind. Now, whether it manifests itself as a result of one's reading of the piece, I don't know. But this is how I put the pieces together—that's the rationale.

Right now, the period I'm writing of, which is boyhood—age fourteen—I have no written memoirs about. I didn't sit down or anything like that: at that age, who the hell would've known I was ever going to write! So it's entirely re-created. But it's also fictionally re-created. The same technique is employed: there's a certain *intrusion,* if you wish, of this old rheumatic individual upon the work that he's doing. And there's sometimes even the present journal: if I'm interested, or if I'm preoccupied with something in the present, that goes along too—everything is grist for the mill, as the saying goes. And what determines it, is simply a matter of how I feel. As I say, I flout the novel technique, which is a story, which is a narrative, where, as a rule, the narrator himself stays outside the picture—the Joycean model: the artist who stands to one side paring his nails.

Interviewer: Like a god.

Roth: Yes, like a god. I think that is bullshit. He does not stay outside. And he was not a god. And all of that that I once thought I modeled myself after, I reject, because it's utterly not that. The man is involved, and there's quite a difference. And he's involved even though he *pretends* to be standing on one side.

(taped conversation,
Albuquerque, N.M.,
April 24, 1985)

Roth: The title, *Mercy of a Rude Stream,* I got from Shakespeare, *Henry VIII.* As I write it now, it seems more and more inevitable that the subtitle should not be "English for Foreigners" but "Advanced English for Foreigners." What I sent Targ was, in a sense, straightforward, getting me started. But as I progressed in the work itself, a certain inevitability, a certain pattern emerged—and I'll put it in just as few words as possible. The pattern that emerges is an anti-Joycean pattern. And in order to be anti-Joycean, you have to use his own techniques. Not entirely, I mean—not in the sense of *Finnegans Wake,* which I abhor. But you have to take advantage of the enemy's innovations.

Interviewer: As Lenin said, right? You have to grab the tools of the oppressor.

Roth: Yes. You grab his tools. You can't do otherwise; otherwise there's no meeting, so to speak. That's why, as I advanced in this particular work, that became for me, you might almost say, its *format.* I think of it now as English again, as something that I am originating—again, the sense of exploration, which I felt so many, many years ago when I wrote *Call It Sleep.* I feel it again in writing this. I am again *exploring* this marvelous language for its tremendous resources, that people—our own writers—seem to have made a fashion, have made a fad, of ignoring.

Interviewer: But why "foreigners"?

Roth: Well, this is the irony, if you wish. Because I think of it too as a help for those who wish to advance their own ability in the reading of English!

(taped conversation,
Albuquerque, N.M.,
February 7, 1986)

Last Respects

February 14, 1987

"Last Respects" is one of the hitherto unpublished pieces that were translated into Italian for publication by various Italian magazines and newspapers when Roth was awarded the Nonino International Prize in January 1987. (The other two pieces are "Assassins and Soldiers" and "The Prisoners.")

In point of fact, only the initial portion of "Last Respects"— amounting to about one third of the whole—was published by Europeo. This is owing to Roth's decision that "Last Respects" should not be published in its entirety during his lifetime. Eventually, it will be included in Mercy of a Rude Stream.

"Last Respects" depicts the aging writer searching for an ultimate assessment of the personality of Eda Lou Walton. To this effect, he elicits testimonials from two of her intimate friends. (Under the fictitious name of Marcia, one can easily recognize Margaret Mead, whom Roth came to know as part of Eda Lou Walton's circle of friends.)

The published excerpt cannot do justice to the formal complexity of the whole nor to the brilliant telescopic effect of the receding perspectives. It does, however, confirm two salient traits of Roth's writing—the richness of language and the depth of characterization.

Gratified, as I said before, that "Last Respects" passed critical muster, and hope affection hasn't distorted your view of it unduly, although I too feel that you're quite able to dissociate the critical from the personal. . . . Occurs to me that because it invokes the great Queen MM ["Last Respects"] would create a stir by its very subject matter. And therefore might be held in reserve, as a "sleeper," instead of sending it out for publication.

(letter from Albuquerque, N.M.,
September 24, 1985)

Since one of the pieces ("At Times in Flight") already has a Martha in it, I've changed the Martha in "Last Respects" to Marcia (sounds more martial).

(letter from Albuquerque, N.M.,
October 2, 1985)

With regards to "Last Respects," I withdraw my "sleeper" suggestion. . . . The piece simply has to be printed, is good enough to be too, and am sure will be—somewhere.

(letter from Albuquerque, N.M.,
November 8, 1985)

About "Last Respects," let it rest just a little while longer. Am not too convinced by it anyway.

(letter from Albuquerque, N.M.,
September 30, 1986)

About "Last Respects," I just vacillate. I wish I could include some of the explicit intellectual give-and-take, the ideology, but, of course, I don't think that way, haven't the mind for it.

(letter from Albuquerque, N.M.,
October 30, 1986)

So he had called her on the phone, screwed up his faltering courage to the sticking point, and heard her secretary's voice answer first, and then her own—tightening when he again announced himself. He would be delighted to see her after so many years—if she would grant him the privilege. Could she spare the time, time in a crowded schedule for them to meet once more? Yes, she could—to his great joy! Did he know the location of the Spice Rack restaurant? No, he didn't, he apologized. He had been away from New York so many years, and so much was new here. She would give him the address; could he find the place? Oh, easily enough! He still knew the city's geography. He would be so delighted to see her!

Why had her throat tightened, he speculated after he hung up the phone. Well, why had *he* been on edge when he called? For the same reason she had been, when she heard his voice: because he summoned up the long-distant past, because he was one of the last surviving witnesses of that past, immune to subtle gloss or omission, one who had been present.

He made his way the next day to the rendezvous. Anxiety to be punctual had gotten the better of him. He arrived much too early, and after patrolling the wintry, clamorous street awhile, went indoors, seated himself at the bar near the entrance, and ordered a tall drink— iced, but that couldn't be helped; he would nurse it along until she arrived. Beguiled by the repartee behind the bar, between the droll young bartender and the covey of waitresses he catered to, Ira forgot to keep his eyes fixed on the door. And suddenly there she stood, the famous lady herself! She appeared vexed, whether because he hadn't waited outside and provided her with proper escort into the premises, or whether she too was worried about the kind of individual she would meet, someone she hadn't seen in over thirty years. Like an ancient seeress, she planted her briery, forked stick in front of her and with glittering eyeglasses surveyed diners and drinkers. Her tongue flickered continually between her lips. Holy smoke, what a tic! Ira slipped hastily from the bar stool. She was like a pythoness of old, pythoness of Apollo, but in a double sense, the way her tongue flicked in and out. What the hell did it mean? "Marcia!" Face to face with her, he ventured to press a kiss on her still unmollified cheek in tribute. "How have you been?"

"Oh, fine. Broken ankle. But otherwise all right. I think I would have recognized you."

"You would?"

"Oh, yes. I'm sure of it now."

"And I you, it goes without saying." He had viewed her on the TV screen a couple of years ago—when she was revisiting the site of her early research in Samoa—so he was prepared to some degree for changes in her appearance: the touch of gray in her bangs under the fur turban, the broader face, and the stockier body in its embroidered black coat. But that snub nose, plainness of features, coupled with a monumental, a caryatid self-assurance would have provided sufficient identification.

A minute longer they stood in the forefront of the restaurant chatting, stretching frail strands across a three-decade gap. Had he brought his wife with him? No, he had traveled to New York alone, a kind of sentimental journey from Albuquerque. How did he like the Southwest? Very much. He had become partial to the desert. And she? Why the unique, briery staff? She disliked a cane, she said: it bowed her down. But a staff prevented hovering and kept her posture erect. Her thumb felt snug resting in the fork of a crotch.

"I see. It's picturesque."

Like two characters on the apron of a stage—he felt—conferring for the benefit of an audience, the patrons and personnel who watched them discreetly or commented behind the backs of hands. God, how she basked in cynosure, how she preened in it—and how he hated it! What an immense relief it was when the waitress offered to show them to the table Marcia had reserved.

"I was sorry not to see you at the National Academy awards." He helped her draw up a chair.

"I was at a conference in Sweden."

"Silly paranoia on my part. I thought you were avoiding me."

"Heavens, no. Why should I?"

"No reason." And yet, why that tightening of the throat when he reached her on the phone?

"And now that you've been resurrected, brought back from obscurity, how do you feel?"

"I feel like Lazarus. Uncertain. Security lay in my obscurity."

She detoured around his wordplay. "You must be familiar with the *American Scholar*."

"Only lately. A few years ago my novel was recommended there for republication by a couple of eminent critics."

"That's right. I did too."

"In the *American Scholar*?" Puzzled, he tried to recollect. He hadn't seen her name among those lauding his only novel. Was she flaunting her sagacity, or was she confused? "One of our neighbors subscribed to the *American Scholar* that year. And his wife called up mine to ask: 'Is that *your* Ira in the *American Scholar*?' If you can imagine that being said with a typical Yankee twang."

"It must have been gratifying to have been the only author mentioned more than once."

"Well, yes, and a shade onerous."

"Why?"

"I was being nudged out of a way of life I had become accustomed to. And in large part accepted."

"Oh, fiddlesticks! You were being nudged out of the rut you were in: the waterfowl farm. Scarcely a proper calling for a man of your attainments. And what of your wife? In the backwoods of Maine. She could scarcely have shared your nostalgia for homespun nonentity."

"Possibly not. But we had each other. And two boys to raise." Resentment mingled with defiance. "I'd rather been the average person, normal, sanguine, part of the consensus, such as I saw about me those twenty years in Maine, than the author of my novel—or any other novel!"

"I don't believe it! You would have had no claim to fame whatever. Accomplished nothing of note!" Her tongue flickered. "Truly been a nobody."

"Well, that's what I'm saying! But what would I have known about it?"

His answer, uttered with such vehemence, must have surprised her, for she made no reply. The waitress brought them each a martini, and they ordered lunch.

She raised her glass. And after her first sip: "How do you account for the spectacular success of your novel following so many, many years in limbo."

"Grace, I guess."

"Grace? That's not a Jewish concept, is it?"

"It isn't? Then I must have borrowed it." He snickered. "Maybe I borrowed it back. Apocalypse. Who knows? I'm only sorry Edith isn't here to witness the success of something she made possible. I'll never be able to repay her."

Her tongue flickered, and with what practiced speed. "What happened to your friend Larry?" she asked.

"Gone. His heart gave out."

"Edith surrounded herself with such pretty boys, as we used to call them."

"Larry certainly was. I wasn't."

"He favored a cummerbund, didn't he?"

"Do you remember?"

"Oh, yes. He escorted Ruth Singletree and myself to our seats the evening Lucy Aires read her poems. It was in that Village tearoom where the NYU Arts Club held its sessions."

"Yes. That's where I first met Edith—through Larry. I think we're about to be served." He directed his gaze at the waitress, who, with tray aloft, waded toward them among the diners.

"Good." Marcia picked up her napkin. "I'd like another martini. Would you?"

"No thanks. I'm a drink ahead of you. I had one at the bar."

The waitress set down their plates, took Marcia's order, and left.

And left. Crows cawed across the sere alfalfa field persistently. A compact blue and white panel truck rolled slowly to a stop in the parking space beside the trailer. Oh, hell! The last thing in the world he wanted at the moment were visitors! But no one alighted from the vehicle. Instead, it rolled slowly onward to the next parking space. Albuquerque Power and Light, Ira read the words as they passed by, saw the young Chicano in the cab train his binoculars at the meter at the other end of the yard, jot figures down on a clipboard, and drive on.

Roth: I wrote "Last Respects" In 1980 or 1981. The meeting with Margaret Mead was in 1970, something like that.

The meeting holds a special significance, and there's another part to it. There Is a part that refers to her first husband. I sort of wanted to get the two stories.

She went to the South Seas Isles, where she wrote her famous book, *Coming of Age in Samoa.* When she came back on the ship, she met a younger man whom she fell in love with. She and her husband discussed at great length whether she should leave him and go with this young man. He had tried to advise her, which is a very strange relationship, right? He had been, up until shortly before, a priest in the Anglican Church, so he was a kind of father adviser still. And I think that, although she wouldn't say so, she was rather displeased by the attitude that he took. She was a dominating woman, dominating in the sense that she had a very, very quick mind. Finally she married this younger man, and L.P., her former husband, married another woman he had met in England. After having been with her in a restaurant, I went to see him in Oregon. We took a long, long drive to the ocean. That's the part that follows.

It is almost as a result of Margaret Mead's divorce, you might say, that I became a writer, because when she divorced him, L.P. found, for his paramour, Eda Lou Walton. Eda Lou had done anthropological work with Navajo Indians, so that's how they had met. I mean she and Margaret Mead were very good friends. At the same time, he had almost made up his mind to marry the woman in England. So you can see he put Eda Lou Walton in a very peculiar position. It seems he even took her to his parents, so it looked to her that he was really serious. (I was a sort of confidant of Walton's. I was just a stupid but very sensitive young man, and she would tell me these things that were going on. I had none of this background. I couldn't understand any of these things.)

Then it turned out that two terrible things happened. One, Margaret Mead came to tell Walton that L.P. was interested in marrying the other woman in England. And I can still remember—I just barged in, I knocked on the door, and when I saw what was going on I wanted to leave. She took me by the arm and she said, "Oh no, you can't leave!" She gave me a newspaper and I sat down in the back, but I couldn't help but listen. The conversation was very civil, very polite—everything my background was not. But when Margaret Mead was putting on her gloves to leave, Eda Lou said, "I'm going to miss him, because he's such a good lover." And Margaret said to her, "Ah, but France is full of wonderful lovers!" And Eda Lou said, "But I am not in France." So I thought that the two women were joking. But as soon as Margaret Mead left, Eda Lou suddenly exploded into weeping.

In my tradition, when people are as worked up as that, they are not polite—they insult each other! So I sat down and I said, "What are you crying about?" And she said, "She's so damn smart!" The interesting thing is that a woman like Margaret Mead, who was so very, very clever, didn't have that tenderness, that softness, to have known that the other woman was suffering. It was not kind.

Episode number two came when L.P. went to the ship to go to England, and Eda Lou Walton realized that this must be the truth: a man wouldn't go all the way to England just to make up his mind which woman he wanted. She wanted to go to the ship with him, but the ship didn't leave until about one o'clock in the morning, so she asked me to accompany her and escort her back home. And I can still remember—he had taken his hat off and they embraced. . . . It's a very romantic situation—aboard a ship, and the Hudson River, and the wind is blowing, the stars are shining, and the lights, and the people are all very happy. . . . And they embraced, and they said good-bye—so it looked all right. I am a terribly naive person.

We walked off the ship, off the boardwalk, and to the Hudson Tubes. When we reached New York, she asked me to get a taxi so that she would not have to ride in the subway. So I got a taxi, and then—God, I never in my life saw a woman cry so much. I never saw that. I was almost ashamed of what the driver would think. His face was like iron, he never showed anything—he must see *that* twice a day. So she cried, and she cried, and she cried. Then she asked if I would stay awhile till she could settle down.

Well, I stayed so late, it was four o'clock in the morning. So I said, "Do you mind if I sleep somewhere here?" I was very shy, you know. So I slept on top of the bed. And she said, "Don't be a goose. Get under the covers!" So I got under the covers.

When I became her lover, it was as if she adopted me. She was a great admirer of talent, and she thought I had exceptional talent, even though, in those years, I hardly opened my mouth, I was so very shy! So, it was she who said, "I will support you." She gave me everything. And I'm only sorry she isn't here so I could say thanks.

She was both a mistress and a mother. It was good, and it was bad. It was maybe good for the writer, but it was bad for the person. He fell in the habit of not being an independent, mature individual who was willing to face the world on his own and make his own living.

Interviewer: In "Last Respects," you say that you have become partial to the desert. Isolation seems to be a recurrent theme in both your writing and your own life.

Roth: This is something I can't answer. I really don't know whether it already started way back in the East Side. I don't remember feeling it then. But after we moved to a neighborhood that was very Catholic—being the little Jewish boy, even though I made friends—I no longer felt a community of interest. Now, whether it starts then and the child does not even know that it's already beginning, I can't say. . . . I lived for *ten* years in Greenwich Village, but I didn't feel I belonged there. I more or less *watched*. I was an observer.

Interviewer: When you chose to live in the country, then isolation was not just a sensation—it was real.

Roth: It was real, yes. I was just making reality out of a profound feeling. If you feel that way, sooner or later you will try to *live* that way.

Interviewer: Did transferring this feeling into reality give you a sense of peace?

Roth: I don't think so. The only thing that gives me any peace is when I sit at the word processor and I think of myself and the world I lived in. The only peace I find is in the intense creative effort. Then I forget myself. That's one.

And my wife. If I lose her, I think that I'm finished. Because she understands me, and she's so good, and kind, and she is so steady. But peace—I lost that.

(Barina, 1987)

The Eternal Plebeian and Other Matters

1987

On January 30, 1987, Henry and Muriel Roth traveled to the town of Percoto in northern Italy, where the next day Roth received one of the most important literary awards in Italy—the Nonino International Prize. This prize is awarded yearly to a foreign author whose work has recently been translated into Italian. Previous winners include Claude Lévy-Strauss, Jorge Amado, and Léopold Senghor.

The ceremony was attended by more than five hundred guests from all over Italy and received wide coverage by the press and the national TV networks. To satisfy the increasing interest in writings by Roth and to highlight their articles about and their interviews with the writer, newspapers and magazines vied for additional material. In many cases, these write-ups included excerpts from Roth's acceptance speech. The longest excerpt was published by the Milan-based daily, Il Giorno.

The present version of the Nonino Prize speech is somewhat longer than the one Roth actually read in Percoto. On that occasion, *in observance of time limitations, Roth reduced his speech by one third.*

As a result of the publicity generated by the Nonino prize, the Italian edition of Call It Sleep, *in its third printing, shot its way up to the best-seller list.*

My friends: Since I am the kind of writer who seems to invite all sorts of disasters and commits all kinds of follies in order to provide himself with raw material for his writing, even when it came to writing a letter expressing my gratitude to the Noninos for having chosen me as the recipient of their splendid award, events ran true to form. When I turned on the printer that is connected to my word processor, in order to print the letter that I had written, the printer balked, the printer refused to cooperate—in fact, what took place was one of those tragicomedies of our modern technological era: the whole system began to behave erratically, grumbling and growling, while refusing to do a thing. So I had to turn off the entire device, and instead of sending my carefully written letter, I sent the Noninos a hasty note of thanks written with a ballpoint pen on a standard aerogram. I hope they received it, and I hope they'll forgive me for the hurried and sketchy way I was compelled to express my gratitude.

In the meantime the system was repaired, and the letter I had intended to send was eventually printed. I have it with me, and with your permission, I would like to read it:

Dear Giannola and Benito Nonino:

At the end of my freshman term in the English class of the college which I attended, we were all told to write a long expository essay on some subject of interest to us. Accordingly, I wrote my essay and handed it in, just as my fellow students did. After a week or two passed, and the professor had read all the essays or term papers, he announced that one of them was of such good quality that he had recommended that it be published in the college literary magazine, *The Lavender,* as it was called. And while he paused for breath, before letting us know the name of the student he had selected for the honor, I found myself musing, who is that gifted young man whose term paper is to be published in the City College *Lavender,* while he is still only a freshman? How fortunate he is to be so talented. And then the professor announced the name of the student whose paper was to be published: his name was Henry Roth. And the title of his term paper was "The Impressions of a Plumber." When I heard that, all I could do was utter an inarticulate cry of amazement: "Wow!"

And so I repeat that same cry now, in my letter: "Wow!" in gratitude for the Premio Nonino which you have bestowed on me. In my outcry are compressed all the emotions that I am capable of uttering in the shortest possible way to describe how I feel about the signal honor you have paid me. I wish I could express my gratitude with a more elegant expletive. But I find that sincere gratitude is a difficult thing to express, at least for me. I hope I can do better when we meet face to face. Perhaps I shall at least learn how to say "Wow!" in Italian. (Incidentally, the professor gave me the lowest passing grade for the course, a D, because I had written an impression, instead of an exposition.)

Please let me extend my best wishes and highest regards to both of you.

(signed, Henry Roth)

Now, I'm sure that the implications of this anecdote must be fairly clear to many of you. If you'll bear with me, I'd like to make them more explicit. They are as follows: I cannot persuade myself that the person standing before you is really worthy of the honors you are paying him. To say it differently, I cannot believe that I, I am the one who is the recipient of this honor; I cannot believe that some mistake hasn't been made—in short, I am the eternal plebeian. I am here; you are here. It is all very real. But it is also a great mistake. I just hope you don't recognize your mistake before I am safely out of this gathering, before I have received my prize, and before I am out of Italy and on the way to the United States—where I have already ordered a new and better word processor and printer.

Now to be as serious as I can on the subject of the writer, especially the writer of fiction, it seems to me obvious that the writer does his best work when that work stems from a strong sense of identity. In order for that sense of identity to remain strong, the writer— or anybody—must feel he belongs: he belongs to a people, to a milieu, to a country. Now there's the paradox, or the quandary that haunts the Jewish writer of my time, which is to say, the immigrant Jewish writer, or the Jewish writer still closely identified with what's called the Diaspora, the dispersion, the Jewish writer once faithfully observant of Judaism. From the moment he begins writing, unless he writes in the language of that Diaspora, of that exile, unless he writes in Yiddish, like Sholem Aleichem, or Isaac Singer, but instead writes in the language of the country in which he lives, he begins to lose identity. To cite myself as an example: in childhood, up until the age of eight and a half, I lived on the East Side. It was a virtual Jewish mini-state. All transactions, work, and play, were conducted in Yiddish. It never even occurred to me that I belonged there. I simply belonged. I was scarcely conscious of any more difference between my identity and that of my little companions than one drop of water is from another. When my family moved from that Jewish mini-state on the East Side to Harlem among the Irish and Italians, where I made many good friends, that point marked the beginning of the end of my sense of belonging, and with it, my sense of identity. After that, except at home, all speaking, and of course all writing, was in English, and it became almost inevitable that *Call It Sleep,* based on a lost identity, would be all the novel I could genuinely write—all the creating I could do from that sense of identity—because at the point where my novel ends, I no longer belonged. In fact, the apocalyptic end of the novel may very well depict what the author unconsciously felt: in the novel the child lives on, but his identity seems to have no future. The same thing it would also appear was true of the novelist: he lived on, but his identity disintegrated.

I am speaking to an Italian audience. The lesson, at first glance, or the thrust of my remarks, seems to apply to Jews. I think it applies to all peoples. But the unassimilated Jew in the Diaspora is certainly the most outstanding example of the moral I am trying to make clear. (Not surprisingly, others besides Jews, native Americans, who lose their sense of belonging when they move from the provinces, you might say to the megalopolis of New York, also suffer a loss of identity, and they show symptoms of the same malaise.) Detach the writer from the milieu where he has experienced his greatest sense of belonging, and you have created a discontinuity within his personality, a short circuit in his identity. The result is his originality, his creativity comes to an end. He becomes the one-book novelist or the one-trilogy writer. There are numerous examples of this phenomenon in the United States. . . .

Now it is for this reason mainly, though there are others—and I hope I offend no one who is listening—that Israel has become so central to my thinking. I see Israel as the place where the Jewish writer can live his entire life with a sense of belonging—and a chance of maintaining his identity intact and perhaps the chance of being a creative writer his whole life long, instead of for just a short period. Even though he may be at odds, he may disagree with the majority of people in his native land, still, the language, the people themselves, the customs, the landscape, the sense of belonging remain the same. He—or she—will not suffer the anguished dislocation, the discontinuity, of those of us in the Diaspora, who once felt—and lost—a deep sense of belonging and the identity that stemmed from it. In short, may the phenomenon of the one-book writer, of which I and many other of my contemporaries in America, and perhaps elsewhere, are unhappy examples, be ended forever. May all people feel at home. May all people feel they belong, and may their sense of identity never be impaired.

That's how it all looks to me. That's my truth. It's hard for me, a nonintellectual, to develop my point any further; nor even if I could, is this the appropriate place to do so. In the years that passed, when the author practically stopped writing, he worked as a machinist in New York and Boston. He moved with his family from city to country, to rural Maine—and I must thank my wife for her courage and compassion in bearing with me all these years—he did every kind of hard work, plebeian work, cutting pulp wood for the paper companies, cutting it by hand; raking blueberries for the canning companies, crawling on hands and knees over the ground, scooping up blueberries; he spent long hours in the night boiling down the sweet sap from the maple trees on his property, boiling down the sap into maple syrup, which he could then sell for some cash. He worked four years as a mental hospital attendant, wondering sometimes who should have the keys to the wards, he or the patients. Finally he became a waterfowl farmer. He hatched and raised ducklings and goslings, and then, when they were grown, he prepared them for market. I don't have to tell you people who work in field and farm that though this is wholesome work, it is also hard work. Perhaps it preserved my sanity—until I could begin writing again. It is writing that emerged out of crisis and tribulation, out of war, the Middle East War of June 1967. It is writing that emerged out of partisanship—for my own people again. It is that partisanship that forged a new sense of belonging and a new sense of identity: Israel's regeneration inspired mine.

In conclusion, I would like to say that although the novel on which this award is bestowed—which has been so brilliantly translated by Mario Materassi—seems to be an urban novel based on a sense of identity formed by early life in a Jewish ghetto, nevertheless, reflection has shown me that I drew my inspiration in the writing of the book from many, many sources, from Mark Twain, from Victor Hugo, from Dante, from Shakespeare and alas, Joyce. And the raw material for the book I drew from the many people of different nationalities among whom I lived and with whom I worked. It was not only the people in the Jewish East Side who supplied me with that raw material. It was the people in Harlem as well. It was the workers in the huge repair barns of the New York subway system—where due to my plebeian nature I worked during the summer vacations from college—who supplied me with that raw material. To all these people, Irish, Italian, native Americans, I owe an incalculable debt. All these people, together with the wonderful European literature that elevated my taste, my discrimination, have contributed to the making of the book for which this award is given. It is on their behalf—on behalf of all mankind— that I accept this award. It is placed in my trust. Be assured that I shall treasure this priceless literary trophy all the rest of my days.

Everyone—I do hope—has recovered by now from that giddy whirl known as Premio Nonino. . . . Have decided—and Muriel supports the decision—that it might buttress my sagging spirits to invest some of my ill-gotten gains in a more advanced computer (word processor), since I'm already fairly familiar with its workings. I hope it produces the desired results: Portrait of the Artist as an Old Fiasco.

(letter from Albuquerque, N.M., February 22, 1987)

Oh, yes, tomorrow my new and greatly advanced word processor is due to be delivered. Great incentive to write a book. Or to die with one's books on.

(letter from Albuquerque, N.M., February 25, 1987)